How the Wallflower Was Won

❖ ✱ ❖

She nodded. "Then it appears that, despite your initial trepidation, we'll do very well for each other."

"It appears so. We're to be married."

They stared at each other for many moments, their gazes holding. She had to appreciate that he approached the topic of matrimony with so level and reasonable an attitude, no disordered emotions, no possibility of hurt feelings.

And yet . . . the more they looked at each other, the more aware of him she became. His long body, his beautiful face. The tangible energy radiating from him, masculine and potent. The unmistakable gleam of intelligence in his eyes, an intelligence that went beyond academic learning into something far more complex. More alluring.

And he was to become her *husband*.

A shiver ran the length of her.

By Eva Leigh

The Wicked Quills of London
FOREVER YOUR EARL
SCANDAL TAKES THE STAGE
TEMPTATIONS OF A WALLFLOWER

The London Underground
FROM DUKE TILL DAWN
COUNTING ON A COUNTESS
DARE TO LOVE A DUKE

The Union of the Rakes
MY FAKE RAKE
WOULD I LIE TO THE DUKE
WAITING FOR A SCOT LIKE YOU

Last Chance Scoundrels
THE GOOD GIRL'S GUIDE TO RAKES
HOW THE WALLFLOWER WAS WON

How the
WALLFLOWER
Was WON

Last Chance Scoundrels

EVA LEIGH

AVONBOOKS

An Imprint of HarperCollinsPublishers

HOW THE WALLFLOWER WAS WON. Copyright © 2022 by Ami Silber. All rights reserved. Printed in the United States of America. No part of this book may be used or reproduced in any manner whatsoever without written permission except in the case of brief quotations embodied in critical articles and reviews. For information, address HarperCollins Publishers, 195 Broadway, New York, NY 10007.

First Avon Books mass market printing: September 2022

Print Edition ISBN: 978-0-06-308628-9
Digital Edition ISBN: 978-0-06-308266-3

Cover design by Amy Halperin
Cover art by Paul Stinson
Cover photograph by Shirley Green

Avon, Avon & logo, and Avon Books & logo are registered trademarks of HarperCollins Publishers in the United States of America and other countries.

HarperCollins is a registered trademark of HarperCollins Publishers in the United States of America and other countries.

FIRST EDITION

22 23 24 25 26 BVGM 10 9 8 7 6 5 4 3 2 1

*To Zack, who always supports me,
even when I think too much*

Kim Lawrence

CLAIMED BY HER
GREEK BOSS

HARLEQUIN®
PRESENTS™

Recycling programs for this product may not exist in your area.

ISBN-13: 978-1-335-73872-1

Claimed by Her Greek Boss

Copyright © 2022 by Kim Lawrence

For questions and comments about the quality of this book, please contact us at CustomerService@Harlequin.com.

Harlequin Enterprises ULC
22 Adelaide St. West, 41st Floor
Toronto, Ontario M5H 4E3, Canada
www.Harlequin.com

Printed in U.S.A.

Acknowledgments

❧ ✳ ❧

*T*hank you to my sprinting buddies, Jackie Barbosa and Jen DeLuca, who kept me motivated, accountable, and caffeinated throughout this process. Gratitude to Claire Chiaravalle for the exceptional sensitivity read, and huge thanks to the Ladies of the Loop (I shall not name it here) for your support and patience when I needed to vent. Thank you to Joanna Shupe, Caroline Linden, Megan Frampton, and KB Alan for years of friendship and entertaining my wild ideas.

I am also extremely grateful to the Bookstagrammers, BookTokkers, and book bloggers who have championed my books through the years.

As always, thank you to my editor, Nicole Fischer, and her willingness to put sweating emojis in her comments, as well as thanks to my agent, Kevan Lyon, for taking care of the dirty work.

And thank you to all the bookish people out there, who read at breakfast and never travel anywhere without at least one book on their person.

Author's Note

❖ ✽ ❖

This book contains a character with a learning disability, and depicts memories and scenes of verbal and physical abuse.

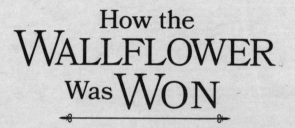

How the
WALLFLOWER
Was WON

Chapter 1

❖✳❖

London, 1818

*B*eing a successful gambler meant manipulating the complex alchemy of risk, calculation, and gut instinct. In the case of the gamble Finn Ransome had made four months ago, however, not only had his wager *not* paid off, it had bitten him right on the arse. With pointed teeth.

Admittedly, assisting his best friend in jilting Finn's sister had seemed like a better idea at the time. Willa and Dom had been miserable in the weeks leading up to their marriage. With the help of his younger brother, Kieran, Finn had prevented what he'd believed would be a horrendous mistake for both his friend and his little sister—yet misery had followed. Estrangement from Willa had also followed, along with a ghastly ultimatum from his family, the terms of which now wrapped around his throat like an iron collar.

Before Finn could consider what the hell to do about any of this, though, he had to survive walking through this disreputable tavern in the tough and gritty riverside neighborhood of Ratcliff. Even the rowdiest of his usual gaming hells couldn't compete with this nameless watering hole. As he carried three pints of dubious ale in severely dented pewter mugs toward his table in the corner, he dodged four fistfights, two men splayed out on the floor, and someone gesturing wildly with a longshoreman hook.

He narrowly avoided the rusty metal point tearing the fabric of his black silk wool waistcoat by twisting nimbly to one side. Unfortunately, the movement caused ale to slosh over the rim of a mug, and the liquid splashed across a seated patron's head.

Scowling, the man rose to tower over Finn, which, given Finn's not inconsiderable height, was impressive. Ale dripped from the man's sandy hair, and he shoved his sodden fringe out of his eyes to glower at Finn.

"Sincere apologies," Finn said with as much even-keeled calm as he could manage given his current squalid surroundings and the fact that a hulking, ale-reeking giant glared at him. "It was entirely accidental, and I'd be more than amenable to buying you a pint as recompense."

"Fancy words and a pretty face ain't going to keep you from a beatin'," the colossus growled. To prove his point, he brandished his ham-sized fists.

"You look like a betting man," Finn said tranquilly. "I'm correct, aren't I?"

His would-be attacker frowned in puzzlement. "I—"

"Of course you are," Finn went on. "You've the appearance of a man who enjoys the thrill of staring Dame Fortune square in the eye and challenging her to do her worst. A daring, confident man."

The fair-haired behemoth glanced down at himself and fingered the button hanging from a thread on his jacket. "I suppose."

"Let us make a small wager, then," Finn continued, giving no hint to any of the fear that prickled along his nape. "If you win, which I've every confidence you will, you get to pummel me into paste. But if *I* win, we go about our evening and part company as friends. The tiniest of bets, which I'm certain you agree to, because you're a wise and quick-witted fellow."

"I—"

"Excellent." Finn nodded toward a patron seated alone at one of the rickety tables, bent over his mug and regarding the room through red-rimmed eyes. "You see that gentleman over there? I wager that he'll be unconscious on the floor within the next fifteen seconds."

"Hatchet Taylor can hold his liquor better'n anyone here." The giant smirked. "He ain't goin' no place."

"So, we're in agreement." Finn set one of his mugs on a nearby table—which likely meant that one of the men seated there would drink it, but sacrifices had to be made—and held out his hand.

The huge blond man stared at Finn for a moment, then spat into his palm and offered it to Finn.

Suppressing a sigh, Finn copied the gesture and shook the big bloke's hand. At least he had a handkerchief tucked into his jacket, which he made good use of the moment his opponent looked toward the aptly named Hatchet Taylor.

The wager had drawn the attention of several patrons nearby, who eagerly watched the exchange.

Their own side bets immediately followed, with nearly all of the tavern's regulars laying odds that not only would Finn lose, he'd also be laid out flat with a single punch to the face.

Finn pulled out his timepiece. Fortunately, he'd had the foresight to wear one of his least ostentatious watches, so he wouldn't attract the attention of every pickpocket between here and Soho. "Fifteen seconds beginning now."

He, the large man, and half a dozen others watched as Taylor drained his mug. Five seconds elapsed. Taylor swayed in his seat, but remained upright. Ten seconds had passed.

Even in the din of the taproom, Finn heard the giant beside him crack his knuckles in preparation for the beating that surely was to come. Finn didn't give him or the onlookers the satisfaction of fidgeting or looking at all uneasy, though, his attention was fixed solely on Hatchet.

Taylor abruptly lurched to his feet. Swayed—but remained standing.

Three seconds remained. Then two. One.

Taylor pitched backward, over his chair. Both man and chair tumbled to the ground. The onlookers were silent, until those that had wagered on Finn cheered. The losers grumbled as coin changed hands.

Gloating was always bad form, so Finn nodded politely to the giant before turning to head to his table. Yet he knew what was coming, and purposefully dropped the remaining mugs he held moments before the huge man clamped a hand on his shoulder. As the colossus spun Finn around, Finn launched his own punch.

His fist collided solidly with the bloke's jaw. The

chap's head spun to the side, his eyes fluttering, though it didn't quite hide the shocked look on his face.

He took a step, sank down to his knees, and then hit the sticky, puddle-strewn ground. A moment later, an impressive snore shook his body.

The bystanders gaped, looking back and forth between the unconscious man and Finn, all of them wearing matching expressions of disbelief.

Finn tugged on his coat, adjusted the folds of his neckcloth, and walked to his table.

His brother Kieran and their friend Dominic Kilburn frowned at him as he approached.

"Where are our drinks?" Kieran asked, eyeing Finn's empty hands.

"If you're in need of refreshment," Finn answered as he dropped into his seat, "get it yourself."

Dom rolled his eyes. "You nobs can't fetch your own ale."

As it often happened when they were in this part of town, Dom's East London accent came out thicker, undoing the elocution lessons that had been drilled into him after his father made a fortune leasing dockyard warehouses.

"I'll get 'em." Dom got to his feet, looming over the table like a standing stone clad in Bond Street fashion, before he stalked toward the bar.

Finn turned to Kieran, who wore the irritatingly contented smile of a man actually looking forward to his upcoming wedding. Well, Finn *assumed* that was what caused his younger brother to seem so revoltingly pleased, since Finn had little knowledge of what constituted a happy marriage. God knew he'd never seen one in his parents' home.

"I'm going to cast up my roast mutton if you keep beaming at the world in that fashion," Finn muttered.

"Celeste and I went to another of Longbridge's parties last night," his brother said happily. "In disguise, of course. We aren't married yet."

"And then you two came back to our rooms and kept me up half the evening with your acrobatics and caterwauling." Though he was nocturnal by nature and had been home last night for only one hour, those sixty minutes had been enough to force Finn to flee his rooms and take shelter at a late-night pie shop around the corner.

Kieran grinned at him with the same unrepentant smile Finn had seen from his brother all their lives, even when Kieran had been caught with French illustrations tucked beneath his mattress. "The stipulation of our family's ultimatum indicated we had to find respectable brides. The fact that mine makes me feel like I could write a dozen volumes of odes is a perquisite."

"Missed sleep is an irritant," Finn said, but added grudgingly, "yet I can't resent your happiness."

Finn's own prospects in locating someone who gave him the same kind of joy were dim. The reason why miracles were called miracles was because they almost never happened.

Three tankards dropped unceremoniously to the table, and Dom threw himself into his chair with the same lack of decorum. Finn sipped gingerly at his ale, hoping that whatever brewing process was employed effectively rid the beverage of most of its impurities. He was comfortable in most of London's taverns, pubs, and alehouses, from Mayfair's most exclusive locales to Whitechapel's more gritty establishments, but this unnamed Ratcliff tavern tested the limits of his own adaptability.

Yet when Kieran had insisted that he, Dom, and Finn meet to discuss their current circumstances, Dom had immediately dictated that they would convene in this place, apparently a few blocks away from the tenement where he'd spent the first eighteen years of his life. Perhaps his rationale had been that, as the conversation was bound to be extremely unpleasant, he needed the comfort of familiar surroundings. Knowing that Dom possessed the personality of an extremely irate bear, Finn and Kieran hadn't much choice but to capitulate.

Still, as Finn eyed Dom over the rim of his tankard, his friend didn't look especially comfortable. In fact, of the three of them, Kieran was the one who appeared the least troubled.

Yet Kieran said, "You two are bollocksing everything up."

"Bugger yourself," Dom shot back.

Finn raised his hands. "Charming as this discussion is going, what, precisely, is intended by convening us here?"

"In four months, Celeste will make me the happiest of men."

Dom muttered at that, likely still attempting to reconcile the fact that his rakehell friend was marrying his sister, but thus far Dom hadn't punched Kieran into Michaelmas.

"However," Kieran went on, frowning, "that leaves only eight months for the two of you to find respectable brides of your own. Our families stipulated that we *all* must marry, or none of us are given a ha'penny more."

"We're well aware of their ultimatum," Finn said sullenly. He himself didn't need the money—his gambling kept him comfortable—yet in good conscience, he couldn't keep Kieran and Dom from their allowances. His brother had few other means of supporting himself, for one thing, and Dom had come from poverty. Finn would be a right ass if he threw his friend back into penury and left his brother without a source of income.

"And yet neither of you have done a ruddy thing about it," Kieran fired back. He glared at Dom. "*You* were the one that jilted *our* sister, *on her wedding day.*"

"And you two helped me do it," Dom spat.

"In our defense," Finn answered after debating whether or not to take another drink of questionable ale, "we believed we were acting in Willa's best interest."

"So was I," Dom grumbled.

Finn *had* believed, on that awful day last spring, that helping Dom flee before the ceremony was for everyone's benefit. Though it had clearly been a love match, his sister and Dom had been wretched in the six weeks leading up to the wedding, with constant bickering, tears, and increasing tension. Willa was too stubborn by nature to call off the engagement. Finn's own parents were trapped in a bitterly cold marriage, and he and Kieran had both thought they were sparing their baby sister a similar fate by giving her groom a means to escape in the minutes preceding the service.

Fortunately, Willa hadn't sued for breach. Dom had been willing to perpetuate the lie that Willa had been the one to call off the wedding, on account of her future groom's riotous and disreputable behavior. She'd fled to the Continent soon after.

Finn wasn't much for correspondence—his writing was concrete evidence to others that his relationship to words was a problematic and fraught one—but all of his letters to Willa had gone unanswered. Clearly, she was furious with her brothers for assisting Dom. Finn had memories of holding her tiny, plump hand as she'd taken her first steps, and boosting her up to reach the biscuit jar on the very top shelf of the dry larder.

But not a word from her. Not in months.

"Assigning blame is pointless," he said to his brother and friend. "None of us are magicians who can manipulate time, and so we can only move forward."

"Forward you two must go," Kieran pointed out. "Unless you count drinking whisky, getting into brawls, and playing faro as courtship, neither of you have done anything to find brides."

At Dom's silence, Finn felt obligated to point out, "I haven't time for swanning around ballrooms and dancing quadrilles with terrified debutantes."

"Yes," Kieran said dryly, "I can see how sleeping all day and prowling gaming hells all night can take precedence over something so minor as the looming prospect of our penury."

"This from the man who considered bedding theatricals as cultural enrichment," Finn answered.

"But one of them was a playwright," Kieran replied. "And I happen to write very emotionally abundant poems, myself, so I consider all efforts well spent."

Dom's hand slapped on the table, startling both

Finn and Kieran. "If the two of you are done lobbing quips at each other like a shuttlecock, I'm for home."

Finn traded a worried look with his brother. True, Dom had never possessed a personality ripe with sunshine, but he used to enjoy running from one end of London to the other with the Ransome brothers. Since that fateful day last spring, though, he'd grown more and more surly, barely able to tolerate anyone's company for more than a quarter of an hour.

"We must address the issue of locating brides for both of you," Kieran said flatly. "Given that we're *all* culpable for finding ourselves in this position, each of us has to do our part to remedy our circumstances."

Dom glowered but didn't object. For his part, Finn did the very important work of using the moisture beading on the outside of his tankard to draw patterns of cleanliness on the filthy tabletop.

"Have either of you any candidates for a potential bride?" Kieran pressed. At their silence, he muttered, "You haven't even made an effort, have you?"

"Not precisely," Finn prevaricated. "I'm still formulating a strategy."

"For a man who handsomely supplements his income through gambling," Kieran drawled, "you're being exceptionally unsystematic about it."

"These things take time."

"We don't have time," was the reply.

Kieran had often been Finn's champion whenever their parents' disdain for him grew exceptionally poisonous, and having his younger brother look at him with disappointment made Finn want to slouch in his seat and avoid his gaze. It was much the same way he used to behave whenever his father lambasted him for his appalling academic performance.

What could Finn tell Kieran, when he himself didn't know why he'd been so slow to begin his bride hunt? For twenty-nine years, he'd lived an unencumbered life. Unlike Kieran—before Celeste—who'd had plentiful lovers, Finn remained alone. When he did find someone to share his bed, it was never for long, and with the understanding that the arrangement would be brief. It was simpler that way.

Assessing risk versus reward led him to one conclusion: it was neater and more manageable to walk a solitary path. When he had physical needs, he found a partner for a night, and then returned to his life, unaccompanied.

"I've someone in mind for Dom," he said abruptly.

Kieran's brows lifted, while his friend regarded him suspiciously.

"This isn't Smithfield Market," Dom said with narrowed eyes, "where you decide I'd like mutton instead of beef."

"I'd never liken a woman to a meat," Finn answered, "but in this case, I wasn't on the hunt when the lady came across my sights."

Kieran rolled his eyes. "Insulting metaphors aside, who's the fortunate woman?"

"Miss Tabitha Scaton."

Kieran had been taking a drink of his ale and promptly spat it onto the table, which actually improved the table's appearance. "The wallflower bluestocking?"

"The same." Finn had met Miss Seaton at a ball several months prior. It had been a brief, but memorable encounter. He had a vivid impression of mahogany hair, a pointed chin, angular cheekbones, and terrifyingly incisive blue-gray eyes, and she'd had little use for a man of his raffish reputation. With a few words and one look of her rapier-like eyes, she'd cut him into a neat pile of shredded black silk on the ballroom floor. She had quit the chamber, carrying a book she'd brought with her, clearly preferring its company to his.

"You'd mentioned her before as a possibility for Dom," Kieran said, appalled, "but I thought you were joking."

"She sounds promising," Dom said with heavy irony.

"Item the first," Finn said, holding up a finger, "she is Viscount Parslow's only daughter. Given that your father would prefer you to wed a woman of the gentry, she fulfills that criterion."

Dom crossed his arms over his massive chest, but didn't argue that point. It had been pure happenstance—at the time it had seemed like good fortune, though that had been a misjudgment—that Dom, a man of common birth, had fallen in love with Willa, an earl's daughter, as she had fallen in love with him.

Naturally, lightning wouldn't strike twice, which brought Finn to his next point.

"Item the second," he continued, holding up another finger, "Miss Seaton is six and twenty."

"And unmarried," Kieran said, nodding with understanding.

"With her bluestocking leanings," Finn added, "it's unlikely that anyone is going to offer for her. She also has a tendency to linger at the edges of ballrooms, placing her firmly in the wallflower classification."

"She wouldn't laugh in my face if I was to propose," Dom said sullenly. "Not much of a reason to request a private talk with her da. I don't even know this woman—why would she want to shackle herself to me, and I to her? We sound nothing at all alike."

"Bringing me to item the third." Finn held up one more finger. "You and Willa were *exceptionally* alike. Perhaps overly so. It was like two volcanoes attempting to share a single dining room. While it might be thrilling initially, it's not especially sustainable for a lasting arrangement."

"Spoken from your tomes of experience," Kieran said wryly.

Finn dropped one of his fingers to make a rude gesture at his brother. After Kieran sent him an equally profane gesture, Finn continued. "Miss Seaton is the diametric opposite of Willa. Prefers the company of books to people, rather than outgoing and social. Cool, rather than passionate. All she would want is a library of her own, and she'd be perfectly content to leave you to your own devices. There would be no possibility of emotional entanglement. No hurt feelings on either side."

That last point seemed to intrigue Dom the most. He leaned back in his chair, which creaked threateningly under his muscled mass, and tilted his head to the side, considering.

Finn had been saving that particular aspect in Miss Seaton's favor—it was exactly the sort of thing that would interest Dom. Finn had witnessed his friend's and sister's heartbreak from ringside. With the potential for further emotional injury looming large, there surely was safety in knowing that love would not, could not, blossom.

"You're awful knowledgeable about this wallflower," Dom noted.

Finn smoothed a hand down the lapel of his coat. "I conducted a small amount of discreet reconnaissance, and the rest is logical inference. A dullard I may be," he continued, "but certain things are obvious, even to me."

His brother opened his mouth as if to object to something, then closed it.

"Why don't *you* offer for her?" Dom asked.

Finn had expected this very point. "Of the two of us, only *you* had a university education. You look like a towering brick edifice, but you won academic awards at Oxford. I merely have a favorite seat at the faro table and wouldn't know scholarly achievement if it kneed me in the groin. Hardly qualifications that would endear me to her as a possible husband."

"'*A fool thinks himself to be wise, but a wise man knows himself to be a fool*,'" Dom quoted.

"I merely know that line because I've seen a performance of *As You Like It*," Finn countered, "and only then to see the actress playing Rosalind wear breeches. Whereas you actually read and studied the play for far less lascivious reasons."

Dom exhaled heavily. "I can't just go to Miss Seaton's house, pound on the door, and demand that she meets me outside with her trousseau."

"Naturally not. There *are* rules." Though he kept his tone even, Finn inwardly rejoiced at his friend's capitulation. At least with the attention on Dom and Miss Seaton, it would give Finn more time before he had to begin his own search for a wife. The thought of trying to woo some woman with his own rather inadequate assets made him want to run. "I'll find some social gathering where she'll be in attendance and introduce you to each other."

"Given what a positive impression you made on her at the Duke of Greyland's ball," Kieran said, "I'm unshaken in the belief that she'll greet you with effusive warmth."

"It wasn't *that* awful," Finn muttered.

Kieran chuckled. "Brother, I was going to call in a stable hand to scoop you up like dung."

"Dom will look like a shining prince by comparison," Finn answered.

"It's already off to a rosy beginning," Dom threw in.

"Am I or am I not a man who earns a substantial amount of money through gambling?" Finn demanded. When Kieran and Dom were quiet, Finn said, "Precisely. So, I know how to pick a winning situation. Trust me, this is going to be exactly what everyone needs, and it will succeed flawlessly."

He put confidence in his voice. Matters of chance often relied on careful assessment, but sheer bravado was also a necessary component.

Miss Tabitha Seaton would make Dom a suitable bride. It might take some maneuvering, and a good deal of finesse to pair them, but Finn would get the job done with the same clear-eyed sense of purpose that he applied to his gambling. When it came to strategy and cunning, he was always successful, far more so than matters of the heart.

Chapter 2

❧ * ❧

$\mathcal{B}$ased on the number of curious or outright alarmed looks aimed in Tabitha Seaton's direction, one would suspect that the presence of a female waiting outside White's was akin to seeing a tigress lying across the front step, waiting to devour whomever was unwise enough to cross her path.

That was ridiculous. For one thing, Tabitha was an omnivore, but she wasn't a cannibal. At least, not yet. Although, given the number of censorious glances shot in her direction, she strongly contemplated devouring at least one of the gentlemen striding past her. It would send a message that her errand was of the greatest importance, and she would not be turned away.

"I don't think he will be coming out any time soon, miss," Olive said worriedly.

"I saw him go in two hours ago," Tabitha replied to her maid. "How long can it take for one gentleman to read a newspaper and drink a glass of brandy?"

She only knew that men did such things in their clubs because her father and brothers had mentioned those activities, but of course, she herself possessed no firsthand knowledge. Something she *did* know, however, was that women were not permitted in White's. It was too late in the day to approach Sir William Marcroft outside his home. She'd been forced to follow him to his club, and then wait for him outside. Sending a note to the baronet to inform him of her presence would be considered gauche.

If she was to have any success in her mission today, she couldn't give Sir William any reason to look askance at her. Yet the best strategy for ensuring that he *had* to talk to her was catching him somewhere relatively public. After all, a gentleman wouldn't snub a lady in the street. Would he?

Despite her extensive knowledge of many subjects, she knew very little about matters related to Society. She'd had a lone and unremarkable Season, eight years ago, and from the outset remained a wallflower. It hadn't mattered to her very much, because she'd had her one source of comfort and happiness existing outside of that world—until one horrible night.

She fought a grimace, struggling to keep at bay memories of that particularly awful evening. Tabitha had been taken to task for it, too, and had learned her painful lessons.

"Oh, miss," Olive said, growing lively, "I think that's the baronet coming out now."

Seeing the man emerge from the club with his distinctive mane of black hair streaked with gray, Tabitha straightened her spine. No time for doubts, even though they nipped at her ankles in an effort to bring her to her knees.

"Good afternoon, Sir William," she said as he descended the short flight of steps to the curb.

He drew up short and stared at her from beneath impressive white eyebrows. "Do I know you, Miss . . . ?"

"Seaton. Miss Tabitha Seaton. You do not know me, personally, but I believe you know my father, Viscount Parslow."

"I doubt your father would be much impressed by his daughter standing outside White's like a shopgirl."

Her face grew hot, but she plowed ahead. "When it comes to enriching the mind, surely such things as social niceties are irrelevant." Before he could offer a rebuttal, she said, "I'm a great admirer of yours, and the Sterling Society."

Sir William's brows climbed upward.

"The Society's collectively authored monograph on applying the pedagogy of ancient Sumer to contemporary education was most edifying," she added. It would have been even more valuable if it had included thoughts on the education of girls, as well as learning for children outside of public schools, but she would keep such thoughts to herself until she'd attained her goal.

The skeptical look on Sir William's face was replaced by grudging interest. Yet he expectantly eyed the lacquered carriage that had pulled up to the curb. A footman was even now climbing down from the box to open the door and usher the baronet inside.

"This is indeed flattering, Miss Seaton," Sir William said, casting glances toward the vehicle. "Yet I'm expected at the Society's headquarters—"

"Which is why I've been waiting for you, Sir William." She would have gone to the Sterling Society's headquarters, except its location was secret to anyone except members. Given the group's reputation for advising members of Parliament and giving counsel to other influential individuals, if their whereabouts were widely known, they'd be inundated by the public. Individuals would insist that the Society advance their particular interests, which would pollute the organization's main purpose: to operate from a place of pure rational thought.

Of course, some might consider ambushing the head of the Sterling Society outside his club to be less than rational. Yet as long as Tabitha kept her voice steady and avoided any appearance of being overcome by emotion, she had a chance at success.

She drew in a balancing breath. "I would like to become a member of the Sterling Society."

He let out a bark of laughter, then sobered when she merely looked at him. "Truly?"

"My credentials are excellent," she said, launching into the speech she'd been preparing for the past month, ever since her intention of joining the Society firmed in her mind. "I have read all of the Ancients, including Plato, Socrates, Aristotle, Pyrrho of Elis, and more, all in Greek, and Cicero, Plotinus, Lucretius, Theodas of Laodicea, and others in Latin. Further, I've translated Montaigne's *Essais* and Descartes's *Meditationes*, and have compiled an index of Pascal's works. Oh, and I've read every book and paper published by the Sterling Society, of course."

She had also studied Maitreyi, Ghosha, Hypatia of Alexandria, Anne Conway, and Mary Wollstonecraft, amongst others, but given the Society's proclivity for reading works by Western men, it would be wisest not to mention this particular area of interest.

"You had a radical-thinking governess?" Sir William asked, slightly alarmed.

"Miss Elgrave's education was limited to drawing and French," Tabitha replied. "I supplemented the rest by reading my elder brother's books. Lawrence went to Eton and Oxford," she added, "and so, I supplied myself with the same education as if I myself had gone to such esteemed institutions."

She omitted that she'd also studied extensively with her younger brother's tutor—that touched too closely to personal matters she'd *never* discuss with Sir William. In truth, she'd only told a handful of close friends about her relationship with Mr. Charles Stokely, and even then, she'd left out the most humiliating parts. There was nothing to be gained by rehashing it, other than reliving her mortification and shame.

Now she waited to see if Sir William was impressed by her self-created education, but he continued to wear an uncertain expression. The best choice was to plow ahead and show the baronet that she was imminently qualified to be a part of the Sterling Society.

"I published a paper," she continued, "on the contributions of women to the development of Classical philosophy, which was highly regarded by a number of exemplary figures in the field." She did not add that the paper had been published under the name "T. Holly," a combination of her first initial and her middle name.

Sir William continued to regard her as though she were speaking an especially obscure Gallic dialect.

"If you're concerned that I'd merely be riding the coattails of my illustrious Society colleagues," she pressed on, fumbling through her satchel until she found the object she sought, "I've many ideas which I'm eager to share with the group. This notebook contains theories, hypotheses, and research notes collected within the past six months alone."

She held up the leather-bound volume, which bulged with its contents that included writing, clippings, sketches, diagrams, and other relevant ephemera. The notebook did indeed represent half a year of extremely hard work. Pride suffused her, expanding through her body as she showed it to Sir William Marcroft, of all people.

She *did* admire him, and the Sterling Society. Though their views were somewhat limited, there wasn't a single organization or institution in England as dedicated to the development of the mind. Their publications had nourished her throughout her adolescence, making her believe that she, too, could spend her life expanding the limits of human knowledge. With shy pleasure, she presented the society's leader her own efforts, contained within the bindings of a humble notebook.

He made a dismissive wave of his hand, as if she'd held up a child's embroidery sampler. Her heart dropped heavily within her ribs.

"Women are *not* admitted to the Sterling Society," he intoned. "Which you would know if you are as much an admirer as you claim to be. Unless," he added with narrowed eyes, "you thought yourself to be an exception."

That *had* been her hope, but that hope was on the verge of being cast to the pavement and shattered like so much fragile porcelain.

"Perhaps it hasn't been the policy *to date*," she said,

forcing herself to smile in what she hoped looked like a calm but friendly manner.

A bald-headed man climbed the steps to White's, sending Sir William a questioning glance, clearly discomfited by the sight of him talking to a young woman outside the esteemed halls of masculine exclusivity. The baronet gave the man a clipped nod, before turning his displeased gaze to her.

"The Sterling Society is a *respectable* institution, Miss Seaton," he said, the edges of his words fraying. "Permitting females amongst our members is hardly decorous, and an *unmarried* female is absolutely impossible."

"Unmarried," Tabitha said thoughtfully. Her attention snagged on that word, and its implications. "What if a woman with qualifications such as mine *did* have a husband?"

"I . . ." Sir William looked back at his waiting carriage. "I suppose so. But she must absolutely be married for her to be given the barest consideration."

"I see."

"Now, I truly *am* late, so if you will excuse me, Miss Seaton." The baronet gave her a brief bow before hastily climbing into his carriage and driving away.

She stood on the sidewalk as more men entered and exited White's. Rather than endure their shocked or scandalized stares, which now felt as lacerating as a face full of brambles, she began walking west, with Olive trailing after her. Tabitha's steps were heavy, despite the fact that she was headed to one of her very favorite places in London. Even though the Benezra Library housed one of the most extensive collections of books on a dizzying array of subjects, and even though the private circulating library permitted membership to any gender, any race, any age, and any class, she was not eager to journey there today. Because she'd have to admit that, despite her very best efforts, she'd failed.

It was several miles from St. James's to Kensington, where the Benezra was located, but she always preferred walking to riding in carriages or hackneys. Her best thinking was done on her feet, which was why she'd developed a rather unladylike musculature in her legs. She didn't mind having strong legs, though, since it was a testament to the amount of thinking she engaged in.

Yet with each step along Knightsbridge, and past Hyde Park on the Kensington Road, all her mind could conjure up was the disastrous meeting with Sir William.

By the time she reached the library's columned portico, her shoulders drooped and she felt as though she'd dragged her heart in an iron cage for the past three miles.

She climbed the steps, pushed open the heavy door, and entered the foyer. The Benezra had once been a private home, with many of the interior walls removed to make room for the shelves and shelves of books, though columns had been added to support the weight of the floor above. Many people sat at long tables for studying. Tabitha greeted the scholars with silent nods as she made her way to the circulation desk.

"Good afternoon," she said to Chima Okafor, the head librarian, when he looked at her expectantly. "Is everyone here?"

"The others are waiting in the study room." The

Igbo language gave Chima's words a melodic intonation. He studied her face, but she hoped her expression didn't fully give away her low mood. "Shall we go see them?"

When she nodded, Chima motioned for Mr. Pagett to take his place behind the desk. Together, she and the head librarian walked together to the study room tucked into the far corner of the building. Her maid selected a book with copious illustrations of the celestial spheres and sat at one of the tables, as she often did whenever her mistress visited the Benezra. Olive was especially fascinated by constellations.

Three more eager faces met her when she entered the study room. Her heart felt as though someone had wrapped heavy chains around it.

"That's a gloomy expression," Diana Goldstein said, peering at Tabitha's face. "Wouldn't you say, Iris?" She turned to the freckled woman seated beside her.

"I've seen storm clouds that look more cheerful, my love," Iris Kemble confirmed, taking Diana's hand in hers and giving it a squeeze. To the outside word, Iris, a former governess, and Diana, a widow who worked at her family's optical shop, were merely good friends who shared a cozy home in Bloomsbury. Yet within this trusted circle of friends, they could be more overt in showing their romantic affection for each other.

"I would never sail through such a storm," Arjun Singh added with a grim nod. A retired lascar, Arjun spoke with authority about all matters nautical. He and Chima waited for Tabitha to sit before taking their own seats.

As concisely as possible, Tabitha related the unproductive conversation with Sir William. While she spoke, the faces of her friends grew more and more despondent, until she said heavily, "He was quite clear that, as an unmarried woman, I'd have no chance at being admitted to the Sterling Society."

"But . . ." Diana appeared both puzzled and angry, which, given her usual even temperament, indicated how upset she was. "Your notebook, and all your wonderful ideas . . ."

"Might as well be lyrics to a nursery nonsense song. Sir William was obdurate."

Grim silence met this statement, and she resisted the impulse to drop her head into her hands, though it was a struggle.

"The Sterling Society is soon to consult with the top members of Parliament on the upcoming education bill," Chima said despondently. "The one that would provide funding for schools in growing urban areas."

Tabitha's hope had been to join the Society so she could advise on that bill. It would be voted on in three months, which hadn't given her much time to join the organization. But she had to try.

Try she did—and failed.

"I'm so terribly sorry." She swallowed hard. "I've let you all down."

The others were quick to assure her that she hadn't done any such thing, but she knew the truth. Her goal was to become the first female admitted to the group, and to make her voice heard when it came to the extremely important education bill. Once she was established within the Sterling Society, she could make the way easier for other people to join the influential organization. People like Diana, Iris, Arjun, and Chima. As the Sterling Society was comprised entirely of white, wealthy Christian men, it hardly seemed to be representative of the greater world, and yet these men were making decisions that affected many people. As the daughter of a viscount, Tabitha had the best chance out of all of her friends to gain entry to the Sterling Society.

If she'd been granted admittance, she could show the members how important it was to include *all* voices in their discussions and proposals. Especially with the clock ticking on this critical bill. Yet Sir William had crushed that prospect as if it was an empty walnut shell beneath the heel of his shoe.

"He *did* say that he might consider a woman for membership if she was married?" Arjun asked thoughtfully.

"He did," Tabitha said.

"Don't look at either of us," Iris said with a wry smile.

Four sets of eyes turned to Tabitha.

She stared back in alarm as worry danced through her limbs. "My Season was eight years ago and I'm surprised that broadsides weren't written about what an unmitigated disaster it was. I wouldn't doubt that children sang songs about it in the lane."

"An exaggeration, surely," Chima said, his eyes kind. "Such a charming, intelligent young woman must have had a bounty of suitors."

"What's valued in women beyond the doors of the Benezra is not what's valued amongst the ton," she answered grimly. "And tall women with a fondness for philosophical and theoretical discourse rank precisely at the bottom of qualities that are celebrated."

During her single Season, she'd never been asked to dance. Not once. She wasn't and would never be part of that world, so it had stung, but not terribly.

The greatest wounding had come from someone who was just as much an outsider as she was. She'd naively believed that she'd possessed enough appeal that Charles would've considered her his ideal mate. Yet even there, she had fallen short.

She swallowed around the knot that suddenly formed in her throat. This wasn't the time to indulge in a display of unwanted emotion. Yet it was a strange quality about past hurts—you could move through life fully convinced that they had no power over you, and yet all it took was a word and you were plunged back into the worst moment of your existence.

"England is a most absurd country," Arjun said, resulting in nods from the others in the study room. "And the weather is terrible. But my wife and children are most attached to it here, and I'm rather fond of the company at the Benezra."

Warm smiles were shared around the table. Here, within the walls of Leonidas Benezra's library, you could find understanding and companionship when there were many in the outside world who offered neither, only exclusion.

Iris murmured, "As you so often say to us, Tabitha, you are capable of great things. We're all certain that you'll find a way."

The knot in Tabitha's throat eased. She looked around the table, regarding each of her friends. Diana had extensive knowledge of Jewish philosophical texts. Iris wrote on the subject of the ethos of the sciences. Arjun's distinct concern dealt with governance under England's zeal for empire, and Chima focused on the rich cultural and philosophical traditions of the Igbo people.

She herself was fascinated by the measures it would take to create a more balanced perspective in canonical works. As a viscount's daughter, she had a privilege that few of her friends had. She had to use what measure of power she possessed to allow more voices to be heard.

The path ahead of her was clear. Her spine firmed, even though anxiety churned in her belly. That was merely emotion, and what had emotion ever gained her but misery? No, she'd lock her fear and uncertainty into a lead-lined coffer, and forge ahead.

"I'm going to do something that will make my mother very happy." She stood, and Chima and Arjun also got to their feet. "I shall finally find myself a husband."

Chapter 3

❖ ❈ ❖

"I'm as unfamiliar with a place like this as a rich man is unfamiliar with an almshouse," Finn muttered as he and Dom stood in the corner of the Earl of Blakemere's ballroom.

Multiple chandeliers hung from the vaulted ceiling, casting glittering light over the dance floor filled with jeweled ladies and polished gentlemen. They were the sort of respectable people he studiously avoided. More highly virtuous guests enacted curious rituals of bows and curtseys and polite talk. It all served merely as glossy lamination over venal motives.

"They serve stronger drink at an almshouse." Dom disgustedly eyed his cup of punch. "What the hell is in this?"

"Virgins' tears and lemonade." The night would have been far more enjoyable if he'd been able to retreat to his favorite gambling hells—at least there, he knew most of the people, and no one looked at him with thinly veiled mistrust. Gamblers knew *everyone* carried the seeds of dishonesty within them, and, consequently, there was a kind of freedom in believing everyone was out to rob you.

Finn never cheated. He'd no need for such tactics.

He couldn't blame the lords and ladies for their suspicion, though. After all, he and Kieran and Dom made themselves scarce from sanctioned gatherings, and the few times that they had been in attendance, excessive drinking and inappropriate behavior followed. There had been one time at a ball when he and Kieran had challenged each other to see how many flowers they could filch from ladies' hairstyles. And there may have been a time—though whisky had muddled the edges of that memory—where Finn had raced Dom down some stairs on a pair of Axminster rugs.

Kieran had been fortunate, or cunning, enough to have Celeste Kilburn rehabilitate his reputation as a rake. Perhaps Finn should have asked his brother's fiancée to work the same magic for him. Yet he'd been too anxious to get this whole *match Dom with Tabitha Seaton* gambit underway to make the request, and so he had plunged ahead by attending the Earl and Countess of Blakemere's ball in the hope of crossing Miss Seaton's path.

"I don't know what this gel looks like," Dom grumbled, as if aware of Finn's thoughts. "Can't keep watch for her."

"I'm not certain she's made an appearance yet." Finn scanned the ballroom, but no woman had Miss Seaton's unusual height, or way of holding herself at a slight remove, as if analyzing the events around her to determine whether or not they were worthwhile.

"Has the major domo announced Miss Tabitha Seaton?" Finn asked a passing footman. For good measure, Finn set his punch cup down on the servant's tray and grabbed a flute of sparkling wine. It was surprisingly good wine, but then, the earl and countess had a reputation for excellent hospitality.

Dom also gave the footman his punch cup, and took two flutes, which he downed in quick succession.

"Yes, sir," the footman answered. "She came in half an hour ago. Haven't seen her since her arrival."

Finn put a shilling on the servant's tray. The footman bowed his thanks before pocketing the coin and moving on to other guests.

"Here but not here," Finn said thoughtfully.

"In the retiring room?" Dom speculated.

"Let us pray she's no need of the retiring room for a full thirty minutes. No, she's somewhere in this house . . . but where?"

What little he knew of Miss Seaton could be contained in a needle case. Still, the first and last time he'd met her, she'd had a book with her, which meant that she wasn't precisely enamored of the company at balls.

"I've a very good idea where she might be," he said to Dom. "Wait here. If my instincts are correct, I'll return directly with the lady."

"Don't leave me here alone." Dom, tall as a draft horse and broad as a barge, held a hint of panic in his voice.

"Nothing's going to happen," Finn soothed him.

"What if . . . they make me dance?"

"Think of it like a barroom brawl, with only slightly less violence."

With a reassuring chuck of his fist to Dom's shoulder, Finn strode away. He skirted the edge of the dance floor, just as he skirted the edge of respectability, and moved out into a corridor. His steps faltered only once, when he passed the cardroom, yet he cast but one longing look in its direction before continuing on. The play wouldn't be deep enough here, anyway.

Though he had never been in Blakemere's home before, it stood to reason that the place he sought would be found on this floor. As he walked, he fell into step several paces behind two young women. They fanned themselves and spoke in low, eager voices about people he didn't know and things he didn't care about.

"I could have *sworn* I saw Lady Georgette dancing twice with Mr. Devaney," the blonde woman said excitedly.

"She would never," her companion insisted. This girl had a crown of diamonds woven into her brown hair, which would have made a handsome bet. "For one thing, Mr. Devaney is only worth two thousand a year."

"And Lady Georgette won't flutter her eyelashes for less than four thousand."

To Finn's surprise, the two young ladies walked through a set of double doors, which was where he had intended to go. He followed at a respectful distance, entering the chamber behind them.

The women drew up short. "This isn't the ladies' retiring room," the blonde said in consternation.

"It's a *library*," her friend added with disgust.

Indeed, it was a most splendid library—if one liked such places. The room was ringed with abundantly stocked bookshelves, and there were so many volumes that they were piled onto every available surface, forming stacks on chairs and tables. Clearly, the earl and countess enjoyed their books.

Though this was where he had intended to go,

unease still worked its way through Finn's muscles. The instinct to turn and run sent currents of electricity along his limbs, but he made himself remain in the room as he breathed in and out. They were just books, after all, inanimate objects that could not, on their own, hurt him.

The women cast him a curious glance, so he feigned interest in the bookshelves, perusing their contents. "Ah," he mused aloud, "a rare first edition of Wilhelm Schnitzel's treatise on drainage systems."

This seemed to deter the women from paying him any mind, so they turned away, which suited him very well. His true focus was on the library's only other occupant.

She was here.

Surely the throb of his pulse was from triumph. His instincts in locating her had proven correct—that was the only reason he felt any kind of excitement in seeing Tabitha Seaton again.

She stood close to the table, her nose buried in the book she held.

"Who's this?" the blonde asked. She and her companion walked deeper into the chamber.

"Miss Seaton, I believe?" Diamond crown said with curiosity.

The woman in question looked up in alarm, evidently caught by surprise. "Oh—I thought—Well. Good evening."

The two young ladies approached Miss Seaton. As they did so, Finn edged nearer, still pretending to be absorbed in examining the books on the shelves.

With Miss Seaton's attention focused primarily on the girls, he had an opportunity to regard her without being rude.

Her deep brown hair was primly pinned up without any stray tendrils to curl beguilingly around her angular face—he'd forgotten that she had a slight cleft in her chin—and her stormy blue-gray eyes were wide with apprehension. He hadn't remembered that she possessed a rather captivating mouth, full and pink.

What would it be like to kiss that mouth? Her lips might be soft and yielding, or assertive and commanding.

The deuce? There was no reason why he should speculate on *kissing* her.

As if aware of the direction of his thoughts, her perceptive gaze arrowed to his.

A quick, hot thrill ran the length of his body.

Her eyes widened. Did she feel it, too—this sudden, unexpected jolt of awareness? Impossible. It was the sort of thing poets wrote about but no one ever actually experienced. Certainly, *Finn* didn't. And not with someone so completely unlike him as Tabitha Seaton.

"That must be quite a naughty book you're reading, Miss Seaton," the brunette said with a giggle. "Look how she hides it from us, Harriet."

Miss Seaton held the volume to her chest, as if she was indeed trying to keep the other women from examining it too closely.

Perhaps the bluestocking had been caught reading one of the Lady of Dubious Quality's racy tomes. An unexpected, intriguing display of passion.

"What do you think the book could be, Flora?" the blonde asked. She and her friend leaned close to get a look at the volume's spine.

"Nothing of note," Miss Seaton said. Her pleasantly husky voice trailed along Finn's nape. She quickly shut the book and stuck it amongst the piles of texts on the table behind her. It was clear she hoped that it would be impossible to identify which one it was amongst all the other tomes with similar covers.

Finn's eye went right to it.

She stepped away from the table. It appeared she was attempting to draw the girls' attention to something else. And it worked, to a point. Harriet and Flora's focus remained on her.

Still, if the two young ladies *did* identify which book Miss Seaton had been reading, it might prove disastrous. Though Finn didn't have much commerce with the world of the ton, he understood enough about it to realize that gossip could work quickly and devastatingly. If Miss Seaton had been reading an erotic novel in the earl and countess's library during a ball, it would be calamitous for her good standing.

The young ladies advanced on Miss Seaton, like wolves stalking prey.

"Was it a French novel?" Flora asked in a wheedling voice. "You can tell us. We promise not to tell anyone. Will we, Harriet?"

"Not a soul," the other girl said without an ounce of sincerity.

"The strangest thing," Finn said, snaring everyone's attention.

He moved toward the table and stood in front of it. As he pointed to the door, directing the girls' gazes, he reached behind him and grabbed the book Miss Seaton had been reading. He hid it behind his back.

"I could have sworn I saw Lady Georgette about to dance a *third* time with Mr. Devaney," he added.

The young ladies gasped and turned to each other.
"We *must* see this," Harriet insisted.

She and Flora hurried from the library without
a backward glance. Leaving Finn alone with Miss
Seaton.

The moment they were out the door, Finn pulled
the book out from behind his back. Was it one of
the Lady of Dubious Quality's stories—which he'd
heard extolled by Kieran—or perhaps something
with ribald illustrations? Hopefully, it had ribald illustrations.

He gave Miss Seaton a knowing smile. His smile
faltered when he saw the frontispiece. He read it
once, but his usual method of using context to figure out what something said failed him. Another attempt at reading the title yielded no results. He tried
to sound it out in his mind. Still no luck.

He looked up at her with a puzzled frown. This
was *not* the daring secret he'd been anticipating.

"It isn't every day that you find a first printing of
Hildegard von Bingen's *Physica*," she said, a hint of
excitement in her voice. "And the Blakemeres just
have it lying around as if it was as commonplace as
Haywood's *Love in Excess*."

"I'm rather dizzy about it, myself." He handed her
the book, and their fingers lightly brushed against
each other. Her gloves lay atop the table, so that the
brief contact had been between bare flesh. Something quick and gleaming shot up his arm from the
minuscule contact, and it careened around his chest
for far longer than he would have believed something
so minor could last.

"A fellow bibliophile?" she asked, her expression
brightening.

"I'm not much of a reader," he admitted.

The look of happiness on her face quickly disappeared, and he was almost sorry that he'd spoken the truth, if only so he could witness how pleasure illuminated her from the inside out for a little longer. But then, he was rather used to seeing that disappointment on people's faces.

Carefully, reluctantly, she set the tome back onto the table, but not before giving it one last yearning glance, typically reserved for parting lovers.

"Unless you fear that Harriet and Flora are collectors of rare books," he said, studying her, "why not let them see what you were reading?"

"Eligible ladies are supposed to be at gatherings such as this to make brilliant matches. Being discovered in the library poring over a medieval Germanic abbess's treatise on the natural world would do me few favors, especially with a reputation such as mine."

She said these last words with a touch of bitterness.

Perhaps that reputation she'd spoken of had something to do with her currently unwed state, and why she was here, in the library, instead of being whirled around the dance floor.

"But I thank you for your gallant service," she added. "Had word gotten out about me and Hildegard, I'm sure I wouldn't make one of those brilliant matches." She narrowed her eyes. "We've met, haven't we?"

"Finn Ransome." He bowed, and she slowly nodded in recognition. "I believe that at our last meeting, you mentioned something about bringing a book to a ball just like this one."

"That sounds like me." Her lips curved wryly.

It was fascinating, her mobile mouth. It moved and

shifted and for some reason, he couldn't stop looking at it.

"I'd made the effort not to bring a book to *this* ball," she went on, "but I took one look at the dancing and immediately regretted my decision."

"Regrets come fast and furious at balls," he said dryly.

"They do seem to flow as readily as sparkling wine," she answered.

"But have a far more bitter flavor."

There were tiny flecks of green in her irises, the green of forest shadows. And there had to be something in his own eyes that seemed to captivate her, too, because she stared into them for a long moment.

He mentally shook himself. The very fact that she considered a library to be her sanctuary was proof that this conversation could not lead anywhere further.

The room continued to loom around Finn menacingly. Fortunately, he was well familiar with the art of bluffing, so he didn't let his discomfort show in his face or voice.

Unlike him, however, she gazed at the shelves with the air of someone coming home from a long journey. Music and laughter drifted into the chamber, and her brief joy fell away, replaced by what appeared to be steely resignation.

"Suitors aren't abundant in libraries, are they?" she asked.

"In my limited experience, swains and bucks favor displaying themselves in the middle of a ballroom. But, again, I'm not considered an expert in that realm." If she wanted to hear his thoughts on the best wagering strategy for the game of hazard, he had an abundance of them.

Yet the word *suitors* from her lips caught his attention.

"Is that your goal?" he asked, as lightly as he could, lest he reveal how much her answer signified. "Finding a suitor?"

"It is." She frowned. "Demure young ladies aren't supposed to be so blatant in their intentions as I am."

"Candor is a better choice than obfuscation," he answered. It was a challenge to keep his voice steady. She might actively be seeking a bridegroom—exactly what he hoped for.

"Clearly, you know less about Society than I do," she replied dryly, "if that's your belief."

A smile touched his lips. But he set it aside—he had an objective, just like Miss Seaton, and fortunately, their objectives aligned.

"If it's a suitor you're seeking," he said, "allow me to be of assistance."

Her brows climbed. They were very nice eyebrows, actually, arched and expressive. "Here we had agreed that eligible gentlemen weren't often found in libraries."

Their gazes met again and something hot and alive uncoiled in his belly. Her tongue darted out to leave a gloss upon her bottom lip.

A rather pretty lip. Both of them, in fact.

Yet those lips had spoken the names of Latinate texts moments ago, and likely frequently formed themselves around words and concepts that would be entirely beyond him. She'd already been disappointed that he'd admitted he wasn't a reader. No need to see more displeased frowns in his long history of witnessing that same expression.

"Please." He gestured toward the library door. "Come with me."

She opened her mouth as though to urge him for details, then seemed to think better of it, and remained silent.

After she retrieved her gloves and tugged them back on, she preceded him out of the library. Air rushed back into his lungs once he'd left that chamber.

He motioned for her to accompany him to the ballroom.

"Must we go in there?" she asked warily.

"It delights me just as little as it does you," he answered, "but needs must."

He held out his arm, and she eyed it for a moment. A strange, taut expectancy traveled the length of his body before she set her hand lightly upon his sleeve.

Even though she exerted hardly any pressure on him, that tautness within him vibrated as though she strummed him like a lute.

She stared down at where her fingers rested on his sleeve, and her breathing hitched while twin stains of pink rose up on her cheeks. Then she inhaled as though purposefully steadying herself.

He ought to do the same. And so, he guided her into the ballroom. Once they were inside the hot, crowded room, her fingers twitched slightly on his arm. The movement was so slight it was nearly imperceptible—but he noticed.

She looked toward the dancers, a hint of wariness in her eyes, but that wariness shifted to confusion as he led her around the perimeter of the dance floor. Toward Dom.

His friend continued to stand by himself in the corner of the ballroom, glaring at anyone who came near. As Finn and Miss Seaton approached, she whispered, "I've seen less intimidating battlements. Thank goodness we're not going to interact with *him*."

"In point of fact . . ." Finn stopped in front of Dom, who regarded him stonily. "Miss Tabitha Seaton, may I present the very eligible Mr. Dominic Kilburn?"

A look of surprise flashed across her face, though it was gone in an instant, and she dipped into a curtsey as Dom bowed.

"Mr. Kilburn is the son and heir of warehouse magnate Edward Kilburn," Finn explained. "The fortune he stands to inherit is substantial. You have all your own teeth, right, Dom?"

His friend grunted in response.

"Are you *advertising* Mr. Kilburn?" Miss Seaton asked pointedly. "Like a bottle of tonic in the newspaper?"

Finn nearly smiled.

"Evasiveness is a luxury none of us can afford," he replied. "Both you and Dom are on the hunt for a spouse, and we needn't pretend marriage is not the intended goal. In my opinion, the perfect solution has presented itself." He gestured between a grim-faced Dom and the skeptical Miss Seaton.

She glanced toward Finn once more. Disappointment seemed to flicker briefly across her face, but surely, he had to be mistaken.

"We cannot begin reading the banns next Sunday," she pointed out. "I know nothing of Mr. Kilburn, nor he of me."

Dom made a low noise of agreement. Come to think of it, he hadn't spoken actual words since Finn had introduced him to the lady. It wasn't promising, but Dom hadn't stalked away, either, so there was still hope.

"Royal marriages have been based upon less," Finn noted.

"God knows I'm no prince," Dom said, finally breaking his silence.

Miss Seaton continued to look unconvinced, so clearly something would have to be done.

"And yet what prince has won academic awards at Oxford?" Finn countered.

Some of the doubt left Miss Seaton's eyes. "Is that true, Mr. Kilburn?"

"A paper I wrote on Spencer's *The Faerie Queene* got a prize," Dom said grudgingly. "Same with an essay on the Baconian method."

Finn knew nothing of Spencer, and the only Bacon he was familiar with graced his breakfast table.

"There, you see," Finn said reasonably. "Common ground."

Yet both Dom and Miss Seaton seemed uncertain. More action would be needed.

"In two days," he said, keeping his tone encouraging, "there's to be a harvest fair held on Parliament Hill. You know it?"

"In Hampstead Heath," she answered. "Best views of London."

"You and Dom can attend together," Finn continued, "and learn more about each other in the process."

Silence from his friend and the lady greeted this suggestion. All right, he'd have to provide further inspiration.

"I'll accompany you," he added. "Less pressure to perform if there's three of us instead of two."

Finn almost never saw daylight hours, and he was hardly the sort of man who frequented fairs. Further, most gaming hells did not offer bobbing for apples or tossing rings onto pins, so he had little experience with these activities. Still, he'd make an exception if it meant taking a step closer to Dom and Miss Seaton's possible engagement.

She appeared on the verge of refusing, causing a rock of apprehension to rattle around his stomach. Yet, to his astonishment, she said, "That's acceptable."

It wasn't a scream of delighted enthusiasm, but he'd take it. He turned to Dom, who continued to resemble an especially stoic oak tree.

"Awright," Dom said at last.

"Excellent." Finn clapped his hands together. "We shall meet you at the entrance to the fair, Miss Seaton. Say, one o'clock?"

"This will be my first fair," she said, halfway between puzzled and interested.

"Mine, too." He blinked with the realization.

"Do you believe anyone there will know?" she asked. "That we're both novices?"

"I suppose not." Why did it please him so much that they would be together, experiencing something for the first time? "Unless we do something dreadfully inappropriate."

"Given that I read in the middle of balls," she mused, "it's entirely possible that I *would* do something inappropriate. I cannot imagine what sort of misbehavior *you* might engage in."

"Fairs are supposedly full of games, and I have

been known to taunt my competitors if I feel it's a good strategy to ensure my win," he said gravely.

"How about this," she offered, and he didn't have to bend to hear her, the way he had to with most ladies. "We'll both act as each other's minders. If you start goading anyone during the egg and spoon race, I'll say, 'Cervantes.'"

"And if I find you engaging in excessive acts of scholarship at the fair, I'll give you a signal. Like this." He coughed once, then rubbed his chin.

She nodded solemnly, though there was a glint of humor in her gaze. "We are in accord."

Dom gave an additional grunt that Finn decided was a noise of agreement, before his friend glanced away. Clearly, the conversation was at an end.

Turning to Miss Seaton, a banal pleasantry formed on Finn's lips, some way to conclude their discussion—but then he was looking into her eyes and his thoughts scattered.

Despite his height, it was easy to gaze into her eyes. They were almost at a level with his own.

Clearly, that's why he kept staring into them and getting lost.

"I . . ." Another crease appeared between her brows as she seemed equally unable to think.

A moment passed, and then another.

Finally, she murmured, "Gentlemen," then gave them a small curtsey. Luckily, Finn recalled enough of his experience with his dancing master many years ago that he knew he was supposed to bow when a lady departed his company. So, he did, with Dom following suit, before Miss Seaton walked away.

Unlike the other young women, who glided around like flower petals atop the surface of a pond, she walked with quick, purposeful strides, as though she was too busy to waste her time moving around like withered flora on water.

His attention was wholly fixed on her, the rest of the room and its occupants fading away as he watched her. She did cut a striking figure, standing quite a bit taller than most of the women, and a few of the men. Finally, she disappeared into the crowd.

Finn blinked, coming back to himself.

"A cheroot on the balcony?" he suggested to Dom.

"Please, God," his friend answered.

In short order, they stood to one side of a long terrace, blowing smoke into the cool autumn evening air. A few gentlemen and some hardier ladies were also outside, though the women wore wraps to keep them warm, and the low hum of flirtatious conversation drifted over to where Finn and Dom had positioned themselves.

Finn drew deeply on his cheroot, the fragrant smoke soothing him. This had to be a new record for the amount of time he'd recently spent at a ball. Gaming hells were so much more comfortable—the tranquil clicking sound of dice being cast, the servants circulating with drink far stronger than punch or sparkling wine, the cheers and cries of people at the tables as they won and lost fortunes.

"She looked at me as if I'd devour her. Like a dragon with a virgin," Dom grumbled, breaking the silence between them.

"Granted, you have a somewhat intimidating appearance," Finn said, yet added in an attempt to be conciliatory, "but she'll surely discover all of your delightful facets and be completely amenable to accepting a proposal of marriage."

"Don't see why *I'm* the one who has to court her." Dom exhaled a thick cloud. "*You'd* make just as acceptable a bridegroom."

"I found her in a *library*, Dom," Finn answered. "*Reading.*"

"Ah," his friend said in understanding.

Finn smiled ruefully. Thank God for good friends who didn't need explanations. Thanks to the stipulations of his father's decree, he *would* have to marry at some point over the course of the remaining eight months. But when that time came, it would be a disaster to tie himself to someone who would eventually look at him across the breakfast table with disgust. Because that's what would happen with Miss Seaton—sooner rather than later.

"You'll have plenty to talk about," Finn noted, "though you hide your intellectual light under a bushel."

"When I first got to Oxford," Dom said, "I thought I'd try to fit in with the nobs. It's what my da wanted. Studied like mad. Won those bleeding awards." He lifted one big shoulder. "It hardly mattered. They still looked at me like someone had dumped a chamber pot in the middle of the junior common room. Didn't see much point in boasting about my brains after that."

"Ah, the revolting snobbery of the young aristo," Finn said. "May I apologize on behalf of all my kind."

"Lucky for you, I don't hold your anemic bloodline against you," Dom answered wryly.

"We all can't have Kieran's good fortune in bride choice," Finn went on. "We must make do with the options we're given."

Dom grunted, and Finn couldn't blame him for his laconic response. It was excruciatingly evident that Kieran was madly in love with Dom's sister, and she with Kieran, but that was a rarity, not the average. Christ knew, Finn's own parents barely tolerated the sight of each other.

A marriage amongst his class was typically more business arrangement than blissful union of two hearts. His own circumstances impelled him to find a bride out of necessity . . . yet it was far easier to consider Dom's matrimonial prospects rather than his own.

Whoever his future wife might be, she couldn't be someone who lived for intellectual pursuits, as Miss Seaton did. He could never be the sort of man she would want, and lashing them together for a lifetime would be a tremendous mistake.

Chapter 4

❧ ❋ ❧

$\mathcal{T}$wo days later, Tabitha alighted from her carriage at the base of Parliament Hill, with Olive following behind her. A breeze blew the ribbons of her bonnet and molded the fabric of her redingote to her body, and the wind would only grow stronger once she actually ascended the hill—a place so well-known for its gusts that people came from all over the city to fly kites here. Even so, Olive fussed with her clothing.

"It's a losing battle," Tabitha said as her maid attempted to smooth her clinging redingote into something a little more modest.

"I can't help it, miss," Olive protested. "Outings with gentlemen don't happen very often, and her ladyship would sack me in a trice if she suspected your wardrobe wasn't up to snuff."

"I suppose it is a rarity." It had been rather unseemly, the way Mama and Papa had lit up like lanterns when she'd told them this morning that she was to visit a harvest fair with not one but *two* eligible gentlemen. But then, they had likely lost all hope that their spinster wallflower of a daughter would ever find herself the object of an interested suitor's attention.

Strictly speaking, Finn Ransome was not an interested suitor. He'd offered himself as a kind of intermediary between herself and Dominic Kilburn, which was fortunate, because Mr. Kilburn was one of the most physically intimidating male specimens she'd ever encountered.

If one judged an individual on the basis of looks, then Mr. Ransome was quite literally one of the handsomest men she'd ever beheld. Physical appearance was immaterial when it came to indicating the nature of someone's character. She'd known many who were considered conventionally attractive but beneath their exteriors beat mean and spiteful hearts, whereas people who might have been dismissed as plain were kind, giving, and creative. And yet even she understood that, as far as exteriors went, Finn Ransome's was exceptional. She considered herself at best an agnostic, but the hand of the Creator seemed evident in him, as though They were showing off. *Look what I can make. Your statues of David don't stand a chance against me.*

He had black hair and dark eyes, with a substantial nose, a full mouth, honed features, and a square jawline that would make most architecture envious. Whatever he did to maintain his physical condition proved itself effective, because he filled out his black jacket and waistcoat admirably. Who knew men had such wide shoulders or such flat stomachs? She wouldn't pretend that she hadn't observed the long lines of his thighs beneath his white breeches.

Appearance *was* inconsequential, though. Yet he'd shielded her from Harriet's and Flora's prying. It wasn't as though he knew or owed her, and yet he'd made certain the two girls didn't have any ammunition in the assassination of her character.

But that's what a gentleman did, wasn't it? Acted courteously toward young women.

She simply wasn't used to the company of robust, eligible men. That had to be why her attention had been pulled to him again and again, why she'd been so powerfully aware of him.

"Miss, it's considered decorous for a young lady to keep a gentleman waiting," Olive said, interrupting her thoughts, "but it would be wise if you weren't *too* late."

Tabitha's mouth twisted wryly. "The implication being I'm not the sort of woman men would be willing to wait for."

"Of *course*," Olive amended, flushing, "Mr. Kilburn and Mr. Ransome will be more than happy to bide a while if it means the possibility of spending time with you, miss."

"It's a fair point," Tabitha conceded. After rising this morning, she'd looked at herself in the mirror and tried to see herself objectively. She lacked the soft and gentle features males of her class seemed to laud, and was unusually tall, which also seemed to be a deterrent to most men.

She wouldn't entertain illusions about her ability to attract a suitor. Sentiment and tender feelings were for other people. Hers was a life of the mind, and she would not, *could not*, be led astray by something as messy as emotions. She'd learned that eight years ago. But you couldn't miss something you'd never had, and everything was much simpler and more logical this way.

Though neither Mr. Kilburn nor Mr. Ransome had said so at the ball, there seemed a certain desperation in the former's need for a bride.

Well, she had an agenda, too. One at which she *couldn't* fail.

With that in mind, she gently shooed Olive away from any further fussing with her clothing and started up the hill. The sounds of the fair were caught on the wind—music played upon country fiddles rather than elegant violins and laughter that was far less genteel than at the ball—as were the scents of fried dough, spiced cider, and animals. People of different classes streamed toward the amusements, so she and Olive joined their ranks, the climb upward steep but not impossible.

She spotted Mr. Ransome and Mr. Kilburn before they caught sight of her. And while nervousness spiraled in her belly at the sight of the massive Mr. Kilburn, her heart thudded when she looked at Mr. Ransome. Today he wore an ink-blue coat with a black velvet collar, and two rows of gleaming buttons marched down the front of his deep gray waistcoat. His breeches were dove gray and tucked into tall, shining boots. His face was slightly shaded by the brim of his tall hat, yet enough sunlight reached his sculpted features to make her suck in a breath.

Appearance is of little account. It was even less important because her interest was not in Mr. Ransome, but Mr. Kilburn. *The inner landscape is what matters.*

The two men were conversing, and Mr. Ransome said something that made a corner of Mr. Kilburn's mouth quirk up, which was, she supposed, the closest that individual ever came to a full smile.

That minuscule show of emotion disappeared when Mr. Kilburn saw her approaching. He nudged Mr. Ransome and nodded in her direction.

She swallowed hard when Mr. Ransome's gaze locked with hers. Even though many yards separated them, as well as countless people on their way to the fair, his dark eyes seemed to reach deep into her and find all the places she tried so hard to keep hidden. As they had at the ball. She'd gone to bed that night convinced that the fascination she'd had with him had merely been the byproduct of being unused to the presence of unmarried men.

Yet she *felt* his regard on her now, aware and alive. Her steps faltered.

You're here for a reason, and he is not *that reason.*

She resumed her usual brisk stride to reach the two men. After bowing and curtseying, they exchanged pleasant but featureless greetings. Mr. Kilburn barely managed a grunt, and Mr. Ransome kept looking at her as though afraid she might turn and flee at any moment.

"Are you ready to experience a fair for the first time, Miss Seaton?" he asked.

She'd half believed that her recollection of his voice had been an exaggeration, and that he sounded like any ordinary man, but, alas, his words were rich and low and reminded her of the kind of shadows where one was tempted to do unwise things. Those shadows had never tempted her before—until now.

"Everything I know of these places comes from books," she answered.

"Don't be afraid," he said.

"I'm not afraid," she replied. "Only curious."

"Curiosity is a valuable commodity," he said with

a nod. "Without it, humanity would never have learned that old grapes make excellent wine."

"That sounds suspiciously like an aphorism."

"If it does, it's purely accidental."

She studied him, this man who was as sleek as a polished stone yet with a vein of something far more substantive running through him. "It's my belief that little you do is accidental."

"The hazards of my profession," he responded.

"Which is . . . ?"

"Surely that can hold little interest to you," he countered with a dispassionate tone. "Not when we're in such a fascinating place, with so much else worthy of your study. I'd wager you could write more than a few volumes on the sociological significance of festivals and fairs."

"Magicians are experts at distraction," she replied. "They direct your attention one place so that you don't notice the mechanics of their tricks. You, Mr. Ransome, are showing me a colored handkerchief in one hand so I won't see you hiding a rabbit in a hat."

He started before visibly smoothing his expression. "What could I possibly be hiding from you, Miss Seaton?"

"That would require further study—but I am a dedicated scholar, Mr. Ransome. And nothing intrigues me more than being told I *shouldn't* do something."

"Motivated by contrariness?"

"Why not?" she countered. "Whole schools of philosophy have been founded on willfulness."

He regarded her with a mixture of interested curiosity and caution. But there was no disgust in his eyes, no derision. Perhaps even a glimmer of admiration.

Her belly fluttered. How rare for her to encounter respect in anyone outside of her friends from the Benezra.

"Let's go, then," Mr. Kilburn said curtly before turning on his heel and marching through the gates that marked the entrance to the fair.

Mr. Ransome forced out a chuckle. "I believe Dom is merely keen to enjoy all that the fair has to offer."

"He seems a man who lives to enjoy himself," she answered dryly.

"Once he was," Mr. Ransome murmured, his expression darkening. Then he seemed to force himself back to good humor. "Dom's eagerness to appreciate the fair will subside within a few moments, and he'll be pleased to escort you to all the attractions. In the interim, I offer myself as a poor substitute."

He held out his arm.

The polite thing would be to take it. And yet she stared at his forearm, uncertainty holding her back, as if touching him again—even through her gloves and his layers of wool and linen—crossed some boundary.

There was no boundary to cross. They were simply people who were put together by circumstance. Any response she had to him could be chalked up to being physically near a young, single man.

A moment later, she placed her hand on his sleeve. The current that ran through her body was merely the product of an overly active mind, which had long been a complaint many had directed at her. And if she thought she heard Mr. Ransome inhale sharply, it was extremely noisy here and she couldn't be certain of any sound, let alone one man's intake of breath.

They joined with the crowds, with Olive following, and were soon in the fair itself. True to the season, it was decorated with garlands of wheat, and gourds were piled festively beside many of the booths. There were games of all varieties, from tossing rings onto bottles to apple bobbing to archery targets complete with miniature bows and arrows. Vendors sold sweet and savory pies, sausages, and paper sacks filled with roasted nuts. The braying of a donkey called attention to the animals, who were led around a small track with children perched atop their backs. She smiled at the flower crowns of asters draped around the animals' ears.

"They must like it," Mr. Ransome mused. "Being made beautiful, if only for a little while."

"'Beauty is a short-lived tyranny,'" she said absently.

"Perhaps so," he answered with a small smile as they walked past the donkeys and their young passengers, "but at least the animals can eat their adornments. Diamonds are so tedious to chew. Do you really believe that beauty is a short-lived tyranny?"

"Socrates did," she answered.

"But what do *you* think? Do you truly think that beauty is both momentary and oppressive?"

She frowned in surprise. "You genuinely want to know my thoughts?"

"Of course I do. That is to say," he added quickly, "Mr. Kilburn and I are both interested in your opinions."

After eyeing Mr. Kilburn's broad back—which was a dozen yards ahead of them—she said warily, "Beauty can be misleading. It dazzles us into false beliefs and tempts us to act unwisely. The very fact that it *is* transitory is part of its power. We're tempted to claim it quickly before it dissipates, and so we're lured into disaster."

Mr. Ransome arched one brow.

Something leaden coagulated in her. She should have known—whilst her friends from the Benezra Library were interested in her thoughts and gave them full consideration, people like Chima, Arjun, Diana, and Iris were rare. When she'd dared give her opinion to people outside her circle, especially men, she'd been met with disbelief or derision. They couldn't understand how someone of her sex could possibly have enough understanding to formulate a complex ideology. And God forbid she ought to express any notion that wasn't entirely sunny—she'd been told again and again that no one appreciated a woman who wasn't a cheerful balm to a man's soul.

"Beauty *is* treacherous," he said after a moment. "There are many things in life that would harm us—if we aren't careful. Then we bear their scars."

She stared at him. Of all the people to say such things to her, she'd never believed Finn Ransome would be the one to do it. What wounds did he carry?

"And those scars make us ugly," she whispered, "whether they are visible or not."

"Or make us stronger, and even more wondrous," he countered gently.

They gazed at each other, and she was held again in the dark depths of his eyes. She'd thought them cool, but now there was a hint of warmth that curled around her.

"Oi!" Mr. Kilburn called over his shoulder. "I'm going to look like a ruddy ass playing ring-a-bottle alone." He headed toward the booth offering the ring-a-bottle game.

Mr. Ransome grimaced, then forced out a laugh when he looked at Tabitha. "A lively fellow, is Dom."

If ill-tempered behemoths could be considered lively, she thought. Yet that was unfair. She hardly knew Mr. Kilburn, and ought to give him some leeway when assessing his character.

"Shall we join him?" Mr. Ransome asked with deliberate cheer. "I was in the nursery the last time I played ring-a-bottle."

"I've read about such fairground games. To understand the nature of public spaces and the necessity for play within the context of structured societal norms."

"We all need a little play in our lives." He took long strides as he spoke, and she appreciated that he wasn't one of those people who meandered around, but walked with purpose. "Else we'd explode like one of those new steam engines when they overheat."

How unexpected, that a gentleman of Mr. Ransome's elegant and leisured disposition might be at all interested in engineering developments. Yet outcomes seldom unfolded as anticipated. Certainly, *he* was proving unexpected.

They joined Mr. Kilburn at the booth, and Mr. Ransome placed three coins into the palm of the woman running the attraction. She handed him and Mr. Kilburn four wooden rings apiece, and then offered Tabitha a set of rings.

"Give it a try," Mr. Ransome said when Tabitha eyed them cautiously. "Put theory into practice."

Gingerly, Tabitha took the rings from the woman, who moved aside to give them all a clear shot at the rows of bottles lined up on a board three yards away. Colorful nosegays rested in a nearby basket, presumably the prizes for whomever was dexterous enough to get their rings around the bottles' necks.

Tabitha studied the wooden pieces, feeling the rough texture. How many people had handled them, filled with excitement and eagerness, perhaps to impress a sweetheart or test their abilities for no other reason than to prove to themselves that they could? Yet when you put so much emphasis on a desired result, and that result didn't come, how did you manage the disappointment? Perhaps if one had a sanguine view of the world, wherein minor setbacks did not become emblematic of a larger, more pessimistic conceptualization—

"It needn't mean anything more than a diversion," Mr. Ransome said softly, breaking into her musings. A small smile peeked in the corner of his mouth. "Simply enjoy the activity without giving it too much thought."

She wrinkled her nose. "That's a rather difficult prospect."

"The task is simple enough for me," he said easily. "I have never struggled with too much intelligence."

What an extraordinary thing to say. It was so alien that she could only gape at him.

She looked to Mr. Kilburn, standing on the other side of Mr. Ransome. His expression had barely changed when Mr. Ransome had spoken so dismissively of his intellectual abilities, and she waited for Mr. Kilburn to refute that statement—but no refutation was forthcoming. Instead, Mr. Kilburn tossed a ring toward one of the bottles and grunted when the ring glanced off the glass.

Mr. Ransome stood loosely, easily, before lightly flicking one of his rings toward a bottle. It wasn't a particularly strenuous thing to do, and yet he imbued the action with a natural and comfortable athleticism. Her stomach fluttered.

The ring hooked onto the bottle's neck, spun around several times, and then slid into place neatly.

"You did it," Tabitha exclaimed.

"The power of not thinking," he answered. "Now, your turn."

It felt entirely unnatural to fling one of her wooden rings toward the target, and it came as no surprise when the ring weakly landed on the patch of grass between her and the bottles. Even so, a barb of disappointment jabbed her. She'd so hoped to be good at this, despite the fact that she'd never done it before.

"Would you like advice?" Mr. Ransome asked. "Though, I'm perfectly content to keep my blathering to myself."

"Your counsel is welcome," she answered, appreciating that he asked rather than simply inundating her with his opinions.

"Keep your focus on the bottle's neck rather than looking at the ring. Might have more success. And don't forget to breathe."

She tried again, following his guidance by looking at her intended target, and letting out an exhalation as she threw. This time, the ring actually pinged off the bottle's neck.

"Excellently done." Palpable warmth once again shone in his eyes.

Her own cheeks grew heated—but it had to be because she didn't deserve his praise.

"I didn't get the ring around the bottle," she protested.

"But you did better than before. You tried, and improved. That's a victory by my standards."

His admiration was a warm pour of liquor, loosening the tension that had knotted through her body, all the more potent because it was so unlike anything she ever told herself.

Clearly, it was less extraordinary for Mr. Ransome, because he turned to Mr. Kilburn. "A bob that you won't make the next three throws."

"Done," Mr. Kilburn answered at once, while Tabitha started at the considerable sum of the wager.

The two men shook hands, and then Mr. Kilburn faced the bottles. He narrowed his eyes, balanced on the tips of his toes, and angled his body. Tabitha held her breath as he threw.

The ring landed neatly on its target.

Mr. Kilburn threw a smug look at Mr. Ransome, who looked unimpressed. "Two more to go."

To Tabitha's dismay, Mr. Kilburn's next two throws landed, the rings clattering in celebration as they worked their way down the glass vessels.

Mr. Kilburn's teeth flashed in a feral smile as he held out his hand to Mr. Ransome. With surprisingly good grace, Mr. Ransome dropped a shilling into Mr. Kilburn's huge, outstretched palm, which he then tucked into a pocket in his waistcoat.

"You look awful chipper for a bloke who just lost a bob," Mr. Kilburn said to his friend.

"Yet you smiled for the first time in months," Mr. Ransome replied.

The large man's smile fell away and he stalked off just as the woman running the booth approached with his prize. Looking puzzled, she watched him go, then faced Tabitha and Mr. Ransome.

"Would either of you like it?" she asked, holding out the nosegay.

Tabitha stepped forward and took the small bouquet from the woman. After taking a moment to inhale its fragrance, she bent down and offered the flowers to a small child clinging to his father's hand.

The little boy reached for the nosegay before his father's voice stopped him. "Posies are for lasses, Freddie."

The child's face fell, but Mr. Ransome spoke. "Oh, but it's quite the fashion for gentlemen of the most superb taste to carry flowers. Isn't that so, Miss Seaton?"

"So it is," she agreed. "Just yesterday I saw Wellington himself with a whole bouquet of larkspur on his way to meet with Lord Liverpool."

The small boy brightened at this, and, after receiving a grudging nod from his father, he took the offered nosegay. He proudly held them aloft as he toddled away.

"We've created the next Brummell," Tabitha murmured as she observed the child disappearing into the crowd.

"Best invest in flower farms now," Mr. Ransome said wryly. Seemingly as an afterthought, he tossed his remaining rings toward the booth's targets, and, one after the other, they clanged down over the bottles' necks.

"You make that look so easy," she said, shaking her head after her own disastrous attempts to get her rings around the bottles.

"As I said, the trick lies in not thinking overmuch.

Thank you, madam," he added when the woman operating the booth handed him his prize nosegay.

Tabitha rocked back on her heels when Mr. Ransome stretched out his hand, offering *her* the small bouquet. "Miss Seaton."

She hesitated. In theory, she was here at the fair to become further acquainted with Mr. Kilburn, not Mr. Ransome, with the possibility that it was *Mr. Kilburn* who might court her. She and Mr. Ransome were simply acquaintances to each other. Weren't they?

If she took the flowers, she'd have a little memento of Finn Ransome. Something to look at and remember him by, including the way the sunlight gleamed off his ebony hair, and his fascinating eyes, and his unexpected kindness.

Emotional attachments were dangerous—and irrelevant. They certainly weren't any part of her plans.

"You are a gentleman of the most superb taste," she said, hoping for evenness in her voice. "The nosegay should remain in your possession. Here."

She plucked several of the flowers from the small bouquet and, after pulling a pin from her hair, moved to affix the blooms to his lapel. As she did so, he bent his head to watch her do it, bringing his face close to hers. His soft, spice-scented breath gently fanned over her cheeks. Her fingers felt ungainly, tremulous, and she had to pull off her gloves to make them work properly. She brushed against the velvet of his collar, improbably warmed by his body.

She barely kept from stabbing herself with the pin before finally managing to get the flowers attached to his lapel.

Glancing up through her lashes, she met his dark

gaze, which touched on her eyes before gliding down to her lips. There his regard remained.

His breath stopped, just as hers did.

Thoughts streamed out of her, emptying from her mind, until there was only a hot, liquid space where her intellect used to be.

One of the donkeys brayed, and at that unmusical sound, Tabitha's awareness returned. She took a step back, while Mr. Ransome did the same. His focused expression softened, and he smiled glossily at her before giving his lapel a pat.

"Now I'm a true arbiter of style," he said, his words composed. "I only wish you had some prize of your own. Ah. This will do." He took the remainder of the flowers from the nosegay and tucked them into the ribbon of her bonnet.

She caught a glimpse of his wrist. Despite his poise, his pulse beat quickly beneath his skin—mirroring her own.

Damn. If she kept these wretched flowers, she might start to have *emotions* about him. The very last thing she wanted. Dangerous things, feelings, which was why she made sure she had little to do with them.

"Let us see the rest of the fair," she announced. Before he could offer her his arm, she strode away.

Chapter 5

❧ ✳ ❧

$\mathcal{F}$inn was at this fair for a purpose, and so far, he'd been doing a right bungling job of it. Of course, having Dom march around like a one-man funeral procession didn't quite help matters, either, not if he was to endear himself to Miss Seaton.

In a few quick strides, he caught up with her, trying like hell to pretend that as she'd pinned the flowers to his coat, he hadn't wanted to pull her close and find out if her lips tasted sweet or piquant. A little of both, he'd wager, and he nearly always won his wagers.

He breathed in and out with purposeful calm. It didn't matter that she was exceptionally insightful, seeing into him in a way few could. It didn't matter that he craved knowing what had put the guardedness in her eyes. Yet that caution in her that kept tugging on him, drawing him nearer, wanting to discover each and every one of her layers.

"Mr. Kilburn's humor today is a trifle bilious," he said, glancing toward where Dom stomped toward a vendor selling mugs of cider. "Yet I assure you, he's the most excellent of men. Steadfast"—perhaps overly so, since Dom had been in the blackest of moods ever since he'd jilted Willa—"generous, and on better days, he's truly quite genial."

Miss Seaton glanced dubiously at Dom before her attention returned to Finn. He struggled not to shift restively beneath her perceptive gaze.

She kept doing that—looking at him as though she saw far deeper into him than anyone else, including Kieran.

He wasn't certain he liked it. But it did unsettle him.

Perhaps attempting to sell Dom on the basis of his personality wasn't the right tactic.

"One couldn't ask for a man with greater prospects," Finn went on. "Kilburn & Company keeps him exceedingly comfortable, and his bride would never want for any material comfort. I believe the family has recently purchased a country estate in Shropshire, with more surely to follow. And Dom's sister is Miss Celeste Kilburn, one of Society's most esteemed young ladies. She's engaged to my younger brother, which, if you value pedigrees, carries some weight. He *is* the younger son of the Earl of Wingrave."

"As are you," Miss Seaton pointed out.

"Well, yes." He was momentarily thrown, but went on, "*Mr. Kilburn*—"

"Seems highly reluctant to become anyone's bridegroom."

In the short amount of time Finn had been speaking with Miss Seaton, Dom had bought and consumed his cider. He shoved the empty tankard at the vendor before stalking away as if being pursued by hounds.

Bloody Dom. He wasn't helping anyone by behaving like a boor.

Finn paid for two mugs of cider and handed one to Miss Seaton. As they both drank the crisp, tart beverage, she regarded him unblinkingly over the rim of her tankard. Waiting for his answer.

Ah, hell. He could offer words full of prevarication and half-truths, but he wouldn't entrap anyone with evasion. Besides, if there was anyone who would surely see right through his attempt at misrepresentation, it would be her.

"There was . . . an incident," he finally said. He turned to face the spectacular view of Highgate, which was Parliament Hill's main attraction, and Miss Seaton also took in the vista. Yet her attention was mainly on him, rather than the spire of St. Paul's, rising up above the skyline.

"Nothing that would besmirch your reputation," he hastened to add. "But it served as a catalyst. I shan't inundate you with details, but the end result is that Dom, my brother Kieran, and myself must *all* find ourselves respectable brides within twelve-month, else we stand to lose all financial support from our families. I have my own income from other sources, so I don't fear losing my allowance. But I won't be responsible for Kieran and Dom being cut off."

Miss Seaton's eyes widened. "What a dire ultimatum."

"A mild descriptor for something that has completely upended our lives. As it stands, that ultimatum was issued four months ago."

"Leaving you eight months to secure wives." She

stared at the view of the City of London, which, on this clear and breezy day, stood out in all its grimy, industrious glory. There'd been a time when Finn had contemplated opening a gentlemen's coffeehouse. When he'd said so to his father, he'd been laughed out of the earl's study. Not before his father had said that ambition was for men with functioning brains, which disqualified Finn.

His parents had been adamant that their sons were amply provided for—financially, anyway—so there'd been no need to pursue work. Not the kind of work that was undertaken during daylight hours, in any case.

As for those other ambitions, notions, and possibilities, he had learned his lesson not to discuss them with anyone, not even Dom and Kieran. Because it seemed ridiculous to strive for something that he couldn't have, and though he could usually count on his friend and brother supporting him, he didn't want to hear them gently tell him to temper his expectations. It would be too crushing. So, he said nothing.

"My brother, as I've said, has already found himself a future wife," he continued. "Which leaves Mr. Kilburn in need of a bride."

"Are you engaged to be married?" Miss Seaton asked with her usual directness.

"No."

"Not yet," she pointed out. "But you will have to be, at some point."

"At some point," he conceded. "I am a particular man set in my particular habits. They will not change when I eventually marry, and few women would tolerate such conditions."

"What *are* those conditions?" she pressed.

"Immaterial." Some women might not mind the fact that he was not and would never be a scholar, but *she* would likely not be one of them. Besides, he'd already discussed with Dom that he'd help secure an understanding between his friend and Miss Seaton, so discussing his own matrimonial prospects with the lady in question was a waste of everyone's time.

He feigned interest in viewing a pond, its mirrored surface scored by the movement of wind across the water. "For the present, my attentions are dedicated to finding a wife for Dom."

"I see," she answered.

"And you must also recognize the necessity for proceeding at a rapid pace."

"My attendance at balls has been sporadic at best," she said, approaching. "Even when I had attended them with any regularity, it wasn't commonplace for prospective suitors to be so boldly offered, the way you presented Mr. Kilburn like a roast on Christmas."

Finn snorted. "Dom wouldn't take kindly to being likened to a chunk of meat. Though I have called him beef-headed on occasion. Have I shocked you with my plain speaking about these matrimonial circumstances?"

"Many hurtful untruths can be tucked into the corners of pretty obfuscation." Her expression was focused, thoughtful. "Plain speaking suits me better."

He exhaled. "Good. That's good. Would you—"

Something caught her eye, and she straightened, an intent frown creasing between her brows. Before he finished speaking, she walked away, heading straight toward one of the booths. A sign above the

wooden structure announced, CAN YOU BEAT BRIT-
AIN'S CLEVEREST MAN? ONE PENNY TO TEST YOUR
INTELLECT. There was a painted sign that showed
a male figure, labeled Mr. Smythe, perched atop a
stack of books.

Here was a challenge Finn would never be able
to overcome. Throwing rings onto bottles was easy
enough for him, and he could hold his own in a boxing ring. Squaring off against an intellectual, however, was a much greater challenge.

By the time Finn reached the booth, Miss Seaton
faced a middle-aged and pale man who filled out his
waistcoat with a prosperous stomach. The look on
his face was exceedingly smug as he said to her, "I
couldn't take your money, miss. It wouldn't be fair at
all—like you were throwing your coin away."

"Let me be the judge of how I spend my money."
She held up a penny, glinting in the sunlight.

When Smythe looked doubtful, Finn added, "Unless you fear that she *will* best you."

Britain's Cleverest Man chuckled indulgently and
plucked the penny from Miss Seaton's fingers, before
making a show of setting the coin on the wooden
railing.

"Be forewarned that your complaints will fall on
deaf ears once I have beaten you," Smythe said.

"You'll hear not a word of protest," Miss Seaton
returned levelly.

Smythe hefted a huge book and set it on the railing. It took several tries to read the spine, but eventually Dom worked out that it said, *The Compleat
Canonical Works of Western Civilization*.

"We're to finish quotes and cite the author, I assume." She tapped the massive tome.

"Just so, miss. Pick anything at random from this book and I will recite it in its entirety. And you, sir," he added, glancing at Finn, "will use this book to determine whether or not we are correct."

A bead of sweat traced down Finn's spine.

"You must judge yourself," he answered. "I know the lady will be honorable."

That answer seemed to satisfy Smythe, and he nodded. Miss Seaton also appeared pleased with Finn's reply.

"As I'm a gentleman," Smythe said airily, "I shall permit the opening salvo to you, miss."

Without opening the book, she said, "'*Friends show their love in times of . . .*'"

"'*Trouble, not happiness,*'" Smythe finished with a smirk. "Euripedes." He nudged the book toward Miss Seaton. "You may check if you'd like to verify that I am correct."

"Unnecessary," she said blandly. "You are right, sir."

"Of course I am," Smythe answered.

Finn never took gambling personally. It was a business transaction for him, no matter how much braggadocio his fellow gamesters displayed at the table. He didn't respond to taunts, either. But the way Smythe seemed so certain of his superiority over Miss Seaton set Finn's teeth on edge. For some reason, it was *vitally* important that she best this pompous braggart.

"It's your turn now, sir," Finn said coolly.

Still wearing his smirk, Smythe opened the book seemingly at random and placed his finger down on the page. He placed a pair of spectacles on the end of his nose, and read.

"*'Pleasures are like poppies spread . . .'*"

"*'You seize the flow'r, its bloom is shed.'* Robert Burns—from 'Tam O' Shanter.'"

Finn's heart cartwheeled when the smug smile dropped from Smythe's face. He resisted the impulse to give Miss Seaton's hand an encouraging squeeze, but damn. That was impressive.

Without delay, she said, "*'Censure is the tax . . .'*"

Smythe's brow furrowed, and he turned his face up to the sky as if the answer would drop from the heavens like shit from a passing bird. Finally, he slowly said, "*'. . . a man pays to the public for being eminent.'* Swift."

Britain's Cleverest Man dragged his forearm across his damp forehead, then Miss Seaton said, "That is correct. From his *Thoughts on Various Subjects*, 1711."

Scowling, Smythe flipped through the pages of his book, and then his lips curved into a vicious little smile when he read, "*'A wise man is superior to any insults . . .'*"

"*'. . . which can be put upon him,'*" she said immediately, "*'and the best reply to unseemly behavior is patience and moderation.'* Or, in the author's original tongue, *'Un homme sage est au-dessus de toutes les injures qu'on lui peut dire; et la grande réponse qu'on doit faire aux outrages, c'est la modération, et la patience.'* Molière, from *Le Bourgeois Gentilhomme*."

Finn chuckled. She sent him a quick little look of triumph, while Smythe glared at him.

He didn't give a fuck about Smythe, but something brightened in him with Miss Seaton's success. Here was someone who clearly underestimated her, yet she would not retreat. She had faith in herself—and, in her way, she rebelled.

"Time to once more test this fellow's knowledge," Finn said to her.

Once more, she eschewed the book. Planting her hands on her hips, she said, "*It is no weakness for the wisest man . . .*'"

"'. . . for the wisest man . . . the wisest man . . .' . . . uh . . ." Smythe reddened as Finn and Miss Seaton waited for his response. Finally, thrusting out his chest, he declared, "*It is no weakness for the wisest man to be merciful.*'"

Finn looked to Miss Seaton, whose expression was smooth and enigmatic, revealing nothing.

Smythe forced out a laugh. "You'll have to try harder to best me, miss."

"You'll have to try harder to bluff, sir," she answered coolly. "The actual quote is, '*It is no weakness for the wisest man to learn when he is wrong.*' Sophocles, *Antigone*. Shall I quote it in the original Ancient Greek?"

"I believe you owe the lady," Finn said when Smythe only scowled deeper.

The Cleverest Man in Britain reached into a metal box and pulled out a penny, which he slapped down onto the railing beside Miss Seaton's coin. Then he grabbed a wooden sign that read AWAY and hung it from a peg before hefting the metal box and storming off.

"Marvelously done," Finn said appreciatively as Miss Seaton put the two pennies into her reticule. "You took a risk, gambling on your intelligence, and you emerged triumphant."

"I should hope so," she answered, though her lips quirked beguilingly as she spoke. "Hypatia of Alexandria knows I've devoted enough of my life to study. Though limiting oneself strictly to works written by European men discounts huge, significant swaths of thought that isn't confined to the West, and to people who aren't male. Even so, I hope what knowledge I have means that it's enough to—" Her words stopped abruptly.

"To what?" he pressed when she moved away from Smythe's booth and he followed. They had completely lost Dom, but at the least Miss Seaton's maid was still trailing them at a discreet distance.

"Do you remember that night we first met? At the Duke and Duchess of Greyland's ball."

"Difficult to forget," he answered dryly. "I believe you said, '*I'm sure you find me as useless to your company as you are to mine.*'"

She had the courtesy to wince. "Social niceties are not my métier. My rudeness notwithstanding, you may recall that I inquired whether or not you knew Sir William Marcroft, of the Sterling Society."

"Never heard of him, nor that Silver Society."

"Sterling Society," she amended. "It's England's most noteworthy and influential intellectual society, and"—she drew a breath—"it's my intention to join that institution."

It made perfect sense that she should seek so scholarly a goal. Yet, as much as he admired her dedication to that objective, it proved that he was the very last man who ought to court her.

His belly clenched, but that was likely the result of skipping breakfast.

"Given that display back at Smythe the Blusterer's booth," he said, "there should be no obstacle to your ambition."

"Do you truly think so?" she asked with genuine curiosity.

"Without hesitation."

Her lips parted, as if his words were a surprise. Clearly, she encountered many people who were like Smythe, woefully underestimating her.

A sizzle of anger on her behalf worked its way down his spine.

She stopped to pay a vendor for a bag of fried yeasted cakes. As she held the bag open for Finn, he plucked out a still-warm cake before popping it into his mouth.

They were quiet together as they ate. The silence was companionable . . . with an undercurrent of awareness beneath. Because he kept looking at her mouth, and the damnedest thing . . . he couldn't stop wondering what her lips might feel like against his.

But when he glanced at her to see if she noticed, her own attention was fixed on his fingers brushing away crumbs from his mouth.

Then she blinked, collecting herself.

Which reminded him—he really ought to do the same.

"When I accosted—I mean, met with—Sir William the other week," she said, resuming her crisp tone, "he was adamant that the Sterling Society would never admit an unmarried woman."

Finn frowned. "Why not seek out an alternative society that has less restrictive criteria?"

"Because . . ." She exhaled in frustration. "Worthwhile intellectual societies are not exactly plentiful, and the Sterling Society happens to be the one with the greatest scope of influence. And if I gain entrance, then—" She cut herself off with a shake of her head. "Suffice it to say that it's vitally important for me to become a member."

"Thus, *your* necessity for proceeding at a rapid pace in search of a potential husband."

"It seems that you, Mr. Kilburn, and myself are all in rather dire circumstances."

"But a solution has already presented itself for you and Dom," he answered evenly. "If I could just locate him . . ."

Despite Finn's height, and Dom's size, it was still difficult to find his friend in the midst of the crowded fair. Most of London seemed to have crammed itself onto Parliament Hill this afternoon, but surely Dom hadn't *fled*. Or had he, leaving Finn alone with the fascinating but out of reach Miss Seaton?

He discreetly studied her, this driven, incomprehensibly intelligent woman. A goodly portion of him feared her—in some ways, she was very much his opposite—but damn him if she didn't draw him in. It was a fool's interest, for so many reasons, including the fact that he'd already told Dom that he wanted to match his friend with Miss Seaton. Going back on that intention would make him a cad of the first order. Bad enough that Finn had encouraged Dom to jilt Willa. He still tasted the metallic flavor of guilt whenever he thought of that morning last spring.

Further, if that display at Smythe's booth had proven anything, it was that Finn could *never* be Miss Seaton's mental equal.

He was used to seeing frustration in his teachers'
faces, and almost inured to the scathing comments
his parents and eldest brother made in his presence.
Yet he didn't relish the thought of seeing her sharp
quicksilver eyes dull with disappointment when he
didn't live up to her expectations.

Chapter 6

✦✳✦

"I'm certain Dom's here, somewhere," Finn Ransome said unconvincingly.

Standing beside him, Tabitha searched the throngs of people for Mr. Kilburn, but her attention wasn't entirely fixed on finding the giant man.

She was far too intrigued by the tall, lean gentleman next to her. True, he was distractingly handsome and virile and all the things that usually made women forget how to breathe properly, but more than that, he hadn't chastised her when she'd announced her intention to join the Sterling Society. He didn't say that it wasn't fitting for a female to be part of an organization devoted to the development of the mind, and he wasn't appalled that her main intention for finding a husband was to gain entrance to said organization. And he'd been extraordinarily encouraging when she'd faced off against that Malvolio, Mr. Smythe.

What a peculiar man. Peculiar and . . . captivating. If one was the sort of person who could be captivated by appearance and insightfulness and a refreshing lack of judgment.

She was far too rational and self-aware to be that sort of person. But if she was . . . then Finn Ransome might lead her into feeling things she did not want to feel.

On top of which, he hadn't said a word about offering himself as prospective bridegroom. Despite the fact that he also needed a wife.

"Oh, is that Tabitha?" a familiar female voice said nearby. "What a delightful coincidence!"

Tabitha bit back a grimace at Diana's incredibly unconvincing attempt to sound surprised. She faced Diana and Iris as the two women emerged from the crowd. Both women wore matching curious expressions as they looked at Mr. Ransome as though he was a prize bull being offered up to stud.

"How charming, running into you so unexpectedly," Iris said once she and Diana reached them. When Diana elbowed her, Iris added, "Tabitha, you must introduce us to your companion."

If Mr. Ransome noticed the patent falsehoods being spun, his genial countenance gave no indication.

"Mr. Finn Ransome," Tabitha said, "these are my friends, Miss Iris Kemble and Miss Diana Goldstein."

"Ladies," Mr. Ransome said with an elegant bow that made even Iris blush. "An honor."

"And where is the other gentleman?" Diana asked.

Tabitha barely resisted the impulse to cover her face with her hand. Instead, she dropped her bag of fried cakes, and they scattered across the ground like the last vestiges of her dignity. "Oh, gracious. How clumsy of me. Would you be so kind, Mr. Ransome . . . ?"

"Of course," he answered, and bowed once more before heading toward the nut vendor.

He was barely out of earshot when Iris said excitedly, "Well done, Tabitha! He's got the face and form of a fallen angel. But excellent manners."

"With a touch of sinfulness in those eyes of his," Diana added. "It will make for most delightful marital obligations."

"Mr. Ransome is not the man I intend to have court me," Tabitha answered, after glancing to make certain that he was some distance away. "Mr. Kilburn has absented himself, but he should return presently."

Hopefully, Dominic Kilburn *would* return, because the whole purpose behind having Iris and Diana "accidentally" meet Tabitha today was to size him up and give their opinion on him.

Diana clicked her tongue. "Are you certain about this? Marriage? It seems an extreme course of action. The financial ramifications alone . . ."

"Have indeed crossed my mind," Tabitha answered. "I'd be losing my fiscal independence, and bodily autonomy. But it's a minimal price if it means that I can become part of the Sterling Society. Think of what we'd all gain once I obtained membership."

"Tell us more about Mr. Kilburn," Iris urged.

"All I know of him is that his father's fortune comes from leasing warehouses along the river. Before that, I believe he and his father worked at the docks."

Diana frowned. "A very different world from yours."

"That's of little consequence." Tabitha exhaled in disgust. "It's absolutely airless, the ton. It was that way eight years ago when I made my debut, and nothing has changed in the intervening years. Everyone's the same, with the same backgrounds, the same beliefs, and woe betide anyone who deviates from that."

"So, it's a comfort, then," Iris said with curiosity. "That he's not from the ton?"

"It is," Tabitha answered confidently.

"Mr. Stokely wasn't, either," Diana noted.

"Di!" Iris chided when Tabitha winced.

Diana looked contrite, so Tabitha hastily assured her, "It's all right. I barely think of Charles anymore."

A falsehood. Even now, eight years later, Charles occasionally snuck into her mind like a thief who sought to steal her equanimity. Most of the time, Tabitha forgot that horrible night. And other times, memories and shame rose up and nearly choked her. As they did now, clogging her throat as though she'd swallowed rocks.

She'd done her best to put that particular night into a special box that she refused to open or even contemplate. But what she'd locked inside continued to scratch against the lid, like a premature burial, and in quiet moments she continued to hear it remind her of her folly.

She'd been so foolish, truly. The blame was on her alone for believing that anyone, even her younger brother's tutor, could possibly want her.

Charles had been young for his profession, hardly a few years older than her, and she'd been drawn to his studiousness, his rigorously thoughtful mind, and—if truth be told—how very handsome he looked in his spectacles. They had begun a friendship that had started over evening conversations about philosophy, lasting late into the night. She'd lived for their chats, breathless with anticipation for the hours after dinner when she and Charles sat in the corner of the parlor and talked of everything and anything.

When she'd had to come out, and endured the tedium of the Season—as well as her status as a wallflower—those conversations had been her balm. She and Charles would talk about Society's snobbery, its hypocrisy and uselessness, and when all the ballroom swains turned their backs to her, with Charles, she felt *seen*. Appreciated.

She'd thought herself in love with him. And she'd hoped that he felt the same about her. Yet it had all been a fata morgana, leading her into dangerous ground.

But instead of a fatal swamp or moor, the treacherous territory had been the study in her parents' home. Tabitha had followed Charles in there one night when he'd gone to find a book they had been discussing.

Reckless with the certainty that he returned her affections, she'd kissed him.

He'd pushed her away, and then dragged his sleeve across his mouth, as though the feel and taste of her disgusted him.

Diana and Iris knew all of this, but they didn't know the rest.

I'm disappointed in you, Miss Seaton, he'd said. *You've let tender sentiment and unruly soul govern you.*

I thought you cared for me, Charles, she'd choked.

You should have expected this. Had you acted with logic and reason, you would have seen no other outcome, and you wouldn't be humiliating yourself in such an appalling display. This is why I had such misgivings about encouraging a female in scholarly pursuits.

But I love you, she cried, plaintive as a beggar. *Don't you love me?*

Whatever you are experiencing, he'd answered, *it's merely an illusion, created by your own feverish expectations. Perhaps if you'd learned to temper your emotions, there might have been a chance for us. As it is, I feel only pity for you.*

It had hurt to be spurned by Charles, but his disappointed scolding wounded her even more. They never spoke again beyond the barest of civilities. Soon after, he resigned and found a new post tutoring a marquess's sons.

After that, she'd made certain to avoid all risks of emotion. For months after Charles left, her only contact with the world had been to immerse herself in books and more books. When her mother had cautiously suggested she try visiting a circulating library just to get her out of the house, she had been reluctant. But learning about the existence of the Benezra Library had kept her from a life of complete isolation.

For nearly eight years, Tabitha had shuttled primarily between her home and the Benezra. She never again permitted herself to form any romantic feelings for anyone.

If it wasn't for her need for a husband to join the Sterling Society, she wouldn't have ever considered matrimony. Why potentially expose herself to that kind of possible emotional attachment, and the potential hurt and chaos it could cause?

But marriages without sentiment weren't uncommon. There would be no chance that she might develop feelings for Mr. Kilburn, just as he seemed entirely shut off to the idea of feeling affection for her, which made him the ideal candidate.

Far more ideal than Finn Ransome.

He continued to hover in her thoughts, like a particularly complex philosophical conundrum. Because there was a terrible possibility she *liked* Finn Ransome, and *that* she could not permit.

"In any event," Tabitha continued, "I'm only attending this fair with Mr. Kilburn. Nothing has been determined, and we aren't walking down the aisle together quite yet."

"I'm not convinced," Iris noted with concern.

"Well," Diana insisted, "if Mr. Kilburn doesn't suit, Mr. Ransome seems a delightful choice."

"He hasn't offered himself," Tabitha answered.

It was better this way. His smile was devastating, and when she looked up into his impossibly dark eyes and saw him looking at her with admiration, something fluttered in her belly.

After today, if she was wise, she would give him a wide berth. Aside from that night eight years ago, she made certain that everything she did was wise.

The man in question wove through the crowd toward her, his steps unerring as he slipped between gaps, his expression intent and focused. Which, she began to see, was his usual approach to life. Nothing was disregarded, nothing dismissed or elided over.

And the way he'd looked at her mouth had been even more absorbed and rapt.

Her stomach quivered again.

"I come bearing fried gifts," he said, proffering another paper bag of cakes.

"A true knight errant." Diana sighed as Tabitha took the food from him.

"More like a knight erratic." He gave a self-deprecating smile. "I would have been back sooner, but it seems that a goodly portion of London has decided it cannot endure a moment without partaking of donkey rides and bobbing for apples."

It *had* grown rather thick with people in the last few minutes. The day was exceptionally fine, a splendid display of early autumn, with crisp breezes and clear skies, but unfortunately it appeared that Mr. Ransome was correct, and most of the citizens of the city were packing themselves onto Parliament Hill.

"Are you all right, Iris?" Tabitha asked. Her friend's cheeks were pale and her lips bloodless, and, despite the briskness of the day, a bead of perspiration ran down from her temple.

"Perfectly well," Iris mumbled.

"I can fetch some cool lemonade," Mr. Ransome offered. "We'll find you somewhere to sit and catch your breath."

"Crowds of this size upset her disposition." Diana took Iris's hand in hers. "Shall I take you home, my love?"

Though she was concerned about Iris, Tabitha's gaze flew to Mr. Ransome. If he hadn't guessed the nature of Iris and Diana's relationship before, certainly he'd know now. Would he be censorious? Disgusted?

"I'll walk ahead of you, Miss Kemble," he said firmly. "Clear a path so you can exit the fair easily."

Diana sent Mr. Ransome a grateful look before wrapping one arm around Iris's shoulders. Iris leaned against her, and when Mr. Ransome did as he promised, cleaving his way through the throng and holding back the masses to make an exit route, Diana led her out of the fair. Tabitha followed, worried about Iris but grateful that Mr. Ransome had proven as good as his word. And he had been perfectly accepting of Iris and Diana's partnership.

At last, they reached the edge of the fair and the bottom of the hill. Mr. Ransome strode out into the street and hailed a hackney. When it stopped, he handed Iris into the vehicle and performed the same service for Diana before tossing a coin to the driver with instructions to take the ladies wherever they desired to go.

He'd handled everything with efficiency, but with surprising compassion.

It would be too easy to like him.

"Thank you for your kindness," Diana said, leaning out of the cab.

Iris lifted her head from Diana's shoulder to say weakly, "I'm sorry to spoil your afternoon."

"We only want you happy and well," Tabitha assured her.

"Crowds *are* terrifically bothersome, and notoriously ripe," Mr. Ransome said. "I've no doubt that a little rest, quiet, and tending by Miss Goldstein will soon set you to rights."

Both Iris and Diana smiled at him before he rapped his knuckles against the side of the carriage, and it drove on. Once the vehicle had rounded a bend, vanishing from view, Tabitha and Mr. Ransome turned to face the entrance to the fair.

"Did you get the approval you needed from your friends?" he asked.

She didn't bother attempting feigning ignorance. "Not precisely. Mr. Kilburn's my potential suitor, but as he made himself scarce, it wasn't possible for Iris and Diana to form an opinion of him. They rather liked you, though," she couldn't help but add.

He shrugged as if what he'd done was hardly worth comment. "We ought to find Dom."

No, that was definitely *not* a little pitch of disappointment in her chest. And she definitely was *not* interested in spending more time alone with him. Dominic Kilburn was her goal, unlike Finn Ransome.

He offered her his arm, and she took it. The gesture meant nothing, only politeness, and she could be just as indifferent to him as he seemed to be to her. Yet as they walked up the hill in search of Mr. Kilburn, she noted that he had a nice, long stride that matched her own, and a purposeful energy in his body.

She kept glancing over at him, watching how he took in his surroundings and the continuous way he assessed each and every detail. Naturally, she would approve of that kind of focus, and if she had to bite back questions to learn more about him, it was simply because she herself was a scholar with a thirst for knowledge. Even of handsome, enigmatic men.

Once they were inside the fair proper, they both surveyed the mass of people.

"I think that's him." She pointed toward a strongman game that consisted of a puck attached to a tower, with a bell at the top and a lever at the bottom. Men of all ages queued up to swing a mallet and strike the lever, sending the puck up the tower to ring the bell.

Making his way up the queue was Mr. Kilburn, his unmistakable broad back straining the material of his expensive coat.

They made their way toward the game, just in time

to see the brawny man in front of Mr. Kilburn fall
short of ringing the bell. The man threw down the
mallet before stomping away, a woman chasing after
him and insisting that everyone knew these games
were unfair.

Mr. Kilburn caught sight of Tabitha and Mr. Ransome standing nearby, and he pulled off his coat before silently handing it to Mr. Ransome. *Gracious.*
In his shirtsleeves, Mr. Kilburn's musculature verged
on terrifying.

Her fingers tightened on Mr. Ransome's arm, and
the feel of him was solid without being excessive.
What would he look like in *his* shirtsleeves? Would
the fabric be snug or drape over his body? She'd
certainly have a better view of how his waistcoat
molded to his torso, which, she could already tell
formed an inverted triangle from the width of his
shoulders to his narrow, flat waist.

The study of anatomy became suddenly much more
interesting. Her own anatomy, for example, seemed
to be doing something peculiar because, despite the
brisk breeze, she grew quite warm when thinking
about Finn Ransome's body.

Appearance doesn't matter. And if it did, she
ought to be ogling Mr. Kilburn, *not* Mr. Ransome.
And she certainly shouldn't fantasize about what his
form would look like in various states of undress.

Mr. Kilburn rubbed his hands together and picked
up the mallet. He glanced at Mr. Ransome.

"Going to bet anyone on this outcome?" Mr. Kilburn asked with a curl of his lip.

"My friend," Mr. Ransome replied, "*no one* would
ever be foolish enough to wager against you in this
contest."

Mr. Kilburn nodded, accepting as fact that he was an oversize brute of a man. He faced the strongman game before raising the mallet over his head, while the nearby crowd watched breathlessly. Even the barker for the game could only gape as all of Mr. Kilburn's muscles strained in preparation for the strike.

For some reason, men felt the need to test their physical strength, and to demonstrate it to everyone around them. It was an exhibition of primacy, a warning to other men, and an inducement to women to select him as a viable mate.

Theoretically, he might be *her* mate. Her spouse for the remainder of her life. If Mr. Kilburn wanted to demonstrate his fitness for being her husband, he might have saved himself the trouble of this display of physical prowess.

"Your mind's running faster than a steam engine," Mr. Ransome murmured, leaning close. "Let's simply enjoy Dom showing off. It's been a while since he seemed eager to do anything." Cupping one hand around his mouth, Mr. Ransome called, "That's it, Dom! Make that bell explode!"

Right. She ought to offer her encouragement, too. "That's the way, uh, Mr. Kilburn!"

As cheers went, hers was somewhat lacking, but she had little experience with urging men to slam mallets onto objects.

With a grunt, Mr. Kilburn brought the mallet down, slamming it onto the wooden lever. It contacted with the puck, which shot up the metal rail before hitting the bell. It sounded with a clear, forceful ring that made the crowd cheer. Mr. Ransome stuck his fingers into his mouth and whistled, and Tabitha clapped in approval.

What would her friends at the Benezra think, seeing her applaud such a primal display?

Rather than accept the audience's ovation, Mr. Kilburn silently took his coat from Mr. Ransome and pulled it on. He waved away the offered prize of a stuffed poppet, his expression stony.

"Are *you* going to make an attempt?" Tabitha asked Mr. Ransome, who looked concernedly at his friend.

"God, no." Mr. Ransome laughed. "I leave such demonstrations to Goliaths like Dom."

"You bring down giants at the gaming tables," Mr. Kilburn growled.

"Lady Fortune isn't a giant," Mr. Ransome replied. "To win her favor, you must dance, not brawl. And I'm an excellent dancer."

Of that, Tabitha had no doubt. But the whole exchange intrigued her. It seemed Mr. Ransome was a frequent gambler, so much so that he was quite skilled at it. She didn't know anyone who played games of chance with such regularity, and a host of questions gathered. Yet before she could ask, Mr. Ransome spoke.

"Diverting as this has been, another outing would be delightful. Give you two more of an opportunity to get to know each other better." He narrowed his eyes at Mr. Kilburn, the wordless implication being that his friend had been largely absent from the day's activities. "We've barely discussed any of your shared intellectual pursuits."

At the least, Mr. Kilburn looked contrite. "Apologies, Miss Seaton. Maybe another time we can talk philosophy. You can tell me your thoughts on Descartes versus Leibniz."

"I look forward to it," she said, grateful. Much as she'd resigned herself to accepting Mr. Kilburn as a suitor, the fact that they had barely exchanged any words today unsettled her. It was one thing to rationally accept that she might wed him in order to gain entrance to the Sterling Society, yet that would mean tying herself to a virtual stranger. "I've quite a lot to say on the theories of substance."

"That topic can be discussed during a private supper following a visit to the theater," Mr. Ransome offered. "In three days, the Imperial Theatre has an excellent program, including a performance of one of Lady Marwood's most popular burlettas."

"Will you be there, as well?" She didn't want to sound so eager for his answer, or his presence. Still, it made sense that she'd want Mr. Ransome to also be in attendance. He could smooth the rough edges when it came to conversing with Mr. Kilburn, and perhaps, in a small way, he could be considered a friend.

Yes, friendship and ease of conversation were the only reasons she hoped he'd also come to the theater.

"Doubt not, Miss Seaton," he said with a bow.

"I shall be happy to attend." A slight exaggeration. She wasn't precisely looking forward to spending more time with Mr. Kilburn, but she *ought* to. And there was the added incentive of being at the theater, a place she seldom ventured since she wasn't familiar with most modern works. It was always beneficial to expand one's cultural knowledge, especially if she intended to be part of the Sterling Society and make recommendations to powerful men on the running of society.

She'd also see Mr. Ransome in his evening finery. Not that that was an inducement.

"Dom?" Mr. Ransome asked pointedly.

After a long, slightly insulting pause, Mr. Kilburn mumbled, "Fine."

"Splendid," Mr. Ransome said through his teeth. Then, with far more politeness, "It will be a lovely evening, Miss Seaton. Dom and I both eagerly anticipate seeing you again."

How much of that was true? Until a few moments ago, she would have said that Mr. Kilburn appeared to barely endure her presence. As for Finn Ransome, he was around simply to ensure that she and his friend didn't sit in strained silence as they considered whether or not they ought to marry.

She had a working knowledge of how the ton operated, yet she was certain that this arrangement with Mr. Ransome—and to an extent, Mr. Kilburn—was highly unusual.

Well, most people considered *her* unusual. How she went about finding a husband would be no different.

Peculiar or not, she hadn't much time to select a groom. The Sterling Society would consult on that education bill soon, and she *had* to be part of the organization by then. Each day that passed made her need for a husband more and more urgent. But who would be that husband, and why did she picture Finn Ransome waiting for her in front of the altar?

Chapter 7

❧ ✳ ❧

$\mathcal{I}$'m so glad you permitted me to dress you in the blue gown, miss," Olive said as she and Tabitha climbed the stairs of the Imperial Theatre. "It does so flatter your eyes, and it will surely make a favorable impression on the gentlemen."

"It isn't too bright a shade?" Tabitha glanced down worriedly at her dress. Since she'd parted company with Mr. Ransome and Mr. Kilburn three days ago, she'd fretted over ludicrous things such as how to wear her hair for their night at the theater, and whether or not she ought to put a tasteful amount of rouge on her lips and cheeks. Her feelings were ridiculous and utterly uncalled-for. "I don't want to be mistaken for a courtesan."

"That will *never* come to pass, miss."

As they went up the next flight of stairs, heading to Mr. Ransome's family's private box, Tabitha sent a wry look at her maid. As courtesans were supposed to appear extremely enticing to the male sex, the fact that no one would ever confuse Tabitha for one of their number was ever so slightly vexing. Couldn't she look even a *little* enticing?

Still, Olive had done the best she could with what raw material had been given to her, and Tabitha would meet Mr. Ransome—and Mr. Kilburn—looking as pleasing as she ever had. It was slightly challenging not to feel like a wren amongst swans as she passed dazzling women and elegant men in their very best ensembles. The theater was more about being seen than seeing, after all.

A hint of worry chewed at her. She didn't relish being looked at, watched, and scrutinized by the people in the audience. And found lacking. She had always come up short with them. She'd made fun of that in her talks with Charles, and they'd both agreed that the value system of the ton was deeply problematic. But then, ultimately, Charles hadn't valued her, either.

The ton's opinion didn't matter, neither did Charles's, not when it came to getting her into the Sterling Society. Yet would Mr. Ransome—Mr. *Kilburn*—like what he saw of her tonight?

At last, they reached the correct private box. Heavy velvet curtains had been drawn back, revealing the box's interior. She peered inside. There were seats arranged within the luxurious space, and her heart jumped like a spring lamb when she saw Finn Ransome seated alone at the railing.

The theater itself was quite noisy since the performances hadn't begun, and though Tabitha advanced quietly into the box, Mr. Ransome stood as if sensing her presence.

Facing her, he was all dark elegance in his black coat and white breeches, which beautifully fit his long form as he bowed.

Oh, damn. She was entirely *too* glad to see him again.

His regard swept over her, his gaze warm and palpable. If the admiration in his eyes was any indicator, then the extra effort she and Olive had put into her toilette had been well worth it. A flush stole across her cheeks, but that had to be from the heat of the theater. She opened her fan and tried to cool herself, though the breeze she created did hardly anything.

At the least, seeing him distracted her somewhat from the anxiety gnawing her stomach.

"We appear to be missing Mr. Kilburn," she noted as Mr. Ransome showed her to one of the seats at the railing. As she looked out at the audience, she felt the same trepidation she had during her Season, and yet having him at her side calmed her. Certainly, handsome, urbane Finn Ransome would draw far more attention than she ever would.

A few people in boxes looked at her quizzically, as though trying to figure out who, precisely, she was. Dimly, she remembered some of her deportment lessons, and offered the curious people polite nods, which seemed to mollify them before their interest turned elsewhere.

Even now, in her evening regalia, she hardly drew any regard. It was almost comical. Certainly, she and Charles would have mocked it. But she set those memories of him into a compartment, shut it, and told herself they were entirely forgotten.

"Dom's notorious for lack of punctuality," Mr. Ransome answered smoothly.

Was she imagining it? The tension in the corners of his mouth, the slight flinty gleam in his eyes?

"Would you prefer to meet here again on another night?" she asked.

He tilted his head, puzzled. "Tonight is perfect."

"It's only . . ." She smoothed her hand down her skirts. "It seems that something is troubling you."

"I . . ." For a moment, he looked almost uneasy, but then he snapped an unruffled mask into place. "I merely don't want Dom to miss the opening act. It's a cat who performs the most marvelous of tricks, including walking on a tightrope. I never knew that cats could be trained to do anything besides look disdainful, so the fact that Sir Salmon can do this is quite astonishing."

"Perhaps the secret is that the cat wants us to *believe* he's been trained, when the truth is that he's only conditioned *us* to have certain expectations of him."

"Quite so, quite so." Mr. Ransome seemed relieved that she hadn't pressed him about the nature of his anxiousness, and together, they looked out at the audience, which was filling up by the minute. "Part of the joy in attending the theater is the spectacle of the audience."

"I would rather *not* be part of the spectacle," she admitted.

"You prefer to be the observer rather than the observed," he murmured. "A sentiment I share. That surprises you," he noted when her brows climbed.

"I thought handsome men enjoyed being admired," she said, astonished.

His smile flashed, made all the more potent by the fact that it seemed entirely spontaneous. "You think me handsome?"

Despite her intention to remain unruffled and impassive, her cheeks went hot. "There are certain criteria of attractiveness, which I recognize that you meet. Objectively, of course."

"Of course. Objectively."

Part of her wanted to bolt out of the theater box and keep running until the night swallowed her. Yet another part of her wanted to touch her fingertips to the dimple at the corner of his lips.

She fought to salvage her equanimity. "You would rather not garner attention?"

"It has never served me well." His smile turned rueful, and shadows slipped into his eyes.

What could that mean? At the fair, he'd confessed that he had been embroiled in a small scandal, but was there something else in his past that put such regret in his eyes? And why did she need to know?

Yet before she could press him on this, he said with purposeful brightness, "I own that I am excessively fond of the performances themselves. You'll find me at the Imperial at least once per week."

Ah, a deliberate change of topic. Intriguing, that he wasn't a reader, but he was a regular theatergoer. One appealed more than the other, but why?

She tucked that information away as one might save a piece of paper bearing a sweetheart's penmanship.

Mr. Ransome isn't your sweetheart.

"My family has its own box at the Royal Opera," she said, but admitted, "though I seldom attend."

"You don't care for theatrics?"

"Admittedly, most of the texts I focus on are of a more academic nature."

"A good story can transport you," he said, voice deep with appreciation. "Take you somewhere far outside of yourself, somewhere beyond your limited experience. And isn't the fundamental nature of the human experience universal? Even when a story isn't real, it can resonate."

This enthusiastic side of him was unexpected. "What are your favorite works? Something martial, perhaps?"

He gave a dismissive wave of his hand. "Men and their wars are topics that hold little interest. Yelling and sword waving and declaring oneself to be a hero beyond measure—it's so tedious."

"Heroism on a more intimate scale," she speculated.

"Give me a good, underestimated character who triumphs over doubt." His eyes were dark and gleaming. "Cinderella, or Prince Hal."

"I'll have to read their stories." She didn't add that she'd do so in order to discover more about him. He kept defying her expectations, which kept her off-balance and uncertain—and yet it wasn't unpleasant. Far from it. As though she rode a kite through the skies, wheeling and spinning—and flying. Each turn and twirl made her giddy.

Despite the activity surrounding her and Mr. Ransome, their gazes locked. A charged current passed between them, making her shiver with awareness.

No. No, no, no.

She *would not* permit herself any interest in or fascination with him. Once, she'd been giddy over a man, yet she was wiser now, more protected.

"Do you think Mr. Kilburn will miss the beginning of the performance?" she asked in a deliberate effort to remind herself of why she was here.

Mr. Ransome pulled out his timepiece. After several moments, he frowned at its face. "He's later than usual. But he'll be here," he added, perhaps for his own benefit as well as hers.

Yet the remarkable Sir Salmon was brought out onto the stage and pranced through his act, and still no sign of Mr. Kilburn. After the theoretically trained orange tabby cat was met with thunderous applause, next came several dancers, and after them, a single-act comedy about an irate Scottish miller trying to grind his wife's dry Dundee cake into dust.

All of it unexpectedly engrossed her, capturing her attention with the silly, the beautiful, and the comic. Perhaps there might be some who would find such entertainments beneath them, but truly, *why* had she denied herself this pleasure?

Mr. Ransome gave a low, rumbling chuckle at something that happened onstage. The sound reverberated low in her belly.

He leaned forward, his expression astute and captivated. It was fascinating to see him like this, almost too engrossed to keep his usual detached expression. As though there was a man of heat and passion beneath the cool reserve.

What would he be like, if he let that reserve slip away to reveal the fires beneath? She very much wanted to see that.

He caught her looking at him, and, before she quickly glanced away, she saw something hot and primal flare in the depths of his dark eyes.

No one had ever looked at her that way. Yet it had to be merely the illumination from the stage lights, and nothing more. She waited for him to return his attention to the stage before discreetly studying the sharp line of his profile.

Tabitha pressed her hand to her stomach, yet it still trembled.

She prayed that Mr. Kilburn arrived soon, because she needed some relief from being alone with Finn Ransome.

GODDAMN DOM.

Finn had been *counting* on his friend showing up. Each unaccompanied moment with Tabitha Seaton became torturous. He was too experienced to show any reaction to her, and yet within, he was alternately hot and cold, altogether too attuned to her every movement, her every sound.

From the corner of his eye, he studied her as she watched the performances. When something particularly amusing happened onstage, a tiny laugh escaped her. Her laughter was low and husky, tinged with surprise, as if she hadn't expected to be so delighted by the antics.

She pressed her delicate fingertips to her lips as though she wanted to contain the noise of her laughter—and the sight of her fingers against her mouth shot heat through him. The sudden need to have her touch *his* mouth rose up, quick and hard, but he shoved that need away. He was only being roused by the capers onstage, making him feel things that he normally didn't feel.

Where the fuck was Dom? The sooner his friend arrived, the sooner he could focus on negotiating pairing them up.

His chest tightened, but he could ignore that.

Something small hit him in the back of the head,

and *that* he couldn't quite ignore. Especially when another little projectile pinged against his head, and then fell to the ground. Finn bent down and picked it up to discover he'd been hit with a hazelnut.

Turning, he started to tell the pest to go the hell away. His rebuke died when he saw Dom peering through the curtain at the back of the theater box. Finn started to demand where his friend had been, but Dom shook his head.

"Would you excuse me for a moment, Miss Seaton?" Finn murmured.

"Of course," she answered, still watching the performance and clearly unaware of Dom's presence. Her maid, as well, seemed too immersed in the show to notice anything amiss.

Finn rose and bowed to Miss Seaton. He found Dom pacing in the corridor, his friend wearing an agonized expression.

"Sorry I threw filberts at you," Dom muttered.

"Better them than coconuts," Finn answered. Though a hundred questions piled up in his mind, he waited. If he demanded answers from his friend, there was a high degree of likelihood that Dom would go mute before running away.

There were a handful of people moving up and down the hallway, but Dom ignored their curious looks as he caromed from one side of the corridor to the other.

"I can't," he finally growled.

"Can't what?" But Finn already knew.

"It isn't her," Dom said lowly. "She's a fine woman. A good woman. And I tried—"

"You didn't," Finn answered lowly. "Not really."

"I've been a churl." Dom scrubbed a hand through

his hair. "Never should have agreed to any of these outings in the first place. I'm not ready—not yet."

"We have less than eight months, Dom," Finn reminded him. "Eight months left, and if we aren't married . . ."

"I'm aware of the consequences." Dom slouched against the wall. "I just need a little more time."

"It's unlikely that Miss Seaton would be willing to abide a long delay." She seemed especially keen to join that intellectual society soon.

"God, don't have her wait for me," Dom said vehemently. "Can you . . . can you apologize on my behalf? Let her know that the fault's mine, not hers?"

Finn nearly retorted that Dom ought to beg for his own forgiveness, especially as the lady in question deserved far better, but the agony in his friend's eyes made him hold his tongue.

"I'll see what I can do," he finally said.

Dom's wide shoulders slumped in relief. "My thanks. You're a good friend."

"Or a fool," Finn said mildly. This was the second time he was assisting Dom in running away from a woman. Ironic, given that Dom was absolutely fearless when it came to facing down a taproom full of bruisers thirsting for blood.

Finn wouldn't ever fully understand the man. Which was . . . sad.

"Never that." Dom looked worriedly past Finn, toward the box where Miss Seaton sat, completely unaware that her potential suitor was bolting.

"Go," Finn urged him. "Seek solace at the bottom of a bottle, or wherever you can find it."

Dom grunted. "The problem is, I can't find it anywhere. 'Night, Finn."

"Good night, Dom."

And then his friend was hurrying away with surprising speed for such a big man. Sadly, the faster Dom went, the sooner it meant that Finn was going to have to tell Tabitha Seaton the bad news: Dom had hightailed it.

Finn's heart thudded as he turned back to the box. What was he supposed to say to her? How could she take it any way other than personally, and why did it pain him so much to think of her feeling rejected?

Something had to be done, and the hell of it was, he wasn't sure what it might be, or how to spare her feelings. But he couldn't let her be hurt, not if he could protect her.

Chapter 8

❖ ✳ ❖

The moment Mr. Ransome left the theater box, Tabitha understood what was happening. Despite the voices of the performers onstage and the laughter of the audience, she could hear his low voice in the hallway speaking urgently to someone who growled in response. She wasn't able to make out exactly what was being said, but she liked to think her carefully cultivated intelligence counted for something, and she readily guessed what the topic of conversation was.

When Mr. Ransome returned a few minutes later, tension emanated from him. He sat down beside her and tried to affect an easy smile. Brackets formed around his mouth, and there was tightness in the corners of his eyes.

He opened his mouth to speak. Closed it.

"That was Mr. Kilburn, wasn't it?" she asked when she could stand it no longer.

"Yes." In a barely audible voice, he added, "Damn Dom."

She looked at the stage without seeing the acrobats currently tumbling across it. "We need to face the truth—he doesn't want to court me."

"He doesn't want to court *anyone*," Mr. Ransome said tightly. "And he can't have the woman he wants."

"There never was a chance." She turned to him, and though she kept her words low so she wouldn't be heard by the other audience members, she asked, "Did you know? That attempting to pair us up was a fool's errand?"

"Had I believed that," he answered grimly, "I wouldn't have offered up my services as—"

"Procurer." When he jolted, she pressed her fingers together over the bridge of her nose. "Forgive me. I need a husband as much as Mr. Kilburn needs a wife, and for similarly unromantic reasons. I suppose it was too much to hope that my first foray in years into the marriage mart would yield a better result than my initial attempts. It's only . . ."

She swallowed around the hot, leaden object that had lodged itself in her throat. "Becoming a member of the Sterling Society is extremely important to me, and soon. Yet at this rate, and with me competing against women far younger than I, I'll never find myself a groom, never be admitted to the Sterling Society."

Admitting failure was like a brand against her heart, marking her forever. She would have to face Iris, Diana, Arjun, and Chima, and tell them that she'd let them down. Closing her eyes against the mental image of their disappointed faces, she prayed that she didn't cry in public, especially not when the act on stage was currently making the audience shout with laughter. The sounds of hundreds of people's mirth became mocking.

Why had she ever believed she could find a man

willing to marry her? Hadn't she learned that people like her—*women* like her—would never be sought after? Not by the men of the ton, not by anyone.

And the fact that she felt *hurt* by all this only proved how little she'd taken Charles's lesson to heart.

"I think . . ." he said, his words low, his brow furrowed as he seemed to be working out a puzzle. ". . . I think I may have a solution."

She forced back her tears. They would do her no good, and what she needed now was rational thought, not messy emotion.

"Go on," she urged.

"You need a man to marry in order to become a member of that organization," he said, thoughtful and deliberate. "I need a wife so that I, my brother, and Dom aren't thrown into penury. I believe the solution has presented itself."

She stared at him, and the depths of his dark eyes.

"Are you suggesting . . . ?" Her breath hitched, and she could barely complete the thought. It was so outrageous. So stunning.

So *exciting*.

No—she didn't have room or need for anything exciting.

"I am." There was a tremor of eagerness beneath his level tone, but he seemed to deliberately master it by the time he spoke again. "Let *me* be your husband, Miss Seaton."

"You had ample opportunity to present yourself as a prospective groom," she noted as steadily as she could manage. "And yet now you change your mind."

"I'd believed that we were too incompatible to wed," he admitted.

She couldn't stop herself from flinching. "I see."

"Because I thought you far superior to me," he said hurriedly. "It would be an intellectual misalliance."

She frowned at his strange notion. Before she could contradict him, however, he spoke again.

"I still think it would be, but we're useful to each other. And that might mitigate our differences."

"That's logical." She appreciated his sensible approach, when inside, she didn't *feel* very sensible. This was a possible resolution to both of their circumstances.

"It takes three consecutive Sundays to have the banns read," he went on. "By the beginning of next month, you could have what you need, and I could have what I need."

"That schedule is suitable." She would have preferred for them to marry sooner, so she could be certain to gain her place in the Sterling Society in time for the discussion of the education bill. But a special license was difficult to obtain, and exorbitant. She'd no choice but to wait the allotted three weeks.

Until then, however, she had plans and preparations to make.

"Granted," he added, "our marriage would be one based on mutual convenience, not sentiment, but you and I don't require such things, do we, Miss Seaton?"

"Tabitha," she said, trying to match his equanimity. "If we're to be wed, you may call me Tabitha."

"Tabitha." He had a way of saying her name that sounded like a promise. "I'm Finn."

"Finn." It *did* feel rather nice to call him by his name, as if she'd been given a key to unlock a secret door. "Before agreeing to this, there's something you ought to know."

"Go on," he encouraged.

She tipped her chin up, and said with purposeful composure, "Any marital union I enter would be one based entirely on expediency. I am not . . ." She drew in a breath. "I am not the sort of person who engages in sentiment and emotion."

"I see," he said pensively.

Perhaps that meditativeness meant that he was deterred. But she had to tell him the truth.

"If we marry," she continued determinedly, "I won't be the variety of spouse who provides much in the way of tender feelings. They aren't my way, and it's simpler to live without them. Naturally, I wouldn't expect you to play the role of doting and ardent husband. This would be a mutually beneficial arrangement—and nothing more."

He leaned back, his gaze contemplative.

Her breath stuck in her lungs. Would he rescind his offer, knowing her stipulations? Many people required affection, if not love, from their spouses. Yet it was something she absolutely couldn't provide. Since Charles, she'd done her best to sever herself from her emotions, and that wouldn't change with the advent of Finn Ransome.

"I wouldn't feel right, moving forward," she added, "if you weren't fully apprised of the situation. I can't let you enter into this marriage with any sense of being misled. Much as I need a husband, you deserve better than half-truths."

"Your candor is appreciated."

He was quiet for a moment, the only sounds coming from the stage and the audience, and yet all she was aware of was his silence, wondering what it could mean.

"Is this to be a true marriage?" he asked lowly.

She regarded him levelly, even as her heart thudded within the cage of her ribs. Naturally, the marital rights had to be considered. Yet the thought of intimacy with him was alternately alarming . . . and electrifying. "What is it *you* desire?"

"Rakishness was my younger brother's province," he answered, his gaze never leaving hers. "Not mine. I've never seen the need to jump from bed to bed. That won't change after we're married."

She exhaled, surprised by her relief. "Affairs and trysts hold no interest for me, either."

"Then we're in agreement. On that front. And in the interest of full disclosure, I ought to tell you that, though I receive a generous allowance, the predominance of my income derives from gambling."

"An uncertain way to earn money." Games of chance were wildly popular amongst the ton, a result of its idleness and general uselessness, but Finn hardly seemed idle and useless.

"Many years past, I discovered that I have a talent for it," he explained, "and it gratified me to know that the roof over my head, the clothes upon my back, and the food in my belly came from my own labors and not my father's coffers. I have some losses from time to time, but nothing catastrophic."

She looked at the audience, now watching a burletta. The hundreds of faces were mirrors, reflecting the pathos being enacted on the stage. She curled and uncurled her hands in her lap, as if she could somehow wring out the right choice from the air. This was such an immense decision, now that she was truly confronting it. And to bind herself to *Finn Ransome* . . .

"Your honesty is appreciated," she finally said.

"And the death knell of my marriage suit," he answered grimly.

"Many marriages are based on deceit," she noted. "Yet if we are truthful with each other from the onset, it bodes well for our union."

Surprise momentarily flickered across his face. "Then you'll marry me?"

"Will you marry *me*," she countered, "knowing that ours is to be an arrangement predicated only on necessity?"

Again, there was a long pause, as he seemed to sort over and consider everything. That silence stretched out. Surely her tensed hands simply indicated that she needed a husband for a specific reason, and not because she feared his rejection.

"Truthfully," he finally said, "it's a relief."

She started. That wasn't the response she'd been expecting. "It is?"

"I'm . . ." He looked upward, as if the words he sought danced around the chandeliers, and his brow creased. But his frown seemed self-directed. "One of the reasons why I excel at gambling is because emotion has no place there. If I approach the table with steadiness and logic, and take nothing personally, I wind up with heavier pockets."

"And you apply that selfsame approach to when you are away from the gaming table," she surmised.

"It suits me." He turned his attention back to her, sharp and direct, in that perceptive, searching way of his—and it was the oddest thing, how her skin felt hot all of a sudden. "Just as your approach suits you."

She nodded. "Then it appears that, despite your initial trepidation, we'll do very well for each other."

"It appears so. We're to be married."

They stared at each other for many moments, their gazes holding. She had to appreciate that he approached the topic of matrimony with so level and reasonable an attitude, no disordered emotions, no possibility of hurt feelings.

And yet . . . the more they looked at each other, the more aware of him she became. His long body, his beautiful face. The tangible energy radiating from him, masculine and potent. The unmistakable gleam of intelligence in his eyes, an intelligence that went beyond academic learning into something far more complex. More alluring.

And he was to become her *husband*.

A shiver ran the length of her.

Applause rose up from the audience, startling her. Strange that she was in the middle of a crowded theater and had entirely forgotten the presence of hundreds of other people.

He started, and blinked, as if he, too, had been caught in some kind of spell.

She'd have to be very cautious. For the last eight years, she'd done an expert job keeping her heart uninvolved. It was like a seldom-read book that she kept high on a shelf, safely gathering dust. The pages wouldn't be torn if no one took it down and carelessly thumbed through it.

She could do this. She could marry Finn Ransome and meet the minimum expectations for being someone's wife. Including sharing his bed.

Her gaze arrowed to his mouth.

It was a most exceptional mouth, wide and full, with an especially voluptuous bottom lip that would give very nicely if she gently tugged on it with her teeth. Or would *he* be the one who liked to bite? Did people nibble on each other's mouths like tea cakes? Did they scrape them over their lover's skin?

Her own flesh prickled at the image of Finn Ransome, nipping his way down her neck and soothing the bites with sweeps of his tongue.

My God, she'd no idea where these ideas were coming from, only that the longer she spent in Finn's presence, the more they filled her head. As the ideas were quite pleasant ones, she didn't chase them away. They settled over her skin like moths made of flame, warming her, sending shivers of awareness all over her as they walked on tiny, delicate legs across her flesh.

"I'll talk to your father tomorrow," he said, his voice deep.

From the huskiness in his words, she could almost believe that he'd read her salacious thoughts. And entertained similarly carnal thoughts of his own.

She couldn't find words, so instead she fabricated a smile, as if everything in her life wasn't about to undergo the most astonishing transfiguration.

The biggest metamorphosis seemed to be emerging within her, and she had no idea who she would be when it was all over.

Chapter 9

❧ ✳ ❧

"Tabitha," Lord Parslow said, staring at Finn across the expanse of his desk.

"Yes," Finn answered.

"You're asking for Tabitha's hand." The viscount furrowed his brow.

"Perhaps you have other daughters," Finn replied, relying on his years of experience hiding his feelings at the gaming tables to keep his expression placid and unbothered, but *damn* if Lord Parslow's incredulity didn't annoy the hell out of him. "But I don't want to marry them. I want to marry Tabitha."

"That is . . . extraordinary." The viscount leaned back in his chair and looked at Finn as though he couldn't quite understand how a wolf in a waistcoat happened to be seated opposite him in his study.

Clearly, Lord Parslow had given up all hope that Tabitha would ever marry. Which was reasonable, since she was already six and twenty and had likely never received another offer before. Even so, the patent disbelief in her father's face and words angered Finn. Did the viscount believe his daughter so unpalatable that no one would want her?

"We can have the banns read beginning this Sunday," Finn said, clipped.

"An abbreviated engagement."

"There aren't any objections, I trust." Finn's tone brooked no argument.

"None," Lord Parslow said at once. "We can begin the legal proceedings immediately, and I've a man who can help you secure a home, unless you would prefer to reside here, in which case, we can begin preparing a suite of rooms."

His words gained momentum, as if he was afraid that to present any delay might result in Finn changing his mind and rescinding his offer.

Parents, it seemed, had little idea of the worth of their children. Well, that wasn't entirely fair. Finn's older brother, Simon, had never been undervalued, but as the heir to the earldom, he meant far more to their father than Kieran and Finn ever did. Finn wasn't even a good spare, or so the earl had often reminded him. But as Simon's wife, Alice, was now expecting, the fear that Finn might accidentally wind up the heir was diminishing by the day. Thank God.

"I'll find us a home," Finn announced, cutting off Lord Parslow's nervous chatter.

"Good, very good."

"So, I've your permission." This was a statement from Finn, not a question.

Finn stood and offered his hand to Lord Parslow. The older man got to his feet and shook his hand, a plainly relieved smile breaking across his colorless face.

"Send all necessary documents to my man of business," Finn went on.

Finn did employ his own man who managed his

banking, given how considerable his winnings could be. He didn't live recklessly, but he did tread a somewhat more unusual path than most men of the ton, and he had to be certain that Tabitha would be well cared for, legally and financially protected so that, if Finn *did* make a horrendous mistake at some point in the future, she wouldn't pay for it.

"We should join the ladies," he added, glancing meaningfully toward the door to the viscount's study. When he'd called late this morning, he hadn't been given much opportunity to see Tabitha. She'd been seated in a parlor with her mother when he had been shown in. They'd barely been able to speak a handful of careful words to each other before the footman took him into her father's study.

"Lady Parslow will be so pleased," the viscount said, now brimming with good humor once he and Finn had shaken hands and thus sealed the bargain.

Finn only offered his future father-in-law a polite smile. It didn't much matter what Tabitha's mother thought of her daughter's upcoming wedding. What *did* matter was Tabitha's feelings about being his wife.

Jesus God. Him, a husband. It was a role he hadn't considered for himself until the ultimatum four months ago, and even then, he'd only been able to consider it in theoretical terms. Now it was to be a reality.

Would he be a good husband? He'd do his damnedest to make certain Tabitha didn't want for anything. Whether she would ultimately grow disillusioned with him, that was unknown. The best he could do was try to keep that from happening for as long as possible—though it *would* happen. He would stake any sum of money on it.

At the least, they were in agreement on the terms of their union. They each served a purpose for the other, expecting nothing more beyond that. It ought to be comforting.

And yet, restlessness and edginess prowled through him, like a searching creature, and damn him if he didn't know why.

He and Lord Parslow exited the study and headed down the corridor toward the parlor where they'd left Tabitha and her mother. The women's low, intermingled voices hovered in the hallway, with faint notes of tension beneath the meandering, aimless conversation.

Both Tabitha and the viscountess looked up when he and Lord Parslow entered. They wore twin expressions of apprehension, making the resemblance between mother and daughter all the more evident. But while the eye color and shape were the same, Lady Parslow lacked Tabitha's insightful, potently intelligent gaze, and he had no expectation of the viscountess saying something that rocked him back on his heels with her profundity.

"I have been welcomed into the family," Finn said, which wasn't entirely true, because as much as the viscount seemed eager to marry off his daughter, Finn hadn't missed the assessing look in Lord Parslow's gaze, trying to make sense as to why a man with Finn's admittedly uncultivated reputation would seek to wed a noted bluestocking such as Tabitha.

Likely, Finn thought sourly, the viscount believed him to be a fortune hunter, who could have no interest in his daughter outside the financial. And while there *was* a compulsory aspect to his marrying, allowing Lord Parslow the belief that only money would make Finn want Tabitha was an acrid brew to swallow.

When Tabitha and her mother rose from the sofa, and Lady Parslow exclaimed joyously at the news, Finn went straight to Tabitha to take her hands in his as he gazed at her with affection. It wasn't entirely for her parents' benefit that he did so.

He jolted as something stirred in his chest, something small but growing. It was a green shoot that strengthened and grew hardier with each passing moment. Looking at her, that tendril grew even more as it burgeoned with life.

No—they'd agreed on the terms. No sentiment. No emotion. He wouldn't go back on his word before they'd even formalized their engagement.

Well, he was very good at maintaining a smooth, unreadable surface, and he could hide anything that might or might not be developing.

She gazed up at him with relief and a touch of gratitude, entirely unaware of the peculiar, unwanted feelings stirring within him. Just as he hoped.

"Everything is settled?" she murmured as her parents toasted their happiness with sherry. "He wasn't difficult about it?"

"Sailors could only hope for such smooth sailing." Finn wouldn't tell her of her father's insulting disbelief. "And you with your mother?"

She glanced at her mother, now onto a second glass of sherry, and Tabitha's nose wrinkled in annoyance. "One would think that I'd authored the definitive treatise on ontology, she was so proud. As if the only way a mother might consider her daughter successful was to *land a husband*, to use her verbiage."

"When you *do* author that definitive treatise on

ontology," he vowed, "I'll be the first to throw you a celebratory gala." He would have to get Kieran to read him several books on the subject, after obtaining a definition of what ontology was.

She smiled up at him, and that growing verdant thing within him sprouted new leaves.

"Your father offered to have us live with him," he said, trying to focus on the business at hand.

"I pray you declined," she answered fervently.

"I did," he replied.

"Thank goodness," she said, smiling.

He liked it an awful lot, seeing that happiness on her face. There had to be other ways to gratify her, and yet . . . they were to be only polite spouses, respectful of each other, but asking for little. A business arrangement with no possibility of ever developing into anything more.

Just as he wanted it.

Yet he warmed when she looked at him with actual pleasure, and even though there would come a time when that pleasure would fade, no good luck streak could last forever. The trick was learning when to stop hoping.

A WEEK LATER, Finn stood with Kieran and Celeste at one side of the drawing room at Wingrave House.

After expressing a mild amount of interest in the fact that their second son was affianced, his parents had insisted that they would host a small engagement party, but he suspected it was more to let their friends know that their unpromising offspring had actually convinced some woman who wasn't an actress to marry him.

Now he observed the festivities with his brother and his brother's wife-to-be.

"They look slightly inconvenienced to be here," Finn noted as the earl exchanged pleasantries with an archbishop and his wife. On the other side of the room, the countess spoke to a quartet of matrons.

"I'd say to give them credit for showing up," Kieran said over the rim of his wineglass, "but the kindest thing would've been for them to just stuff a wad of cash into your hand and be about their business."

"I thought they'd be pleased that you met the conditions of the ultimatum," Celeste said.

"Believe the phrase my father said was, *Tie her up quick so she doesn't have time to regret her decision that she's marrying a half-wit.*"

Celeste winced, and Kieran snorted because he of all people knew the sort of names his parents had lobbed at him for most of his life.

"I've done my best to keep her interaction with the earl and countess to a minimum," Finn said wryly. "So far, I've been successful, but God knows what Christmas is going to be like."

"Perhaps you and Tabitha can start a new tradition," Kieran offered. "All holidays are spent in isolation—I think Oliver Longbridge has an estate on a tiny Scottish island that he'd be willing to let, if the terms are favorable."

"Sounds promising." His gaze sought out Tabitha, as it had every few minutes since the onset of the party. She talked with Miss Kemble and Miss Goldstein, as well as an East Indian man, and a Black man of considerable scholarly mien. From the animated look on Tabitha's face, she was likely telling them about the stack of books he'd presented to her before the party had begun.

Yesterday, he'd gone to the bookseller with a list of volumes that Miss Goldstein had recommended to him when he'd solicited her help in finding the right tomes as an engagement gift. The bookseller had discussed the merits of each tome as Finn had paid for them, and he'd tried to listen attentively, storing up bits of information in case Tabitha wanted to talk to him about them. His stomach had churned, though, to be in the presence of so many books.

Still, it had been worth it to see how she smiled when he'd given them to her. As if he'd given her a piece of the sky. It might be a marriage made strictly for the sake of convenience, but surely a small gift didn't violate the terms of his agreement with Tabitha.

Perhaps he ought to be with her, here at the party. After all, they were supposed to give the appearance of an enamored couple, especially given how brief their engagement period was to be.

He found it no hardship to go to her, his steps growing lighter the nearer he came. She smiled at him, and the lightness within him grew.

They stood side by side as she introduced him to her friends. Miss Goldstein and Miss Kemble he knew, but he shook the hands of Chima Okafor and then Arjun Singh.

"We know each other from the Benezra Library," Tabitha explained.

"Then you have spent many hours together," Finn said with a nod.

"Indeed," said Mr. Okafor, "I am on the verge

of giving Miss Seaton her own key, so she needn't waste time waiting for me to unlock the library every morning, and could stay as late as she desired."

"As her friends," Mr. Singh added, "we request that you take her on as many outings away from the library as possible."

"Surely you aren't so weary of me, Arjun," Tabitha said with mock affront.

"Our affection for you is undimmed," Mr. Singh replied, eyes twinkling. "But there is a very big world out there, one that exists beyond the pages of books. Perhaps Mr. Ransome will be able to exert some influence that us mere friends cannot."

Miss Goldstein arched a brow. "You mean, that a *husband* could influence."

"Would it help if I said my overbearingness came from a place of deepest fondness and respect?" Mr. Singh asked.

"Not in the slightest," Miss Kemble answered.

"It would be in your best interest to cede the field of battle," Tabitha advised with a laugh.

Mr. Singh held up his hands in what appeared to be a show of surrender. "Madam, I yield."

Finn smiled as he watched this exchange. It was clear that Tabitha did have a fine group of friends around her, and, in truth, it eased his mind to know that she wasn't isolated. Yet from the way Mr. Okafor had described her visits to the Benezra Library, Finn would be lucky to see his wife at all. Especially if Finn's own routine was primarily nocturnal.

They didn't *need* to see each other, not truly, and yet maybe, hopefully, their paths might cross from time to time.

They had time *now*.

"If I promise that we host your friends at our future home," Finn said, turning to her, "would you be so gracious as to come with me?"

"Only if that promise includes providing them with many cakes from Catton's," she answered.

"Do you ask for their benefit, or your own?"

"In the demand for more Catton's cakes," she said pertly, "everyone benefits."

"Then I am happy to agree to your terms."

He offered her his arm. It was rather nice, how readily she took it now. Yet when she touched him again, even with politeness, electricity sizzled through him, as if he still hadn't grown accustomed to the feel of her.

And, given the way her breath hitched softly, she wasn't used to the feel of him.

Glancing up, he noted her friends watched them with interest. Just as Kieran and Celeste observed them intently.

"I'm feeling like one of those pickled specimens they keep at the museum," he murmured low enough so that only she could hear.

"Let's away before the dissection begins," she whispered.

Together, they strode away from her friends. She frowned in puzzlement as he kept going, taking them out of the chamber and then down the corridor. They moved out to the terrace, and then into the garden. It was a brisk day, a harbinger of the approaching autumn, which kept the guests inside.

"I thought you were going to introduce me to your family's acquaintants," she said with surprise.

"I'd never subject you to anything so tedious," he answered. "Not when Baron Corborn is so fond of talking about the number of pheasants he's slaughtered, and Lady Hurst will demand that you compliment her in as fulsome a manner as possible."

"My thanks for depriving me of both of those experiences," Tabitha said, her lips curving.

"It occurred to me that there's still so much about each other that we don't know, and I'd hate to think you were wedding yourself to a stranger."

She nodded thoughtfully. "I do so love a new subject of study."

"Doubtful that I'm as enriching as one of your scholarly tomes," he chuckled, "but you may consider me an open book."

They walked amongst the ornamental bushes, which had lost their blossoms, and beneath the branches of trees whose leaves were fading into rust and gold. Despite the efforts of the gardeners to keep the garden as rigidly tidy as his parents preferred, some crisp leaves were scattered across the gravel paths like fallen soldiers.

He was acutely aware of her beside him: the pressure of her fingers on his arm, the small tendrils of hair that curled at the nape of her neck, how the hem of her gown sometimes brushed against his boots. As they strolled, she would occasionally stop and examine the decaying flowers, or test the texture of a brittle leaf.

How fascinating, the way she looked at the world. As if she wanted to study and learn everything that existed beneath the canopy of the sky.

"I've written to the Sterling Society," she said, breaking the silence, "informing them that I'm now engaged."

"So, they should accept you for membership," he answered.

Her brows lowered, and she spoke with frustration. "Not precisely. Sir William Marcroft said that a discussion on that subject wouldn't happen until *after* I've actually married."

"A few more weeks," Finn said, "and then it will be done."

He didn't do anything as inane as pat her hand consolingly, because no one ever actually felt better from such a ridiculous gesture.

"It's only . . ." She exhaled tightly. "I want everything to be settled so I can become a member quickly."

"There's a reason for your urgency, I take it," he noted.

For a moment, she hesitated, as if weighing whether or not to let him into her confidence. It shouldn't have mattered and still . . . giving him her trust felt vitally important. That wasn't part of their agreement, yet he felt it all the same.

"A vote is coming up soon," she finally explained.

He quietly let out a breath, pleased that she believed she could confide in him.

"An important one?" he asked.

"To me, it is. Parliament might allocate finances and resources to the creation of more schools in urban areas."

"Makes sense," he said thoughtfully. "Cities are growing daily, and they'll need places for children to learn."

She seemed gratified that he understood and agreed with her. "The Sterling Society is consulting with several high-ranking members of Parliament on that bill. But the society is comprised of a rather . . . restricted range of people. Men who have a limited way of looking at the world."

"And you would like to introduce a more expanded mindset," he said with a nod.

"I would be the beginning of what would be a considerable metamorphosis for the Sterling Society. That's my hope," she added quickly. "But it's vitally important that a new voice is heard as the society advises on something so significant as this education bill."

"Consequently, the need to marry quickly."

She regarded him, caution in her gray eyes. "You must think me naive, or radical, to attempt this."

"I know so many people of our class who want everything to stay exactly the same," he mused. "It benefits us to keep all the fortifications in place. But to work to tear those fortifications down . . ."

She continued to look at him warily.

"I admire it," he finally said.

"Truly?"

"Truly."

Tension eased from her gaze, and out of the set of her shoulders. Clearly, she'd expected him to criticize her ambition, and he was glad that he defied that expectation.

It was fascinating, how intent she was on this single goal.

"How seriously should I take Mr. Singh's request?" Finn asked. "To take you on excursions away from the library?"

"I admit that I do consider the Benezra something of a second home," she confessed. "Or rather, it *is* my home, and my parents' residence is merely where I eat and sleep and occasionally exchange pleasantries with my family. And perhaps there's some element of truth to the fact that I spend most of my waking hours reading or writing about what I've just read."

He couldn't imagine someone so different from himself, but this wasn't to be a match between two soul mates, so perhaps it wouldn't be as disastrous as he feared. "We already know that you hadn't been to a fair until Parliament Hill. The experience wasn't *too* unpleasant, I hope."

"Not at all," she answered at once. "It felt rather nice to actually *attempt* something rather than simply read about it. Even if my efforts at ring-a-bottle were meager."

"You *did* best Britain's Cleverest Man," he pointed out.

She pressed her lips together, and he shook his head.

"No need to hide your pride," he insisted. "If I did something that commendable, I'd run down the streets, waving a pennant and yelling, 'I'm bloody marvelous.'"

"Thank you," she murmured, "but you're a man. Men can show everyone that they're pleased with themselves and everyone calls it *confidence*. When women display satisfaction in themselves, they're labeled as *vain*."

"I hadn't considered that." He inclined his head. "I'd never argue against your own experience."

Even so, she did permit herself a hint of a smile, and it drifted around him like perfume, muddling his senses.

He stopped to pick up an acorn, and handed it to

her. She studied it carefully, turning it this way and that, before tucking it into her sleeve.

"If you *could* take an expedition to anywhere in London," he pressed, "where would you go?"

A crease appeared between her brows. "I . . . don't know. I think I've worn a path between my house and the Benezra."

He said nothing, but set aside this piece of knowledge, to consider at a later time. Undoubtedly, he didn't have Kieran's penchant for ranging far and wide across London, but he was a single man with a comfortable income, and took advantage of where both of those attributes could take him.

"And what of you?" she asked. "You said that the majority of your livelihood derives from gambling."

"It does," he answered carefully. She hadn't voiced an objection to it earlier, but perhaps, upon further thought, she didn't like the notion that her husband earned his coin through chance. Though—it wasn't truly chance with him because he knew precisely how to play the games so that he almost always emerged the winner.

Yet she simply nodded, and he exhaled.

"Surely gambling doesn't take up all of your time," she said with curiosity.

"Oh, I spend my hours in the usual pursuits of gentlemen," he said dismissively. "Visits to the pugilism academy, conversation and drinks with my brother and Dom, attending the theater."

"That's . . . surprising," she confessed as they paused to watch a squirrel scamper along a tree branch. "You've such a vast amount of astuteness, I would've thought that those activities would grow wearisome."

He stared at her, frowning. Surely, she had to be mistaken in her assessment of him.

She continued, "There's nothing *wrong* with those pastimes, but a man like you could apply himself to so many things. I'd hate to think of your mind growing fallow."

"Believe me," he said, dryly, "wasting time is all I'm good for."

"Isn't there *something*?" she pressed. "A tiny sliver of a goal, a morsel of a dream? You know that it's my hope to join the Sterling Society, and what I intend to do once I'm admitted. I'm not a professional gambler," she added in a coaxing voice, "but I'd wager that you're nurturing your own ambition."

Against his every trained response, his face heated. He hadn't told anyone, not Kieran, not Dom, not even Willa. And yet this woman noticed something in him that he'd carefully concealed, at times from himself, because he dared not have any hope that someone like him could ever accomplish more.

"There is something . . ." he heard himself say. "It's foolish. And I haven't given it *that* much consideration."

"I'd be honored if you told me," she said softly.

"Occasionally . . ." Getting the words out of his mouth was a challenge. They seemed to want to crawl back down his throat. "I think about opening my own gaming hell. As I said," he added hastily, "foolish."

"Not if it's something you truly want to do," she countered, her voice level. And it was her simple, straightforward way of speaking that made him pause. If she'd been eager or overly approving, he could have dismissed whatever she said as mere well-intentioned hyperbole, or patronizing. But she seemed to mean what she said.

"Do you think so?" he asked.

"You have considerable experience with gaming hells, so you would know what would be required to run them. And you aren't a frivolous person, so it wouldn't be based on the notion that such a business would be easy to establish, and effortless to run."

Hope and excitement trilled in his chest, but he wouldn't reach for them, not when they were so illusory. "There are so many gaming hells in London. Surely this city doesn't need one more."

"The distinction being that it would be *your* gaming hell," she noted. "And that would make all the difference."

He didn't know what to say to this, too stunned by her faith in him to come up with a smooth and collected reply. She was the most intelligent person he'd ever met, and if *she* believed that he might be able to accomplish something on that scale . . . perhaps it wasn't a foolish dream after all.

Or . . . he was so adept at hiding who he truly was, he'd fooled even her.

The pale sunlight traced the angular lines of her profile, her pointed chin contrasting the fullness of her lips. She was indeed a sharp woman in many ways, and the more he came to know her, his need to understand even more of her climbed higher. Yet it might take lifetimes, and he wouldn't ever truly grasp all her dimensions.

His gaze returned to her mouth. It was unexpectedly sensual, ripe and pink. She pursed her lips as she contemplated a starling winging overhead, and a quick, hot streak of desire ran through him, taking his breath.

This was to be an arrangement of convenience, not passion. But still . . . his awareness of her grew with each moment, his body asking him questions he shouldn't answer. Yet he craved those answers. Craved *her*.

He must have made some sound, because she turned her attention to him. Her eyes widened briefly, and surely, whatever she saw would appall her. Except it didn't. Because the surprise in her gaze shifted, growing hotter. And that desire that had touched him grew even more potent and demanding.

She glanced past him, looking toward the house, and then peered around the garden. "Are we alone and unobserved out here?"

"It's too cold for the guests," he answered.

"And the staff?"

"The gardeners will have been told to make themselves scarce lest anyone from the party comes out. As for housemaids and footmen . . ." He studied the windows that faced the garden. "I see none, and they dwell too much in awe of the butler and housekeeper to linger at windows."

She took his hand and led him toward an arbor. Foliage still clung to the trellis, and though it was turning brown as the season progressed, the structure provided coverage from anyone who might happen to stroll by or look from the house.

"Sit there," she directed, nodding toward a stone bench beneath the arbor.

Intriguing, this commanding side of her. And arousing.

He did as she directed, and she stood in front of him. Instinctively, he widened his legs so that she could position herself between them. Hunger streaked through him as the fabric of her skirts brushed his boots and buckskin-covered thighs.

"You've something in mind," he murmured.

She took what appeared to be a steadying breath before placing her hands on his shoulders. His stomach contracted at the feel of her, but he clamped down on his body's demands. However this was to play out, *she* must be the one to lead them both.

"I would like to kiss you," she said, before adding, "if I may. If we're to be married in the fullest sense of the word, we ought to grow accustomed to being intimate with each other."

Her prim but direct words arrowed hotly through him. "A very good notion. And if *I* may . . ."

When he curved his hands around her waist, she sucked in a breath. Truth be told, he did, too, because he wasn't wearing gloves and it was truly incredible to feel the shape of her, the dip inward and flare of her hips. At Parliament Hill, he'd caught glimpses of her form as the wind had pushed her gown against her body. But now he could discover her with his very sensitive hands, and soak in her warmth.

"You may," she said, voice low.

"Come a little closer," he instructed huskily, and when he urged her nearer with his hands, she came forward. Beneath his hands, he marked the fast movement of breath through her, and her excitement and nervousness surged from her body into his.

Though he sat and she stood, he was tall enough that he barely tilted his head back to angle his face up to hers.

After one more glance behind her, she brought her lips to his.

He held himself still, despite the sudden roaring urge to claim her mouth, while she explored him. She took her time, brushing her lips back and forth across his as if learning him anew. When she stroked her tongue across his bottom lip, then dipped it into his mouth, his body flared fully to life as if waking from hibernation.

He opened to her, giving her entry, and she took it, slicking her tongue against his with a sensuality that drugged him. Moment by moment, she grew bolder. He met her strokes, drinking her in as though she was the only sustenance he might ever need. It certainly felt that way, as lust tore a ruthless path through him, a kind of madness that shook him to his depths.

Her hands moved from his shoulders, gliding up his neck so that she cupped them around his head, her fingers digging into his hair and tilting him in the precise position so she could kiss him deeper.

Her confidence grew from moment to moment as she explored how to take what she wanted. He would give her anything she desired, and he prayed that what she desired was him.

She gave a soft moan, and that sound seemed to bring her back to herself. Pulling back slightly, she gazed down at him, her pupils wide and dark.

"I thought . . ." She inhaled unevenly. "I'd always believed the greatest pleasures came from the intellect. That bodily sensations were nice enough, yet never the equal of what the mind could produce. But my hypothesis has just been proven wrong."

"Why don't you have legions of suitors at your

feet," he said, his voice rough and jagged, "all clamoring for the briefest taste of you?"

Her lips pressed into a rueful half smile. "You are the only one who ever wanted one."

"The world is comprised of fools," he said vehemently. "And the bucks of the ton are the biggest fools of all."

She stroked his hair back from his forehead, and for a moment, she seemed on the verge of kissing him again. Then, to his regret, she straightened and stepped back. "We ought to return to the party."

"Tell me something."

She tilted her head. "Tell you what?"

"Anything. Preferably the driest, most impenetrable philosophical theory."

"Why?"

He leveled his gaze at her. "Because I need to regain some semblance of control over myself before returning to mixed company, especially if that company contains my mother."

"I . . . *Oh*."

He groaned as she glanced down at his groin. "Please don't look there or we'll be here until tomorrow morning."

"Yes, well . . . perhaps a discussion of Stoicism would be the most appropriate." Twin spots of delectable pink appeared on her cheeks as she purposefully looked up at the arbor. It was and yet was not a comfort to know that she battled arousal, too.

"Though it has its roots in Greece," she began, "most of the Stoic philosophers we study today were associated with Rome, specifically the emperor Marcus Aurelius, the political figure and playwright Seneca, and the once enslaved Epictetus. In fact,

Epictetus said, 'The greater the difficulty, the more glory in surmounting it. Skillful pilots gain their reputation through storms and tempests,' which is an excellent way to encapsulate Stoicism, as we can see how the principles of virtue ethics—"

"Better now," he gritted out.

He'd made a grave error. If, in fact, Finn had actually listened to Tabitha muse about philosophy, his cock would have gotten considerably harder. But as she'd spoken, he'd had to purposefully think of extremely unerotic things, such as the mouthful of spoiled mutton pie Kieran had once dared him to eat. Which he had, winning him a whole pound, and then spent the rest of the night and into the following day in the privy.

Such musings had the desired result, and now he could stand without brandishing an aggressive cockstand. He held his arm out for Tabitha, and as they made their way back inside to celebrate their upcoming nuptials, it became increasingly clear that there was so much more to this woman who would become his wife, more than he'd believed—and underestimating her had been a grave mistake.

They had *agreed*. There would be no excess of emotion, no attachment. And the more she came to know him, the more she would see how damaged he was.

She would devastate him if he let her. So, he couldn't let that happen.

Chapter 10

❧ ✳ ❦

*W*iser minds than Tabitha's had written and reflected on the subjective nature of time, and she felt woefully inadequate to express how it could pass both in an interminable crawl as well as within the beat of a hummingbird's wings. Theoretical musing was all well and good but she was beginning to learn that nothing surpassed actual experience.

Over the next three weeks, the banns were read, and during that time, she and Finn spent more time together. He took her to Catton's, they went for drives in a sleek, open-topped carriage, which he had purchased in advance of the wedding, they strolled through Hyde Park. Everything an engaged couple might do—though she noticed that Finn seemed to have them do activities that she'd never done before.

He was at all times polite, scrupulously polite. But they never again spoke of things that went deeper than the surface, so no discussion of dreams or hopes or anything truly substantive. They were always friendly and cordial and only that.

And . . . they hadn't kissed again. Was she relieved or disappointed?

Relieved, because their one and only kiss had wreaked havoc on her sense of reason. She often found herself staring off into nothingness, lost in memories of his lips on hers, the stroke of his tongue against her own, and how her body had blazed hotter than a room full of braziers at the feel of him.

She'd ached for more. He had been so encouraging of her ambition, and he kissed her as if he truly enjoyed it. As if he wanted to devour her, and she *wanted* to be devoured.

She had originally proposed they kiss because it seemed logical to get used to being physical with him. At best, she'd hoped that it would be mildly pleasant. At worst, she'd learn that it was something she could endure.

But it had been more. Much, much more. And so very dangerous. The stipulations of their marriage specified that their union was one only of convenience. If she started mooning after him, she invited pain, especially when he adhered to their terms of passionless cordiality.

Caring for him would break their agreement, and she couldn't do that. Protecting herself was paramount.

Besides, she told herself sensibly, there was no room in her life for messy sentiment. The moment she was married, she would press Sir William to make her one of the Sterling Society. And then she could truly begin her work.

"This is the morning," her mother sang, coming into her room as Olive finished doing up the row of tiny buttons that ran down the back of her wedding gown. "Ah, look at you. How lovely you are."

With her mother standing behind her, they both studied her reflection in the cheval mirror.

The gown was the soft blue of a robin's egg, worked on the sleeve and along the bodice with twining silver embroidery, and silver brilliants were tucked in her upswept hair. She examined herself with curiosity—it was as if she was about to play a role onstage, that of the adoring bride, and wore the appropriate costume for that part.

Yet she *was* going to be a bride. This was real. Even if they weren't going to be a typical married couple, she was truly going to wed Finn, and the more she looked at herself, the faster her heart beat. How was it that her mother couldn't see it pounding beneath the silk of her bodice?

"When he sees you walking down the aisle toward him, he'll consider himself a lucky man." The viscountess fussed with the hasp of the pearls clasped around Tabitha's throat.

"I'm fortunate in my choice of groom," Tabitha answered sincerely. There weren't many men of his class who would accept a scholarly wife, and one with ambition that went beyond the domestic.

In truth, they *both* had something to gain by marrying, and she had to remember that rather than let her head be filled with daydreams of dark, clever eyes and lush kisses.

"Come," her mother said, guiding her toward the door, "he's waiting for us at St. George's."

The ride to the church was blurred, particularly because the fashionable veil her mother had insisted on filmed her vision with gauze, yet even if Tabitha hadn't worn it, the world would have a strange, dreamlike cast. It made no sense that Tabitha felt at all nervous, there was no cause for it. And yet her mouth was dry and she could barely hear her parents' conversation over the roar of blood in her ears.

She was handed down from the carriage, and then she proceeded up the church aisle on her father's arm. The faces of friends and family watched her walk on unsteady legs toward Finn, who stood before the altar with the priest and his younger brother. There was a definite family resemblance between the brothers, but she only saw Finn, excruciatingly handsome in his claret-hued coat and slate gray waistcoat. The freshly shaved planes of his face were sharp in the morning light, yet his eyes were kind as the bouquet shook in her hands and they both recited their vows.

They promised to love, comfort, honor, and keep each other, in sickness and in health, and to forsake all others. They vowed to be faithful to each other as long as they both lived.

The words felt peculiar, unnatural. Particularly the bit about loving each other. There was no possibility of that. They'd agreed there wouldn't be, and yet something danced along her skin as she swore to love him, and he swore the same.

But then they exchanged rings and he kissed her, his lips so soft and so gentle. He whispered, "Now I'm Mr. Britain's Cleverest Woman," which made her laugh. That seemed to be his purpose, and his eyes gleamed as he gazed at her.

She was still laughing as he escorted her up the

aisle. Finn's mother looked vexed by a display of mirth at a wedding, yet Tabitha barely noticed.

Her laughter faded as she realized what had just happened.

She was married now. To Finn Ransome.

The wedding breakfast at her parents' house sped by, the hours chased forward by the fact that at the end of it, she and Finn would climb into a carriage for their journey to an inn in Blackheath. The plan was to spend the night there, and then return to London, and their new home in Chelsea.

The atmosphere in the house wasn't precisely raucous, but it was busy and noisy enough to jar her nerves. Guests came forward to offer their felicitations—she knew some of them, but not everyone—and wherever she looked there were faces and more faces. Many of them were likely in attendance for the food, and for the prestige of attending a fete given by Viscount Parslow. Somewhere in the midst of all this were Diana, Iris, Arjun and his family, and Chima and his fiancée, though she couldn't see them now.

"How are you bearing up?" Finn asked in a moment of quiet, as they stood together in a relatively peaceful corner of the parlor.

"Well as can be expected," she answered. "People keep winking at me. I want to ask if there's an excess of pollen in the air, and offer them my handkerchief."

A corner of his mouth lifted. "Not the season for pollen. But it is the right time for innuendo, since I've been the recipient of many elbows in my ribs and knowing looks. We can both recover on the road to Blackheath."

"Like soldiers retreating from the field of battle."

"I'm ready to wave the white flag if you are," he said wryly. "Shall we go?"

There had been a sense of comfort in being around him, but at his words, her peace scattered like startled birds. The next stage of her life—that of a married woman—was about to begin. She could tell herself over and over again that this union was simply for expediency, yet her composure refused to believe it. Just as her body insisted on responding to his nearness.

It was bewildering—and frightening. She had more control over herself than this. Yet all that control evaporated in his presence.

After telling a servant to make the carriage ready for departure, Finn tucked her hand into the crook of his arm. "Are you ready to quit your parents' home for the last time?"

"Not precisely the last time," she felt obligated to point out. "We've plans to dine with them on Friday."

"Not much for symbolic gestures," he noted, his words dry.

"I'm not much for fancies," she had to agree. But she wouldn't tell him that she'd tucked the acorn he'd given to her into her glove, so it rested over where her pulse fluttered in her wrist.

Together, they headed toward the front door, with the guests following boisterously behind them. Her mother stopped dabbing at her eyes long enough to embrace her and wish her a safe journey, while her father shook Finn's hand.

Finn searched the guests, and she could only speculate that he was looking for his own parents. Yet the earl and countess didn't appear. Did she imagine the resignation in his gaze? His expression smoothed so quickly it was difficult to tell. But he brightened when his brother emerged and slapped him on the back.

"Remember, it's ill-bred to rob carriages when you're on your honeymoon," Kieran Ransome advised.

"I haven't done that in ages," Finn answered.

Tabitha gaped at him. "Did you truly hold up a carriage?"

"It hardly qualified as robbery," Finn said with a dismissive wave, "and it was years ago."

"But—"

She fell silent when Dominic Kilburn shouldered his way through the well-wishers. It was the first time she'd seen him since the fair at Parliament Hill, and his expression was grimly set as he bowed to her.

"It wasn't personal, Miss Seaton," he said gravely.

"I took no offense, Mr. Kilburn," she answered, which was true enough. The demons he battled belonged to him alone.

"Finn." Dominic Kilburn offered his hand.

She exhaled when Finn shook it.

"Try to be good to yourself," Finn said gruffly.

Mr. Kilburn's brow lowered, as if the notion of being good to himself was a distressing one. He made some grumbling noises before letting go of Finn's hand and trundling away.

"Are you ready to go?" Finn whispered to her.

"Please."

"We thank you for your well-wishes," he said to the lingering guests. "And for now, farewell."

Before anyone could delay them any longer, Finn

escorted her outside to their waiting carriage. More of the celebrants came out to wave as Finn helped her into the vehicle, and she'd never been so grateful as she was when he climbed in after her, shut the door, and then rapped on the roof to signal that they were ready to depart.

"I haven't Iris's intense fear of large gatherings," she said once the carriage was en route. "Yet I think I'm rather out of practice making conversation with so many people."

"It *is* exhausting," he answered.

Silence fell, and they swayed as the carriage rocked from side to side. Her mind kept approaching the thought that she was now married, but whenever it neared the notion, it spun away and she tried to find rationality by mentally cataloging her personal library.

Beside her, Finn radiated gentle heat, which steeped into her. It was . . . nice to have someone beside her, someone at her side. Much as she appreciated her friends from the Benezra, they all had people to whom they belonged. Diana had Iris. Chima was engaged, and Arjun was devoted to his wife, Sarah. In her way, Tabitha had been alone for a very long time. And right now, Finn's solid form next to her provided an anchor in the midst of what had been a tumultuous, trying day.

Weary, she started to lay her head upon his shoulder, then tensed.

"It's all right," he murmured. "The morning has been long and, if you were like me, last night's sleep was scarce."

"I kept imagining all the things that might go

wrong," she admitted. "That I'd belch uncontrollably during the vows. Or that the priest would show up drunk, and instead of performing the wedding service, he'd try to baptize us with whisky from his hidden flask."

"It wasn't the priest who had the flask." Finn reached into his coat and pulled out a slim metal container. "Kieran gave this to me right before the ceremony, but I haven't touched a drop of it."

He uncapped it and held the flask out to her. "A drink to celebrate our mutually beneficial arrangement?"

She gingerly plucked the container from his fingers and sniffed at its contents. A sharp, earthy scent shot up her nose. "What kind of spirits?"

"Whisky, but not the good stuff, damn Kieran."

"I've never had whisky." Today—and tonight—would hold many firsts.

She put the flask to her lips and tipped her head back. Liquid filled her mouth, pungent and vegetal. When it hit the back of her throat, she coughed, her eyes and throat burning.

"Slowly," Finn advised. "Inhale, take a sip—a *small* one—and then exhale after you swallow."

The process went much better when she followed his instructions, the burn turning into a rounder, softer warmth that spread through her chest and in her belly.

She offered the flask to Finn. He took it and drank with smooth motions that proved he was well familiar with drinking from such a container.

"I'd like more," she said when he slipped it back into his coat.

"Did you eat anything at the wedding breakfast?"

"A bite of cake and . . ." She frowned. "Nothing else."

He patted his chest as he secured the flask in its inside pocket. "You know your own limits, but all the same, I'd rather not have to carry you into the inn and have everyone there think I was some villain from an opera, kidnapping and drugging the heroine before forcing myself on her."

"Are these the kinds of stories I miss out on by not attending the theater?" She sat back. "That sounds rather thrilling."

He chuckled ruefully. "I'll ask the innkeeper if he has a black cloak and plumed hat I can borrow so I can look the part of a proper villain. Though," he added, sobering, "I'd never force myself on you. Not tonight, not ever."

"That's . . ." She swallowed, and became very interested in the stitching of the carriage squabs. "Considerate of you."

A weighted silence fell. She and Finn regarded each other, and it seemed that they both became aware of what was to come that night, the atmosphere in the carriage becoming strained and fraught.

The best thing to do would be to consider it rationally, calmly, just as she approached any new topic of interest. Nothing was ever too frightening or intimidating if she took a measured approach.

"We *are* going to consummate the marriage," she said in as steady a voice as she could manage. Then she added, in a slightly less sure tone, "Aren't we?"

The carriage rocked as he moved to sit opposite her. Bracing his forearms on his thighs, his gaze was serious and intent as he regarded her carefully.

"What do you know of sex?" he asked.

Her cheeks warmed. "I've . . . read a few texts."

"*Fanny Hill?* Books by the Lady of Dubious Quality?"

"*I modi* by Aretino," she confessed. "It was, er, plentifully illustrated."

His brows climbed. "Illustrated, you say?" Then he shook his head. "The acquisition of that book will be discussed later. So, you know what follows when two people go to bed together."

"Yes," she answered, "well . . . a bit. Certain parts go into certain parts."

"And there's pleasure," he added.

She could not believe she was having this conversation with a man, but he was *her husband*, and if any two people ought to talk about sex, a husband and wife certainly ranked high on the list.

"For the man," she said. Once outside the Benezra, she'd overheard two women selling oranges talking candidly about carnal matters, and they had made fornication sound exciting but not entirely satisfying.

"For *everyone*," he amended. "If it's done properly."

The interior of the carriage was *quite* warm and she wished he would produce the flask again so she might have something, anything, to drink. "And do you, er, do it properly?"

Heat flared in his eyes, and she felt the promise of that heat all the way through her body, strumming along her most sensitive places. But then he appeared to deliberately bank it.

"I've been told so," he answered.

"Quite . . . encouraging." She didn't like this awkwardness, or admitting to anyone that there were some areas of knowledge where her own understanding was insufficient. Mustering her courage, she tipped up her chin and looked him directly in his eyes. "I've had orgasms, you know."

"Have you, now?" Despite his unruffled expression, fire glowed again in his gaze, as if he couldn't control his response to her.

Nothing for it but to brazen it out, however truthfully. "When I'm alone as I bathe. Sometimes at night before I go to sleep. And occasionally in the morning, before Olive comes in."

She'd never admitted it to anyone, and she couldn't tell if her racing pulse was from fear, mortification, or excitement.

"You like them enough, by the sound of it."

"They're pleasant," she said primly. Then, because she could not seem to stop herself, "And you? Alone, I mean."

"Almost every day," he said, his words surprisingly raspy.

"Ah." More heat pulsed in waves through her as she imagined Finn, languid in his bath, or stretched out, naked, in bed, pleasuring himself.

"I will do my best to give you more than *pleasant*," he added lowly. "This might be a marriage based on necessity, but I don't want you merely enduring our nights together."

"That's appreciated." The air in the carriage was thick and warm, and she fought to draw it into her lungs. This was *supposed* to have been a matter-of-fact conversation about the terms of their marriage, but it kept slipping from her control. There was something ungovernable about the attraction she felt for him—and the most alarming thing was that it just might be mutual.

"Is this what husbands and wives speak to each other about?" she asked, striving for steadiness.

"We aren't concerned with what others do, only what *we* do."

She pressed a hand to her quivering belly. Would tonight ever arrive, and was she afraid of it, or eager for nightfall?

She didn't know, and could only fumble in the dark.

Chapter 11

꒜ ✳ ꒜

$\mathcal{F}$inn knew what fear looked like. He'd seen it often enough when sitting opposite someone at the gaming hell. When they tried to smother their involuntary expressions but couldn't suppress the tiniest of winces as they were dealt a card they didn't want, or the tight creases in the corners of their mouth as they feigned a confident smile.

He'd also seen the quirk of a gambler's lips as they attempted not to show that they were pleased about their hand, or how they'd drum their fingers on the baize-covered table in an attempt to hurry the betting along, so they could win big.

His new bride would make a terrible gambler— everything showed in her face. Apprehension. Alarm. Eagerness. No matter how much she fought to hide it and appear the levelheaded scholar, he sensed her unease as they continued for the rest of the journey to their inn.

While he'd promised her that he would make their first time in bed together good, the truth was . . . he was scared out of his wits.

Because he *had* to make certain she enjoyed herself. He'd heard too many stories of frightened brides lying stiff and unmoving beneath their rutting husbands, leaving the poor women unsatisfied as the men got what they wanted.

It would be different with him and Tabitha. This might be an arrangement, but he meant what he said. She'd find pleasure in their bed.

Tension crept up as they got closer and closer to Blackheath. By the time the carriage approached a handsome red-brick-fronted inn, Finn was fairly certain Tabitha levitated above the vehicle's cushions.

"I've a surprise for you," he announced when the carriage rolled to a stop.

"What is it?" She seemed eager to seize any distraction.

"I'm no scholar," he said as he opened the door and climbed out, before turning to help her down. "Yet I believe the nature of a surprise means that it must be concealed from the one who is being surprised."

"You are a scoundrel." She slipped her hand into his as she emerged from the carriage. Without thought, his fingers curled around hers, and they fit perfectly.

"I have been told so, yes."

A peach-cheeked woman in an apron and wearing a ring of keys at her waist emerged to greet them. She introduced herself as Mrs. Kemp, while her two teenage sons assisted the footman in retrieving their luggage.

"Felicitations, sir and madam, on your nuptials," a Black man said warmly when they entered the inn.

He handed them each a ceramic mug. "I'm Josiah Kemp, and I welcome you to our inn."

Finn and Tabitha both sipped at their beverages, and exchanged smiles at the delightful flavor of spiced wine.

"Would you care to be shown to your room?" Mrs. Kemp asked.

"I was told that there was a *special feature* of your inn," Finn answered.

Mr. Kemp beamed. "This way, if you please."

They were led down a corridor, past an exceptionally stately taproom, where travelers and locals sat at polished wooden tables as they supped and drank. Finn paid more attention to the tight set of Tabitha's shoulders, the rigidly upright line of her back. Uncertainty poked fingers in his belly—hopefully, she'd enjoy this surprise.

Mr. Kemp stopped outside an open door, and motioned for Finn and Tabitha to enter. After sending Finn a curious glance, she went inside, and he followed.

She sucked in a breath as she turned in a circle. "Oh. My goodness."

The room contained numerous full bookshelves, as well as several chairs and lap rugs. It wasn't a massive chamber, but it appeared well stocked for any traveler's reading needs.

"Not many inns boast their own library," Finn said, trying to hide how he curled and uncurled his hands. "But I made certain to find one that did."

Tabitha turned in a circle, her eyes wide. Yet, to his relief, the tension had left her shoulders, and true happiness shone in her face. He sent up a quick but sincere prayer of gratitude that his instincts had been correct.

"It's marvelous," she exclaimed.

"My own collection," Mr. Kemp said. "I was a sailor for many years and always bought books on leave, and since then, I have continued to expand my library."

Tabitha went to one of the shelves and pulled down several books. "*Northanger Abbey* and *Persuasion. Frankenstein; or, the New Prometheus.*"

"That one is a very new acquisition," the innkeeper said. "And now I'll leave you to enjoy it."

When Mr. Kemp left, Finn regarded Tabitha, trying to hide the uncertainty that continued to prod him. "Do you truly like it?"

"Oh, Finn." She went to him and, after glancing toward the door, she cupped her hand around his face. "It's like a second home."

At last, he permitted himself true relief. Not only that he'd accurately determined what she might like, but that she didn't throw his gesture back in his face because he'd once again strayed from the terms of their agreement. No matter how hard he tried to remain polite and indifferent, he couldn't stop himself from wanting to please her. Wanting to see pleasure and joy illuminate her face. Wanting . . . wanting things he had no right to want. And yet he wanted them all the same.

FINN HAD WAITED in the taproom as Tabitha had bathed in their chamber, and when she had emerged, he also washed away the grime of the road. Once they were both refreshed from their travel, they made their way downstairs for supper.

"Would you care for a private dining chamber," Mr. Kemp asked at the entrance to the taproom, "or will the common room suffice?"

Finn glanced at Tabitha. While the inn's library had soothed her after the tension of their journey, the tightness in the corners of her mouth had returned. Was she thinking about their first time sharing a bed? Being alone with him as they dined might make her even more uneasy, and he'd do whatever was necessary to make her feel comfortable.

"The taproom will suffice," Finn answered.

The tiny lines of tension around her lips softened. So, he'd made the right decision.

Mr. Kemp showed them to a cozy settle in the corner, so that while they were surrounded by other guests and regular patrons, they had a degree of privacy.

"The menu is limited," the innkeeper explained once Finn and Tabitha had taken their seats. "But I can vouch for its excellence. My wife makes an excellent pumpkin and pheasant pie, and we've roast lamb with potatoes and greens of the field."

"The pie sounds quite appetizing," Tabitha said. "And I'd like an ale, please."

"I feel morally obligated to have the lamb," Finn added. "An ale for myself, as well."

Mr. Kemp bowed and left to fetch their food and drink.

Once they were alone, she arched a brow at Finn. "Morally obligated?"

"When given options," he explained, "two people

cannot both select the same dish. They must be different from each other. It's the rule."

"Not my rule, certainly," she said with a laugh.

"That's how it's always done with me and Kieran," Finn clarified, enjoying the rare sound of her laughter. "Our whole lives. Then, we both can try the other person's dish. Although," he went on thoughtfully, "it becomes a competition to see who ordered the best dish. If *he* wins, he's insufferable and gloats the remainder of the meal."

"But he didn't actually cook it," she objected.

"Never stopped him from crowing about his superiority."

She laughed again, the sound throaty and expectedly rich. Damn, he could get very used to craving her laugher and spending far too much time and energy trying to coax it from her.

"Brothers are exceedingly ridiculous," she said, shaking her head. "Everything is a competition. My own brothers were constantly vying to be taller than each other. They used to hang from tree branches to see if they could stretch themselves longer. As it turned out," she continued with a lift of her lips, "I grew taller than both of them."

"I hope you lord it over them every chance you get."

"Well," she said, her smile turning slightly wistful, "that would presume that I converse with my brothers with enough familiarity to tease them."

Anger on her behalf made him sit up straighter. "Are they cruel to you?"

"On the contrary. They're courteous and respectful, as if I was an acquaintance they occasionally encountered on the street. Pleasantries are exchanged, and then we all go about our separate paths. The truth is," she said on an exhale, "I've never quite fit in with my family, and I've given up any hope that one day they might accept me as I am."

She sounded resigned to it, and yet his heart gave a sympathetic squeeze. "Other than my younger brother, Kieran, and my sister, Willa, I'm entirely convinced my family wouldn't notice if I vanished from the earth. My father would continue to pay my allowance and I'd receive the same gift of a writing set that he sends me every year."

It was intimate—too intimate—to reveal. Yet in the snug confines of the settle, with the rest of the world shut out so that it did feel like he and Tabitha were fully alone, it wasn't quite so terrible to show her this one small, vulnerable part of him.

He fully anticipated she would deny it, or offer him some palliative words that surely it wasn't as bad as all that, and that he exaggerated how poor relations were with his parents. Except—her gaze was sympathetic, and her hand slid across the table to weave her fingers with his.

Her touch seemed to reach all the way into him, as if she'd gently, carefully, cradled not just his hand but his heart. Part of him wanted to snatch his hand back and curl it protectively against his chest. Another part of him wanted to hold on to her for as long as he possibly could.

Which wasn't very long. The moment Mr. Kemp and one of his sons appeared with their supper and drinks, Tabitha pulled back. Finn almost reached for her again, missing her touch immediately, but instead smiled politely at the innkeeper and his boy as their food was set before them. Savory smells curled delectably within the confines of the settle.

"I wish you hearty appetite," Mr. Kemp said before he and his son backed away.

Tabitha bent close to the pie in front of her and examined the decorative pastry pieces that adorned it. "This is very clever. It looks like a picnic basket. Perhaps," she went on, eyes glimmering, "I've won dinner."

She looked entirely too enchanting, with her cheeks slightly pink from the steam rising up from her food, and her gray gaze sparkling. The strongest urge to close the distance between them gripped him. More than anything, he wanted to lean across the table and kiss her. To hell with the food—he wanted to taste *her*.

He had to remain in control of himself, so he turned his attention to his own dish.

"Granted," he allowed, "yours has a slight visual advantage over my humbler lamb and vegetables, but the true test is in the taste."

"We'll use our superior discernment to determine the winner," she answered.

They were both quiet as they each took a mouthful of their separate meals. Then he cut a piece of lamb and potato and set them on her plate, and at the same time, she put a morsel of pie on his dish. Again, there was silence as they each tasted the other's food.

There was a soft, welcome domesticity to it, enclosing them both. And yet beneath it, he was at all times conscious of her mouth, and the small sounds of pleasure she made as she ate. They were instinctive sounds, low and husky, very much like the noises she might make in the throes of passion.

Not for the first time, he imagined making love to her. Before they'd kissed in his parents' garden, he might've suspected that she would be cool and reserved, merely accepting sex as some tedious biological act. But after that kiss . . . he knew she'd be full of fire, responsive and eager.

His body went taut as his pulse hummed. Because he wanted her. Wanted her with a hunger he'd never known before—and it shook him to his marrow.

He had vowed to make their lovemaking good for her, yet he could give her pleasure without losing his heart to her in the process, couldn't he?

What he *couldn't* do was reach across the table, wrap his hand around the back of her neck, and claim her mouth in the base, primal way he desperately wanted.

He needed to focus on something else, anything else. Turning his attention to his meal, he noted that their food was delicious, both the lamb and the savory combination of pumpkin and partridge.

"I believe we have tied, madam," he said on a sigh. "Alas."

"Why *alas*?"

"Because I was very much looking forward to insisting upon a prize from you if I emerged the victor." The words flew from his mouth before he could stop them, and he cursed himself for getting carried away.

Her cheeks grew rosier as she stared at him. Breathlessly, she asked, "What sort of prize? The sort a bridegroom might demand from his wife on their wedding night?"

He'd no idea how to answer, not without revealing how much he desired her—and possibly terrifying her in the process. What he wanted of her went far beyond their bargain. Unless she wanted more, too . . .

"We trust everything's to your satisfaction," Mrs. Kemp said, appearing beside their table.

"It's all excellent," he answered.

Tabitha smiled and nodded, though she kept glancing at Finn, as if she craved his answer to her question. As if she craved *him*. The thought was exciting, and daunting. He would lavish on her every desired pleasure.

"ARE YOU ALMOST ready?" Finn asked through the closed door to their bedchamber. "The other guests are looking at me suspiciously, as if I might rob their rooms."

"Five more minutes," came Tabitha's muffled response.

He tried not to pace in the corridor as he waited for her to finish changing for bed. They'd concluded their supper with no more discussion of bridegrooms claiming prizes from their wives. For the rest of the meal they had been well-mannered and courteous.

Thank God the other patrons of the inn hadn't shouted encouragement at Finn as he escorted his bride upstairs. One ribald comment would surely have made Tabitha run out the door and into the night.

Now he waited and listened to the sounds she made as she prepared for their first time sharing a bed. Mrs. Kemp had helped her disrobe, but left the room as Tabitha donned her nightgown. He pictured Tabitha's sleek, bare limbs as she slipped into something soft and gauzy.

His cock surged, and he made himself stare at the

framed pictures of botanical specimens to calm himself. He'd scare the hell out of her if he barged into their bedchamber with a vehement erection.

He took several deep breaths, but they didn't steady him as much as he hoped. Excitement coursed through his muscles, as a sharp, pulsing desire gathered. Perhaps wanting her as much as he did defied the terms of their agreement, and yet this hunger gripped him, growing keener by the moment.

The door opened.

She peered around it, her face flushed, and her hair spread around her shoulders. "Come in."

Discreetly as possible, he rubbed his palms on his breeches before striding into the room. He barely saw the fire burning low in the grate, or the finely carved washstand. His attention shot to the sizable bed, and then to Tabitha, who shut the door to enclose them in their bedchamber.

Firelight danced over the waves of her mahogany hair, and played in the soft folds of the white wrapper that she pulled close around her body. The sight of her magnificently long bare feet peeping out beneath the hem of her nightgown shot a surprising bolt of pure lust through him. Though he enjoyed all parts of women's bodies, he'd never before found anyone's feet erotic—until tonight.

Her toes curled, tiny indicators of her uncertainty, and his attention glided up her body, lingering briefly on the tender, small swells of her breasts, before he found her watching him cautiously. Then she shivered.

"You're cold," he noted with a frown. He strode to the fire, which was flanked by two armchairs. He sat, then motioned for her.

Slowly, she approached. When she started to sit in the other armchair, he said, "Not there."

"Then where?"

He patted his thigh.

Her eyes widened. "I thought sitting in laps was something only children did."

"I think you'll find this position to be quite adult." He tapped his fingers on his thigh again.

She looked doubtful, but lowered herself down to sit on his lap. He bit back a groan at the feel of her arse against his leg, and the press of her barely clad body to his. It wouldn't do to scare the lady out of her wits, especially because she perched on him as if he might catch on fire at any moment, and she would need to leap up to save herself.

At this rate, he just might burst into flames.

"Put your arms around my neck," he instructed.

After giving him another hesitant glance, she did as he directed. Her diminutive breasts shifted beneath the fine fabric of her wrapper and nightgown, but instead of cupping them as he hungered to do, he placed a hand on her waist, and another below her knee, hoping to imbue his touch with comfort.

The feel of her was anything but comforting. She was satiny and warm, her gentle curves exquisite against his harder, firmer body, which grew harder and firmer by the second. God, he was made to fit so snugly to her like this.

"Am I supposed to do something whilst I sit here?" she asked.

"Feel free to rest your head on my shoulder," he suggested. When she did so, he murmured, "Taking a breath might be advisable."

She let out a long exhalation, her body tangibly

relaxing against his. Her hair brushed against his cheek, silken and abundant, and it carried a lemony scent. More arousal poured through him.

"The day's been exceptionally long," he said as evenly as he could. "We've had to perform for many people, but this, now, this is for us."

"I'm not used to it," she said softly. "Having someone be so considerate. I don't mean to imply that my family was *inconsiderate*, only, as I said, they've never quite known what to make of me. So many puzzled looks, as if they had expected someone else, but wound up with me, instead."

"I'd wager the feeling was mutual." Though his words were light, he held her protectively, as if he could shield her from anyone who didn't appreciate her.

She chuckled, and the gentle sound passed from her body into his. "The fault isn't all theirs. I couldn't understand why they wanted to make *conversation* at breakfast and dinner, when reading was so much more enjoyable."

"You're welcome to bring books to the table whenever you please."

"The best part about books is having someone to discuss them with," she said with a smile in her voice.

Tension shot along his limbs. Someday, she'd learn the truth about him. Until then, he'd give her what he could, and hopefully prolong the inevitable.

Slowly, very slowly, he glided his hand back and forth across her knee. The fabric shifted and bunched beneath his fingers, but it was so finely woven that it offered scant barrier against the feel of her. At the same time, he stroked the curve of her waist, warm and supple as she leaned close to him.

"That's nice," she whispered.

"Since our kiss in the garden," he said, gravelly, "I wanted to touch you. I kept seeing you in these prim gowns and all I could think about was the texture of your skin, how soft you'd be."

"You're the only one who considers me soft. I always believed I was nothing but points and angles."

A smile touched his lips. "Delightful geometry." He moved his hand to the hem of her nightgown, his fingertips grazing along her shin. "May I?"

"Please."

He considered himself a sophisticated man. He wasn't a libertine like Kieran, but he'd experienced many of life's pleasures. Yet nothing compared to what it was like to touch her naked leg, long and sleek, beneath the filmy cotton of her nightclothes. His breath caught as he stroked over her knee to reach the tender flesh of her thigh. Her own breathing came quickly when his palm stroked along her bare skin.

Fine tremors shook her body, but she didn't pull away.

"It's been hours since we kissed to seal our bond," he said lowly. "A brief kiss, at that. Since then, I've wanted nothing more than to savor you again."

He brushed his lips across her cheek. Then made a low sound of pleasure when she turned to press her mouth to his. They took small sips of each other before the kiss quickly deepened, and she opened to let him in. The flavor of her was fruity and sweet from the ale they'd consumed at supper, yet it was her own taste that made his head spin and his cock thicken, especially when her fingers wove into his hair.

As the kiss heated, she shifted and writhed against him, brushing her breasts across his chest. He stroked up her thigh, going higher, while his other hand skimmed up her ribs until, at last, he cupped her breast.

She jolted, gasping into his mouth, yet she pressed tighter to him. He murmured in approval as he found the taut peak of her nipple and rubbed his fingers back and forth across it, firming it even more, drawing sounds of surprised pleasure from her. And when he gave it a gentle pinch, he swallowed her moan.

He caressed along her inner thigh, the softest skin imaginable, and then, ah, bless, he reached her hot, damp sex. She inhaled sharply before her legs drifted open.

Careful to take his time, he petted her mons and outer lips, the flesh searing and plump, growing riper by the moment, until he slipped a finger into her crease.

"Ah, fuck," he growled when he found her lush and wet. He'd been right—she *was* responsive and eager, and having her in his arms was wondrous. That *he* could make her feel this passion stoked his pleasure even higher.

When he reached the stiffened nub of her clitoris and circled it with his thumb, she gave another moan. His mind emptied as he traced her folds and rubbed along her soaked flesh, making her arse grind against his aching cock. All the while, he continued to stroke her breast and lightly pluck at her nipple.

He removed his hand from her cunt long enough to lick his fingers—good Christ, did she taste incredible—before returning his attention to her pussy. As his thumb moved glossily over her clitoris, he eased a finger into her passage. It was incredible to be inside her like this, to feel her around him so intimately. As if this communion was a secret shared only by them.

She jerked in his arms, and he stilled.

"Stop?" he rasped.

"Hell, no," she said throatily. "Keep going."

He kissed her hungrily as he stroked up into her. Within, she was snug and scorching hot, and his cock throbbed in anticipation of being inside her. He found the swollen place within her, loving the mewls she made every time he glided over it. Her legs widened even more. To prepare her for him, he added a second finger into her channel, and she bucked in wordless demand.

"Look down," he growled. "Look at what I'm doing, how you can't get enough."

She did glance down, and moaned. Tucking her head into the crook of his neck, she confessed, "I don't know what's happening to me."

"You're chasing your pleasure, love. Let it happen. Fuck my fingers until you come." He could hardly believe the words coming from his mouth, and yet to be with her like this, to feel her against him, around him, unleashed something dark and primal within him. As if he was tapping into his truest self, and only she could make this happen.

"So crude."

"And yet you're riding me even harder."

She *was* wild against him, pushing her hips up and down as she made blissful, unrestrained sounds. How incredible that he could give her such ecstasy.

"God," he snarled, scraping his teeth along her

neck, "I love seeing you like this. Out of control. Needing to come so badly."

"Finn . . . I'm . . ."

"That's it, love. Come apart. You're safe. You're safe with me."

She tightened around him as she cried out, her body going taut with her climax. He was incredibly close to coming in his breeches, but it didn't matter if it meant watching her mouth slacken and hearing her sounds of release and taking the trembling of her limbs into his own body.

He wanted more. More of her and her bravery in opening herself so completely to him—not just physically, but with this gorgeous, fearless vulnerability. No one had ever given themselves so completely to him, trusting him in such an intimate way, but she had. It was a precious gift, one he would hold close for the remainder of his days.

He continued to thrust his fingers into her luscious cunt, until she cried out again, this time with even greater force. Only when she collapsed against him did he relent. He pulled from her body and gently curved his hand over her mound, petting her, soothing her in the aftermath.

More tremors wracked her. Taking his fingers from her breast, he laid them tenderly around her throat, turning her so he could kiss her deeply.

Christ almighty. The most intense sexual experience of his life, and he was still fully clothed.

"That wasn't covered in Aretino," she said, her words flatteringly slurred.

"There's always more to learn," he answered.

"You seem to know everything."

"Not everything, love." He traced one finger down the curve of her cheek, humbled to his marrow that she'd trusted him enough to be so unrestrained. "I suspect I might be completely incinerated when I'm inside you, but I won't know for certain until we try."

Her cheeks were pink, her eyes glassy, yet she managed a smile. "I'm always eager to expand my basis of knowledge." She pressed kisses along his jaw. "Take me to bed."

Chapter 12

❧ ✳ ❧

Tabitha didn't consider herself an especially diminutive person—she was taller than most women she met, and it wasn't uncommon for her to look eye to eye with many men—but she felt small and delicate when Finn gathered her in his arms, stood, and carried her to the bed.

Thank goodness he held her, because she didn't think her legs could bear her.

Despite her brazen words to him a moment before, urging him to take her to bed, as he laid her down upon the mattress, she pressed her face against the pillow and covered her eyes with her hand.

The mattress dipped as he sat beside her. "No need to hide, sweet."

"I was so shameless." The way she'd pushed her hips onto him, pursuing her release as though it was the only thing that mattered, and the way she'd kissed him, open-mouthed, greedy, and pressed her breasts into his hands . . . She'd enjoyed her self-administered orgasms, but she'd never been utterly in thrall to the need to come.

The way he touched her, knowing what she needed when she herself did not . . . There was magic in Finn's hands. As if he *knew* her in a way no one ever did.

"Shame is simply a way in which those in power try to hold us back, by tricking us into controlling ourselves."

She peered through her fingers. "Who said that? Mary Wollstonecraft? William Godwin?"

"Finn Ransome." His smile flashed, wicked and sensual, and impossibly, her sex ached with need. How could she want more after everything that had happened tonight?

He braced his hands on either side of her head and bent low, brushing his lips across her cheeks and the bridge of her nose.

"We can stop for tonight, if that's what you desire," he said, deep and husky.

His mouth stroked across hers, and she could not stop herself, pushing up slightly to press her lips to his. Something about this man reached past each of her defenses, slipping between the plates of armor that shielded her heart.

A barb of fear lodged in her, but then he deepened the kiss and the anxiety dissolved.

"Is that a yes?" he breathed between strokes of his tongue.

"It's a yes." She would face the consequences later. Now . . . now she wanted him. She gripped his wide shoulders, holding tight to his firm muscles as if she could anchor herself to the world by clinging to him.

He caressed her face, her neck, his thumb trailing in the hollow of her throat to summon shivers of pleasure. As he kissed her, he skimmed his hands down her arms and molded them to her breasts. When she gasped from his touch, he said on a growl, "You undo me in every way."

"We undo each other," she managed to gasp as his lips glided down her throat.

He stopped and made a grunt of frustration when he encountered the barrier of her nightgown. Straightening, he fingered the lace-trimmed neckline. "This needs to come off."

"I believe in equality," she said, tracing the buttons of his waistcoat and slipping one through its opening. Her face warmed at her bold words and bolder actions, but she tried to take heart from what he'd said earlier. She wouldn't let anyone make her feel ashamed for her desires.

"Mrs. Ransome, I am obliging." His lips curved as he pulled off his coat.

She stared at his long, blunt fingers as he swiftly undid the buttons of his waistcoat, another wave of heat surging as her body recalled the feel of them in her most intimate place. Talented fingers, no doubt shaped by handling cards and dice and gaming chips, but even more skillful at handling her.

He stood to strip out of his waistcoat, and her gaze was riveted by the thick, long shape of him pressed tightly to the front of his breeches. His boots were quickly removed and flung aside before he pulled his shirt up and over his head, and it, too, was cast aside.

"Good Lord," she couldn't stop from exclaiming as she gazed at his bare torso.

She'd thought statues and paintings had been exaggerations of the male form. No one had arms that were carved with sinew. Or such defined and beautifully hewn pectoral muscles, or actual ridges leading to their flat abdomen, or those two sharp lines angling from their hips that led straight to the groin.

But her husband did.

"What in God's name are you doing walking around like . . . like that?" She waved toward his alarmingly beautiful body. "I . . . You . . ."

A corner of his mouth lifted. "Much as I adore hearing you talk, reducing you to speechlessness makes all those sweaty, agonizing hours at the pugilism academy worth it."

She tried to think of something intelligent to say, witty or trenchant, but all she could do was salivate.

"Shall I continue?" His fingers hovered over the fastening of his breeches.

She nodded.

He undid the fall, revealing his erection.

She was forced to sit on her hands to keep from reaching for him. The aforementioned illustrated Aretino, as well as those statues in the museum, had prepared her for seeing a penis—but illustrations and bronze and marble couldn't compare to a . . . to a . . . well, there was no other word for it but *cock*.

And, heavens, was it delicious to look upon. It would likely feel even better in her hand, and yet . . . it was supposed to fit inside of her?

Her alarmed gaze flew to his, as he watched her staring at him.

"It's impossible," she whispered.

"You of all people should know that nothing is impossible." But when she continued to gape at him, he said soothingly, "We took care to make certain your body would be ready for me. I'll be as gentle as I can. But I understand if you're afraid."

"I'm not afraid," she said at once. "Not exactly. I'm only thinking of logistics."

"Ah, therein lies the heart of the matter." He removed his breeches.

She had glimpses of his long, muscled legs, and briefly as he turned away to discard the last of his garments, his most delectably firm buttocks, before he stretched out beside her, propping himself up on his elbow.

"The operative word you used was *thinking*," he said, smoothing his hand along her hip. "Let's give your mind a rest tonight, and simply let yourself feel."

"I can't shut it off like a water valve."

"Perhaps I can assist in that matter." He cupped the back of her head and kissed her ravenously. She clung to him, her fingers digging into hot, smooth flesh. Her legs moved restlessly, thighs rubbing together as she sought to soothe the need that built higher with each stroke of his tongue against hers.

She was lowered to the bed, and he paused in his kisses long enough to rasp, "I need you naked, sweet."

"I need that, too."

They both worked to remove her wrapper and nightgown, then she was nude. He pulled back to gaze at her. The way he looked at her with sharp, dark desire, she felt no shame in her nakedness. Especially when he slicked kisses over her collarbone, going lower, until his lips fastened around one of her nipples. He flicked his tongue over the tight point while his hand stroked and pinched the tip of her other breast.

Gasping, she arched into him, and held his head

in place as he lavished attention on her. Her eyes drifted closed at the onslaught of sensation, but she forced them open so she could watch the candlelight gleam in his black hair as he licked and sucked her.

Yet she couldn't keep her eyes open when he took one hand and slid it down her belly, until he found her wet, aching sex. He slid through her folds to circle her entrance, his thumb rubbing back and forth over her clitoris. She moaned his name when he slid one finger, and then another, into her—before he started to thrust.

Noises tumbled from her. Noises she could scarce believe she made, and yet there was no stopping them. Not when he moved the way he did and suckled on her breasts, and then he found that place in her as he had before. She hadn't even known such a spot existed in her body but he stroked over it with each thrust of his fingers, and light gleamed behind her eyelids and through her body every time he massaged it.

Her release erupted with the force of a gale, obliterating any sense of herself. She couldn't stop the long keening cry ripped from deep within her, nor the sounds she made when he brought her to climax once more. And again.

"Finn," she gasped. "My God, Finn."

He kissed his way back to her mouth, drinking her down like a man who survived on nothing else but the taste of her.

"I want you now," he said, guttural and rough. "Do you want me?"

"Yes, Finn. Yes."

He was sleek motion as he positioned himself above her, bracing himself on his forearms. Of their own volition, her legs opened wider to accommodate him. There was the briefest moment of panic when the crown of his cock fitted to her entrance, her body going taut. Though he'd made her ready for him, could he really fit inside her? Would there be pain? What if she couldn't carry through with this, and everything, including their marriage, fell apart? How—?

"Don't think," he murmured against her lips. "Just feel. Breathe with me."

Eyes locked, they exhaled together. As their breath mingled, he slid slowly, gradually into her.

He was thicker than his two fingers, and she automatically winced at the intrusion.

"Am I hurting you?" he said, his jaw tight with concern.

"It's not pain." Talking, forming words with him inside her was strange, yet she was able to explain, "I'm learning. Learning you. Learning us. And I'm learning . . . I like this. Very much."

"There's a lass." He was seated to the hilt in her, completely filling her, and his hips were still as he seemed to understand that she needed time. Yet he rumbled, "Christ, you feel good."

"So do you." Her body loosened, accepting him. She experimented, moving slightly so that he stroked deep inside her.

"Oh, fuck," he snarled.

"Exactly," she gasped.

He drew back before thrusting forward. She moaned at this wondrous sensation, far more profound than his fingers, this incredible joining of their bodies. He did it again, adding force to the movement.

A wild noise escaped her as ecstasy blossomed. She

jolted with each plunge of his cock, her sounds growing louder and wilder the fiercer he became.

"This is what you like, love." His words left in rough gusts with each stroke into her. "This is how you want to be fucked."

Her eyes rolled back, pleasure billowing with his raw language. And when he continued to drive his hips with unrelenting demand, she pushed herself into him, wanting more and more.

He shifted slightly, so that each time he surged forward, he ground against her swollen clitoris. Over and over until, astonishingly, she came again.

Moments later, he jolted, his entire body drew tight. He threw his head back as her name left his lips on a long, jagged groan.

He held himself above her as they gasped and sweated together, and then slowly pulled out before lying beside her. Reverberations echoed in her body while her heart tried to relearn a steady, sedate rhythm. She didn't have high hopes for it ever returning to normal, not after what she'd just experienced.

She leaned into his touch when he brushed damp hair off her forehead. He pressed a kiss between her brows before rising from the bed and striding to the washstand. Only a fool would miss the opportunity to look at his nude body, and she was no fool. She watched all that gorgeous sleek movement as he used the water pitcher to wet a cloth, and then return to the bed.

His movements were gentle and tender as he cleaned her, using soft strokes between her legs to wipe away his seed that spilled from her and ran down her thighs.

Once he seemed satisfied by his efforts, he set the cloth aside. He climbed back into the bed and leaned against the headboard, then gathered her in his arms. She pressed her face into his chest, the crisp curling hair tickling her cheek. His heart thumped beneath the spread of her fingers, and she smiled at the flatteringly quick pace.

"Would you like some wine?" he asked. "I could send for something to eat."

"This is perfect." And it was, nestled in the protective strength of his arms, her body soft and pliant in the wake of so much pleasure. "The sounds we made. I hope we didn't disturb anyone's sleep."

"I'm confident we woke the building. Which means we did it properly." He stroked his fingers down the side of her face. "All right?"

"I am," she said, truthful. "And you?"

His chest vibrated with a chuckle. "No one's ever asked me that before. And I can answer quite honestly that I've never been better."

"Not even when you've won piles of money at the gaming tables?" She tilted her head back to look at him.

"I could win the whole gaming hell and it wouldn't feel like this." He rubbed his cheek against the crown of her head. "That was my first time as someone's first time, and I thank you for the wondrous experience."

Wondrous. It had been. From the moment he had her sit on his lap until now, every moment had been extraordinary. The physical pleasure had surpassed anything she'd ever known, yet more than that, his kindness and grace throughout reached into the most hidden, carefully guarded parts of herself and held her securely.

Nothing in her life had prepared her for this. For him.

It would be quite easy to care for him, far beyond the boundaries of their agreement. She wanted to lean into the sensation, and the warmth that spread through her and encircled her heart. All the things he'd given her today and tonight had been magnificent. Yet that didn't mean he had deep, profound adoration for her. He was a good man, and had done his best to make sure that she felt comfortable in their marriage.

Even so, it would be a mistake if she read more into this than he truly meant. And it would only open the door to a pain that she already knew would devastate her when he didn't reciprocate her feelings. She knew that pain too well.

"Are you certain you don't want some wine?" Finn asked. He rubbed his hand up and down her arm in what must have been an attempt to chase away the gooseflesh that pebbled her skin. "It might warm you up."

"I'm only tired."

"To bed, madam," he commanded with a smile.

"We *are* in bed." She tried to keep the edge out of her voice, but she wasn't certain how successful she was in the effort.

"To sleep, then." After blowing out the candle, he pulled back the covers, and they both slid beneath the bedclothes.

When she curled onto her side, away from him, he curved his body around hers, his arm secure across her waist. Sheltering her. Protecting her.

She squeezed her eyes shut. Her throat tightened and she wanted so badly to curl into him. But she couldn't, not if she wanted to keep herself from giving him her heart.

A heart he'd already said had no place in their marriage.

With Charles, she'd thought them perfectly matched, but when he'd rejected her so coldly, she had realized that she hadn't truly known him. She'd been half in love with an inhuman ideal. Finn, however, was so real to her. She learned more about him day to day, moment to moment, breath to breath, and what she discovered was becoming frighteningly important.

How could she stop herself from caring about him? From falling into feelings that Charles had insisted muddled her judgment and led her so terribly astray?

"Good night," he murmured sleepily behind her. "Mrs. Ransome."

"Good night," she managed, "Mr. Ransome."

Holding herself still, she counted his breaths until they came farther and farther apart. At last, he was asleep.

Ten more minutes, she waited. When she was certain he slumbered, she eased from the bed. It was a difficult task to dress in the half-light given by the fireplace, but she managed a reasonable approximation of slipping on her shift, lacing her stays, and pulling on her gown. She didn't bother with stockings. Every time she moved, the floorboards creaked, and she kept casting worried glances toward the bed, where her new husband slept.

She stilled, staring at him in repose. God above, he was splendid, and as he rested, the wariness that made his features so diamond sharp eased. It would be such a pleasure to lose hours like this, watching him, beautiful as he dreamt. What did he dream about? If only she could slip inside his mind and know his every thought, if only she could delve into his heart and understand everything he felt.

She shook herself. They had an agreement, she and Finn, and she wouldn't renege on it. She wouldn't let sentiment and emotion fog her mind, and she couldn't leave herself exposed and defenseless when he pushed her away.

Even so, she cast him one last look before she crept from the room, and made sure the door made no noise as she shut it behind her.

Chapter 13

❖ ✳ ❖

She was gone.

Finn snapped awake when he reached for Tabitha and discovered that her side of the bed was empty. For someone used to sleeping alone, he shouldn't have been expecting to find anyone beside him. Yet he searched for her, his hand sweeping back and forth across the sheets, and when he didn't come into contact with her warm, slumbering form, his eyes opened and he bolted upright.

He spun his legs around to sit on the edge of the bed, and the soft fabric of her discarded wrapper and nightgown brushed against his feet.

Peering into the semidarkness, he saw no sign of her in the bedchamber.

Fear dug talons into him, and he rose to gather up his own clothing from the floor. After lighting the candle, he hastily pulled on his shirt and stepped into his breeches. Her luggage was still in the room—but the garments she'd worn that day were missing.

Fuck. Fuck. Had she been kidnapped? Or, *God,* had she realized that she'd made a mistake in marrying him, and fled into the night?

He went cold all over, imagining her out alone, defenseless, roaming the countryside in the pitch-black night. All sorts of terrible things and people were out there, any one of them capable of hurting her.

Taking the lamp, he went out into the corridor. He'd rouse Mr. Kemp from his bed and organize a search party. And if, by the grace of God, they found her, if she *had* fled from their marriage, he would cede to any of her demands, so long as she was safe.

But where *did* the innkeeper and his wife sleep? Surely not on the floor with the guest rooms. Likely they'd be on the ground floor, near the kitchens.

Finn pounded down the stairs, heedless of any noise he might make. The inn was dark and silent, save for a clock that chimed three o'clock, and he strode past the empty taproom, down the hallway to reach the kitchens and hopefully the private chambers of the Kemp family.

As he sped, he passed the open door of the library. Light spilled into the hallway, so he peered inside, half afraid to hope.

His heart spasmed.

Tabitha sat in one of the chairs, bent over an open book, a small lamp burning beside her.

His breath left him as sharply as if he'd been punched in the stomach. Relief came so quickly he was faintly queasy.

The last time he'd known that kind of fear, Kieran had been a small boy. His brother had fallen off the roof of an outbuilding of their family's country estate and had lain unmoving on the grass. Finn had raced to the main house to call for help, the whole time certain that his brother was dead. But by the time Finn had returned with the butler and several footmen, Kieran had been sitting up and complaining that he'd dropped the custard tart he'd brought up to the roof.

Finn had been so relieved he'd had to hide in the stables so no one could see him cry.

Tabitha was here, she was fine. *Thank God.*

She seemed to be so absorbed in whatever it was she read, she didn't notice him sagging against the doorframe. Licking one of her fingers, she turned a page and nodded as if in agreement with something written in the text.

"Tabitha," he said, his words scraping his throat.

The book flew from her startled hands and landed on the floor with a thud.

"Finn. My gracious." She pressed her palm to the center of her chest. "You startled me."

He strode into the library, then stopped midway between the door and where she sat, as if an invisible hand held him back. "I woke and you weren't in the room."

"This library is so extraordinary, I had to take advantage of it." She bent down and picked up the book, frowning slightly as she smoothed a crease in a page.

"Ah." He stood there, relief and fear draining from him so that his limbs were weak, made more unsteady by the creep of embarrassment. It was foolish to have been so worried, when the most obvious answer had been right in front of him.

She looked at him now with a small smile but there was a slight tension around her mouth.

His wife had slipped from their bridal bed to . . . to read.

The stab of hurt made no sense. She *was* a scholar, after all, and they *had* entered into this marriage not on the basis of sentiment but convenience. There was no reason why he ought to feel wounded by her visit to the library—yet he was.

"Do you wish for company?" he asked.

"Please don't deny yourself sleep on my account," she answered at once.

The readiness of her reply stung, but he nodded. "Enjoy your reading."

She looked on the verge of saying something, but then she also nodded. "Have a good night."

He went to the door and lingered on the threshold, hating himself for wanting her to tell him to stay. When she was silent, he resignedly gave up hope and left the library.

It wasn't in the terms of their arrangement that they would actually develop feelings for each other. Their only stipulation was fidelity. She could do precisely as she pleased, and he shouldn't expect anything more than that. What did he expect, in any event? That she'd suddenly developed ardent feelings for him in the span of a few weeks? He wasn't the sort of man who people cared for, certainly not so swiftly. If at all. This only confirmed what he already knew about himself.

Or so he told himself as he climbed the stairs to the room. Once in the bedchamber, he stripped, blew out the candle, and then slipped back into bed. It was much chillier now with no one in it.

He sat up and relit the candle. Sliding out of bed, he padded to his luggage and rifled through the various items in it until his hands encountered a small rectangular box, which he removed. He returned to the bed and sat cross-legged upon it before opening the box.

The deck of cards within it fit comfortably in his hand. Shuffling them came as naturally as other men shaved, and once he was satisfied that they were sufficiently rearranged, he laid them out to play a game of patience. One game turned into another, and another.

In his infrequent imaginings of his wedding night, he'd never pictured himself like this, his only company a deck of cards.

At least the cards never turned him away.

The following morning, Finn awakened to find Tabitha up and in the process of dressing. She had her back to him, so he watched as she slipped on her traveling costume, though she struggled to do up the fastenings.

He propped himself up on an elbow and tried to ignore the heaviness that weighted in his chest at seeing her like this, as though he wasn't in the room, as though their incredible lovemaking hadn't happened.

"I can assist with that," he said, his voice gravelly soon after waking.

She spun to face him, and she looked slightly guilty, as if he'd caught her doing something she shouldn't. But these were the conditions of their marriage, which they'd both agreed to.

"It would be appreciated," she said, and her own voice was low and rasping from the early hour. "The inn sounds quite busy, and I hadn't the heart to ask Mrs. Kemp to leave her duties to attend to me."

"I'm always at your disposal." He slipped from

the bed—and her eyes widened as her gaze traveled down the length of his body. He wore only a pair of fine linen drawers, which hung low on his hips, the drawers themselves providing minimal coverage over his groin.

She stared at him as her cheeks turned pink, her lips parted, and her pupils widened. At least she wasn't immune to his physical form, but that provided little comfort in the wake of the strain between them.

"I'm ready to play the role of abigail," he said coolly.

Shaking her head, she seemed to come back to herself, and presented him with her back and the tiny fastenings of her gown that awaited his ministrations. He began to fasten them, slipping the small fabric-covered buttons through their loops.

His stomach clenched—this was such a tender, domestic thing to do, and yet he had to remember that he ought to treat it as impersonally as possible.

"You're very deft at this," she noted.

"I've considerable experience—"

"Oh," she said quietly, almost as if she was disappointed.

"—handling dice and cards and playing chips," he finished. Despite his insistence that he wasn't some sort of rake, it appeared that she'd forgotten, and imagined him undressing, and then dressing conquests? Perhaps he ought to have been, so that he'd find this moment less poignant. "My hands are trained to work with delicate things."

His body stirred in recollection of how silken and glossy she'd been against his fingers, her moans of pleasure. And she must have been thinking the same, because a rosy stain crept along her neck.

"I hope I didn't disturb you when I came back to our room last night." Her words attempted an impersonal tone, but there was breathlessness beneath them. "You didn't awaken when I got into bed."

"I wasn't aware that you had returned." He finished the last of the buttons, his hands admirably steady, and he congratulated himself for not stroking his lips over her soft nape as he wanted to. That was the sort of thing affectionate newlyweds did, and they weren't that.

She faced him, though she seemed intent on staring at his shoulder. "Part of you must've known, because you wrapped an arm around me and pulled me close."

"Ah." His jaw tightened. Damn it. Even when unconscious, he wanted her.

"I . . ." Her gaze lifted to his. Quietly, she said, "I liked it."

Hell, when she said things like that, his sense of direction went spinning, and he couldn't find his true north.

The urge to haul her against him surged along his limbs. Yet even so, the more he craved the feel of her, the more painful it was when he recalled that this was a business arrangement.

"If we want to reach London before afternoon," he said, moving past her to collect his clothing, "it would be best to break our fast soon, and get back on the road."

"Of course," she said with a tight nod. "I'm going to write Sir William Marcroft as soon as we arrive, and let him know that I'm married now."

Yes—there was a purpose to their marriage, and he couldn't forget that. She would get what she desired, and he had fulfilled the requirements of his family's ultimatum. Everyone got what they wanted.

Except, as he dressed and she packed up her belongings, all he felt was hollow.

THE RETURN JOURNEY to London was passed in almost total silence. Every mile was taut and strained, and Tabitha tried to keep her attention on the scenery out the carriage window, rather than study the clean, distinct line of her husband's profile.

I wanted to stay, she almost said. *I was afraid, and when you held me in your sleep, I knew why I was afraid.*

She didn't say any of this. He'd seemed quite content with the impersonal nature of their marriage, so she couldn't—shouldn't—ask for more. Yet it hurt to see the chill in his eyes, as if they were back to being mere colleagues rather than husband and wife.

But the way he'd touched her last night . . . the things he made her feel . . . not merely physical pleasure, but that she was someone to be cherished. Surely mere obligation and male pride couldn't be his only motivation. Could it? She knew more of life from books than experience.

At last, the carriage was pulled to a stop outside a dignified two-story town house in Chelsea. Apprehension danced through her as Finn helped her down from the vehicle to show her their new home. This was to be the place where they lived the rest of their lives together.

"I hope it will suit you," he said as he led her to the front door. A footman bowed when they crossed the threshold, and the waiting housekeeper and two maids curtseyed.

"It has a roof and my parents don't live beneath it," she answered, "so it suits me wonderfully."

The housekeeper introduced herself as Mrs. Stilton—"Like the cheese," she helpfully informed them—and the footman as Edgar, and the maids as Cora and Dilly, then she led Finn and Tabitha on a tour.

"It's all quite lovely," Tabitha whispered to him after Mrs. Stilton showed them the dining room, furnished with a long and handsome mahogany table and eight matching chairs. "But how can we afford this?"

"My income from the gaming tables keeps me very comfortable," he replied. "However, the funds to let and furnish the place were a wedding present from my parents. At the least, they've never been scarce in supplying me and my siblings with money."

Rather than admire the silver candle sconces on the walls, she looked at him. This wasn't the first time he'd alluded to a cold relationship with his family. The casual, offhand way he spoke of the aloofness between them made her wonder what was at the heart of it, and what he'd had to endure from his parents. They had barely been present at the wedding. Tabitha had actually exchanged only a handful of words with the earl and countess.

She hesitated to ask him for an explanation—perhaps she didn't have a right to press him for such personal details.

But if he'd insisted that he didn't want emotion in their marriage . . . did that come from something in his past? Something that had to do with his up-bringing?

"What's this room?" she asked instead as they neared a chamber that faced the tidy back garden. It was safer to discuss the house than the mountain of uncertainty between them.

"Ah, that." He appeared briefly uncertain, then his expression smoothed over. "This was one of the features of the property that impelled me to lease it."

He waved her into the room.

Tabitha's breath caught as they stepped inside together. She was surrounded by floor-to-ceiling bookcases. Some of the shelves already held books, whilst others stood empty. Many small crates were stacked in the center of the room.

"You keep surprising me with libraries," she whispered. Oh, God, she was in terrible danger, and she swallowed hard around the knot in her throat.

"You like them," he said simply. As if what he said didn't delve right to her heart.

To keep herself from throwing her arms around him and showering him with grateful kisses, she walked to one of the shelves to examine a book. "Where did these come from?"

"The person who decorated the house bought the lot of them from a dealer—someone was liquidating their collection."

"They certainly had eclectic tastes," she said, returning the volume to the shelf. "Though whoever they were seemed to have a predilection for the gothic and sensational."

"Lurid tales?" he asked hopefully. "Full of suggestive and shocking scenes?"

"Having never read them before," she said with

a touch of regret, "I can't vouch for their contents. The beauty of an unread book is that we can imagine whatever we want for its subject matter. And then it's even better when we *do* read it, and find that it surpasses anything we could have conjured up."

She fell silent when he regarded her intently.

"Apologies," she said stiffly. "I forget myself when I'm talking about books."

"I . . . It's . . ." His gaze was warm. "Wonderful."

Unable to stay away, she quickly crossed the room to him. "You've done so much for me, Finn. I'm grateful. Truly grateful. I don't think anyone's ever given me so much."

He tipped up his chin, yet a tiny, careful smile snuck through to hover around his lips. "I'm glad you like the library."

The moment lengthened as they stared at each other. There was an ache within her—reaching, yearning for something she shouldn't want.

Then he cleared his throat and glanced away. "I have some business matters to attend to. Mrs. Stilton can show you the rest of the house. We'll meet again at dinner."

She nodded, and he started for the door. But she couldn't let him go without being fully honest.

"Finn." When he turned to face her, she gave him a cautious smile. "Thank you, truly. For the house. For my very own library. For . . . for everything."

"My pleasure." He drew in a breath as if he would say more, but whatever it was he'd planned on saying, he banished with a shake of his head. "Enjoy your afternoon."

Thankfully he left quickly, before she did something foolish. Like ask him to cancel his appointments so they could spend more time together, and begin to hope for things that wouldn't come to pass.

TABITHA SPENT THE remainder of the afternoon exploring the rest of the house, which she found smaller but much more comfortable than her parents' home. There were three bedrooms, but when she looked into a clothes press in the biggest bedchamber, she discovered his garments. She ran her fingers over his shirts and stroked over the crisp fabric of her neckcloths and fought against the urge to bury her face into them to see if they carried his smoky scent.

There was a second clothes press in the room. Perhaps Finn was attempting to rival Brummell in the scope of his wardrobe. She really oughtn't look—how silly to want to touch his clothing, like she was some lovestruck girl—yet she opened the cabinet. Just a peek. To satisfy her curiosity.

Opening the cabinet, her gaze fell on the distinctive russet color of her favorite pelisse, carefully stacked on a shelf. Turning, she noticed her hairbrush and a few bottles of toilette water on a dressing table—beside a mahogany case with the inlaid initials *F.A.R.* on the lid.

So. They were to share the bedroom.

She pressed a hand to her thudding heart. She *could* move her clothes to another room. After all, many married people kept separate bedchambers. But maybe . . . maybe sharing a room with Finn might be all right, and she wouldn't grow too attached to the idea of watching him shave every morning or discussing quotidian, domestic matters with him as they both undressed at the end of the day.

And maybe she could keep her emotions well removed from sleeping in the same bed with him, and from growing too attached when they made love.

She shut the door to the wardrobe and took a steadying breath. It would be fine. There was nothing to be afraid of—and if she looked forward to having his arms around her all night, well, she wouldn't dwell on that.

What she *did* need to focus on was writing to Sir William Marcroft to let him know that she was now married, and to press him for setting a date for her meeting with the Sterling Society so they might discuss when they would admit her.

She went down to the library—her heart squeezed again at the thought that Finn had provided her with her very own library—and found a desk with writing supplies in it. It took a good half an hour for her to compose a letter that wasn't too importunate or overly reticent, but write it, she did, and then handed it to the footman to deliver immediately. With any luck, Sir William would respond immediately. It would soon be time for the Sterling Society to consult on the education bill, so she hadn't the luxury of a delay.

Once the footman had gone, there was nothing left to do except wait patiently, hoping Sir William replied. And try not to be too eager for Finn's return.

She failed at both.

A FOG HAD crept in and the sun had already set by the time Finn returned home. Welcoming lamplight bathed the entryway to the house as the footman took his hat and walking stick.

"Where is Mrs. Ransome?" he couldn't help but ask, brushing the damp off his coat. *Hell*. He forced himself to take his time and not chase after her the moment he crossed the threshold. He'd deliberately stretched out his excursions to prove to himself that he was not and would not grow overly attached to his new bride.

He'd visited Joaquin Mendoza, his man of business. There, he'd casually inquired about the amount of funds necessary to finance opening his gaming hell. It wasn't a surprise to learn that he had been careful with his money, and now had enough to actually start an establishment of his own.

Still, doubt prickled him. Could he do something so monumental? Something that demanded considerable intellectual prowess?

Tabitha believed he could do it. Yet she didn't know how he struggled with reading, which surely had to be one of the most critical elements to running a business. Telling his wife that her husband was not, and would never be, a scholar caused ice to sheet down his back. Nothing made her happier than libraries, which were places that he avoided.

Except he'd found himself in them an awful lot ever since she'd come into his life.

After finishing with Mendoza, he'd gone to his club and purposefully lingered over a game of billiards with Dom. He'd challenged Dom to another game, but his sodding friend declined before stalking off into the night. Finn had had to sit by himself and nurse a glass of whisky, musing on how grim and dark Dom had become, which surely had to do with lingering feelings for Willa.

They had been in love. Perhaps Dom was *still* in

love, and that was why he was so bleak and sullen. If his friend wasn't so miserable, it was almost enviable, to have that kind of emotion for anyone, and to have once known that someone shared the depths of your feelings.

He'd concentrated on the bottom of his glass rather than think of Tabitha—though it wasn't a successful strategy. The whisky had tasted strangely bitter, so Finn hadn't asked for another round. Instead, he'd reluctantly left the club and headed back to Chelsea.

That reluctance had burned away the closer he got to home. He'd sat forward on the cushions of the carriage, as if he could somehow propel the vehicle forward by his will alone.

Now he called upon years of training himself not to show emotion as he waited for the footman's answer.

"Madam is in the library."

"I see." Very calmly, Finn removed his gloves and handed them to Edgar. "I'll be there presently."

He paused for a moment in front of a framed mirror, taking time to make certain his neckcloth still retained its crisp folds and that his hair hadn't gotten too windblown. Fortunately, he'd had his hair cut in the days before the wedding, otherwise it had a tendency to curl when it grew too long.

Although, perhaps Tabitha might like running her fingers through his curls, especially when they kissed.

He squeezed his eyes shut, though the taste of her mouth reverberated hotly through his body. Storming into the parlor and pulling her into his arms to kiss her passionately wouldn't be appropriate. A few deep inhalations set him to rights, and when he felt reasonably in control of himself, he moved down the corridor that led to the library. He actually walked rather than ran down the hallway.

He paused in the doorway to the library, barely concerned with the laden bookshelves, the two wing-back chairs beside a small table, or the tasteful cherrywood desk. All he saw was her, standing in front of the fire, a book in her hand but her attention fixed on the flames that danced in the grate. The light graced her sharp features and gilded her cheeks—how was it possible that she'd gone so many years without anyone offering for her? He hadn't spent much time circulating amongst respectable society, but surely it was comprised of fools if she hadn't had a sweetheart or admirers gathered in the street to await a glimpse of her.

Since he'd parted company with her this afternoon, she'd changed from her traveling costume into a silk gown of cornflower blue.

Tabitha must have heard him as he hovered on the threshold, because she turned to him with a welcoming smile. It was an unexpected gift, that smile. The hours apart from her fell away.

She went to him, and while she didn't embrace him, she did stroke her hands across the breadth of his shoulders. His breath stuttered at her touch. "I began to despair that you mightn't return home for dinner."

"Undomesticated I may be, but I'm not so churlish that I'd leave my wife of twenty-four hours to dine alone."

"You had appointments?"

"My man of business." Should he tell her about what Mendoza said? She might recant, and say that she'd been mistaken, that Finn couldn't possibly be capable of owning and operating his own establishment regardless of his financial status.

Better to get that disappointment out of the way.

Even so, he turned to face the fire so he didn't have to see the skepticism on her face. With purposeful lightness, Finn said, "Mendoza believes I'm solvent enough that if I so choose, I could open a gaming hell."

"That's . . ."

He braced himself, waiting for her to say, *unwise* or *foolish*.

"Wonderful," she finished enthusiastically.

His body jolted. Surely, she hadn't said . . . ?

"Truly?" he couldn't stop himself from asking. He glanced at his wife. Her eyes shone with excitement, resounding brightly in his chest.

"If anyone is qualified to run a gaming establishment," she went on with an eager nod, "it's you. I'm certain if you chose to open one, it would be a roaring success."

"You don't think I'm too . . ." He cleared his throat. "Feckless? Irresponsible? Or—" He had to push the word out, lodged as it was in the deepest layers of himself. "Stupid?"

She stared at him, her expression disbelieving. "None of those words apply to you." A frown pleated her brows. "Who has called you those things?"

He waved his hand dismissively. No need to go into *that*—he'd already revealed too much. "If you honestly believe I could do this—"

"I do," she insisted.

"Then perhaps . . . perhaps I should." He could almost imagine it, could just begin to picture himself at the head of his own gaming hell. It was still too outrageous to fully grasp—he, the man who had been ridiculed for his lack of intellect for most of his life—yet there was a glimmer of possibility, and hope that he could truly do something with himself. But he never would have dared to permit himself to consider it. Not without the belief and support of Tabitha.

Chapter 14

❧ ❋ ❧

"We could look for available properties," Finn said to Tabitha as they sat opposite each other in the dining room.

"I could purchase a map of the city," she said thoughtfully. "We can narrow down the locations you think would work best."

"It's a vast city," he mused. "And some areas are more abundant with gaming hells—but if we choose a site that's too scarce, no one's going to come."

She toyed with a cluster of grapes on her plate. The meal had been excellent, and they continued to linger at the table long after most of the dishes had been cleared away.

Tabitha took a sip of her wine and studied her husband across the table. In the past hour as they'd talked more of establishing his own gaming hell, the transformation in him had been astonishing—and wondrous. He'd appeared at the threshold to her library remarkably cautious, wary, full of doubt. The words he'd used to describe himself had been so strange, so very unlike the man she knew, yet he'd spoken them from a place that seemed deeply embedded within him.

There was a history there, a painful one, and she ached with the desire to tell him it was all right—he could reveal himself to her; she'd keep him safe. Perhaps she didn't deserve his trust—but maybe she could earn it.

When she'd given him her full confidence . . . it was like a bright fire blazed to life within him, burning away old doubts. He was so animated now, the veneer of cool remove gone, and she adored watching true excitement animate his features. He wasn't merely handsome, he was gorgeous with self-assurance and eagerness.

She squeezed her thighs together as desire pooled between them. Last night felt so long ago, yet her body continued to hold the feel of him around her, *in* her.

Unaware of her libidinous thoughts, he leaned back in his chair. Her mouth watered at the picture of masculine grace he made.

"The trick will be determining what would distinguish my gaming hell from the scores of others that pepper the city. I could be whimsical—indoor carousels and flower-crown-wearing donkeys with trays of drinks on their backs." His eyes gleamed with humor.

"And ring-a-bottle and bobbing for apples," she added with a laugh. "A carnival-themed gaming hell. I speak from my extensive experience with carnivals, having been to a grand total of one."

"Emerging victorious from your battle with Britain's Cleverest Man." The most intriguing dimple appeared next to Finn's mouth when he smiled, and she wanted to press her lips to it. "Though inveterate gamblers reserve most of their intellect for calculating odds at hazard. The rest is pure porridge."

"With yourself as the exception," she pointed out.

He merely smiled in response. "There's one element in a gaming hell that will always draw patrons. Self-indulgence."

She raised her brows. "Is hedonism such a common trait in London?"

"Self-indulgence is one thing everyone with money has in common." He made a wry noise. "In that, *my* family is no different. You've never met a group of people less able to control their impulses than the Ransome siblings. Except my elder brother, Simon, of course. He's a prig."

"Again, you are the exception," she noted.

"Hard-won maturity," he countered, then smirked. "Or some form of it."

His words made her frown slightly, yet she said, "Kieran's no profligate, surely."

"Before Miss Kilburn exploded into his life, he was the very definition of a libertine."

She tried to reconcile the man who clearly worshipped his future bride with someone immoderately dedicated to pleasure. They seemed incompatible. But surely Finn knew his brother better than anyone, so she'd have to accept him at his word.

"And your sister, Willa?" Tabitha asked. "She's abroad, but I hope to meet her and see if your theory about the Ransome family intemperance holds true."

A shadow passed across Finn's face. "Willa has her reasons for staying away. I wouldn't presume to make her return home before she's ready."

They were silent for a moment, and she cursed

herself for accidentally bringing up something that clearly pained him—though she couldn't know what it was about his sister's absence that he found so troubling. Possibly they were close. While her brothers had always treated her with relative politeness, they were much puzzled by their bookish sister and gave her a wide berth. She had thought Charles accepted her, but in that, she'd been horribly mistaken. Only her friends at the Benezra appreciated her for who she was.

Until she'd met Finn.

It wasn't part of their agreement, and yet these moments with him wrapped her in warmth, and acceptance, even as she was acutely aware of his potent physicality. The way he'd touched her last night, the pleasure he'd given her . . .

Heat climbed into her cheeks and coiled through her body.

Seeking to ground herself, and bring a smile back to his face, she said, "If you are, as you say, dissolute, you're one of the most abstemious dissolute people I've ever encountered."

"It depends on what I'm being tempted by." He didn't smile—instead, his gaze heated as it lingered on the exposed skin above the neckline of her gown. "When it comes to bluestockings who encourage me to open a gaming hell–carnival hybrid, I find myself battling the most shocking urges."

Her pulse sped up. The things he said to her, destabilizing in the most delicious way . . . and she forgot the reasons why she had to maintain distance between them.

"If you're so tempted by my inadequate occupational schemes," she said, striving for a lighter tone, "imagine what you might do if you spoke with someone who truly understood the workings of business."

"How little credit you give yourself," he answered huskily. "I could go to dozens of experts in the field for their advice, but it's what *you* think that matters most."

"Surely I'm not so wise." Her words were breathless.

"I trust your wisdom," he said, holding her gaze with his, "but, more than that, you've no obligation to listen, to *care*. And yet you do. I'm not used to that," he admitted quietly. "Not from anyone."

The vulnerability in his dark eyes pulled her from her chair as if she was magnetized by them. Instinctual force drew her across the dining room to stand beside him.

Her heart pounded faster and faster, and when she stroked her hand down his jaw, stubble rasped against her fingers. The sheer masculinity of him made her breath come quickly, yet his openness with her made him all the more intoxicating.

She grazed her thumb across the fullness of his lower lip. He opened his mouth to lightly nip at her thumb. She swallowed thickly as need gathered between her legs and in her breasts.

It blazed bright and quick, the desire between them, even here, in the dining room. She was dizzy with it and with him.

"Leave us, Edgar," he said without taking his gaze from her.

She sucked in a breath.

The footman, who had been standing silent and carefully unseeing from his place next to the sideboard, quickly slipped from the room.

They were alone.

Finn pushed his place setting away, silver and porcelain clattering to the floor, but he didn't seem to care about the noise. Instead, his eyes burning like midnight, he clasped her waist and lifted her to sit on the table in front of him. He braced one hand on the table, and his other cupped the back of her head, bringing her mouth to his.

He tasted of warm wine and sweet grapes as they kissed greedily. It was as though they hadn't consumed a meal at all, the way they devoured each other. This man knew how to *kiss*, seducing her, lavishing her with his undivided attention, as though he'd waited his whole life to savor her, and only her, like this.

She held tightly to him, need building quickly within her as they kissed, stoking fires that had smoldered all day. What did it matter if the footman or other servants knew what they were doing in here? What did anything matter but the feel of Finn, so demanding and tenderly dominant, enraptured by her.

He dragged his mouth down her neck, and she held him to her skin, loving the sensations he brought to life within her. One of his broad palms cupped her breast, lifting it to rise above the neckline of her gown. His teeth scraped at the sensitive skin and she shivered.

"All day," he said throatily. "From Blackheath to London, from Chelsea to the City, I've thought of nothing but this. Been half-hard for hours, wanting you."

"And now?" she gasped.

"Now I'm fully hard."

A gasp slipped from her lips. *She* did this to him.

This careful, controlled man was deliciously wild and crude because of *her*.

She ventured a glance toward his groin. The thick ridge of his cock jutted against the placket of his breeches, and a hot wave of longing delved between her legs and made her breasts ache.

"Thought I never wanted anyone more than I wanted you last night," he rumbled, caressing her breasts and dragging his lips against the fabric of her bodice. "I was wrong. Because now I know the perfection of what you feel like, against my fingers, around my cock."

"*Finn*," she moaned, her blood roaring.

"What I *don't* know," he went on, stroking his hands up her calves and gathering up her skirts, "is what you feel like against my tongue. What your cunt tastes like."

She gasped. "People *do* that?"

His gaze was wickedness incarnate as his hands paused just above her knees. "*I* do. And I want *us* to. I've dined tonight, but what I'm burning to feast upon is you."

There had been hints in books she'd read, but there had been no illustrations showing it in Aretino, and she should have been shocked, or appalled by the notion. Instead, she couldn't recall ever being so wet.

For all the need in his eyes and sharpening in his features, he held himself still. Waiting.

"I want that," she said, unsteady with arousal.

His jaw tightened, and then he kissed her again, mouth open to consume her. He broke their kiss to focus his attention on lifting her skirts, taking armfuls of the blue silk and gathering them at her waist. She could scarcely believe her legs were being bared in a dining room, but shock dissolved into desire as he kissed his way along her stocking-covered calves, going higher, past her garters, until his lips pressed into the skin of her bare thighs.

And then . . . oh, God, then . . . He paused as he stared at her quim.

"Look at you," he said, rough and low. "Look at how beautiful you are."

"Not the . . . words . . . I would have used," she said, her own words ragged as she watched him gaze at this hidden place. It felt too exposed—and yet she trusted him.

"But you *are* beautiful." He brushed his fingers over the hair curling on her mons. "Here. And these pretty lips." He nuzzled at her outer labia. "And this gorgeous pink flesh, glistening and eager. That little pearl of your clitoris. I can't wait any longer. I have to . . . have to . . ."

She moaned as his tongue slipped glossily through her folds.

"God almighty." His words rumbled against her. "The way you *taste*."

He licked her again, his lips nimbly caressing her, and then he circled her clitoris with his tongue, forcing a mewl of ecstasy from her. His eyes remained open, focused on her face, as he continued to lap and suck at her quim. Whenever she moaned, he delved deeper, feasting on her just as he'd promised. Already the beginnings of her climax collected in silvery filaments through her body.

She cried out when he thrust two fingers into her passage. It became impossible to hold up her weight under this onslaught of pleasure, and she collapsed onto the table, her back pressing into the wood as she arched and writhed beneath his attention. He devoured her as he pumped his fingers into her. Sounds escaped from him, feral growls that urged her higher and higher, until she came with a long, throaty moan.

He was relentless, his fingers deep within her as he sucked on her nub. Another climax fractured her and she gripped tightly to his head, holding him to her as he went on licking her, unrelenting in his demand for her pleasure.

Limp, wrung out, she let her hand slip from her grip in his hair. He lifted his head and she inhaled sharply to see the sheen of her arousal across his lips and shining on his chin.

"I have to fuck you, love," he rasped. When she managed to nod, he stood between her thighs and tore open his breeches. His freed cock curved thickly, a shining bead of moisture slipping from the slit.

She stared hungrily at the sight of his large hand in a tight grip around his cock. His eyelids lowered as he guided his shaft up and down through her slick folds, coating himself in her wetness.

She clutched at his shoulders, his muscles flexing beneath her hands, as she panted with eagerness. Then, with one sure, hard stroke, he plunged into her. Pleasure jolted through her body, radiating out from the place where he was buried within her, and it expanded outward with each thrust.

Needing him as close as possible, she hooked her ankles at his waist.

"That's it, sweet," he growled, gripping her thighs. "Hold me all the way inside you."

The table rattled as he worked his hips and yet she barely noticed the noise. All that mattered was him, fucking her with steady, purposeful drives. It was wondrous, and not enough. They had to join in every way. He needed to be as deep within her as possible, until she forgot everything about herself and knew only them together.

She pressed herself into him in silent demand.

"You want more?" His voice was searing. "You need me to fuck you harder? Is that it, love?"

She made an inarticulate noise, half whine, half command, uncaring that she sounded utterly wild. She wasn't herself and she was more herself than she'd ever been.

"Give me the words, Tabitha," he said, stern and autocratic even as his breath gusted from him.

"Please, Finn." Even in the throes of her frenzy, she couldn't quite bring herself to say what he wanted. Releasing herself in that way—it was too much.

"Tell me what you want, sweet, or I'll fuck you slow and steady all night."

That sounded rather wonderful—but not now. Now, her body primed from the climaxes he'd already given her, she ached for another devastating release.

"Fuck me," she moaned. "Hard as you can."

"Hold tight to me."

She did, and he clasped the table in a grip so tight his knuckles turned white before unleashing a series of thrusts so exquisitely brutal she had no choice but to abandon herself to pleasure. Vision hazy, she saw the chandelier above her, its light reflecting back within her as Finn fucked her like the devil himself. Their bodies made crude, delicious slapping sounds, filling the elegant dining room.

Reaching between them, he stroked her clitoris in tight circles.

"Come, Tabitha," he said, fierce. "Come around my cock."

His words unleashed the tempest within her. The force of her orgasm made her bow upward, and the many lights of the chandelier fractured into thousands of glittering diamonds inside her.

Yet his hips didn't stop. He thrust and thrust, summoning another climax from her, and then he went taut as he growled his own release.

She cradled him against her as he rested his head on her breasts. Shudders continued to move through her, yet they slowed and lessened, leaving her liquid while she continued to lie on the table.

My God, she thought. She hadn't known it could be like this. Nothing in the entirety of her existence could have prepared her for him.

"You are," he said in a gratifyingly spent voice, "the most magnificent being I've ever known."

She would have said that he had completely devastated her, but forming words was impossible, so she embraced him tighter. Perhaps her body could communicate what language couldn't.

He kissed his way up her chest, along her neck, until he reached her mouth. As he did so, he pulled from her. She missed having him inside her, but purred when he took his handkerchief and gently cleaned between her thighs.

"You see to me so nicely," she murmured. "Even better than Olive."

"I should hope the services I provide are not redundant with those of your maid." He tucked himself back into his breeches.

"Oh, you are quite unique." She brushed back his dark, thick hair from his forehead. It had become damp and curled, standing up in delightful tufts from where she'd dug her fingers into his locks.

He kissed her again, his large hands stroking over her face, and her heart clutched at the tenderness in his eyes.

"I'll be right back," he murmured against her lips, then walked to the sideboard to grab the decanter of wine. When he returned, he poured them both full glasses. "Refresh yourself, for the night isn't over."

"You want *more*? After . . . after . . ." She glanced at the table, and its ruined landscape of scattered dishes and cutlery.

"Apparently, when it comes to you," he said, his regard hot over the rim of his glass, "my appetite has no limits."

"I thought you weren't a voluptuary," she murmured.

"I wasn't." He shook his head at himself, as if hardly believing it. "Evidently, you become one upon meeting the right person."

"Isn't the adage, 'Reformed rakes make the best husbands'?"

"In our case, the best husbands become rakes."

Despite her many climaxes, excitement shimmered within her. She took a long swallow of wine but it did nothing to cool the fire that blazed from the wicked promise in her husband's eyes. How was it possible that she, Tabitha Seaton, could turn any man into a libertine, especially *this* man, who kept himself so tightly leashed?

They opened something within each other, something she'd never realized existed in herself. He helped her to see more and more of who she was, and who she *could* be.

Once they had both drained their glasses, he set them aside and helped her off the table. He threaded his fingers with hers.

"I can carry you upstairs," he offered roguishly.

"That will scandalize the servants."

His smile was wolfish. "Sweet, if they're scandalized by that, after the way we shook the walls with our fucking, then they'll be better suited to someone else's household. Besides," he added at her stunned, aroused gasp, "they had best brace themselves. You and I have only just begun."

Her husband made good on his vow.

After they retired to their bedchamber, Finn removed his clothes, revealing his luscious form, and then leisurely undressed her. He proceeded to slowly make love to her, his kisses deep and lingering, his strokes long and unhurried. He pleasured her deliberately, relentlessly, her ecstasy building higher and higher. When her climax finally crashed through her, she sobbed with its force, and his growl of culmination shook her body like an earthquake.

They lay together quietly afterward. Yet as his breath slowed and his limbs loosened in the moments before sleep, her heart beat faster and faster. Invisible knots coiled in her belly and climbed up her throat.

Sex was one thing—she could tell herself it was merely a physical act, a biological imperative that overrode sense. Yet once they lay down together in the profound intimacy of sleep, there was no hiding behind passion. He had been within her body, but as they shared a bed, the way mates did, he was also in her heart.

From moment to moment, she felt her heart opening to him. If this continued, the potential for hurt would swell as big as a mountain, casting a long shadow that engulfed her.

She had to stop these feelings from growing. It was the only way to keep herself safe, to keep herself from losing control of her heart and stumbling once again into rejection and pain.

Eventually, mercifully, he slept. Looking up at the canopy of their bed, Finn's arm slung across her in unconscious claiming, she could scarcely draw a breath.

She slipped out from beneath him. Though the bedchamber had been warmed by the now-dying fire, cold prickled her skin as she went to the clothes press and pulled out a nightgown and wrapper. She tucked her frigid toes into slippers. Lighting a candle might wake him, so when she crept out into the hallway and shut the door behind her, she was plunged into darkness.

The servants had gone to bed, and there was no one around as she used her sense of touch to guide her along the corridor and carefully, cautiously, make her way down the stairs. All the while, her pulse was a furious pounding. Would he wake and find her missing? How could she explain herself to him? She only knew that she had to step back and shelter herself.

So here she was, fumbling through her own house like a burglar.

Still unfamiliar with her new home, she waited in the foyer for a moment, allowing her eyes to adjust to the faint street light that crept in through the transom above the front door. The world came into view in gradual smudges, and she eased down the ground floor hallway until she reached the library.

There would be no chance of a light disturbing him in here, so she lit a candle in a silver holder and carried it to the bookshelves. Her heart quieted as she looked at the rows and rows of books, especially her personal collection that she'd gathered and acquired over the years, like seeing old friends who would never reject her.

A pulse of longing and affection moved through her as she gazed at the shelves. Finn had given this to her, such a thoughtful, attentive gesture. Could he possibly care for her more than the terms of their bargain? Or did it simply mean that he was considerate, and making her happy ensured that his own life at home would be comfortable?

Damn it, she didn't know, and her stomach clenched at the thought of asking him what any of this meant.

There was comfort and familiarity, though, with her books. She could find shelter here. So, she walked to one of the shelves to peruse their contents.

She ran her fingertips over the spines of the books until she found Anne Conway's *Principles of the Most Ancient and Modern Philosophy*. There were several chairs in the small library, so she curled up in one and opened the book. She'd lost count of the number of times she'd read it, but there was reassurance in the familiar words, like easing into a warm bath of ideas that gently surrounded her. With an exhalation of relief, she began to read.

The candle had burned down by half by the time

she heard the creak of floorboards in the corridor. She looked up, and her chest contracted when Finn appeared in the doorway. He wore an untucked shirt and breeches, but nothing else, and he ran his hand through his already tousled hair as he looked at her with puzzlement.

"You can bring books up to the bedroom," he said, padding into the chamber. "No need to risk breaking your neck to come down here after midnight."

"I wouldn't want to wake you by lighting a candle," she explained.

"Sleeping during daylight hours was my common practice for over a decade." He stood beside her chair, and she gripped her book tighter to keep from reaching for him. "If the sun didn't disturb me, a candle surely won't."

"You've done such an admirable job of securing me my very own library," she said, looking up at him with what she hoped was a polite smile, rather than the sharp longing that pierced her when he was so close. "Coming down here is no hardship."

He nodded at that, the corners of his mouth lifting slightly. "Return to bed?"

"I've just reached a very interesting section." She held up her book. "It may be some time before I go up."

The beginnings of his smile faded, and there was coolness in his eyes. "I shan't disturb your study, then."

He stroked her hair once. She started to lean into his touch, then caught herself and pulled back. It hurt her to do so, but she had to if she wanted to remain unscathed.

A moment later, he left the library. She didn't return to her book right away. Instead, she listened to his progress down the hallway, and up the stairs. Even then, when she was certain he'd returned to the bedchamber, she sat staring at nothing, swallowing down her words that demanded to call him back.

Finally, she began to read again—though she barely saw or processed the text before her. They blended into shapes and forms without meaning, and it took her a solid ten minutes before she realized that she'd been reading the same paragraph over and over again.

She glanced up once more when the sounds of footsteps came from outside the library. Expecting a servant, she prepared a courteous reply to the anticipated question as to whether or not she required anything. That reply died as Finn reappeared at the entrance to the room.

This time, he was fully dressed. His clothes were unrelentingly dark, his coat, shirt, waistcoat, neckcloth, breeches, and boots all black. A gold watch chain and stickpin were the only elements that broke up the midnight hue of his garments. He'd combed back his hair so that it looked lacquered and glossy. He was severe and beautiful, his gaze dark and remote as he stood in the doorway, regarding her.

Her belly leapt, and she pressed a hand against it in a futile effort to calm herself. There wasn't a moment where he wasn't stunning to look upon, yet dressed as he was now, he was so astonishingly handsome, her eyes stung.

"That doesn't look like the kind of ensemble one

wears to bed." She hoped for levity, but only sounded forced and thin.

"As I said, I've been nocturnal for the better part of a decade," he answered, and though his posture was relaxed, she sensed tension coiling through his long body. "Sleep at this hour is more unusual than common, so reverting to my old habits comes easily."

"I wasn't aware anywhere would be open now."

"You'd be surprised how much of the city lives in darkness."

She nodded stiffly, but she was the one who'd deserted their bed first. It was pointless to feel any sense of hurt. Yet it cleaved through her, sharp and cold. It only proved that she *was* too attached to him, if his distance could hurt her so much.

"It's not advisable for you to wait up," he continued.

"Will I see you at breakfast?"

"It's possible."

She opened her mouth to ask him where he was going, but she'd no right. No right to urge him to stay, even though she ached to go to him, kiss him. But that was dangerous.

"Then I shall see you in the morning," she said. "Or possibly not."

He lingered in the doorway. Then he bowed and disappeared into the darkness of the hallway. A moment later, the front door opened and closed, followed by the noise of his key in the lock. She strained for the sound of his boots on the pavement, but the library was tucked too far back from the street to make out anything.

Where was he going? She had no claim in asking, and yet she burned to know. It was entirely possible that she'd effectively pushed her husband into a lover's arms.

It was pointless to try to read again, not now. The shelter she'd sought in books was illusory. They could do nothing about the fact that she was already half in love with Finn. Keeping him at a distance was the only way she could ensure no further hurt.

Chapter 15

❖ ✳ ❖

$\mathcal{F}$inn sat at the breakfast table as the servants bustled around him, setting out plates, arranging covered dishes that smelled of poached eggs and broiled fish on the sideboard. Edgar poured him a cup of coffee, saying nothing about the fact that Finn's clothing still carried with them the scent of tobacco, whisky, and the fog that stubbornly clung to the streets even as the sun climbed.

He and Tabitha had been married a week, and a more confusing seven days he couldn't imagine. During the day, she would either study at home or else go to the Benezra, and he would be occupied with his own personal and business affairs. It was pleasant enough, each of them comfortably making space for the other. Sometimes they took luncheon together, sometimes not, the meals enjoyable and full of engaging conversation.

The evenings had become both delightful and dreadful. He knew no greater pleasure than making love to her, sharing ecstasy, and holding her close—and then waking to find her gone, holed up in her library. Never had his arms felt so empty.

Rather than face the deserted bed, he'd go out to his usual gaming hell haunts and not return until dawn was streaking the sky. Same as he had last night.

Finn now took a sip of coffee and rubbed his face, but weariness sat heavily on his shoulders. It had been a successful foray at the tables, but he didn't feel any of the usual excitement and liveliness that followed winning.

He'd tried to study the workings of the gaming hell, too, taking mental notes about what worked for that particular establishment, and what he'd do differently. But his mind had barely functioned enough to gamble, let alone consider his future. A future that *she* encouraged.

At present, he barely kept himself from slumping in his seat, closing his eyes, and drifting into an exhausted doze even as the servants continued to scurry around the breakfast room. When his eyelids lowered, he saw Tabitha sitting in the library, and how he'd as usual forced himself to stay at the gaming hell far longer than he wanted, because he couldn't face having her side of the bed remain vacant.

As much as his bride enjoyed fucking him, sharing a bed with him was something she did *not* desire. The wisest thing would be to set up one of the spare bedrooms for himself. Many genteel couples had separate bedchambers, and he and Tabitha could be just the same.

He'd been expecting her rejection, but that didn't make facing it in truth any easier.

"Ah, you're here for breakfast," Tabitha said, coming into the room.

He straightened and opened his eyes, nodding at

her politely. But damn, if he didn't want to go to her
and pull her into his arms.

"I am," he answered instead. An ache gathered in
his chest while he watched the line of her back as she
served herself breakfast from the sideboard.

"Might I fix you a plate?" she asked over her
shoulder.

"Coffee suits me well enough at this hour."

"I always awaken famished. Clearly," she added,
showing him her plate piled high with eggs, kippers,
toasted bread, and stewed apples.

The table in the breakfast room was smaller than
the one in the dining room, so she was nearer to
him when she took her seat. She nodded at Edgar,
who poured her tea, and, after sending Finn a quick
but strained smile, began eating with the appetite of
someone who dug trenches for a living.

"You're just getting home," she noted, eyeing his
clothes.

He drank his coffee rather than reply. After leaving the gaming hell, he hadn't been in the humor for
going to a tavern, which was his usual practice. Instead, he'd walked along the riverfront, watching the
boats make their way up the thick, dark water, and
observing the mud larks wading through the muck
to find something, anything, they could sell.

"Was it a good night?" she asked carefully.

"No better or worse than any other."

"Wherever it is that you go," she said lightly, "it
must be exhausting."

"What makes you say that?"

She nodded toward the cup he held tightly. "You
always drink an abundance of coffee as if it was your
sole means of staying upright."

"I've never cared for tea," he answered.

There was a pause, and she asked casually, "Where *do* you go?"

He hesitated. "Hither and yon."

How could he tell her that he fled to the few places where he'd always felt most comfortable—gaming hells? Such places filled the gap that she left behind when she absented herself from their bed. It wasn't precisely something he could admit to her.

She took a massive bite of toast. It truly was impressive how much food she could consume and so methodically. No doubt the immense operational capacity of her mind required fuel, and his lips curved as he considered how the kippers she chewed might result in a groundbreaking intellectual theory that could alter the course of history.

She was, in every way, vastly superior to him. He'd done his best to conceal from her what a faulty, fallible creature he truly was. A man who danced at the edge of respectability, whose own parents barely tolerated the sight of him. And now his wife was the same.

He set his cup down and stared at the remainder of the coffee within it. The beverage soured in his stomach—it was best not to drink any more.

There was a knock at the front door, and Edgar went to answer it. A minute later, he returned to the breakfast room, and carried a letter to Tabitha.

"It's from Sir William Marston, of the Sterling Society," she explained excitedly as she broke the wafer.

Finn watched her as she read the missive. She went from curiosity to excitement to apprehension all in the span of a minute. Biting her lip, she set the letter aside as she distractedly stared into the distance.

"What does it say?" he finally asked.

"The Sterling Society has commanded my presence," she said pensively, then added with a hint of alarm, "in five days."

"That's good. Means you needn't wait overly long to see them and be admitted."

"But . . ." Her chest rose and fell and she looked troubled. "I need to study and prepare."

He could well understand her concern. After all, this was something she wanted very badly. "While I've no doubt that you will excel in this," he said steadily, "your library is at your disposal. And if there are any texts that you require, they can be either purchased or else we can send the footman to the Benezra to check out anything you might need."

She nodded, though she seemed slightly distracted.

"Is there something else?" he asked with concern.

"They are demanding my presence, but . . ." Her gaze locked with his. "They insist I come with my husband."

Hand unsteady, he reached for his cup and drained it, certain that he wasn't fully awake to understand exactly what she was saying. But the coffee only heightened his alarm.

"*You* are the one they're admitting." He strove to keep the panic out of his voice.

"Given that I will be the first ever woman they are allowing into their organization," she said, picking up the letter again and rereading it, "they feel it would be unseemly if I were to visit them unaccompanied."

"Surely your maid would fit the bill," he protested. "Or the footman."

"In their words," she said, frowning in concern,

"'a husband would provide appropriate supervision.'"

Finn's stomach churned. "I see."

Despite his efforts to remain as placid as possible on the outside, some of his worry must've shown on his face, because she said quickly, "Doubtless they'll only concern themselves with my scholarly credentials. Your presence is merely a formality."

He *wanted* to believe her. Still . . . "The wisest course of action would be for me to undertake a small amount of studying, myself." The words were thick in his mouth, tasting of sludge.

"Finn," she said, earnest, "the Sterling Society is *my* ambition, not yours, and I can't ask this of you. You haven't even been to bed."

"It's because this is your ambition that I've got to prepare immediately." Even as his back went cold and slick with sweat, he pushed to his feet. "We should adjourn to your library and begin."

Somehow, he'd have to find a way to endure poring through book after book. His head throbbed, and that sense of frustration and panic he felt whenever he had to read had already begun to well. But he'd push on. His studies at Eton hadn't been important, not truly, but *this* was. Because it mattered to her.

Finn's face was ghostly pale, making the shadows beneath his eyes stand out even more. He was silent as he followed Tabitha into the library, and tension emanated from him like silent drumbeats that echoed in her own heart.

"Are you certain you don't want to rest a little first?" she asked with concern.

He shook his head. "Sleep won't be possible, so I might as well be here. Point me in the direction of the books you think I'll need to familiarize myself with."

Another protest formed on her lips, but his expression was implacable, so she walked to the shelves and began pulling down texts that might possibly come up during the meeting. It wouldn't be wise—or fair—to overload him with too much. Better to keep things confined to the essentials. After grabbing a few books, she brought them over to where he waited, all but pulsating with unease.

"Here are some Classical and Roman philosophers," she said, handing the volumes to him. "St. Augustine, Thomas Aquinas, Avicenna, Descartes. All translated into English."

He took each book, but as his stack of texts grew, he seemed to grow even more ashen. A bead of perspiration trickled down his temple.

"Finn," she said gently, "if you're unwell—"

"Healthy and hale as a sailor," he answered at once.

He *did* look a little seasick. Yet he seemed determined to sail forward.

Flipping open one of the books, his gaze scanned the page. It lingered there for a long time as a frown appeared between his brows.

He didn't turn the page. In fact, he seemed to look at the same one for several minutes, his frown deepening.

"I've heard," she said brightly, "that the best way to learn something is to teach it to someone else."

His tortured gaze moved from the book to her.

"If I may," she added, gently taking the volumes from him, "you would be doing me a tremendous favor if I could read aloud to you. The information will penetrate my mind better if I absorb everything verbally."

He looked at her skeptically. "Are you certain?"

"Absolutely," she answered with what she hoped sounded like conviction.

She waved him to one of the chairs. Slowly, warily, he sat, his cautious gaze on her the whole time. Once he was seated, she took the other chair and set the stack of texts on a nearby table. She took the first book from the top of the pile and opened it.

"*Metaphysics*," she read, "by Aristotle. '*All men by nature desire to know . . .*'"

He leaned forward, bracing his forearms on his thighs. His expression shifted from guardedness to interest, and the more she read, the more intent and attentive he became. It was fascinating to watch, yet she had to retain her own focus as she read. They moved from one text to the next, and then the next, covering centuries of philosophy in a matter of hours.

His weariness seemed gone. Indeed, he asked her many insightful questions, posing sophisticated thoughts and ideas that would have merited their own monographs.

"Free will is essential, then, in determining whether or not one's actions have worth," he said after she'd reviewed the principles of St. Augustine.

"Predestination robs us of our ability to choose a virtuous path," she agreed. "What's the value in our choices if they're made for us?"

He nodded thoughtfully, as if tucking away the information into a vast mental library. And it *was* vast—of that she'd no doubt.

They continued on, pausing for luncheon, before

resuming their studies. What she'd said to Finn had been true—the more she read to and discussed with him, the more her own understanding was enriched. She'd studied with her friends from the Benezra, but the fact that he'd voluntarily done this for *her* benefit warmed her like sitting beside a fire. A very handsome fire that possessed a remarkable mind and a talent for making love to her.

She shut a copy of Avicenna's major works and studied her husband. It was late in the afternoon. Luncheon had refreshed both of them, yet Finn sat low in his chair, his long legs stretched out in front of him, his hands folded across his flat stomach and his eyes shut as his chest rose and fell.

"Are you asleep?" she whispered.

"Only if sleep counts as being awake with your eyes closed," he answered.

"I'd hate to interrupt that," she said with concern, "but you could not-sleep in bed for a few hours, and we could resume our studies after supper."

His lids cracked open, and his irises were shining obsidian. "Madam, is this an attempt to seduce me? Because ruses aren't necessary, not if *you* are doing the seducing."

Heat coursed through her at his husky words. "Tempting, but I need to hold on to my focus, at least until the meeting. I become exceptionally *un*-focused whenever we . . ."

After the things they'd done together, it was remarkable that she could still blush, and yet her cheeks flamed.

His gaze darkened, his jaw going taut with barely banked desire. "It's a distraction we share."

A wave of need surged in her, but giving in to it

would only cloud her mind and confuse her heart. "I was thinking more along the lines of an actual nap."

"Ah." Disappointment flickered across his face, which he quickly hid behind a wry smile. "I've never had the ability to nap. When I wake from them, my tongue feels coated with pitch and my thoughts are even stickier."

"Perhaps that won't be as refreshing as I'd hoped." She stood and stretched—Finn watching her with avid interest—before going to one of the bookshelves. "I've something else in mind."

She pulled out another book, and he arched a brow. "*More* study?"

"A novel full of suggestive and shocking scenes. I skimmed it after unpacking my books, and I think we might enjoy it considerably. While I can't vouch for the excellence of my dramatic skills, I'll endeavor to do my best. Try not to laugh at me when I sound silly, giving everyone different voices. I should warn you that it might not be as enthralling as the theater," she added, her nose wrinkling. "Perhaps you'll find it dull and wish yourself anywhere but here."

She held her breath, half-afraid that he'd dismiss her offer, and call it silly. After all, there wasn't anything to be gained by reading to him from a sensational novel. Except . . . she wanted to. Studying academic texts together was meaningful, yet this was just for pleasure, something they could share for themselves alone.

"There isn't a chance of that happening," he said sincerely.

She exhaled, tension within her loosening. "We could adjourn to the parlor for a change of scenery—and more comfortable seats."

He was on his feet at once. "I enthusiastically endorse that suggestion. As does my arse."

A shocked laugh escaped her, and he threw her a roguish look that made her heart pound.

They left the library and made their way upstairs to the parlor. Once in the comfortable, pretty room, she took a seat on the sofa.

He sat beside her, crossing his leg over his knee and stretching his arm out along the back of the couch. She perched primly next to him, though she didn't move away when he brushed his fingers along the line of her spine. The sensation trilled through her like music.

"Shall I begin?" she asked.

"I am all bated breath. No, I truly am," he added at her skeptical look.

She cleared her throat. "*The Monk: A Romance*, by M. G. Lewis, Esq. M.P. 'Scarcely had the abbey bell tolled for five minutes, and already was the Church of the Capuchins thronged with auditors . . .'"

As she read, she glanced quickly at him over the top of the book. The words stuck in her throat as she saw the rapt attention on his face. He seemed *enthralled*, his gaze fixed on her as if she was the sole illumination in a world of darkness.

Chapter 16

❖ ❋ ❖

*F*ive days passed, the days filled with study. He struggled as best he could with the books he reviewed—though she never urged him to go at a pace that wasn't comfortable for him. Yet it was worth it to spend time with her, especially when they discussed what they'd read, and she seemed genuinely interested in what he thought. Often, she read to him.

In the hours before dinner, they would pause in their intellectual pursuits and she'd again read to him, but she'd forgo the scholarly work in favor of *The Monk*. Though he enjoyed the thrilling, lurid tale, sharing the story with her was the best part. They would talk about it over dinner, speculating on what would come next.

And their bed was aflame with shared passion. Yet she continued to retreat to her library afterward, and he would go out to the gaming hells.

It would have been one of the happiest times in his life, if not for this continual coming together and breaking apart. As if, over and over, he sighted a welcoming shore, only to be blown back out to sea again.

At the end of five days, it was time for the appointed meeting with the Sterling Society.

Finn and Tabitha stood outside a tasteful building nestled between other tasteful buildings on a tasteful street in Mayfair. It looked like any of the homes that faced the pavement, save for the small brass plate affixed outside its red door, which read, PRIVATE, in type so small one would need a quizzing glass to make out what it said. Tabitha had told him that the Sterling Society liked to keep their whereabouts secret, so it only took him a few moments to decipher the miniscule lettering. Even so, it seemed as if the people within deliberately intended to obscure their presence—you would only know about them if you *knew* about them.

He opened his mouth to voice this to Tabitha, who had her hand on his arm, but the vibrations from her body traveled through him. Her face was pale, her normally sharp features keener than a blade, and his chest squeezed in response.

"They will absolutely adore you," he assured her.

"I'd rather have acceptance than adoration," she said, voice unusually faint.

He covered her hand with his and gave it a squeeze. "Of course they'll accept you. They'd be ruddy daft not to."

She shot him a grateful look, yet the breath she let out was ragged and unsteady, its jagged contours running over his heart.

"You're going to level them with your intellect," he insisted gently. "Just think of your bragging rights when you make every member of the organization babble like infants."

"Thank you—but I'm not thinking of my pride.

This isn't only for myself, but for all the others who deserve to be heard." She inhaled and straightened her back, tipping up her chin as she did so. "Let's go in."

Damn, but he admired her.

The previous days had been extraordinary. Even now, he felt humbled and awed and thankful for her. Perhaps she suspected that he struggled with reading—God knew that he hadn't done a bang-up job of hiding it lately. She'd been kind enough not to confront him about it, though, and when she'd first offered to read to him, well, he'd fought not to pull her close and shower her with tears of gratitude.

Sharing ideas with her had been incredible. It was as though, without the barrier of the written word, the world had become deeper, richer, his mind opening like a door leading to a vast palace.

And he'd adored it when she'd read to him from *The Monk*. The story was gratifyingly salacious—but precious because she'd taken time away from her studies to give him something strictly for pleasure.

Maybe, just maybe . . . they might be able to move beyond the limitations of their marriage arrangement. Maybe she could come to truly care for him. The way he did for her.

God—she meant so much to him. He jolted with the realization. How he lived for her rare smiles, her flashes of humor, her astonishing mind, and incendiary passion.

Now wasn't the time to tell her any of this. Not with her dream so close within their grasp.

They approached the door and he knocked. A short while later, a man with a fringe of hair and wearing the sober garments of a butler opened the door. He regarded them for a moment, and Finn fought the urge to squirm beneath the butler's thorough scrutiny.

"Mrs. Tabitha Ransome," she said with admirable steadiness, given how he could still feel her shaking, "and Mr. Finn Ransome, here to meet with Sir William and the other members of the society."

Finn handed the butler a card, which the man studied for a moment before stepping back to permit them entry. As they did, a footman came forward to take Finn's hat and walking stick, but the servant appeared baffled when Tabitha handed him her bonnet. The footman shot the butler an uncertain glance.

Clearly, no one in this establishment was used to dealing with women. Either as members or visitors.

"Put it with the gentlemen's items," the butler instructed lowly.

Holding her bonnet away from himself as if it was a flaming pudding, the footman hurried out of the entryway. The butler turned to Finn and Tabitha and said in a dry, disinterested voice, "Follow me."

He proceeded down a hallway lined with portraits of men, their costumes covering the span from current times all the way back to when long wigs and lace collars were in fashion. As they walked past them, he saw Tabitha looking at the disapproving paintings. Her body grew more and more rigid with each passing portrait.

What must it mean to her, to be one woman facing off against decades of influential men? Yet she continued to walk forward, as if all those years of masculine power didn't deter her.

Goddamn it, she was incredible.

Yet her fear was palpable. There had to be something he could do to help, a way to take the teeth out of this meeting.

"The placards have neglected to mention a very critical element about each portrait," Finn murmured into her ear.

"And that is?" she asked, a note of tremulousness in her voice that made his heart ache.

"These are all portraits of the winners from their annual sausage-eating contest. See that fellow in the bagwig? He ate fifty-seven sausages in the span of five minutes. Never was a man so joyous in the moments before he died of gastrointestinal distress."

A laugh escaped his wife.

Finn smiled to himself. At least he could help relieve a fragment of her apprehension.

They crossed the threshold into a large sitting room, where they were met with nearly a dozen sober-faced men that ranged in years from middle-aged to old. All of the men were dressed finely, though some wore garments of almost severe simplicity, and none of them looked as though they ever worried about whether there would be enough to cover the cost of rent.

Some were standing, while others were seated, many of them caught in the middle of reading books so sizable they made sweat slick down Finn's back. While no one appeared particularly delighted by the presence of the newcomers, nobody glared with open antagonism. No. Check that. There was a snowy-haired man by the fire who looked at Tabitha as though she'd offered to eat his favorite hunting dog.

"I've been in gaming hells that are far more hostile," Finn confidingly whispered in her ear. "Confidence is all that's needed to win these blokes over."

She nodded before smiling at the men of the Sterling Society. As she did so, a tall man with an impressive mane of black and silver hair approached. He had the air of someone who was burdened with too much knowledge whilst also being surrounded by people who knew far too little.

"Miss Seaton," he said with a cursory bow.

"Sir William," she answered, curtseying. "It's Mrs. Ransome now. Which is what enabled us to meet today."

Sir William inclined his head, as though that minimal effort was the most he would expend on admitting he was incorrect.

"Allow me to present my husband," she went on, "Mr. Finn Ransome."

Sir William appeared only mildly interested, until one of the other scholars chimed in, "The Earl of Wingrave's son."

Leading with his connection to his father wasn't Finn's ideal way of meeting someone, but it did make Sir William's expression become slightly more attentive. Finn fought from rolling his eyes in exasperation.

"An Oxford man?" the older gentleman asked.

"No, sir," Finn answered evenly.

"Cambridge?"

"No, sir." He would take his own advice and remain confident in the face of their interrogation.

"St. Andrews? Edinburgh?"

No hope for it but to give them the truth.

"I did not attend university, sir."

There was a collective gasp in the chamber. Finn didn't wince, didn't blink. He knew better than show anyone what their opinion meant to him—that was the quickest path to defeat. And he didn't give a stoat's arse about what the Sterling Society thought of him.

Out of the corner of his eye, he watched Tabitha. His stomach unclenched when he saw that she didn't seem shocked or appalled by his admission, thank God. But this wasn't about him and *his* credentials.

"I do not believe a university education is the sole criterion of whether or not someone has anything of intellectual value to contribute," he went on steadily. "My wife's breadth of knowledge is considerable, and her ideas are exceptional, even though she has been prevented from attending university."

He looked at Tabitha, who sent him a small smile of gratitude—which was all he needed.

She turned her attention to Sir William. "We earlier discussed some of the works I have extensively studied," she said, "and I've been delving into a line of inquiry for half a decade."

"What *is* that line of inquiry, Mrs. Ransome?" Sir William asked pointedly.

"The development of canonical thought," she answered at once. "Its origins, and the forces that shape it, and the pedagogy of the canon."

Hell, he loved hearing her wax cerebral. Each word from her lips shot through him hotly. He didn't think he could feel arousal in this temple of dry erudition, but she was in all ways remarkable.

The suspicion in Sir William's eyes slowly cleared, and he appeared reluctantly impressed. "Come, I will introduce you to the rest of the society."

"That would be lovely," Tabitha answered—and the corners of her mouth lifted in the smallest sign of gratification.

They spent the next quarter of an hour meeting men who, to Finn's eyes, seemed interchangeable, but to each one, Tabitha had something to say about their particular work. She'd read *all* of their books, monographs, and articles, and spoke to each branch of study with the precision of someone who had given each idea considerable thought.

Finn had his own opinions about the things they discussed, but today wasn't about him or what he thought. This was for Tabitha, and by the time they finished meeting the last person in the organization, she was making sly jokes about German philosophers that made the members chuckle. Finn also laughed, though he didn't know anything about Hegel and thought Kant wasn't a word you could say in front of a lady.

Watching her confidence grow was like seeing an entire garden blossom. There was so much life, so much potency, and he couldn't help but marvel at it. At *her*.

"Much as I would enjoy prolonging our visit," Sir William said, hooking his thumbs into the pockets of his waistcoat, "I'm afraid the society is scheduled to discuss policy this afternoon with a rather august Parliamentary figure."

"Of course," Tabitha said. "That's part of the esteemed work this institution is known for."

"When shall we return?" Finn pressed. The best time to increase pressure on someone at the gaming tables was when they felt at ease and confident.

Sir William glanced toward one of the younger members of the society—who appeared to be in his midfifties—and the man produced a leather-covered notebook.

"Our agenda indicates that we will have a group discourse this Friday afternoon," the man said over the rim of his spectacles.

"That will be an excellent time for you to join us." Sir William glanced at Finn. "*Both* of you."

"My contribution will surely be minimal," Finn objected politely. "It's Mrs. Ransome's presence that will enrich your organization."

"Having a woman within the Sterling Society's walls is already a breach of our usual protocol," Sir William said with a sniff. "Much as Mrs. Ransome might impart, to preserve decorum it's necessary for her to attend with her husband." *Even if that husband is you*, seemed to be the silent addendum.

Finn opened his mouth to object, but Tabitha gave her head a tiny shake, and so he said, "I defer to the society's dictates."

"Friday's discourse will be perfect," Tabitha added.

"If you'll just . . ." Sir William looked meaningfully toward the door, where the butler waited.

Finn bowed and Tabitha curtseyed, and together they retreated from the sitting room. As they walked down the corridor, toward the front door, they passed a man who looked familiar.

"Is that . . . ?" Tabitha whispered.

"Lord Sidmouth," Finn answered lowly, "former Prime Minister and now the Home Secretary."

Her eyes widened, and though Finn wasn't overly invested in politics, even he was taken aback at the rarified company the Sterling Society kept.

They were escorted outside by the butler, and then climbed into their waiting carriage. Before Finn entered the vehicle, he said to the coachman, "Take the long way home."

"Yes, sir."

Once they were both inside the carriage and it had rolled into motion, with Tabitha seated beside him, she asked, "Why did you tell him to go the long way?"

"Because it's going to take me a very long time to tell you how marvelous you are." Needing to touch her, he stroked his fingers along her cheek.

She cupped his hand with her own as she leaned into his touch. "I suppose I should demur and say it was nothing but . . . it was very much something."

"It was Something with a capital *S*," he insisted. He brushed his lips across her forehead, and soared inside when she didn't pull away. Instead, she inhaled deeply, as if drawing his nearness into herself. "By the end, they were all your lapdogs."

She gave a small laugh. "A slight exaggeration. There was that one gentleman, Mr. Everett, who still glared at me like I was a rat on his dining table."

"His brain is rat-sized if he can't see what an excellent addition you'd be to their group."

She looked up at him, her gaze soft and warm. "You were utterly brilliant."

"Me?" What a stunning notion. "I was only decorative."

"Far from it," she said firmly. "You astutely refuted Sir William's insistence on a university education, and . . ." Her eyes shone. "You supported me the entire time. It's not possible for you to understand the depth of what that means to me."

"I'd be a fool not to support the finest mind in England."

"Not the finest mind," she murmured. "Me. Your wife."

"All the same person," he said, sincere. "Without a doubt, they will beg to add you to their ranks."

"God, I hope so."

The fire in her words made him pull back slightly so he could see her better. "This means so much to you."

"It does," she answered resolutely.

"Why? Forgive me for asking," he added, "but I'm genuinely interested. Ambition and goals have been things I've sorely lacked in my life, and to see you burn with so much passion for something—I truly want to know what motivates you."

She clasped his wrist as she stared up at him, determination in the line of her jaw and brilliance of her eyes. The sight stole his breath.

"You may have noticed that every man in that room was essentially a duplicate of all the others," she explained. "The same class, the same gender, the same skin color. A sea of sameness."

"And you'll break with that sameness," he mused.

"It has to change," she said firmly. "Yet it's not enough for me to speak *for* someone. They must be able to speak for *themselves*. All I want to do is facilitate that."

"Thus," he concluded, "you infiltrate the Sterling Society and create a metamorphosis from within."

She looked at him warily. "But this system helps people such as you and I. You aren't going to take me to task for trying to dismantle it?"

He mulled over what she said, her goals, her intentions. And saw things in ways he'd never seen before. It hurt, to consider the costs of his privilege and unfair advantages, but nothing ever got better without facing hard, painful truths.

"Yes, I *do* profit from it," he said with a nod, "and I think it's a damned good idea to raze the empire to the ground and start over. If we can reach that outcome by making you part of the Sterling Society, then I'll do whatever it takes to make it happen. We'll study all day and night. Hell, I'll set up camp outside their front door with a bin full of burning rubbish, and refuse to leave until they take you on."

"Oh, Finn." Her eyes were bright as sunlight on the sea, gleaming with appreciation. "Thank you."

"You're grateful for something anyone would do," he countered gruffly, even as her words warmed him. "It's perfectly ordinary, what I'm doing."

"I wish you could see how truly extraordinary you are," she murmured. "But I can show you."

He held very still as she leaned up to kiss him. She was soft and silken against him, yet as need built quickly within him, he let her set the pace, taking them where she wanted them to go. When her tongue slid between his lips, a bolt of pure lust roared through him. He groaned and stroked his tongue against hers.

The slick touch seemed to light a charge within her. She deepened the kiss, her hunger stoking a conflagration inside of him. Unable to hold back any longer, he cupped her head with his hands and kissed her with every ounce of the need that had been growing within him all afternoon.

She responded at once, her lips ravenous and demanding as she gripped his arms. Heat tore through him at her eager responsiveness, such a sharp contrast from the restrained scholar she had been moments before, and that contrast fueled his desire, turning him half-mad with wanting.

Her fingers dug into him tighter as she kissed him avidly, and she pressed her chest to his, her breasts soft against him. His hands were everywhere, stroking along her face, down her back, cupping those selfsame breasts, and caressing her arse. Whenever he touched and kissed her, his demand for her grew tenfold. It didn't matter how or why, only that she was here with him, and that she seemed to want him as much as he wanted her. He would be grateful for whatever she shared with him.

She scraped her fingernails across his jaw, then slipped underneath his high collar and neckcloth to scratch along his throat, making shivers of pleasure dance over his skin. Molding her hands to his chest, she made pleased little sounds, and when she dipped between the buttons of his waistcoat to fondle his taut, twitching abdomen, lightning struck him. His cock was hard, aching, and God, they were too far from a bed—and she was still in many ways innocent to the ways of sex. Fucking her in a carriage might be too shocking, much as he burned to lose himself between her thighs. He was mad with her and the need to be as deep inside of her as he could, to connect with her as intimately as possible.

Then she was gone, and he blinked at her absence. He blazed with hunger for her and missing the feel of her in his arms, but if she wanted to stop, he'd do as she wished.

To his astonishment, she was reaching for the curtains, and a moment later, the interior of the carriage was shaded and hidden from the outside.

"What are you doing?" he asked thickly, daring not to hope.

"I can't wait until we're home," she said huskily. She glided her hands over his torso again. "I need to feel you *now*."

He let out a rough, rueful chuckle. He should have given his ingenious wife more credit. But when she looked at him in puzzlement, he said, "Just blessing providence that you agreed to accept my marriage suit."

"Your fortunes are about to get even better." She cupped the length of his erection through his breeches, stroking him until his hips pushed up into her hand. And then, God above, she unbuttoned him and pumped his bare cock as the carriage rocked from side to side.

Yet before he could thank whatever celestial beings watched over him, she sank to her knees in front of him.

"I don't know how to do this," she whispered. Her gaze was fastened on his cock, red and swollen in her fist, and she licked her lips as she leaned closer. "But I do love learning new things."

That she was willing to try something new thrilled and humbled him to his core. Yet all ability to speak beyond guttural growls disappeared as her lovely pink tongue darted out to lick the crown. He gripped the squabs to keep from clutching her head, his fingers digging into the cushions when she sucked the crown of his cock into her mouth, and then went lower, her lips wrapping around the shaft as he slid deeper into her.

His heart squeezed when her gaze flicked up as if she was gauging his reaction, hoping to please him.

"Fuck, yes," he rumbled. "That's it. So good. Suck me, love."

A flush spread across her cheeks—he loved that she seemed to revel in his crude words—and she closed her eyes as she did precisely what he desired, licking and drawing him into her as if nothing gave her greater pleasure.

"God, you're taking me so deep." He couldn't stop the flow of words from him, how she drew out his basest, most primal self. "And you like it, don't you, love? You like sucking my cock."

She moaned around his shaft, her efforts redoubling.

"No one ever gets to see you like this, sweet," he rasped. "Only me. Only I know how good the scholarly Tabitha Seaton is at this, delightfully wicked creature. Throating me like you can't get enough."

When her hand crept up her skirts to caress between her legs, he had to shut his eyes, or else he was going to fill her mouth with his seed. The thought was too arousing, and he dragged in air to keep himself from exploding and ending this magnificent torment.

Still, he *had* to watch her touch herself, seeing her studious demeanor burn away in the fire of her desire. And he couldn't look away as she moaned around him, her hand moving faster and faster between her legs, until she went still and came with a long, loud sob that reverberated up his cock and into the deepest part of him.

She would ruin him utterly, and he'd revel in the destruction.

"Stop, sweet," he panted when she began to suck him again. When she looked up, her lips plump and glossy, he bent down and kissed her, giving free rein to his carnal adoration of her. "I need inside you."

"You've *been* inside of me," she pointed out cheekily, though she sounded hoarse from the ferocity of her climax.

"I need my cock in your cunt."

She jolted, and yet his earthy language only seemed to inflame her further, her lids lowering and her breath speeding.

Glancing around the carriage, she said, "It's impossible to lie down in here."

"Do you remember the illustrations from Aretino? The one of Mars and Venus?" At her surprised look, he said with a grin, "I tracked down a copy and studied the pictures. Very informative. Limited, but informative."

"I know that illustration of Mars and Venus." She flushed a deep rose, no doubt recalling the image where Venus rode the god of war's cock. "And it always made me hurry to bed."

With a growl, Finn lifted her up so that she straddled him. He gripped his cock, placing it at her entrance, as their panting breath mingled. She braced her hands on his shoulders. Their gazes locked, and in that moment, there was only them, lost in each other.

He craved more, and thrust up. She sank down so that he saw the play of hunger and tenderness in her eyes as he filled her. Hope unfolded within him—perhaps she felt something for him beyond lust. God, how he wished it to be so.

Neither moved when he was seated to the root, and he was damned from that moment, because nothing in his many years upon this sinful Earth ever felt like this, ever inhabited him so completely as his monstrous, overwhelming, and worshipful adulation for her.

The carriage bounced as it hit a rut. Both he and Tabitha moaned as the movement made him thrust within her. The motion broke the spell that had fallen. She rode him hard as he pumped up into her, their movements fast and frenzied. His hands were hard on her waist, holding her as he fucked this woman, who astonished and delighted and terrified him in equal measure.

"Put yourself where you need to be," he said, guttural. "However you want, whatever you require. Take everything. Use me up."

She angled her hips so that she ground her clitoris against him, her hips pounding against his as she gave herself fully to pleasure. Enthralled by the beautiful play of sensation and feeling on her face, he watched her the whole time. He loved that he could give her this, and rejoiced when she cried out and shuddered with her climax.

Two more strokes were all it took for him to follow her. His head tipped backward as he came hard, fire tearing up his spine and incinerating him with the force of his release. It went on and on, and seemed to trigger another orgasm in her, softer this time as she moaned lowly against his chest.

They held each other, bodies quieting, intimacy all around them like a protective cocoon. She pressed kisses to his jaw and nuzzled along his neck, making contented little sounds that went straight into a compartment in his heart.

His clothing clung to his sweat-dampened skin but he didn't give a damn about it. He didn't hear the traffic. He didn't care if anyone outside might have guessed what had happened in the carriage. All that mattered was her, with him now.

Hope uncurled from the center of his chest, spreading through him in tentative coils, and he feared that hope as much as he reached toward it.

He'd gambled on marrying and, in the process, had lost his heart.

Chapter 17

✢ ✱ ✢

Tabitha wasn't certain how it had happened—she was too dazed in the wake of making frenzied love with her husband in a carriage to pay attention to much—but somehow, she and Finn returned home, went inside and up the stairs, and then made it to their bedchamber.

It was only afternoon, the sun only just beginning its descent, the house full of busy servants, and the street outside noisy with traffic. The world went industriously about its business. In spite of all this, Finn took her straight to bed.

She didn't utter a word of complaint or say anything about how ordinary people didn't make love during the day. Because she was learning that little mattered outside of the world she and Finn created together.

As they'd spent hours together, learning each other's bodies, discovering what gave the other pleasure, her heart filled with sunlight. She recalled how, in the midst of her fear in meeting the Sterling Society, he'd been so kind and attentive, making her laugh to put her at ease. He'd drawn the members' attention to her accomplishments, as well. She hadn't liked the way Sir William had been so appalled at Finn's lack of university education, but before she'd been able to object, Finn had smoothly guided the conversation back to her. And while she'd met the men who comprised the group, she'd been most aware of the one beside her, her husband.

He truly couldn't know how much his support signified to her. Including the way that he'd listened to her and appreciated her intention when she'd explained why it was so crucial for her to become part of the Sterling Society.

He'd been with her the whole time, offering her strength, making her burn for him. So much so that she'd acted like the veriest wanton in the carriage. And here at home.

They now dined in their room, a simple meal of roast squab and potatoes with marmalade cakes for dessert, as Finn admitted that he'd told the cook that marmalade cakes were his very favorite.

"There's no use in pretending surprise," he said across the small table set up at the foot of the bed. "When I myself engineered the surprise."

"That does take some of the element of the unexpected from it," Tabitha answered, admiring the way he looked in the firelight.

Both had donned simple, lightweight garments, and her gaze kept straying to the vee of his chest exposed by the open neck of his shirt. Crisp dark hair curled there, tempting and masculine. Only thirty minutes before, that hair had rubbed deliciously across her breasts as Finn had covered her with his body, anchoring her to bed while jolting her with powerful thrusts of his cock.

"Madam," he said playfully, drawing her attention up to his face, "have a care for how you look at me, for as much as I'm enjoying this meal, it would take very little for me to forgo it in favor of fucking you."

Despite everything that they had done together—including fellating him *in a moving vehicle*—a blush spread across her cheeks and through her body.

"Insatiable." She shook her head in mock reproof. "Had I known that my husband would have such a prodigious sexual appetite, I would have spent the weeks leading up to our marriage in intense physical conditioning so I could match his stamina."

"Something I must point out." Long and loose-limbed, he stretched out in his chair, looking every inch a potent, sensual male. It was impossible to not ogle the firm shapes of his thighs encased in softest buckskin.

"And that is?" She took a bite of cake. He was right, a marmalade cake was a delightful end to a meal, slightly bitter with almonds and Seville orange, and pleasingly chewy.

"Whatever exercise you took in those three weeks seems more than adequate, because you have equaled me in our marathon lovemaking. I daresay," he drawled, "you wear *me* out, as I am always the one to fall asleep first, whilst you have enough energy to pursue your studies afterward."

Her gaze slid to the fire, pushed away by guilt. Explaining to him why she felt compelled to run to her books was beyond her. How could she put it into words, and relive her humiliation and devastation, without exposing herself in the most vulnerable way?

Yet as she feared the strength of the bond between them, she craved it. Craved *him* in a way that stole breath and thought at the idea of not touching him, not kissing him, not feeling him move strong and fierce within her body. Or the closeness between them that their lovemaking created.

It was a wide and dangerous world, where nothing was certain, yet she could almost believe they had in each other someone who truly knew and saw them for who they were. How she wanted it to be true.

Yet, when she had asked Finn where he went every night, he'd equivocated. And that sent a chill through her. What was he hiding? She feared the truth because . . . she'd begun to lose her heart to him.

The realization burst through her like a river breaking free of its dam, almost drowning her.

She craved his presence, his smiles, his keen insight, his humor, and his kindness. He was careful and controlled, and yet so open and free with her. Never did she feel more herself than when they were together.

Was it possible that he had feelings for her, as she did for him? Could she trust her husband, if he refused to answer her about his nocturnal whereabouts?

There was so much that told her she could, and yet there was still a part of him that remained in shadow. He went out after she retreated from bed, but *where* he'd gone, he refused to say. Was there something he concealed from her?

He'd claimed he was no rake, and that he'd be faithful, but it was unlikely that a man would admit to his wife that he had many lovers, or that he wouldn't adhere to his wedding vows. He might even have a mistress.

Nausea roiled through her at the thought of sharing him with someone else. She wanted him all to herself and prayed that he needed the same from her.

She had to know, to remove this last barrier between them.

LATER, SHE WAITED until after Finn had nodded off before slipping from the bed. For a while, she'd feared that he wouldn't sleep, and he'd seemed to fight it. But the rigors of the afternoon and evening had taken their toll, and when he at last slumbered, she quickly donned a simple dress. She shot glances toward the bed where he sprawled, yet he didn't waken. Once she was clothed, she slipped her wrapper on over her gown before making her way down to the library.

In the library, she picked a book at random, barely seeing the author or title, before settling into a chair. As she did, she pulled her wrapper tight around her, to make certain it concealed what she wore beneath. If he did come downstairs, she couldn't let him know what she planned.

The clock ticked the minutes away. All the while, the beat of her heart was an unsteady, erratic presence within her, but even if it had been steadily pumping away, she wouldn't have been able to pay attention. The efforts she made to read were a farce, yet she kept up the pretense until she heard someone in the corridor.

Finn appeared at the door, already dressed in his unrelievedly dark garments. Her breath caught in her throat at the picture he presented, emerging from the shadows.

"I should be home just after dawn," he said evenly.

"I'll see you at breakfast," she answered.

He turned away, then paused, as if he had something more to say, before striding down the corridor. As soon as she heard the front door open and close, she threw off her wrapper and uncovered the dress she'd been hiding beneath. She might not be able to go to all the places where he went, but she could be prepared.

Opening the front door, she retreated when she saw Finn in the process of climbing into a hackney. She was outside as soon as the vehicle pulled away from the curb. There wasn't time to feel nervous about hailing a hired conveyance on her own at night, and when one came to a stop, she urgently called up to the driver, "Follow that hackney."

"Best get in before we lose 'em," the driver said, eyeing the door to his vehicle. "And hold on."

Tabitha jumped in and gripped the worn seat as the vehicle lurched into motion. Her heart continued to slam against her ribs during the trip through the darkened London streets. She scarce paid the passing scenery any notice, though she caught occasional glimpses of lamplit people, some dressed for revelry, others wearily heading home after what had likely been a long day's labor.

Unfamiliarity with being out alone at night made it difficult to determine just *where* they headed. Until they passed Grosvenor Square, and she recognized that they were in Mayfair. Wherever her husband was heading, it was located in London's most exclusive neighborhood. What could be here? A party? A woman?

The vehicle came to a jolting halt and she had to brace herself against its interior walls to keep from tumbling to the grimy floor.

"Hackney dropped off a rum cove," the driver called down to her.

"What?"

The driver clicked his tongue. "The hired vehicle deposited its passenger, and he's a finely dressed man. He went in there." The man pointed to one of the stately houses lining the street.

Legs unsteady beneath her, she climbed out of the hackney and handed the driver a coin.

"Want me to wait?" he asked.

"I don't know how long I'll be." She didn't know what awaited her inside.

He shrugged before giving the reins a snap. The hackney drove on, leaving her standing alone outside, her breath misting in fast, anxious puffs. Damn, in her haste she'd neglected to bring a cloak or wrap or even gloves, and her skin pebbled in the chill night air.

She could still return home and find the warmth of her own bed. But if she did, she'd never find peace, agonizing that Finn had found affection in someone else's arms.

Before she could talk herself out of it, she walked quickly up the walkway and knocked on the door.

To her surprise, a liveried footman admitted her, his gaze professionally disinterested as she stepped inside. She rubbed her arms in an attempt to chase away the cold—or agitation—that made her shiver. Fortunately, the footman pretended not to notice.

"The tables are located that way, madam," he said politely, gesturing toward a large chamber at the end of a corridor.

"Yes, of course," she said, though she'd no idea what he meant by that.

She walked down a corridor, following the growing din of many voices. Wherever she was, it was much more boisterous than any ball or soiree she'd ever attended. Her palms went clammy and her throat was a desert. Yet she kept going, drawn forward by the unrelenting need to know if she'd made a terrible mistake in giving Finn her heart.

The corridor opened up into a large, spacious room. There were tables arrayed throughout, and, upon closer inspection, she saw they all offered different varieties of games of chance. Servants bearing trays of refreshments wove through the crowd. At one end of the room, a very elegant Black woman bedecked in sapphires watched the floor with the air of an empress surveying her empire. She kept her sharp attention on the men and women surrounding the tables. People shone in their splendid evening regalia—her own dress much plainer and duller in comparison.

Yet that didn't matter. The reason for her presence tonight made his way through the chamber. Though Finn had his back to her, she would recognize his broad shoulders anywhere, and his uniformly dark clothing set him even further apart from the crowd. He moved with precision, navigating the throng with the kind of directness that came from experience. And the people gave way to him, stepping aside as though yielding to his natural authority, with many interested gazes of all sexes following him as he strode toward one of the tables.

This was a gaming hell. He'd gone to a gaming hell—not a lover's arms.

Thank God. She sagged in relief. All her terrible fancies had been for naught, and she felt a little foolish that she'd been so fearful.

She ought to go, and yet she couldn't stop staring at him.

This was his element. Far more than a ballroom, or the sitting room of the Sterling Society, or indeed anywhere else she'd ever seen him. Despite her anxiety, a bolt of desire pierced her to see him so utterly in command, so perfectly controlled and self-assured.

When a woman in teal and diamonds approached him, smiling invitingly, Tabitha's stomach clenched.

Finn spoke to the pretty woman politely, briefly, before continuing his progress. He didn't spare her any more attention.

A breath left Tabitha, a knot of tension unwinding within her to have definitive proof that he didn't come to this place in search of amorous company. In search of someone who wasn't his own wife.

He took his place at a table where someone dealt cards to half a dozen patrons. Tabitha moved from the doorway deeper into the room to get a better look at what it was that happened at the table. Money was placed in the center of the table, then the dealer laid down two cards in front of each gambler, including Finn. The dealer put one card face down in front of himself. Some of the players seemed to motion for another card, whilst others waved away the offer. Finn gestured to receive another card.

Then the dealer gave himself a card, and several groans plus one cheer rose up from the table when the dealer's face down card was revealed.

Finn was too far away for her to make out his expression, but he didn't cheer and he didn't groan. His posture remained easy—even when he received some of the money that had been offered up at the beginning of the game. So, he'd won.

He tilted his head, as if trying to hear something, though it didn't seem like anyone was speaking to him.

The crowd shifted, swirling around him. When it dispersed, he was gone.

Strange. She hadn't seen him get up, and as she scanned the room, she couldn't find any sign of him. Wherever he'd gone was a mystery.

She ought to go. There was nothing left for her to see here—she had her proof of his fidelity, and she had plans to make. Namely, how she might introduce the fact that she cared for him far more than their initial agreement allowed. How he might take her news, she'd no idea, but she couldn't keep her feelings suppressed any longer.

She turned to leave. And collided with a broad, unyielding chest clad entirely in black. A man's large hand grasped her upper arm, the hold firm.

Her stomach pitched. *Oh, God.*

"Tabitha."

She looked up into Finn's face, his eyes nearly black with an unreadable emotion.

She fixed him with a bright smile that she hoped masked the utter panic swirling in her belly. "Good evening, Finn."

"Jesus," he muttered.

Before she could reply, his hand tightened on her arm and gently but resolutely tugged her toward a quiet corner, then faced her, his expression impassive.

"*How* did you get here?" he demanded lowly. "Is everything all right? What are you doing in this place?"

"You've inundated me with questions, and I don't know which to answer first," she said, attempting humor but only sounding tight and shrill.

Despite the commotion of betting and revelry around them, his attention was wholly on her. While she usually enjoyed being Finn's sole focus, right now his unblinking scrutiny unnerved her, and she did her best not to squirm like a thief caught with their hand in the vault.

"Let's begin at the beginning," he said, gaze intent. "Are you well?"

"Yes, perfectly well." She tried to smile again.

His chest rose and fell as if he was only just permitting himself to exhale. With unnerving calm, he said, "Tell me how you found this place."

"I hired a hackney and followed you," she admitted. "The driver went *very* fast but I managed not to fall out as we rounded corners."

"Thank God for that. I don't fancy trying to fish my wife out of a London gutter."

She couldn't tell if he was jesting or not, so she went on smiling inanely.

"Why are you here?" His jaw was tight as he asked this question. "Did you not trust me? You believed I was off somewhere carousing and whoring like a libertine?"

"I—" She pressed her hand to the base of her throat, where her pulse continued to pound beneath delicate skin. All she wanted to do was hide, yet there was no hiding now. She owed him the truth, even as she recognized it in herself. "Forgive me. You deserve better. Only . . . I was jealous."

He stared at her, a crease between his brows, and she kept talking to make sense of it and make sense of herself.

"There's no excuse for my behavior," she went on.

"You haven't given me true cause to doubt you, but I did."

When he said nothing, heaviness sank within her. Quietly, she said, "I shouldn't have followed you without your permission. I'm sorry, Finn."

He was still silent, so she went on, "I think I was the one who pushed you here. I'd leave the bed because . . . in those moments after we made love, I could feel it, growing in myself. So big I could scarce take a breath. And it frightened me."

"What frightened you?" he asked lowly.

She swallowed hard. "You've come to mean so much to me. And I was . . . hurt in my past. Very badly, by someone who I thought I felt deeply for. I didn't want to feel that pain again. I walled myself off from it, hiding in libraries behind my books."

"And when you began to feel something for me . . ."

"I ran," she admitted. "And shoved you back, at a distance. There was no one to blame but myself that you retreated and wouldn't answer about where you would go."

His jaw tightened. "That culpability is mine. I thought . . . you might think less of me for coming here."

"Why should I?"

"Places like this," he said after a long moment, "are where I go to feel secure. I didn't want to admit that I needed safety. It makes me look weak." He confessed this in a low rumble, as if ashamed.

Her heart clutched hard, a palpable pain that radiated outward. "If you didn't feel safe with me," she said urgently, "that's *my* error. And it's *my* error that I pushed you to concealing the truth from me. Your silence made me unreasonably suspicious and frightened."

It was hard, so hard, to confess all of this, yet she had to, if there was to be any chance of moving forward.

Yet his continued muteness devastated her. She'd pushed him too far, held herself back too much, and now she had to face the consequences.

"If you're angry with me," she said in a choked voice, "I understand. I'll go."

She started to move past him. His hand shot out and gripped her wrist, and she looked up at him, afraid of what she might see—fury, distaste, dismissal. As she had seen on Charles Stokely's face eight years ago.

But Finn's gaze was warm and his full mouth softened into the gentlest of smiles.

"Stay," he murmured. "Please. Stay."

She swallowed around her heart, which had leapt up and situated itself in her throat. Blinking, she searched his face for any sign that he was angry or disgusted, but all she saw was gratitude and affection. His hand slid from her wrist to weave their fingers together. Like her, he wasn't wearing gloves, and the press of skin to skin intoxicated her far more than any brandy or wine.

"Truly?" she whispered.

"All you had to do was ask me, love," he said softly. "I would have told you. Because"—he took a long inhalation, as if steeling himself—"I've feelings for you, too."

"You do?" Her chest contracted with rising hope.

"You weren't the only one afraid to speak the truth," he admitted. "I didn't want to break the stipulations of our bargain. I thought that what I felt for you wouldn't be reciprocated."

"It is." Elated, she lifted up on her toes and kissed him. The feel of his mouth against hers was silken and wondrous, the answer to the question she had been too fearful to ask. She pressed against the length of his body. He was so wonderfully solid and steady, and when he kissed her back deeply, she melted into him.

She'd been foolish to compare him to Charles. They were nothing alike, and by holding on to her past hurt, she'd kept Finn at a distance. That changed—tonight.

"Shall we go home?" she asked breathlessly.

"I want you in my bed," he rumbled against her lips. "But before we go—I want to show you this place. Show you my world. Will you stay with me here? For a little longer."

Joy winged through her, that he would want to share this important part of himself with her. "I will."

"Then," he said, stepping back to tuck her hand into the crook of his arm and drawing her away from the corner, "let's discover it together."

Chapter 18

❧ ✳ ❧

"Where to begin?" With Tabitha beside him, energy pulsed in Finn's body, as if he escorted a ray of moonlight through the gaming hell.

The night suddenly bloomed with possibility, whereas earlier that evening, he'd been focused only on his goals—namely, winning enough to make his time here, away from her, worthwhile. Now, however, he looked around the large chamber with its vaulted ceilings and numerous chandeliers and wagering people, and saw not obligation but potential.

"I could play a few of the games," she suggested, gazing around her with sparkling, astute eyes. He adored seeing how she took in everything with inquisitive openness. "Experience what you experience when you're here."

"Practice without theory inevitably leads to disaster." He waved over a servant with a tray. "Whisky for me, and for the lady . . ." He looked expectantly at Tabitha.

"Whisky for me, as well," she said. Glancing at Finn, she added with a smile, "I've tasted it only once but I'm ready for more."

The servant bowed before going off to fetch them their drinks.

"By all means," Finn said, walking them past a table where a roulette wheel spun, "let us experience everything tonight has to offer. Most people come here to wager on as many games as they desire, and enjoy themselves thoroughly in the process."

"But that isn't what *you* do," she said, looking up at him.

"I do take pleasure in it," he allowed, "but that isn't what brings me back night after night. The pursuit of blunt drives me to the tables."

"Surely there are more secure ways of earning a living." She inclined her head when the servant returned with two whiskies and took her glass from the tray.

Finn also grabbed his drink. Once the servant was gone, Finn held up his glass. "To unexpected turns."

"And wherever they might take us." She clinked her glass against his, and they regarded each other over the rims as they drank. His gaze locked with hers, resonating in the deepest part of himself.

That she hadn't trusted him enough to follow him was vexing. Even so, he hadn't been fully open about where he went each night. More conviction was needed between both of them.

Part of him rejoiced in the fact that she'd been so possessive of him, she'd actually followed him tonight. There was something primally thrilling about inspiring jealousy.

She *cared* for him. *She* cared for *him*. Every way he thought of it, it grew more and more astounding, more unexpectedly wonderful.

The whisky had nothing on the way her words

made him feel. Hot and alive and gleaming, like an ember on the verge of turning to flame.

And yet . . . she didn't know *everything* about him. Her feelings might change when she finally learned that her husband struggled to read.

His joy muted, as if that ember was trapped beneath a glass dome.

For now, he would take what he could. And he would be happy with the memory of this moment when it inevitably ended.

After finishing his drink, he handed it to another servant before leading her to stand at the periphery of a hazard table. Here was something he *could* share with her that held no possible rejection.

"I love the sound the dice make," he murmured to her. "Even in the noise of the room, I can hear it. It dances along my spine and makes it seem as though everything's right with the world."

She tilted her head to listen and smiled when a player cast the carved ivory pieces across the baize. "It's rather homey, isn't it? Like crockery in a kitchen, a comforting sound."

"Hadn't thought of it that way, but you're right." He smiled down at her, his wonder of a wife. Yet he couldn't spend the remainder of the evening mooning over Tabitha—though the idea had merit—so he returned his focus to the game being played in front of them.

"How do you win at games like these?" she asked.

"People come swaggering into gaming hells thinking that bluster and sheaves of blunt are what's necessary to emerge on top," he explained, "but that's never the case. Having your mind in the right place, having a careful approach, that's what's important and what's always drawn me to it. Make plans, think things through, understand the mathematics and the odds. That's how you win."

"It's like the way you are outside of the gaming hell," she said thoughtfully. "Almost nothing done rashly, everything viewed through the lens of strategy. Even your relationships with other people."

He started at her comment. Hell—was she right?

"Insightful," he said, slightly dazed. "And accurate."

There went his pulse, hammering eagerly at the knowledge that she saw him so deeply. He stared at her as she watched the table, fascinated by the line of her profile, and the depth of her concentration.

Someone exclaimed in dismay at their luck at a nearby table, bringing his attention back to the room.

She glanced at one of the players. "So that man there, the one who's sweating as he throws . . ."

"Too wild," Finn said confidently. "Not enough consideration or confidence. The worse it gets for him, the more anxious he becomes, and the less deliberate his play."

He pitied that bloke, because there was no way out of that spiral except winning, but there was no winning until you regained your equilibrium.

The man kept running the cuff of his sleeve across his brow and rubbing his hands on the front of his breeches.

"'*No passion so effectually robs the mind of all its powers of acting and reasoning as fear,*'" she noted, then added, "Edmund Burke."

"Just so," Finn said with a nod. "This bloke's approach is all wrong. And the beauty of this work is that it's alchemy of both the precise and the nuanced.

You have to read the game, but you read people, too, and pay attention to what's said and what isn't said. You've got to be analytical and instinctual at the same time. And patient, and keep your memory sharp, as well."

Her attention left the game, and instead, she contemplated him with a thoroughness that was at once alarming and arousing. Cards and games of chance were safe, and he knew how to remain placid and collected, never letting anyone or anything disturb his equanimity. Yet with her gray, serious eyes on him, seeing to the very center of his being, he barely kept from rubbing his hand along the back of his neck or clenching and unclenching his hands—both surefire tells at the card table.

He'd never wanted to be seen as much as he did at that moment, while at the same time, he feared what might happen if she could see down into the soul of him, who he truly was. A restless, trembling yearning ached in his heart, wanting so much from her, but afraid of the thing he most desired.

"The way people underestimate you," she said at last. "It's *criminal*."

He was nine and twenty years old, and had seen and done things that would scandalize eighty-eight percent of polite society. Even so, her words brought a flush to his cheeks, and he looked up at the carvings in the ceiling so he didn't do something ridiculous, like weeping openly in the middle of a busy gaming hell.

To be sure, he wouldn't have been the first person to sob in a gaming hell, but he'd never done it before, and this night wouldn't change that.

Still, he had to take several deep, rough breaths

before he could look at Tabitha's face and see the understanding and *respect* in her eyes.

He'd earned the respect of so few. To have it from her . . .

Yet he might lose it if she only knew the truth.

He swallowed hard, pushing past the rise of fear that wanted to choke the joy from this moment. "You've heard me expound on theory, and next comes practice." He motioned toward a table where they played loo.

"I know nothing of these games' rules," she said, a crease of worry forming between her brows.

"I'll guide you as you play."

"Aren't you playing, too?" she asked in surprise.

"I'll fare better as a guide if my attention isn't divided."

A silent blessing echoed in his mind as he led her to the table. When he'd arrived at Jenkins's tonight, his spirits had been low—she'd left their bed again, and he'd begun to despair of ever truly reaching his wife—and yet having her here with him now brought him higher than he'd been in a good long while. Perhaps ever. Not even winning all the money in the gaming hell's coffers could ever approach this feeling. As long as it lasted, he would hold tight to it. There would be time to mourn its inevitable loss later.

Finn explained the rules to loo as concisely as possible. Tabitha took it all in, asking questions as needed, until, at last, she said, "I'm ready to try my hand at it."

It was three card loo, and after the dealer staked

the pot, they dealt out cards for each of the other players, before revealing the trump suit for the round. Tabitha picked up the flow of the game quickly, announcing that she would play, and the players went around the table, attempting to win the trick.

Tabitha won several times, sending surprised but pleased glances at Finn, standing behind her. He loved watching her apply her mind to something new, and she seemed eager to embrace the opportunity not just to add to her vast knowledge, but to learn about *him*.

"Best thing to do," he murmured in her ear when her winnings grew yet again, "is to leave when you're on top. Most fail when they hunger for more."

"A sensible strategy," she said with a nod before collecting her chits to cash out.

After she exchanged her tokens for money, they headed home. Both were quiet together as they rode home in a hired carriage.

She snuggled close to him, resting her head on his shoulder, and he wrapped his arm around her as naturally as if his whole life, he'd held her closely.

"Do you need to go to your library tonight?" he asked as lightly as he could, as if he didn't hold his breath in hope and fear of her answer.

"Straight to our bed," she answered.

Finn exhaled and drew her even closer as any lingering uncertainty evaporated. The world contained only them, with her beside him, yawning delicately as the excitement of the night sifted away.

He'd never felt such relief as when they reached their home, and she wove her fingers with his to be led upstairs. By the time they were back in their bedchamber, she swayed on her feet. As he helped her out of her clothing, she couldn't even open her eyes, and once she was undressed, he tucked her between the sheets. He stripped, taking a moment to wash quickly, before climbing in beside her.

She turned to him at once, making soft, sleepy noises. When she settled into the shelter of his arms, he pulled her close. She was soft and warm, and his heart swelled as she burrowed against him. In moments she was asleep.

Replete to his very marrow with her closeness, he looked up at the canopy as he held her. The sun was starting to rise, and the pattern of the fabric became more and more visible with the growing light, intertwined vines with dainty flowers sprouting here and there. The decor's selection had been left to someone else, and it mattered little to Finn, so long as it pleased Tabitha.

She couldn't see the canopy now, fast asleep as she was. A tiny snore escaped her, and he smiled to himself because, like almost everything she did, it charmed him.

His eyelids wanted to shut, yet he forced them open to keep his own rest at bay. He didn't want to sleep just yet. Didn't want to have this moment with her at the end of what had been an incredible night, and then wake later to find her gone, either to the library or somewhere else. Somewhere that wasn't here, with him. She'd said that she hadn't needed to go to her library, but she could always change her mind.

But the bed was so comfortable, and the feel of her nestled close was so soothing, especially the gentle puffs of her breath across his chest, that, struggle as he did, he couldn't stop himself from falling asleep.

He started awake sometime later. It was difficult to determine how long he'd been slumbering because the room was still cloaked in shadows—the curtains were still closed, blocking out the daylight—and he rolled over, bracing himself for the empty space where Tabitha had lain.

Except she was still there.

She looked at him, amusement in her eyes, with her hair rumpled. Truthfully, she was rumpled everywhere.

"Hello, beautiful," he murmured to her.

"I must look like a library book that's been circulated one too many times," she said on a laugh.

"You're ravishing." There were little creases in her face from the pillow, her features lightly slack since it seemed she'd wakened not too long before him, and the tiniest bit of sand in her eyes—and never had she been lovelier.

"And famished," she confessed.

"We will feed you without delay, madam."

"Do you think there are any of those marmalade cakes left?" She propped herself up on her elbow.

"If there aren't, I will make some myself. Actually," he amended, "I know nothing of cookery, but I will stand over our cook and be very strenuous and vocal in my insistence that she bake some for you." He slipped from the bed and donned a robe before tugging on the bellpull. When she started to rise, he held up a hand. "Stay precisely where you are. You're not to move—unless it's to throw back the covers and display yourself in the most lascivious manner."

"Like this?" She flung the blanket away, revealing her delicious nudity. But alas, she hauled the bedclothes up to her chin when there was a tap at the door.

He spoke to the maid through a crack in the door, instructing that a meal was to be prepared and brought up as soon as possible, before returning to his blushing wife.

"My foray into exhibiting myself was short-lived." Only the top of her face was visible above the blanket as he sat beside her.

"We'll have ample opportunity to repeat the event. Thrown-back covers and all. Now that you're in my bed," he said, bringing his lips to hers, "I have no intention of ever letting you go."

Chapter 19

❧ ✲ ❧

"Ah, Mr. Ransome, Mrs. Ransome," Sir William said as Tabitha and Finn entered the Sterling Society's sitting room two days later. The armchairs were arranged in a circle, all of them occupied but for two, standing ready for the newcomers. "Do join us."

The members rose as Tabitha came into the chamber, though some barely lifted themselves from their seats, and quickly sat as soon as she took her chair. Well, she knew it would be a difficult climb, and some men's grudging politeness wouldn't deter her. It was imperative that she keep herself focused on her goal.

Only yesterday, she'd met with Diana, Iris, Arjun, and Chima at the Benezra. It had been a brief gathering, but a necessary one, since the education bill was coming up soon in Parliament. She and her friends had discussed what her approach would be when the Sterling Society was consulted, after which, she fully intended to bring them into the organization's ranks.

Nerves tightened across her skin as she sat—the stakes could not be higher—yet when Finn sent her a reassuring smile and wink, some of her fear eased. *He* believed in her, and *she* believed in herself.

After a servant came through with tea—Finn looked slightly appalled at his cup, likely wishing it contained at the least coffee if not whisky—Sir William cleared his throat.

"Last week, Mr. Dunne raised a very salient point about empiricism versus rationalism," he began in an oratory voice.

"A wise man proportions his belief to the evidence, according to Hume," someone said.

"But that supposes that our senses are themselves perfect," Tabitha said calmly, "and the human machine is faulty at best."

The group erupted into vociferous debate. Tabitha joined in, offering her own interpretation of various texts and philosophical stances, while Finn remained silent, his attention wholly fixed to her. She could have sworn that there was a carnal hunger in his eyes as he gazed at her, but it wasn't as though she and the Sterling Society were discussing anything prurient.

She focused on the discussion. "'*Everything that you receive is not measured according to its actual size, but rather that of the receiving vessel,*' according to Sor Juana Inés de la Cruz."

"You're quoting a *woman*?" Sir William asked with a frown. "And a papist one from the ends of the earth at that?"

Tabitha drew in a steadying breath. "Her ideas are exceptional, regardless of her gender, and I fail to see how her country of origin would compromise the validity of her thoughts."

Leather creaked as the men shifted in their seats, and they traded speaking glances with each other.

"Here in the Sterling Society," Sir William said loftily, "our discourse is built upon only the strongest of foundations. The greatest minds of our society. Socrates, Boethius, William of Ockham, Hegel."

"To be sure," Tabitha said, struggling to speak in as mild and pleasant a voice as possible, lest she be dismissed as an overemotional female, "the doctrines of those learned men are admirable, but you're excluding over half of the population's thoughts because of their sex. And the West is but one small part of a much larger world. As your Shakespeare said, 'There are more things in heaven and earth than are dreamt of in your philosophy.'"

Several of the members gasped, while another sputtered in outrage.

"You must read *Wollstonecraft*," Mr. Dunne said tautly.

"I do," she answered levelly, even though anger already simmered through her. "And Hypatia of Alexandria, and Maitreyi, and Rabia of Basra."

Finn beamed at her, while the other men in the room rumbled agitatedly.

"Mrs. Ransome," Sir William gritted, "the Sterling Society refuses to acknowledge inferior opinions."

"Inferior because of their content," she answered through clenched teeth, "or because of who posits them? If it is the latter, your own methodology is suspect, because you allow yourself to be blinded and prejudicial on the basis of your limited hearts and even narrower minds. Which I once again bring you back to Sor Juana Inés de la Cruz's observation about the size of the receiving vessel."

Outraged shouts greeted her calm pronouncement. Finn looked to her, but she shook her head, and he remained seated but ready to spring into action should she require it. Oh, how she wished she could unleash him, and herself, on these pompous churls. But much as it pained her, she had to remain in complete control of herself. All it would take was a slight shift in tone, and her ideas would be completely invalidated by these men.

A handful of them coughed pointedly into their fists, which seemed to be some variety of signal, because Sir William folded his hands in his lap, his movements deliberate.

"Mrs. Ransome," he intoned, "before your arrival today, your forthcoming presence was hotly debated. In truth, there was not a single member who was in favor of you becoming part of our esteemed organization—myself included."

Finn scowled, looking absolutely murderous, and numerous men looked at him with alarm.

"I see," she said, still holding tightly to her composure, even as her stomach clenched with rage. "Was there ever a moment where I was genuinely considered for membership? Or was this a parody from the moment you and I discussed the possibility outside your club, Sir William?"

"Inviting you here was a purely intellectual exercise," he answered with a sniff, "to see if women could theoretically be included amongst our ranks. Having you here today has proven our hypothesis: women have no place in the Sterling Society. You never had the chance to become one of us."

Tabitha stared at him. The baronet had planted the idea of accepting her once she was married, but that had been a lie. It had all been a false, patronizing charade. Her hopes, her intentions, all meant nothing in the face of Sir William and the Society's bigotry.

Red filmed her vision and fire coursed through her body. They had wasted her time, Finn's time, and made her dance like a bloody marionette, secure and smug in their knowledge that they would forever bar her, and anyone who wasn't exactly like them, from having her voice heard. And Diana, and Iris, and Chima, and Arjun, they would be silenced because of these . . . these . . . *buffoons*.

She got to her feet, and was grateful that her legs didn't shake with fury beneath her. Finn was beside her in a moment, his presence large and secure, but it didn't escape her notice that none of the members of the Sterling Society rose. She didn't give a rat's arse about gendered codes of conduct, yet the men's decision to remain seated was an obvious slight.

"If all you do," she answered icily, "is regurgitate the thoughts of other people who look like you and inhabit your selfsame minuscule inch of the planet, then I cheer your demise, which will happen sooner rather than later."

Finn held out his arm, and she took it. As the indignant cries of the Sterling Society rang all around them, she and her husband made their way steadily toward the door.

"Just a moment, love," Finn murmured to her, pausing on the threshold to the sitting room. He faced the red-and-purple countenances of the members. "In case this hasn't been made abundantly clear, gentlemen, go fuck yourselves." He turned back to her. "Shall we, my dear?"

She managed a nod, and together, she and Finn quit the building. Outside, she took great gulping breaths as rage scoured her.

"How dare they?" she snarled, finally able to give

way to the incendiary anger pouring through her. "How *dare* they?"

"I'm going to be presumptuous," he announced, and he didn't even wince as her nails dug into him. He carefully disengaged himself from her and went to their waiting carriage. To the coachman, he said, "We're walking. You can return home."

The coachman touched his fingers to the brim of his hat before driving off, leaving Finn and Tabitha on the sidewalk outside the Sterling Society's headquarters.

"Come, love." Finn bravely offered his arm again, and a moment later, they were walking down the streets of Mayfair.

Her angry strides were quick, and she barely paid heed to the traffic they wove through or what the buildings looked like or indeed anything at all. It was monstrous, this fury that churned within her like some mythical beast spawned by a Titan, with many heads that spat fire to incinerate anyone foolish enough to cross her path.

Finn said nothing, merely keeping pace beside her on his long legs. Yet he guided her through the city, heading eastward, wordlessly directing her down particular streets and turning certain corners.

"Where are you taking us?" she said through the haze of her wrath.

"Somewhere that will come as a relief," he answered cryptically.

She was too unsettled to demand more of an answer, but after a solid thirty minutes of walking, and her anger not at all abated, she looked around and saw they were in a slightly raffish part of town. The brick facades of the buildings were stained with soot, and one was even missing a few of its windows.

Finn stopped outside a large structure that boasted a thick, slightly warped wooden door, which stood ajar. There was no sign announcing what was inside, but he shouldered open the door without a moment's hesitation and beckoned for her to follow him into the shadowed corridor.

She stepped inside, and was at once greeted by a ripe, humid, *human* smell. It wasn't entirely unpleasant, but it was tangy and heavy, and grew stronger as she trailed after Finn down the hallway. The sounds of men grunting was punctuated with the occasional shout and not a few profanities.

The corridor opened to a vast, soaring space, and she paused when she saw the two boxing rings set up in the middle. Within the rings, men practiced their pugilism, sparring with each other. Some of the men wore breeches and untucked shirts while others were bare chested, and all of them gleamed with sweat. Which explained the smell. Around the rings, men performed gymnastic exercises, while others shadowboxed, and others threw their fists into leather bags suspended from heavy wooden frames.

Some of them glanced in her direction, but if they were surprised by seeing a woman in this temple of masculine aggression, their craggy faces—many sporting crooked noses—gave no sign.

Finn lifted his hand in greeting to a large man with shaggy red hair, who was in a corner training a lean Black man. The redhead looked at Tabitha with raised brows, but then shrugged before resuming his work.

Finn still hadn't said anything to Tabitha, but she followed him when he tipped his chin toward one of the corners of the pugilism academy. He stopped beside a large leather sack, almost as tall as her, that hung from a chain suspended in another wooden frame. After pulling off his coat and laying it on the ground, he positioned himself on one side of the leather bag, holding it in place.

"Go on," he said with a nod.

"You want me to hit that?" She eyed the large sack, which looked rather ominous up close.

"Since planting a facer on Sir William isn't a possibility," he explained, "bringing you to my pugilism academy and letting you have a go on the heavy bag seemed the best alternative. So, go ahead. Give it a wallop."

She stared at him for a moment, her mind struggling to free itself from the net of anger ensnaring it. "I've never thrown a punch in my life."

"It can be very cathartic. Just be sure not to tuck your thumb between your fingers, or you might hurt yourself, and use your body, not your arm, as the source of your power. Otherwise," he said with an encouraging grin, "do as you will."

Even in the midst of her fury, she was grateful for him, and his rare insight.

She looked back and forth between her curled hand—thumb on the *outside*—and the bag. It wasn't at all typical for a woman to practice pugilism, and some might consider it uncouth and vulgar. But those voices were the selfsame ones as the men of the Sterling Society, who didn't think females had any place in the realm of ideas.

After removing her bonnet and setting it aside,

she unbuttoned her pelisse and draped it on top of Finn's discarded coat. She approached the bag, assessing. What was the best way to do this? How could she maximize her admittedly negligible physical strength?

"Thoughts have no place here," Finn said from the other side of the bag. "This is entirely emotion. Whatever you're feeling, put it into your punches."

She let fly. Her fist collided with the bag, ramming into its side. And while it barely moved from the force, the sensation of her hand colliding with *something* and the resulting jolt up her arm and into her body filled her with a wild, furious pleasure.

"Picture Sir William's face," Finn suggested. "Imagine all those smug, supercilious bastards smirking at you."

Her fist slammed into the bag again and again. She imagined the satisfying crunch of cartilage and bone, the spurt of blood. It was vicious and violent and *wonderful*.

"*This* is for giving me false hope," she snarled with each blow. "*This* is for your bigotry. *This* is for being a bunch of. Pompous. Short-sighted. Bloody. Asses."

She punctuated every word with another hit, raining punches on the bag until she panted. Sweat clung to her body and her arm ached and her fists hurt. Yet her anger dulled to a matte sheen rather than gleaming with freshly polished rage.

Gasping, exhausted, she stepped back and planted her hands on her knees. Finn went to his coat and pulled out a flask, which he uncapped before handing to her.

"You travel . . . everywhere . . . with this?" she asked, sniffing its contents. The peaty, round scent of whisky swirled, and she took a sip, though it was difficult to drink when her breath came so quick and fast.

"I'm a man used to taking care of myself."

She gave the flask back, watching the column of his throat above his neckcloth as he downed a healthy dram. He eyed her, then picked up a wooden stool nearby and set it next to her. Grateful for a place to rest, she sank down onto it. No doubt she looked appalling, and Olive would be horrified to see what had become of the coiffure she'd carefully styled earlier in the day, but it didn't matter.

Breathless, she admitted, "I've never . . . actually *hit* anything."

"How did it feel?"

"Good. Very, very good." She stared at the interior of the boxing academy but what she saw was the sitting room of the Sterling Society, and the ring of complacent, self-congratulatory male faces that looked at her as if she was some distasteful aberration displayed in a carnival tent. "But it isn't enough. Nothing's going to be enough. Those damned men."

Finn swore roundly. "Say the word, and I'll go back and make them digest their own teeth. I can do it, too. I come here three to four times weekly."

She was able to smile a little. "It's unexpected but delightful, this vicious side of you. No," she said with a shake of her head, "it will only prove to them that their suspicions about us were right, and I won't give them any fuel to their bigoted bonfire. What I cannot stomach is how they toyed with me. From the beginning, I was merely a moth they wanted to stab with a pin so they could study me. Everything I did to gain their acceptance and admittance was a fool's errand."

For a long time, Finn was silent. The only noise came from the men practicing their boxing skills, with a periodic shout or curse.

She glanced up at him. His arms crossed over his chest, almost protectively, and his expression was shadowed and distracted.

"A fool's errand," he said lowly. "Including this marriage? After what you said to me at the gaming hell?"

Her eyes widened. She shot to her feet and took his hands in hers. "No, Finn. No. One of our reasons for marrying may have been illusory, but I don't regret it. I never regretted it." She dragged in a breath. "I hope you don't, either."

"Not for a moment." His dark gaze held hers.

Though the furious beating of her heart had slowed after she'd rested, seeing how intently her husband looked at her, it sped up again.

I love you.

The words burned in her mouth. Yet . . . she could not say them. Security always seemed out of reach. Even though she had admitted to him that she cared for him, saying those monumental words was too much. Poisonous fears whispered to her that there *was* no safety, not even from the man she'd come to adore beyond all rationality.

Chapter 20

❧ ✳ ❧

*T*hat night, Finn watched worriedly as Tabitha sat listlessly at the dining table. It seemed that though the time at the pugilism academy had been cathartic for her, a heavy melancholy came soon after.

She picked at her food, moving the squab from one side of her plate to the other.

"If there's something else you'd rather dine upon," Finn said with concern, "say the word and I'll ask Cook to prepare it."

"I'm afraid that anything she makes will suffer the same fate." Her efforts at smiling died quickly. "Appetite is difficult to come by. I keep feeling like I failed—myself and my friends. I won't be a part of the discussion about the education bill, either. And the Sterling Society will go on as it always has, using their extremely limited perspective when advising those at the very top. Nothing will change."

Her words struck him hard. He hated seeing her so downhearted over someone else's abysmal behavior.

"Firstly," Finn said, leaning forward to take her hand, "you did not fail. Those jackasses failed *you*. They failed the nation by pigheadedly staying the same. If anyone should be sitting dejectedly in their dining rooms, it should be Sir William Marcroft and the rest of that collection of carbuncles."

She chuckled, yet she still looked dejected. "And secondly?"

"Secondly," he added, squeezing his fingers around hers, "the work you and your friends want to undertake is important. We'll find a way to make it happen."

She looked at him warmly, and he was grateful that he could give her that much, at least. But it wasn't enough.

"Maybe there is some way," she allowed slowly. "But my mind's a jumble now, and I can think of nothing."

His own brain churned, but before either of them could ponder this further, there was a knock at the door. The footman left to answer it, leaving Finn and Tabitha to look at each other in puzzlement as to who might call at so peculiar an hour.

A familiar voice sounded in the entryway.

"Mr. Kieran Ransome to see you, sir," Edgar said, standing at the entry to the dining room, but before he'd finished announcing their visitor, Kieran was already striding in.

Mist beaded on the shoulders of Kieran's coat and in the dark waves of his hair—his brother had confessed that Celeste enjoyed the long-haired poet aesthetic, and so his brother had obligingly grown it longer—and he walked straight to the sideboard to pour himself a glass of wine.

"Don't trouble yourself on my account," Kieran said over his shoulder.

"I assure you," Finn drawled, "we aren't."

"Is everything all right?" Tabitha asked with a worried frown.

"Depends on who you ask." His glass full, Kieran strode to an empty chair at the dining table and pulled it out before the footman could perform the service for him. He dropped into the seat and stretched his legs out, a gesture so habitual and familiar to Finn because they'd both been doing the same thing their whole lives. Upon further reflection, Willa did, too, much to their mother's annoyance. Which was probably why Willa did it so often.

"If you ask our parents," Kieran continued, plucking a grape off a platter and popping it into his mouth, "everything is in shambles and the world will never recover."

"And if we ask *you*?" Finn wondered.

Kieran grinned. "Everything is marvelous. Offer me your felicitations, because I'm to be married."

"Congratulations," Tabitha said, "but aren't you already engaged? Unless," she added in alarm, "someone other than Miss Kilburn is to be your bride."

A look of horror crossed Kieran's face. "Dear God, never say such a thing."

"Apologies," Tabitha said, appearing both contrite and confused.

"Stop tormenting my wife and tell us what the hell you mean," Finn growled.

"I mean," Kieran said as he planted his elbows on the table, "that Celeste and I decided we didn't want to wait any longer, and since the banns have already been read, we've moved the wedding up to this Sunday."

Finn leaned back in his chair and sipped at his wine. Changing the date of the wedding was a surprise, and not a surprise, given that Celeste and

Kieran burned so hotly for each other. Any delay would seem intolerable, regardless of them sneaking around together. "Thus, Mother and Father's horror."

"Precisely. All of their elaborate plans for the wedding wherein they could display their wealth and privilege to London society have been scrapped in favor of a small ceremony, with an intimate breakfast of immediate family to follow. After which, Celeste and I will depart for our bridal journey in Scotland."

"Oh, they must've been livid," Finn chuckled, and his brother joined in.

"Apoplectic. It was one of those rare moments when they agreed with each other—nothing like mutual disappointment in their progeny to bring a couple together."

"We must never let family stand in the way of joy," Tabitha said, smiling.

Finn's heart jumped eagerly at that sign of happiness in her, especially in the wake of this afternoon's debacle at the Sterling Society. Perhaps having her at the wedding would lift her spirits, at least for a little while. Anything he could do to chase the shadows from her eyes.

"Is there anything we need to do or bring on Sunday?" he asked. "Pyrotechnics? Acrobats?"

"Sal volatile for your mother?" Tabitha added.

"Only yourselves." Kieran's expression sobered. "You'll stand with me, won't you, brother? I can think of no one I'd rather have beside me when Celeste honors me with her hand."

Finn sipped at his wine, hoping it would ease the lump that had formed in his throat. When he felt reasonably confident that he could speak without weeping, he said, "Nothing would honor me more."

His brother's own eyes looked suspiciously damp. But he threw back the last of his drink and grinned before getting to his feet. "Excellent. I shall see you this Sunday, when I ascend to the rarified ranks of men who have achieved everything they've ever desired."

Finn rose and shook Kieran's hand, genuinely pleased for him, and yet he couldn't resist glancing toward Tabitha, who watched them. She looked at Kieran with fondness. When she gazed at Finn, that fondness turned to something hotter.

Hopefully, she would find a moment's pleasure at Kieran and Celeste's wedding. He hated this powerlessness he felt in the wake of the Sterling Society's rejection—but he vowed it would be temporary. He'd fight and persevere and be Tabitha's champion, ensuring that whatever her heart yearned for would be hers.

FINN HADN'T EXPECTED seeing his younger brother get married would affect him so strongly. And yet here he was at the wedding breakfast, which was being held in the parlor of his parents' home, watching a beaming Kieran and rosy-cheeked Celeste accepting toasts from the guests, and furiously concentrating on keeping his tears at bay. He was forced to turn his back to the room so he could collect himself.

"A little something," Tabitha murmured, handing him a handkerchief.

"Don't know what the bloody hell is wrong with me," he muttered as he dabbed at his eyes.

"The bond you share with your brother is a rare one," she answered gently. "There's no shame in being happy for him."

"But to *cry* about this." He was disgusted with himself and quickly blotted away any suspicious moisture from his cheeks before handing her back the square of cambric.

"The journey between tears and laughter is a short one, and we hardly know we're making it until we've arrived at our destination." She tucked the handkerchief into her reticule.

"Who said that?" He thought back to the works they had reviewed in preparation for meeting with the Sterling Society. "Aeschylus? Montaigne?"

"Tabitha Ransome," she answered with a small smile.

He grasped her hand in his, giving it a squeeze, as gratitude for this extraordinary woman nearly made him weep again.

The newlyweds broke away from the throng of guests to stride toward them. Bride and groom moved like one entity, a new being created from their bond, and when they reached Finn and Tabitha, their happiness was palpable like unseen sunlight.

"Felicitations," Tabitha said warmly.

"Well done," Finn added, gruff with emotion.

His brother would have no formality, and pulled Finn into a quick, hard embrace.

"The same boy who wrote childish poems in praise of toasted cheese is a husband," Finn said, voice thick as he thumped Kieran's back.

"I still love toasted cheese," Kieran answered, his own words suspiciously rough. "But I love Celeste more."

"What bride could ask for a greater tribute?" Finn chuckled.

"Given how much he loves toasted cheese," Celeste

said with twinkling eyes, "there isn't anything else I want. Though," she added as she looked toward a corner of the room, where Dom stood alone with a glass of sparkling wine, "if I could test my fortune by asking for something else on my wedding day, seeing my brother happy again would be my next wish."

Finn's heart sank to see Dom so melancholy. This was no time for anyone to be solitary.

He waved Dom over, and after his friend drank down his wine in one swallow, he lumbered toward them.

Dom looked as though he was trying to appear happy for the bride and groom, but there was a grim cast to his mouth when he came to join their group.

"I'm glad for you, Star," Dom said, pressing a kiss to Celeste's cheek. Glancing at Kieran, he added, "You don't deserve her, and if you do *anything* to make her unhappy, I'll revive the custom of drawing and quartering, only I'll do it with my bare hands."

Kieran grimaced but nodded. "No need for threats, ogre. Making my bride happy is to be my sole task for the rest of my life."

Dom gave a clipped nod, though a corner of his mouth lifted as if he was pleased by Kieran's vow. He glanced back and forth between Kieran and Celeste, and Finn and Tabitha.

"And then there was one," Dom said lowly.

Finn and Kieran shared a look. As they had often done since they were boys together, a wordless communication passed between them, one in which they were both in agreement. They wouldn't force Dom into marrying anyone.

"You two and your damned silent conversations,"

Dom grumbled. "Scheming to drag me to the altar. Know this: it won't happen."

"We're aware of that," Finn replied.

Dom looked back and forth between them. "Ain't you planning on how to get me leg-shackled so everyone gets their blunt?"

"Why would we," Kieran said, shaking his head, "when it's evident you'll have Willa or no one?"

Expression grim, Dom waved a servant over and took another glass of wine, which he downed quickly.

"We did you both wrong," Finn added. Regret was sour in his mouth and stomach.

Dom's lips twisted into a grim half smile. "You spared her a miserable fate, chained to a wretched boor like me for the rest of her life. She might've been angry with you, might *still* be angry, but she'll see in time that her brothers saved her from making a horrendous mistake. And someday," he added on a rasp, "she'll find someone better, someone who deserves her. I'll be the first to offer my felicitations."

The bleakness in his friend's face was a cold, cutting blade in Finn's chest. Tabitha gave his hand a sympathetic squeeze.

"And what of you?" Finn asked.

"Me?" Dom's massive shoulders lifted in a shrug. "I'll get what *I* deserve, which is a lifetime of being lonesome. I'm sorry about the blunt, though."

"Who gives a rat's arse about the money?" Finn said hotly, and Kieran nodded. "Allowances are nothing compared to your happiness."

Dom's brow creased heavily, and he appeared a man bereft. Finn and Kieran started forward to offer their friend some kind of solace, but he held up a hand, and they remained where they were.

"Forgive me," Dom said ruefully. "This is a joyous day, and I won't taint it with my self-pity. Blessings on you both."

He gave one abbreviated nod before weaving through the crowd with surprising dexterity for one so large.

Everyone in the group of four fell silent. There was no way to undo the past, but perhaps there was some way of remedying the wrongs that had been done.

"I think you're being summoned for more toasts to your health and good fortune," Tabitha said after a moment. She nodded toward a group of well-wishers who were motioning for Celeste and Kieran to join them.

"I'm never going to decline an opportunity to drink someone else's wine," Kieran said before adding with a wide smile for Celeste, "And celebrate my bride, of course."

"Of course," she said with a laugh.

Together, the newly married couple headed toward the celebrants. Finn shared a smile with Tabitha to see his brother and wife so joyous.

His pleasure guttered like a candle flame when, at the conclusion to the toasts, his father headed straight toward him. Finn looked quickly around the room, assessing if he and Tabitha could slip away before the earl reached them. Thus far, he'd done a decent job of keeping her apart from his parents. Hopefully, he could continue to separate them . . . preferably for eternity.

Except the parlor was thick with guests and well-wishers, blocking off any exit routes.

Damn.

The earl drew up in front of him and gave Finn

his typical up-and-down scan, assessing his middle son from the top of his head to the toes of his boots. Finn kept his back straight, his gaze level. He'd done this too many times to show any reaction, which was precisely what his father fed upon.

Yet he couldn't stop himself from gripping Tabitha's hand tighter. She glanced attentively between him and his father.

"A lovely ceremony," she said to fill in the now awkward silence. "The bride and groom are radiant with happiness."

The earl flicked a look over his shoulder toward where Kieran and Celeste were accepting congratulations from the guests. "He met the conditions," his father finally said. "A rare thing for him to meet expectations."

"We both have," Finn couldn't stop himself from pointing out.

"Suppose you have," the earl allowed. "Yet no one gets a farthing until that common friend of yours weds. You'd better see to that, my boy."

Despite his anger at his father's habitually dismissive tone, Finn clamped his lips together. This was a battle he'd never be able to win, and he certainly didn't want to wage it in front of his wife.

"I've every faith in Finn's abilities to accomplish whatever he sets out to do," Tabitha said insistently. "He's a born strategist. I am a member of the Benezra Library and have met many remarkable scholars, and I can say with conviction that minds like his are rare, indeed."

Before Finn could draw any pleasure from her words, his father's expression turned acidic and wry. It was like standing on the shore, watching a ship slowly sink, and being unable to do anything to save the crew or the vessel.

"We cannot be thinking of the same individual, madam," the earl said dryly.

Finn's gut clenched. *Please, no. Don't say another word, old man.*

"Finn Ransome," she answered. "Your second son."

"The only person I know who meets that description barely made it through Eton and only on the good grace of my deep coffers," his father said with a smirk. "You will never find him at your library, that's certain, or associating with its remarkable scholars."

Finn didn't blink, didn't wince or flinch or any of the dozens of responses he'd trained himself not to do over the course of his nine and twenty years. He merely kept a pleasant smile tacked in place as he watched his parent demean him to his bride. He waited for Tabitha to grimace or look at him with disappointment.

"The beauty of marriage," she replied coolly, "is that our spouse is liberated from the burden of being everything to us. They can be our companion and friend, and yet we may rely on others to meet our different needs. Certainly, *family* has its shortcomings."

The earl gaped at her, while Tabitha only stared back.

As for Finn, it was all he could do to keep from sweeping Tabitha into his arms and kissing her in front of the entire wedding breakfast. In an instant, he'd gone from abject misery to the heights of joy.

Except—now she knew the truth about him and his intellectual shortcomings. Thanks to his own father.

"My dear," Tabitha said, turning to him, "the atmosphere is rather close in here. I require some air."

"Permit me." He offered her his arm.

She took it, and they strode from the chamber. He took her along the corridor, and then up, up, up the stairs, until, at last they reached a narrow room, occupied by four small desks, with an adult-sized desk positioned in front of them.

Finn started. He hadn't realized where he was going until they stood within his childhood schoolroom—the site of so much of his youthful misery. It made sense, bringing her here, to see her confront the truth of who he truly was. As though this room bracketed his wretchedness.

He dragged in a breath and then another, the scent of wood and old paper bringing him back to the years where his tutor, Mr. Bowles, made his life a living hell.

Finn tried to speak, but memories came thick and fast—Bowles refusing to let Finn eat until he'd read an entire chapter of a primer aloud, Bowles swatting him across the back of his head when he stumbled over words, and the worst, Bowles describing in great detail to Finn's scowling father that his middle son was and would always be an utter dunce—and his voice failed him.

"They never see us for who we truly are," she murmured in the quiet. "We're always children to them, and even then, it's who they believe us to be rather than our genuine selves."

He exhaled, but the tightness in his chest didn't loosen. Stepping away from her, he walked to the tutor's desk and stared at it. The view was too familiar. He'd stared at that wooden surface many times, counting the small scrapes and gouges, as Bowles caned him for his *laziness and willful refusal to apply yourself.*

"My father's correct," he finally ground out.

"Many people struggle with reading, Finn," she said gently.

Years of hiding his responses kept him from starting at her understanding. And yet he was shaken to the core. Turning to face her, he asked, "When did you suspect?"

"Small signs here and there," she said, her words careful as she slowly approached him. "You didn't want to read Mr. Smythe's book at the fair, and when we were preparing for meeting the Sterling Society. It's nothing to be ashamed of."

"I was, though, for years," he said, lowly. "I think, in many ways, I still am. It took me so much longer to read something than my siblings, and then later at school. And when I take up my quill, well, it becomes obvious that my approach to the written word is . . . well . . . troubled." Jaw tight, he admitted, "They called me so many names, my parents, and teachers. *Lazy, stupid, dolt.*"

"You're none of those things," she said fiercely.

Much as he longed to believe her, there was still so much fear and doubt within, as though underworld creatures lurked at the back of a cave. They lived here, in this room, haunted by the boy that was Finn.

The boy that still dwelled within him.

His shoulders moved up and down in a stiff shrug. "Only Kieran and Willa believed that I was just as capable, just as intelligent. They told me I was worthwhile when others wanted me to hate myself. As my father said, only my family's copious amounts

of money enabled me to finish Eton, but it was decided that university would merely be a waste. I was
so relieved, I wept."

She came toward him, cautiously, as one might approach a trapped wolf. But then she reached out for
him, threading her fingers with his.

Hope . . . tentative hope began to shine light on
those fears, pushing them back into the shadows. Yet
uncertainty held fast.

"It was purely by chance that I discovered my skill
at gambling," he continued.

"There are odds to calculate," she said in a matter-
of-fact tone, "and strategies to employ. I remember
everything you told me at the gaming hell. It's no
surprise you'd excel at gambling. But, Finn, I've
heard you say the most terrible things about yourself,
and they aren't true."

The knots around his chest eased, only slightly.
"Habitual, I suppose. Demean myself before anyone
else can, and rob their insults of power."

"Your armor does more damage than the weapon
it's intended to protect you from," she said sadly.

"Now you know." His words were heavy and final, and he couldn't look directly at her. Instead, he
focused on the motes of dust clinging to the high
window. "I'd understand if you're disappointed that
the man you married takes an hour to read a single
page of text. If you'd rather . . . live apart."

She stepped closer, moving so that he had no choice
but to look into her eyes.

"Finn Ransome," she said, her brow furrowed, "do
you think so little of me that you'd believe I would
walk away on the basis of *that*?"

"You know Miss Goldstein and Miss Kemble from

being members of a *library*." It hurt to speak, but there came a time when you had to show your cards. He didn't know if he could survive her rejection—if he did, he'd bear the scars of it for the remainder of his days.

"My God, Finn." Her throat worked, and her eyes were bright as though tears gathered there. "The *pain* they've caused you."

He ducked his head, overwhelmed by the understanding in her gaze. He'd never let anyone know how much hurt he'd survived, or how its malignancy could seep in at any given moment, reminding him of those long-ago days where he'd fought tears as the beaks at Eton had forced him to read aloud in front of the whole class, or when his father would make him stand in front of his desk and receive a blistering lecture about how he was a blight to the family name.

Either you're obstinately lackadaisical, or else you're a simpleton, the earl had snapped. *Neither prospect reflects well on the Ransomes, the title, or me.*

"Hear me, Finn." She stood in front of him and bent down slightly to peer into his downcast face. "I am *proud* to be your wife, and anyone who dares suggest to me that you're somehow less than me for any reason at all, I will . . . I will . . . well, I don't have much physical strength, but I will give them an extremely articulate and multipronged argument as to why they're no better than a clump of fungi clinging to the underside of a decaying log."

The heavy gates within him opened. It was a wonder the small schoolroom wasn't filled with the groan of their rusty hinges. Yet it felt like an unbolting, like a new beginning, with a much larger world opening up to him, one where he might not ever be completely liberated from the pain of his past, but his steps through that world would be much wider and freer—especially with Tabitha beside him.

She knew everything about him now, and she was still here. She hadn't turned away or sneered or rejected him, and *that*, that was miraculous.

A chuckle resounded from deep in his chest. "I would very much enjoy seeing you call the earl a toadstool."

"Given my poor tolerance for spirits, if you give me enough negus, I will likely do just that."

He looked around the schoolroom, and it was just a room now, narrow and dusty—with all its shadowed corners illuminated by her light.

"Thank you," he said gruffly. "I . . . ah . . . I haven't much familiarity with being defended."

"What a brutal place this world is, especially to the young."

She cupped his face, and he pressed a kiss into her palm, grateful to his core that he'd had the foolish but ultimately wonderful idea of trying to match her with Dom, and that Dom had been unable to properly court her. Against all odds, Finn himself had managed to win his own wife.

Chapter 21

❦ ✳ ❧

When they had returned from the wedding breakfast, he'd taken her straight to bed, heedless of the fact that it was the middle of the afternoon and traffic on the street could plainly be heard in their bedroom. She had no cause for complaint, however, not when he'd been so thorough with his mouth and hands and . . . cock.

Oh, dear—her language had grown quite direct and colorful as of late. Especially when it came to the marital bed. Or the marital table. Or marital chaise.

"Is the studious Mrs. Tabitha Ransome giggling?" he asked, stroking down the length of her unbound hair. It spilled across his chest and she loved to see the contrast of her brown tresses amongst the black hair curling like calligraphy on his pectorals.

"My vocabulary has become decidedly more Anglo-Saxon in the last few months," she said as she looked up into his face. His dark eyes were heavy-lidded with drowsy satiation. And no wonder. He was a very vigorous lover. Again, no complaints.

"That's true," he answered. "I seem to recall you demanding, *Fuck me, Finn*, not thirty minutes ago."

She playfully tapped a finger on his nose in remonstrance. "A gentleman would never remind a lady of such breaches of etiquette."

"Good thing that though we may be of genteel birth, we're both intent on demolishing that world."

She lifted up to look him more fully in the face. The last traces of afternoon light filtered in through the curtains, gilding him with the setting sun's final rays. Her breath caught at the sight of her husband—it didn't seem to matter how many times she beheld his inhumanly handsome face, she would always be awestruck by him.

But it was his *heart*, far more than his face or form, that was most beautiful, and that's what made her melt inside whenever she saw or thought of him.

"I've an idea that could be like a cannon to the walls protecting that world," she admitted.

Wrapping his arms more securely around her, he sat up, bringing her with him. "To say I'm intrigued would be a vast understatement. What do you have in mind, love?"

"The Sterling Society slammed their doors in my face," she said intently. "But that doesn't mean I have no other means of pursuing a cause that means so much to me."

"Tell me more," he urged.

"The Platinum Collective," she answered, barely able to suppress her excitement. At his intrigued look, she explained, "An intellectual society comprised of whomever wants to join—no barriers to membership. We'll meet and discuss all the relevant and important subjects of the day, or explore issues that have not yet been brought to the public eye. We'll talk of matters that relate to women, to all races, to those who aren't wealthy and powerful. And then we'll collect our thoughts and findings and present them to policy makers who can and will create real change."

Her hands on his chest faintly shook with her eagerness, yet what would he think of her idea?

She lost her breath when he leaned down and kissed her deeply.

"Love," he said when they finally drew back from the kiss, "that is an *excellent* notion."

"Joining the Sterling Society was a lofty and challenging goal," she said, uncertain, "but founding my *own* organization is a vast ambition, a wager that's anything but certain."

His smile flashed, making her heart stutter. "The odds are steep, but that makes the win all the greater. And I will be your backer, through every step."

"Oh, Finn." She kissed him again, pouring all her adoration into the press of their lips. Her body heated at once at the feel of him passionately responding, yet she would have to set her desire aside for a moment. Pulling her mouth from his, she said, "There's so much to do. Plans that must be made."

"Fortunately," he answered, "we have two of Britain's finest minds on the case."

She warmed to hear him speak so positively of himself, so different from his old self-denigrating stance. Maybe she had some hand in his transformation, yet the true credit belonged to him, in facing his past and moving forward so bravely.

"Tomorrow," he went on, caressing her back, "we'll look for a headquarters for the Platinum Collective. I've more than enough blunt to cover the cost of rent for several years."

"We'll *both* be responsible for that expense," she insisted. "I've some money of my own, and if this is to be the realization of my dreams, I need to have a hand in its creation."

She half expected him to object, but he nodded. "Understandable. And until a suitable location is found, your collective can meet here. Granted, it might be a touch cramped in our snug parlor, but it's a beginning."

She grazed her fingers across his jaw and felt the delicious prickle of his stubble. Gratitude wrapped around her, enfolding her as strongly as his embrace. "You're a wonder, you know."

He wrapped his hand around her fingers and kissed the tips. "It's not so difficult when one has an excellent model."

THEY TOURED SEVERAL potential locations the following day. Finn was exceptional in helping to coordinate all the efforts needed to establish the Platinum Collective, including finding an estate agent who understood the organization's particular needs.

Mr. Tahiri, the estate agent, showed them several properties, and she found the perfect one near Covent Garden. By five that afternoon, she held the one-year lease to the Platinum Collective's headquarters. A celebratory dinner was held at their home, with Diana, Iris, Arjun, and Chima ringed around the table, toasting to the future of the enterprise.

It was determined that they'd all canvass neighborhoods like Spitalfields and Cheapside to find new members for their group. Finn would continue to lend his support by attending to the organization's financials and other logistical elements.

That night, as she sat at her vanity table and brushed out her hair, she said to his reflection in the mirror, "I don't want the Platinum Collective to take you away from your own work. There's surely much to be done in establishing a gambling hell."

"A fascinating thing." He stood behind her and gently took the brush from her hand before running it slowly through her tresses. She purred at the sensation. "The more I heard you talk about your goals for the collective, the more I began to realize that what London *doesn't* need is another place for its citizens to squander their blunt. But what the city *does* require—hell, the whole nation—is the Platinum Collective. Yet an enterprise of that scale requires considerable administration."

His hand stilled, and he met her gaze in the glass, eyes deep and sincere. "If you'll agree to it, I'd like to offer my services as the collective's financial manager."

"Oh, Finn." She spun in her seat and stood to wrap her arms around him. "It would be a blessing to have you be a part of it."

"Are you certain?" He looked at her intently, clasping his hands low on her back. "This is very meaningful to you, and I don't want to barrel my way into it like a bully."

"You're the furthest thing from a bully," she quickly assured him. "Yet I don't want you to regret giving up something important, something for *you*."

"This *is* for me," he answered with a smile. "I'd love nothing more than to shatter the walls protecting the aristocracy, and this way, I won't go for their coffers, but their consciences. If you'll have me."

In answer, she pressed her lips to his. They didn't speak again for a very long time.

Later, resting in his arms, she could hardly believe her good fortune. Her friends, her husband, all of them believed that this mad scheme of hers might work. With their support, and her own determination, the possibility that they were right gleamed before her.

IT TOOK A full fortnight before the Platinum Collective had its first meeting. Between furnishing the headquarters, traversing the entirety of London in search of members, stocking the research library (with Chima's expert guidance), and the dozens of other tasks involved in the formation of a new intellectual society, those two weeks were the busiest but most satisfying of Tabitha's life.

Meanwhile, Finn was working closely with his man of business, Mr. Mendoza, to ensure the efficient financial running of the collective. They were both up at dawn and collapsed into bed just after midnight, awakening and falling asleep wrapped in each other's arms. No longer was she compelled to desert their bed in the middle of the night. She found all the comfort and security she needed in his embrace.

He was in all ways extraordinary through the process. With his thorough understanding of money and odds, he managed the majority of the Platinum Collective's financial matters—though always consulting with her before making any decisions. He accompanied her on many forays through the city as they gathered keen minds eager to have their voices heard. At times, she would be completely immersed in the business of forming the organization and forget to eat, yet he always appeared in her library with a tray of hot nourishing food that could be consumed quickly before she resumed her labors.

It was late one night, shortly before the Platinum Collective's first gathering, when she sat hunched at her desk, formulating an egalitarian but organized system for running meetings. Her back ached and her eyes burned, and when she stretched her arms overhead, she groaned from the stiffness in her muscles.

"I've precisely the remedy for that," Finn said, leaning in the doorway. He'd taken off his coat and waistcoat, and had rolled up his shirtsleeves to reveal the corded muscles of his forearms. He crossed one booted ankle over the other.

Even through her bleary vision, she could recognize how delicious her husband looked.

"Does it involve ingesting large quantities of whisky?" she asked. "Because while it might be a temporary cure, my head in the morning wouldn't appreciate the tonic."

"What I'm proposing will cause no megrims." He uncoiled from the doorway and prowled toward her, offering her his hand. "Come, madam, or I'll be forced to throw you over my shoulder in a most wild and indecorous manner."

"I wouldn't precisely mind . . ." As active and fulfilling as the past few weeks had been, there had been one highly unpleasant secondary effect. She and Finn had barely made love, both of them either too busy or too weary to give their time in bed the full attention it deserved.

A slow, wicked smile curved his lips. "All in good

time. Now it's time to quit your desk for more soothing environs."

"Will you tell me exactly what I'm heading toward?" she asked as she stood and took his hand.

"And deny myself the pleasure of surprising you?" He shook his head. "A few moments, and all will be revealed."

Smiling, she let him lead her out of the library and up the stairs. As they approached their bedroom, she said wryly, "Taking me to bed requires no subterfuge. I'll go willingly."

His gaze was heavy-lidded and hot, but he said, "One thing at a time, love."

"I—Oh." Her droll reply died when she reached the bedchamber and saw what awaited her.

All light in the room had been banked, save for the blaze burning in the fireplace. It cast flickering golden illumination on the bathing tub, which had been set up in the middle of the chamber, and gilded the steaming water that filled the bath. Herbs floated on the water and filled the air with woodsy fragrance. Beside the tub was a small table, and perched on that table was a mug filled with a hot drink, with two iced biscuits arranged on a little painted china plate.

"Finn—it's wonderful," she murmured as he drew her deeper into the bedchamber.

Her husband looked pleased, yet said, "And it will not wait a moment longer. Now, let's strip you posthaste. No need to summon Olive. I'll happily perform the task."

She obligingly presented him with her back when he made a spinning motion with his fingers. He was brisk and efficient in removing her garments, though she shivered when he pressed kisses down the length of her revealed spine.

He pulled away with a muttered curse. "Can't let myself get distracted."

"Distract yourself," she urged. His smallest touches could set her aflame, and she blazed after the days and nights that they hadn't made love.

Yet he stayed maddeningly on task. In short order, she was nude, but the warmth of the fire kept her from being chilled. His heated eyes were far more warming as he gazed at her bare body.

"Into the tub with you, baggage," he ordered her.

Her nipples tightened into points at the imperious tone of his words, as if he'd brook no argument.

What else might he order her to do? Would she comply, or would she make him battle for domination?

"I'd no idea you were so . . . commanding."

"There are many sides to me, love," he said huskily, "just as there are layers to you. We'll explore them all, but first, there is the bather and the one being bathed." He unwrapped a bar of soap, and the scent of honey uncurled seductively. "In you go."

"I can bathe myself," she felt obligated to protest.

"Your ability in that task isn't in question," he returned, motioning toward the filled tub, "yet grant me the pleasure in attending to you."

Her stomach clenched in eagerness. "See how obliging I am."

She lowered into the tub, and as the hot water surrounded her with its herbal fragrance, her muscles began to slowly unknot in gradual waves. As she sank down, the heat permeated her body, reaching deep into where she ached with exhaustion. Peering into the mug beside the tub, she noted that it was filled with chocolate. She took a sip and hummed in appreciation before nibbling on the iced biscuits.

Finn had truly provided everything.

He knelt beside the bathing vessel and pushed his sleeves up even higher. His smile was rich and intoxicating, making her dizzy.

"I'll never get tired of seeing you on your knees for me," she teased.

"Isn't that the usual way of worshipping goddesses?" He took the cake of soap and dipped it into the water before working up a lather between his large, dexterous hands. More honey scent swirled around her.

"Me? A goddess?" She made an undignified sound. "There isn't much call for goddesses with their noses buried in books."

"There's always a need for wise celestial women," he countered. After setting aside the soap, he ran his lathered hands along her arms, kneading her as he went.

She groaned and closed her eyes at the wonderful sensations of his large hands on her, releasing the knots in her muscles.

"And," he added in a husky voice, "there's so much more to you than books. You're curious and open and you've got a warrior's heart. Yes—you're another Athena. Gray-eyed warrior goddess of wisdom."

"Only this Athena isn't chaste," she reminded him.

"Thank Olympus for that." He nipped at her neck, summoning her desire with each bite. To her regret, he pulled away and resumed bathing her.

His strokes along her skin were long and sleek and expert, and soon, she was boneless, draped against the back of the tub as she was inundated with the alchemy of relaxation and arousal. Wordlessly, he urged her to lean forward slightly, and when she did, he kneaded her back, his touch the faultless blend of firm but gentle.

All the while, having him touch her again licked fire through her, heating between her legs and making her breasts heavy.

"You make a perfect bathing attendant," she said on a sigh.

"I live to serve," he answered.

"Are you certain it's only selflessness that motivates you?" She cracked open her eyes to see the thick ridge of his cock taut against the front of his breeches. Her hands twitched with the need to feel him, to test the limits of his self-control as she stroked him to madness.

"No one is ever completely altruistic. For example," he said throatily as he glided his hands around her torso to caress her slick breasts, "this is definitely for me."

A long, low moan escaped her as he molded his hands around her, and she cried out in pleasure when he lightly pinched her nipples. She arched up, offering more of herself to him.

"Definitely not chaste." Despite his teasing words, husky need thickened his voice.

As he fondled her breasts, he slid one hand down her torso, going lower over the roundness of her belly, and lower still, through the hair curling over her mound. Aching with the need for more, she opened her legs as wide as the tub could accommodate.

"She demands a tribute, this goddess," Finn rumbled.

In response, she angled her hips up, urging his hand closer to where she needed him most.

He seemed to understand her silent demand. Leaning down, he bit her neck again, holding her in place as his fingers slipped between the folds of her quim. She let out another cry as he traced her lips. He circled her entrance while his thumb rubbed in glorious circles around her clitoris.

Pleasure gathered in hot, drugging surges, and she spun into it, losing herself to everything but the feel of him. Yet she continued to ache and pushed herself against his hand.

"You want more," he growled approvingly.

"Finn, please," she heard herself beg.

"I'll take care of you, sweet." His breath was jagged and fast on her neck, and she loved that he was just as affected by pleasuring her as she was to be pleasured.

She moaned when he thrust two fingers into her.

"Ah, there she is," he said, his words both rough and honeyed. He stroked into her, setting her alight as he found the place inside her that made stars bloom behind her eyes. "Right there. Just how you want it. Isn't that right, goddess?"

When she didn't answer, too lost in sensation, his hand stilled. She made a whine of protest.

"Answer me," he demanded. "Isn't this how you love it? Me fucking you with my hand."

"Yes—I love it," she gasped, gracelessly shoving herself into him. "I love it when you fuck me. But don't stop."

He thrust into her again, forceful and commanding, and she arched up as ecstasy gathered like a storm. "I'll give you everything, love."

He was relentless as he plunged in and out of her, working her without compromise. She had to grip the sides of the tub to keep herself upright, and it gave her the stability she needed to grind her hips down on him, abandoning herself to him.

Release crashed into her mercilessly. A sound escaped her, unrestrained, as he fucked her through her climax and then another and one more. She was buffeted by pleasure. Only when she fell back limply did he finally yield, sliding his fingers out of her.

It was impossible to want more. Yet when he licked his fingers clean of her lingering taste, he growled his pleasure, and a rush of need swelled to life.

"If I *am* a goddess, I insist on another offering." She reached out and cupped his firm cock through the fabric of his breeches.

"Anything. All of it." His expression turned fierce, and he held the back of her head to angle her for a deep, ravenous kiss. As his tongue stroked against hers, hunger tore through her. She clung to the front of his shirt, the fabric bunching under her palms, his body taut beneath.

Water from her soaked into the cambric of his shirt until it was plastered to his torso. The translucent fabric clung to his planes and ridges.

"I'm getting you wet," she murmured dazedly.

"Don't fucking care," he snarled. With spectacular ease he pulled her to standing, and then scooped her up into his arms. He truly was heedless of the water streaming off of her body as he carried her to the bed.

He set her down on her feet, and with delectable authority, he turned her around and planted her hands atop the counterpane. Her face flamed at her lewd position, bared so primally to him. She chanced a look over her shoulder and all sense of propriety liquified . . .

He'd pulled off his shirt and opened his breeches. His cock was in his hand as he stared at her with fierce desire. He stroked himself with a punishing grip, and the sight of Finn pleasuring himself whilst looking ravenously at her made her slick and needy.

"Finn," she urged, arching her back so that she displayed herself more fully.

His gaze was fastened to her quim and he growled when a trickle of her arousal slid down the inside of her thigh.

"You need my cock to fill you up," he said, guttural. He stepped close, snugging his hips to her. "Isn't that so?" He stroked the head of his cock through her soaked lips, teasing at her entrance but not delving inside. "It's *my* cock this wise goddess needs."

"Give it to me," she moaned. "Please please please—"

All words, all breath, all thought vanished as he plunged into her with one thick, powerful thrust. She gasped at being so completely full. With each of his exquisitely forceful strokes, she grew more and more wild, losing all control of herself.

One of his hands gripped her hip, hard enough that he would leave marks, but the idea enflamed her beyond reason. He brought the other around to massage her clitoris in time with his surges into her.

She came again, so loud her throat ached with the force of her cry. He continued to pound into her, until he shuddered and snarled from his own climax. Gasping, he curved his body over hers, as if sheltering them both from the tempest of their need for each other.

They both panted in the aftermath. She gave a small, pleasured shiver when he nuzzled between her shoulder blades and kissed her slick skin. Slowly, incrementally, he slid from her body.

"Did I defile you too terribly, goddess?" he asked huskily.

"In this case," she managed to answer as she turned to wrap her arms around him, "worship and defilement are the same thing."

He cupped his hands on her hips to bring their steaming bodies close. The adoration in his eyes stole her breath—there would never come a time when she wouldn't love seeing how he looked at her. And her own heart surely shone in her eyes, because he dipped his head to kiss her in long, lingering tastes.

They finally drew apart before he guided her to the bed. Still throbbing with a combination of satiation and happiness, she climbed in and settled beneath the sheets, which felt cool and crisp around her.

He drew the counterpane over her, before going around to his side of the bed and sliding in beside her. As he pulled her close, he murmured, "Even deities need their sleep if they're to remake the world."

She was replete, full beyond measure of emotions so vast and all-encompassing, she felt herself stepping into a realm she'd never truly experienced before.

She loved him.

There was no sure way to know when it happened, only that it had, by gradual degrees until she didn't quite understand what it was to *not* love Finn. His smile made her smile, his thoughts brought her joy, and his pain reverberated within her as if it was her own. The moments they were together brought her a kind of happiness that she hadn't known before. It was as if she'd discovered she could conjure moonlight with a wave of her hands, a new magic that had been waiting for just the right moment, just the right person, to be unlocked.

She was in love with her husband.

Her breath caught at the realization.

"Sweet?" he asked drowsily behind her.

Only then did she realize that she'd actually gasped aloud.

"Oh, I only remembered something that I need to do in the morning," she said, wincing at the banality of her answer. "It's of little consequence."

She had thought herself in love with Charles, but that was a wan and pallid hue compared to the burst of vivid color of her feelings for Finn. And God, how she longed to tell him and lay bare the whole of her heart.

Yet words continued to echo, as loud now as they had been eight years ago. *Whatever you are experiencing, it's merely an illusion, created by your own feverish expectations. Perhaps if you'd learned to temper your emotions, there might have been a chance for us. As it is, I feel only pity for you.*

Finn wasn't Charles. She *knew* he cared for her, and yet, what if Finn didn't love her back? She wouldn't be able to endure that, and her unreciprocated love would sit between them, like a piece of meat carved from the bone, growing cold.

Chapter 22

❧ ✳ ❧

For the next two days, Finn felt drunk—in the best possible way.

Tabitha slept every night in his arms, never leaving the bed to hide in the library. She trusted him with helping to create the Platinum Collective. She was unguarded and affectionate with him.

It was simply too good to be real, and part of him dreaded the moment when it all went away. Surely it had to disappear, because he didn't deserve her, and he alternated between moments of unmitigated joy and naked terror, waiting for everything to vanish.

Now he and Tabitha stood outside the Platinum Collective's headquarters, which was a plain-looking structure on a row of similar buildings. Simple coverings hung in the windows, but the distinguishing feature was the painted sign beside the front door. Having seen it many times, he already knew what it read, but pride still surged to see the bright gold words on a blue background shining in the afternoon light.

Platinum Collective
All are welcome

The door opened, and Miss Goldstein poked her head out.

"Tabby," she said, "we're ready to begin."

Voices came from behind Miss Goldstein, a lively discussion already taking place.

Tabitha shot him an apprehensive glance—and in response, he pressed a kiss to her cheek.

"It's going to be a triumph," he assured her.

She gave him a quick smile, then inhaled and tipped up her chin as she stepped inside. He followed in her wake, hoping she could feel the waves of admiration emanating from him to bolster her.

Miss Goldstein trailed after them, explaining, "Our recruiting efforts were phenomenally successful. We were aided in our efforts by William Rowe, the political writer."

"Is he here?" Tabitha asked excitedly.

Finn was unfamiliar with this Rowe, but, judging by Tabitha's reaction, he was a person of considerable significance.

"Having a very intense conversation with Arjun," Miss Goldstein said with a chuckle. "But you can see that for yourself."

They all walked toward the back of the house. A few of the walls were freshly plastered, and there was sawdust upon the floor, but they had been busy enlarging the rooms to accommodate everyone.

And everyone, it seemed, was there. They stepped into a large room that faced the narrow backyard, and Finn's throat thickened as he beheld the scene.

People filled the chamber, of all genders, and many races. Some were dressed finely, but many wore the serviceable garments of laborers, clerks, and tradespeople. Some sat on chairs, others on crates, and some on the floor—more furniture was clearly needed—while others stood as they were engaged in intense conversation. Mr. Okafor, Mr. Singh, and Miss Kemble were familiar faces, but he didn't know anyone else. He suspected, however, that the angular man talking to Mr. Singh was in fact the celebrated Rowe.

Tabitha's face was radiant, magnifying his own joy. She'd done it. She had truly made her ambition come to pass.

A shrewd-eyed blonde woman appeared, and she nodded her greeting to Finn and Tabitha. "I'm Eleanor Balfour, the owner and editor in chief of the *Hawk's Eye*."

"Lady Ashford?" Tabitha asked, looking slightly stunned.

The other woman waved her hand dismissively. "I always forget I'm supposed to call myself that, but yes, I am the Countess of Ashford."

"Thank you for coming, my lady," Tabitha said as she curtseyed and Finn bowed. "I hope you will be unbiased, should you choose to write about the Platinum Collective."

Lady Ashford gave Tabitha a look of respect. "That is assured, Mrs. Ransome."

After the countess moved on to try to locate some seating, Tabitha shot Finn another look of concern. "The stakes just got higher."

"True enough, but I'll take that wager."

"Going into a gamble blind?" she asked, arching a brow.

"Oh, no, love," Finn said with confidence, "the game has already begun, and if ever a wagering man could be certain of an outcome, I'm certain of *this*. Now," he added, nodding toward the packed room, "are we ready?"

After taking a deep breath, she drew up tall and straight. "It's time for everyone to be heard."

THE FOLLOWING AFTERNOON, after the delivery of the latest edition of the *Hawk's Eye,* Finn took Tabitha to Catton's bake shop so they might read the paper's account of the Platinum Collective's first meeting. Finn's rationale was that either Lady Ashford had positive things to say about their group, in which case a celebration would be in order. Or, if her comments were negative, there would be an abundance of cake for consolation.

They took a seat toward the back of the shop so there would be fewer ears that might overhear their conversation.

Hands faintly shaking with trepidation, Tabitha picked up the paper and read aloud.

"'*Whilst the Platinum Collective is an extremely young organization, with the usual complement of growing pains that such youth would engender, it is the opinion of this periodical that if it adheres to its principles and maintains its clarity of purpose, very soon the Platinum Collective will be one of the most significant and prominent societies of its kind in London—indeed, in the whole of the nation—which it duly deserves.*'"

Tabitha flashed an exultant smile at Finn, and he grinned in response, his heart tumbling like an acrobat in his chest to witness her triumph.

"Can't ask for a better critique," he said, jubilant.

"There's more," she added. "Perhaps my favorite part. *'It is also the opinion of this periodical that it is high time for the formation and influence of progressive institutions that better reflect the varied mosaic of Britain, unlike the S—S—intellectual association, they of stale mind and staler methodology who have too long held sway over the state's policy makers.'*"

Finn let out a low whistle. "Bloody hell. Lady Ashford went straight for the Sterling Society's bollocks."

Tabitha meticulously folded the newspaper and set it beside her plate, smoothing her hand over the printed sheets with deliberate care. Despite her measured movements, her lips went up, as if she could barely contain her happiness.

"I know that I'm not supposed to be pleased about that," she said with resolute calm. "*'Rejoice not when thine enemy falleth, and let not thine heart be glad when he stumbleth,'* but . . ." Her eyes were bright as she gazed at Finn across the table of iced cakes.

"The hell with the Sterling Society," he finished for her.

A tiny laugh escaped her, but she clamped her lips together, holding it back. "What I *need* to focus on is our next meeting, and if we can reach members of Parliament before the education bill is voted on."

"Taking a moment to savor your victory and those buffoons' defeat is allowed, love." He picked up a cake with a white sugary glaze, adorned with a pale yellow icing flower and set it on her plate. "Devour this as if you were eating Marcroft's pompous, over-privileged heart."

She made a shocked noise. "Finn Ransome, you are positively mythological in your pursuit of vengeance."

"When it comes to destroying my wife's enemies," he replied intently, "I'm happy to shock the gods."

After eyeing the cake for a moment, she lifted it to her lips, and then stuffed it into her mouth to chew it with vicious pleasure.

A matron at a nearby table looked on with horror at Tabitha's uncouth display. The older woman gave an appalled huff before rising and quitting the bake shop.

Finn and Tabitha shared a look before dissolving into laughter. Something brilliant and joyous took flight in his chest. She still hadn't said that she loved him, yet he counted himself the luckiest son of a bitch in London, if not the world. They were equal partners in their marriage, advocates for each other, and energetically passionate in the bedroom. Truly, he couldn't imagine that his life could get any better.

Words hovered on his lips, words he longed to speak.

I love you.

The truth of them resonated through him like music. Though he and Tabitha had entered into this marriage for the sake of expediency, he'd done what he had thought himself incapable of doing. He'd fallen in love with his own wife.

The urge to tell her blazed as bright as a fire. And yet, he couldn't say it aloud, no matter how his heart brimmed with adoration for her. She cared for him—that was certain—but the prospect of finally uttering the most important words in the world filled him with uncertainty. What if he spoke them, and she couldn't answer in return? Shouldn't he be happy with what she *had* given him?

So many risks, so much potential disaster.

He could gamble thousands of pounds on a single game, but wagering his heart . . . that was where courage failed him.

Chapter 23

❖ ✳ ❖

They sat at the table in the breakfast room the following morning, sunlight pouring in through the opened curtains and gilding the cutlery and beverage service so that the chamber felt touched by a heavenly hand.

Tabitha smiled at Finn seated opposite her. He looked exceptionally handsome this morning, drinking his coffee and carefully writing in a small notebook, occasionally looking up with an abstracted frown as he contemplated something, before returning to his notes. He had confessed to her that he never let anyone see his writing, which revealed his complicated, embattled relationship with words. Whatever he wrote now was for his own benefit, so she left him to his work as she shuffled through the newspapers stacked beside her plate.

She liked how quiet they usually were in the mornings, both of them preparing for the day, each of them making plans and readying for the tasks that lay ahead of them. In the wake of the Platinum Collective's first meeting, there were things that needed attending to,

but before any of that could be addressed, she would
familiarize herself with current events.

Turning to the *Times*, she read through several articles before a headline on the fourth page caught
her eye.

A burning cold sheeted through her.

"Dear God," she exclaimed, appalled.

"What is it?" Finn asked as he looked up in alarm.
"Is everything all right?"

"*'An Open Letter from the Sterling Society*,'" she
read aloud, "*'concerning the formation of the Platinum Collective, a dangerous new organization that
threatens the well-being of the nation*.'"

"The hell?" Finn frowned in puzzlement.

"*'We*,'" she continued to read, her voice shaking, "*'the undersigned, are writing to express our
deep misgivings, nay, alarm about the latest threat
to British peace and stability. The Platinum Collective has recently formed with the sole intention of
supplanting known and respected individuals from
the very highest echelons of society with an upstart
throng comprised of figures from the lowest and
most common associations whose only ambition is
to undermine England's foundations and create the
selfsame atmosphere of bloodthirsty anarchy so recently observed in France*.'"

Finn shook his head. "Those blunderers."

"It goes on." She fought for calm. "It would almost be amusing, their reductive and facetious argu-
mentative strategy. Their case against us is a jumble.
Is the Platinum Collective a menace to the security
and prosperity of England, or is it an inconsequential trifle? They intimate that we are both."

She tried to laugh but it came out sounding like broken porcelain.

"God above," she said shakily. "We're ruined. Utterly destroyed. Sir William and his cronies have publicly obliterated us."

"Not precisely," Finn began, far calmer than she would have expected, given the circumstances.

She surged to her feet and threw the newspaper to the floor as hot anger poured through her. The rage she felt after the Sterling Society had dismissed her was a tiny ember compared to the conflagration of fury she felt now.

"He thinks we're going to simply lie down and accept his abuse. It's not going to happen. We'll retaliate. I don't know how, but we will. I'll stage a protest outside their headquarters, I'll take to the streets and let all of London know that the Sterling Society is nothing but a bunch of snobbish bullies. I'll—"

"Tabitha." Finn stood and walked toward her, hands held up in a placating gesture. "There's no need for any of that."

"But . . . but," she sputtered. "How can you be so *calm*? When Sir William has declared *war*?"

"He's going to destroy himself," Finn said levelly. "Marcroft has taken the first step to completely undermine the Sterling Society's reputation. By issuing that statement, he's drawn attention to the fact that his group of fucking snobs are afraid of you, afraid of what you represent, afraid of your power."

She stared at him, her heart pounding and acid churning in her belly. His words pinged off of her like hail against a window.

"*They* look the fools." Finn took hold of her shoulders and looked into her eyes. "And if you could get hold of your emotions, you'd see that."

She reared back as what he said now struck her with the force of a boulder. "*What?*"

"It's elementary logic," he continued, as if he hadn't lanced her with a burning spear. "When you calm down you'll recognize—"

Sucking in a breath, she was thrown back to that night eight years ago, when her feelings had been so callously dismissed by someone she cared about. She was drowning, submerged in the past, and choked on the bitter deluge of memory.

Had you acted with logic and reason . . . humiliating yourself in such an appalling display . . .

If you'd learned to temper your emotions . . .

And Sir William, and his cohorts, casting her aside, sniffing that a woman could never have the right quality of mind, that she would never be *one of them*.

No. *No.* She wouldn't be invalidated again. Betrayed again.

Fight back, instinct shouted at her. *Hurt him as he hurt you.*

"This isn't a gambling hell," she bit out. "The strategies that work at hazard don't apply to the world of intellectuals."

Finn jerked as if slapped. His jaw tightened and he took a step back. In a low, tight voice, he said, "I see."

She spun away from him. "I don't know if you do. The last man to tell me to *get hold of my emotions* hurt me badly. But to hear it from *you* . . . who I cared for. Who I trusted. Who I thought accepted me . . . My heart is broken."

The urge to weep wracked her, yet if she gave into tears, she might never stop. The hurt within her grew and grew, consuming her in its serrated mouth.

Miserable, wounded, she fled the breakfast room, hauled open the front door, and sped down the street.

Chapter 24

❧ ✳ ❧

Stunned, Finn stood alone in the breakfast room, staring at the space that his wife had occupied before everything had fallen to pieces.

What had just happened? There had been words, so many of them, all of them hurtful.

The *look* on her face when he'd urged her to be calm and take control of her emotions, the raw pain in her eyes—God, he'd never wanted to see it, and he sure as hell didn't want to be the source of that pain.

She'd wounded him, too, and for a moment, he was breathless with the shock of how speedily and directly she'd cut him to the quick.

And all the time he was standing here like a clod of earth, she was outside, fleeing.

Cursing himself, he bolted from the breakfast room. She'd left the front door open, but by the time he crossed the threshold to the outside, she was already halfway down the block. He dashed after her.

All that mattered was reaching Tabitha. His attention was firmly fixed on her retreating back, until he slammed into a watchman.

"The deuce?" The watchman grabbed his arm. "Sir, have a care where you're walking."

Finn tried to break free from the man's hold, but the blighter was strong. "I have to go."

"You cannot simply barrel down the street," the watchman insisted. "It's quite ungentlemanly."

Goddamn it, Finn didn't have time for this. His wife was nearly a block away, her figure growing smaller by the second.

"Tabitha," he called to her, desperate to make her stop.

She reached the end of the block and paused long enough to send him one last, agonized glance, before she disappeared around the corner.

"Sir," the watchman said forcefully. "I must insist that your pace be more sedate."

"Shit," Finn spat.

The man's forehead furrowed. "This is a fine neighborhood, sir, and such language isn't appropriate. Neither is your haste."

Finn seethed, furious with the watchman, but more so with himself. He had to apologize to Tabitha, if she'd listen—yet how could he blame her for running away when he'd been such a complete and utter ass?

"I'll let you go, sir," the watchman continued, "but consider this a stern warning."

"Fine, fine," Finn snapped. He didn't waste any more time with the watchman and ran to the end of the block. But there was no sign of Tabitha.

Edgar appeared beside him, looking remarkably calm, considering the mistress of the house had just fled and the master had dashed off in pursuit, only to be admonished by a watchman.

"Do you want the carriage, sir?" the footman asked evenly.

"No time." Finn hailed a hackney. When a vehicle stopped, he shouted an address at the driver. "An extra shilling if you get there in the next ten minutes."

After climbing in, he held on tightly as the hackney hurtled through the city. All the while he kept his gaze trained on the passing streets, seeking any sign of Tabitha, preparing to launch himself out of the vehicle if he should spot her. But there was no sign of her. His gut churned the whole way, and by the time the hackney stopped outside her parents' home, it was as if his own fear and self-directed rage had poisoned him.

Careless of the amount, he threw a handful of coins at the driver on his way to dash up to the viscount's front door. It must have been a sizable sum, because the driver exclaimed, "Cor, gov, want me to wait?"

He didn't answer. Instead, he pounded his fist against the wood, until a stoic footman opened the door.

Before the servant could greet him, Finn demanded, "Is she here?"

"Who, sir?"

Finn shouldered past the footman and into the entryway, calling, "Tabitha! Tabitha!" He ran into a parlor, but finding no sign of her, he emerged and started up the staircase. "Please, Tabitha—we must talk."

"My gracious, Mr. Ransome," the countess said, emerging from what he had to assume was her personal apartments, "what a tremendous din, especially for this hour of the day."

"Is she here?" he demanded. "Tabitha?"

The countess's elegant brows arched. "You mean you don't know the whereabouts of your own wife?"

"Is. She. Here." With every word, he took a step toward Lady Parslow, and Tabitha's mother took an alarmed step back, until she retreated into a private parlor. "Please," he remembered to say, "I just need to see her."

"Whatever you've done," the countess said, tutting, "it must have been quite dreadful for you to shout my house down in search of her."

"It was," he answered grimly. He shuddered when he thought of how utterly overbearing he'd been. "But I swear I'll make amends, no matter the cost. Whatever she desires. I'll give it to her."

Rather than answer him, Lady Parslow walked to a slim decanter perched atop an equally delicate table, and poured herself a glass of golden-brown liquor. She offered a second glass to Finn, but he shook his head. He'd no time for or interest in drinking anything until he'd found Tabitha and begged for her forgiveness.

"My daughter is the sort of person who thinks before she feels," the countess said after sipping her drink. "She is hardly a passionate creature."

Which only proved how little Lady Parslow knew her own offspring. And Finn, fool that he was, had taken the opposite tactic, treating her as though she didn't have a right to her feelings.

"Please, my lady. If you could tell her I'm here, I merely want to speak with her."

"I've received only two letters from her since your wedding," the countess announced. "And have seen her even less. She isn't here."

His heart dropped. "Where might she have gone?"

"We have never been particularly close, my daughter and I." A shade of unhappiness passed behind Lady Parslow's eyes. "We never exchanged confidences, and so I'm just as baffled as you as to where she could be. Unless," she mused, "she went to that library she always patronizes. It seems to be something of a haven for her."

"Thank you, my lady." Finn gave a clipped bow, then headed for the door.

"Mr. Ransome," the countess said, and when he stopped to face her, she added, "The reasons you and Tabitha married were far from what the young people might call romantic. It was more mutual expediency. And yet, even I could see that there was . . . something between you two. Something that went beyond convenience. I hope that you haven't destroyed that."

"That's my hope, as well, my lady."

He was back on the street moments later, and, true to his word, the hackney driver waited for him.

"Where to, gov?"

"The Benezra Library."

FOR ALL THE anxious nausea that plagued Finn as he'd entered the library, it was nothing compared to the sick despair that nearly leveled him when he learned that she wasn't there. Mr. Okafor had no answer for Finn when asked about Tabitha's whereabouts.

As Finn stood outside the library, stewing over where he could find his wife, a fine drizzle started, quickly turning into a stronger rain. Within seconds, he was drenched to the skin.

"Home, gov?" the driver asked hopefully.

Finn wouldn't give up. Not now, not ever. And he recalled hearing Tabitha give an address to their coachman when she went to visit Miss Goldstein and Miss Kemble. Thank God for his exceptional memory, because he recalled the address.

"Gordon Street, Bloomsbury," he directed to the driver.

"Right you are, gov," the hackney driver said, resigned.

Traffic slowed as the rain worsened, and by the time they reached Gordon Street, impatience and anxiety had gnawed holes in Finn's chest. He didn't wait for the vehicle to come to a full stop before he launched himself out the door and toward the narrow town house.

He used the brass knocker to rap sharply and urgently on the door. A minute later, Miss Kemble appeared, clasping a shawl around her shoulders. Her expression turned cool as she regarded Finn.

"She isn't here, Mr. Ransome," Miss Kemble said before Finn could ask. She blinked as she spoke—and Finn knew a tell when he saw one.

Behind Miss Kemble, a shadow moved in the corridor.

His heart slammed up his throat.

"If you see her," Finn said, knowing Tabitha listened, "if you speak to her or write or have *any* communication with her, can you tell her . . . tell her . . . I'm so sorry. So terribly sorry. It ruins me to think that I hurt her. Because I would sooner eviscerate myself than cause her a moment's pain. I'd thought I was helping, but I was behaving no better than any of a score of boorish men. I should have listened better, spoken better."

His chest heaved as he struggled to find exactly the right words to amend the appalling hurt he'd caused her.

He should speak to her of how much he loved her— but it didn't seem right to say the words again this way, through an intermediary, and as an instrument of his own guilt. When he *did* speak those words to Tabitha once more, he would do so to her face, expecting nothing in return.

"The house is hers," he continued. "I'm vacating it immediately. She doesn't need to hide from me, or from anyone."

"Where will you go, Mr. Ransome?" Miss Kemble asked. "That is, if I see her, and she wants to reach you?"

"My brother's new home is in Marylebone," Finn decided immediately. "He and his bride are on their wedding journey—" He swallowed hard around those words, thinking of Kieran and his well-deserved happiness with Celeste, and how Finn had taken his own joy and smashed it to pieces. "The address is 38 Weymouth Street. If she's in need of anything, anything at all, or she wants to reach me, she can find me there. No matter the hour, if she sends for me, I'll come."

"*If* I see her," Miss Kemble said, "I shall let her know."

The shadow in the hallway disappeared. His words hadn't moved her.

He turned his face up to the rain, wracked to his marrow with remorse.

"Thank you, Miss Kemble." He turned away and found himself beside the hackney.

"Home now, gov?" the driver asked. "It's awful gruesome out here now."

"My thanks," Finn answered, "but I'll walk." Nearly two miles stood between here and Marylebone, but he couldn't sit idly in a cab as his world fell to pieces. He would send for his things later.

The cabman whistled. "Sure about that? You might drown with the rats if you're on foot."

Yet Finn was already stalking down the street, uncaring of where he went or whether or not he'd be washed into the Thames with the rest of the worthless debris.

As Iris closed the front door, Tabitha eased out from her hiding place in the drawing room. She dug the heels of her palms into her eyes to force back the tears.

"It's all right, Tabby." Iris walked softly to her. "There's no shame in crying."

Tabitha had heard everything Finn had said—his contrition seemed genuine, and it was clear he knew she was listening—and yet her heart contracted with a sharp ache at the thought of how he had resorted to the exact same patronizing stance as Charles, and even Sir William. How had Finn ever thought that she'd simply swallow down her hurt as he patted her on the head? That treating her in such a fashion wouldn't hurt her unbearably? She'd thought he knew her, *saw* her, but perhaps that had been an illusion cast by their fiery chemistry in the bedchamber.

He knew how to give her pleasure, desired her, and claimed to love her, but that meant nothing, not when he demonstrated with his patronizing words that he had no faith in her.

Tabitha blanched when she thought of what she'd said in response. They'd both struck terrible blows to each other. Regret was acidic in her belly, and she despaired that they could find their ways back to each other.

It all seemed so lost now.

She tried to force down the tears that wanted to spill from her eyes. "If I do start to cry, I mightn't stop."

"Whatever feels best to you," Iris said with a gentle smile.

"That's the thing," Tabitha answered, sinking to the floor as sorrow turned her bones to iron. "Nothing feels best. Nothing will ever feel right or good again."

Chapter 25

❧ ✱ ❧

Tabitha tugged on her redingote to keep the chill morning air from sneaking between the fastenings. Her efforts were futile, and as she sprinted between her carriage and the front door of the Platinum Collective, the bitter breeze made her shiver.

Then again, she hadn't felt warm since yesterday, when she and Finn had been so hurtful to each other. At home, she piled on shawls and blankets, but nothing could chase the cold from deep in her body. It was worst in bed, where the mattress seemed far too big, too empty. She tried to sleep in the middle of the bed rather than remain on her usual side, and Olive used a brass bed warmer to keep everything nice and toasty for her.

None of those efforts had any effect. She spent last night hardly able to sleep, trembling with cold. And when she shuffled wearily to breakfast, the vacant side of the table only reminded her of everything she'd lost.

So, she fled to the Platinum Collective, seeking purpose.

"I see I needn't have brought my key this morning," Chima said as he approached. A colorful knit scarf was wrapped around his throat, and he carried several books under his arm.

She unlocked the door and together they stepped inside.

After lighting lamps, they moved into the small kitchen at the rear of the building. Tabitha's steps dragged, but Chima was all efficiency as he put a kettle on to boil and took down two earthenware mugs from the cupboard.

"The vote on the education bill is approaching," he noted, bringing out the tea caddy.

"Thanks to the Sterling Society," she said grimly, "no one in Parliament will come to us for counsel before they vote on it."

"I'm not so certain about that," Chima noted. "There hasn't precisely been a groundswell of support for Sir William's establishment."

Tabitha straightened. "Truly?"

Her friend nodded. "Sir William's aggression in denouncing us wasn't as well received as he might have expected."

A note of hope rang in her chest, like the opening tones in what might be a song, or even a full orchestral piece. Finn had said that might happen, before he'd ham-handedly told her to manage her emotions.

Wrapping a cloth around her hand, she took the hot kettle off the hob. "If only we had the support of some noblemen, the way the Sterling Society has."

"It's true," Chima allowed. "Yet we might still find a way to be heard."

She pondered this as she went through the steps of brewing tea. A funny thing, the making of this beverage, using dreadfully hot water to extract something delicious and reviving. The tea wasn't complete until it had been exposed to extreme conditions that could damage more fragile things.

But people—marriages—weren't tea leaves. And tea could be ruined with water that was far *too* hot.

Things had been so much easier and simpler when she lived entirely between the pages of books. Retreating into her beloved texts tempted her, yet it was too late. Because of Finn, she was out in the world, experiencing all its majesty and heartbreak, and there was no going back.

"The hell are you doing here?" Dom demanded, dropping into the settle opposite Finn. The furniture was old and in much need of repair, and it listed beneath Dom's impressive size like the nearby drunkards that slouched in their seats.

Finn looked up from his—third? fifth?—tankard, and regarded his friend through drink-filmed eyes. Indulging in this much drink had never been his practice, but a man could change and evolve over the course of his life.

"This is a public house," Finn explained, carefully enunciating his words, yet doing a poor job of it. "Emphasis on *public*. Anyone might consider themselves one of the patrons."

"Patrons." Dom glanced around the Ratcliff tavern. "Fine way of saying *sots*."

Finn waved his hand. "A minor distinction."

"You're certainly one of their number tonight." Dom braced his elbows on the wobbling tabletop. "Can't see as how their company would be preferable to your bride's."

Finn winced before downing the remainder of his drink and signaling for another. The publican wove through the men passed out on the floor to refill Finn's tankard, slamming an empty one down in front of Dom.

"Don't want none, Archie," Dom said curtly.

"You came in here, Kilburn," the publican answered. "If you ain't drinking, you're leaving."

"A pint, then," Dom replied, grudgingly, "but no more."

Foam and ale sloshed over the rim of Dom's tankard as, glaring, Archie filled it before stomping off, unconcerned whether or not he stepped on anyone along the way. A few outraged grunts and curses rose up before settling down to the tavern's glum silence.

"This being your old neighborhood," Finn said dryly, "I see where you get your charming temperament."

Dom leaned back, the wood creaking ominously beneath him. "You could've gone to one of your toff taverns and spared yourself."

"This place suits my humor." Finn glanced around at the grimy walls, the low-hanging ceiling, and the handful of men slumped at their tables as they clutched their ales. In one corner, two blokes were half-heartedly punching each other, which no one tried to stop.

"Surely the gaming hells of London miss your presence," Dom noted.

"I like it here." How could he be expected to have any possible ability at the gambling tables when he'd keep hoping that he would look up from his cards and see Tabitha standing beside him? "Maybe I'll wake up with a knife in my back."

"A man can hope." Dom was quiet, then said, "If I'd a bride waiting for me at home, I sure as hell wouldn't be in this open sewer of a place."

"Oi!" Archie yelled in annoyance from behind the bar. "Watch what you say about my pub, Kilburn."

"Don't tell me this place isn't a pile of shit, Arch," Dom shouted back.

The publican considered it for a moment, and then shrugged before returning to leaning on the bar and glaring at the customers.

"There's no bride waiting for me," Dom continued, grim. "There is for you, though."

"I wouldn't wager on that," Finn answered heavily.

Dom narrowed his eyes as he studied Finn. "What the precise fuck did you do?"

"Can always count on you to cut through the rubbish and get to the heart of the matter. The truth is . . ." He dragged in a breath. "I was an utter ass to Tabitha, and I don't know if she can forgive me—or if I deserve her forgiveness."

Dom attempted to stretch out his legs, but the cramped situation with his seat kept that from happening. "Spill your story."

If there was anyone Finn could unburden himself to, someone who knew all the ridiculous, terrible, foolish, and sometimes admirable parts of himself, it was Dom. They'd met many years back, when Dom had met Kieran at Oxford, and then later when he stumbled upon Finn and Kieran attempting to liberate several bottles of wine from a marquess's cellar during a ball. Apparently, the same notion had occurred to Dom. Between the two younger sons of an earl and the son of a warehouse magnate, they shared a mutual existence on the fringes of polite society, and had formed a close attachment ever since then.

The three of them had torn a path through the wilder sides of London, carousing with the mutual abandonment of men who didn't quite belong. That carousing had quieted when Dom and Willa had become engaged, but the shared experience of those years had remained.

Other than Kieran, there wasn't anyone Finn trusted more.

"I'd tell you," Finn said, "but you'll likely want to punch me at the end of my tale."

"I want to punch your pretty aristo face no matter what," Dom replied after taking a healthy swallow of his unhealthy drink, "so might as well confess all."

So, Finn told him. Everything, from the beginning, leaving nothing out except intimate details. But the reasons for Finn and Tabitha deciding to marry, the initial distance between them, and all that had transpired with the Sterling Society, that, Finn recounted.

He didn't spare Dom the details of what he'd said to Tabitha after they'd learned of the Sterling Society's letter in the *Times* denouncing the Platinum Collective. The wound had to be torn open to be cleaned. And it was why Finn was here.

As Finn spoke, Dom said nothing, but his expression grew more and more grave, a deep crease appearing between his brows while Finn brought his friend up to the moment when he walked into this Ratcliff tavern.

When Finn was done speaking, his throat burned and a hard, aching knot dwelt in the center of his chest. He looked at Dom. His friend looked back.

There was a long silence—the only noise coming from the two men in the corner who had moved on from attempted punching and were now rolling around on the floor, clumsily trying to strangle each other.

"It's comforting, really," Dom finally said.

"What is?" Finn demanded.

"That the most intelligent man I know could so thoroughly bollocks up something. Makes me feel like if *you* made such a godawful mistake, then the rest of us can be forgiven for our own massive blunders."

"Thank God, I've given you some solace," Finn grumbled. Then, "You think I'm the most intelligent man you know?"

Dom flicked that question away with a swipe of his hand. "Now you've got to use that swollen brain of yours to fix everything."

"This swollen brain isn't functioning at its optimum capacity," Finn said bleakly. "It hasn't for a long time."

Dom leaned forward and motioned for Finn to do the same. When Finn did so, Dom rammed the heel of his palm into Finn's forehead.

"Fuck," Finn snapped, rubbing at the sore spot on his head, "is that because I'm an idiot?"

"We've already established you're not an idiot. It's to shake loose whatever's jamming the mechanisms in your head. But you treated her the shite way it sounds like all the other men in her life have treated her."

"She said that someone in her past had done the same thing I did," Finn admitted, his throat burning. "Someone she had feelings for. So, I was no better than that fool. I really *am* worthless, like everyone always said."

The urge to howl his pain tore through him, and yet he forced it down, the way he always forced down what he felt, because his parents and teachers had always used his emotions against him. *Now you cry, instead of doing your work, you lazy creature. Your tears won't move me.*

Slowly, slowly, Dom slid his enormous hand across the table to cover Finn's.

"I lived more than most men in my thirty years," Dom said gruffly. "Encountered so many people. Some good. Some bad. I was convinced that every last nob I met was a vile, self-serving bastard who couldn't think beyond his own coffers and cock. When they'd see me coming, they'd turn away, or sneer at me and my wide shoulders. Then," he said with a hint of a smile, "I met the Ransome brothers."

"Two more vile, self-serving bastards," Finn said with a hoarse laugh.

"To be sure, you were spoilt and selfish," Dom agreed, "but you saw me as a *person*. And you'll never know what a gift that is until people deny you your humanity."

Finn stared at his friend, taking in his impassioned words. "Maybe my parents and teachers were right. Maybe I'm just no good."

"Don't tell me that," Dom fired back, "when I know bad men. When I *am* a bad man."

The coal in Finn's throat burned, but he didn't want to swallow it down, when his friend was opening himself up like an animal being butchered.

"Dom—"

"You've got a way to help her, don't you?" Dom demanded, pulling his hand away.

"I do . . . only . . ." Finn clenched his jaw. "I can't face her. Can't face seeing how much I've let her down. I've seen that look on so many faces in my life. I stopped caring if my parents thought me a disappointment, but when I saw it on *her* face . . . I barely survived that once. I can't do it again." Finn's hand tightened around his tankard. "It's not possible."

"Mark me," Dom said hotly, spreading his hands on the pitted wood of the tabletop, "there's nothing, *nothing* I wouldn't do to have the chance to fix the wrong I did to Willa. I've lost her for good, though, and that's how it's supposed to be. Yet if I could eradicate the hurt I caused her, give her something, anything, to ease her pain, if I had the opportunity that you have . . ." He glowered down at his hands as if he saw something staining them. "I would *fucking take it*. So, *face her*, goddamn you."

Finn stared at his friend, seeing the suffering etched plainly on his rugged face. Witnessing Dom's anguish was itself a torment, because there was nothing Finn could do to help him. Or was there? He'd have to think on that later.

As the ale cleared from Finn's mind, resolve firmed his spine and pumped in his heart. If he did go to Tabitha, he could undo a fraction of the damage he'd wrought. Whatever misery Finn faced in seeing that sense of betrayal in her eyes, it didn't matter, so long as she was given the happiness she deserved.

Chapter 26

❧ ✳ ❧

Tabitha lingered in the doorway of her library but, despite willing her feet to move, they refused to cross the threshold. Going inside and sitting in the space that Finn had specially created just for her felt like trying to push her way through a wall made of thorns. Rather than shred herself on them, she turned away. Perhaps she could study in the parlor.

No—she and Finn would go there when she read to him.

The bedchamber was replete with his presence, and the dining room brought back vivid memories of his mouth on her, his body in hers as they made the table shake.

There wasn't a room in this house that wasn't steeped in him, in them.

He'd been gone three days, the longest three days in the whole of human history. And every day, she went straight to Platinum Collective headquarters, remaining there from first thing in the morning, until she locked the doors at night. Which left the hours after dark for her to move restlessly through her own home. She could impose herself on Diana and Iris, but spending excessive amounts of time with a couple who were so clearly in love and happy would only reinforce her own loss. And surely the women wanted their privacy without her morose presence casting a pall.

"Madam?" the footman asked as she passed him in the corridor. "Are you dining tonight?"

It was a worthwhile question. She'd only picked at her supper until, yesterday evening, she'd skipped the meal entirely. Come to think of it, she hadn't eaten much for breakfast, and did she have luncheon?

"Not this evening, Edgar. In fact, you're welcome to have the rest of the night off. Tell the staff that they're also free to do as they please."

"As you like, madam." If the footman was eager to enjoy his freedom, he didn't show it. Instead, he bowed and withdrew to inform everyone else in the household of their liberty.

Perhaps she should just go to bed. There was an additional bedchamber set aside for guests. She wouldn't sleep, but it was either that or keep moving from one empty room to the next.

Her feet paused on the steps as a knock sounded on the front door. Since she'd sent Edgar away, the responsibility of greeting visitors fell to her, but she couldn't imagine who might be calling at this late hour, and with the cold autumn fog lying so thick and heavy on the streets. All wise people were snug at home.

She opened the door, and her heart leapt into her throat to see Finn standing there.

A wild, reckless happiness sped through her like a beast liberated from its cage. But she chased it down and herded it back into its prison, because to let it run free would devastate her.

Pleasure lit Finn's face, but he, too, seemed to stamp it out.

They both stared at each other for a long while, and her gaze alit on small details: the heavy coat he wore, filmed with mist, the desolate look in his midnight eyes.

Three days without looking into those eyes had been an eternity. To see the sorrow there was a pain she hadn't anticipated. He suffered, too. As much as she did.

But *he* had been the one to cause the empty expanse between them.

"Where's Edgar?" he asked. His voice sounded rusty as a seldom-used iron gate, and yet she yearned for it with a bone-deep longing.

"I gave him and the rest of the staff the night off."

"I see."

More silence.

She kept her feet planted rather than rush to him and throw her arms around him in the hopes that he would hold her closely and tell her that he had faith in her, accepted her for who she was, and everything could go back to the way it had been before. Before he'd shattered her heart.

Yet there would be no going back to the time before she loved him. Despite everything, she loved him still. That would be part of her forever until she released her hold on this world and slipped into the infinite and unknown.

She collected herself enough to motion to the entryway behind her. "It's dreadful out."

He hesitated for a moment before stepping inside. Though he took off his hat, he didn't remove his coat.

"I'm here to offer my services," he said stiffly. "As a

strategist. Whatever you need to ensure that the Platinum Collective emerges the victor."

"It's the collective's fate that concerns you," she said heavily.

"Yes," he said, then, "but no. The world needs to see what you've made, that you've created something so important. I want to make certain that happens."

She gulped in a breath, fighting for composure. "Thank you. I . . ." It was odd and terrible, talking to him like this, so formally, and yet it seemed impossible to return to how they had been before, when they both trusted each other.

"I was thinking," she went on, "of writing a measured but pointed rebuttal and publishing it in the *Hawk's Eye*."

He nodded slowly, considering her words. "Might I offer a suggestion?"

"Please," she said, grateful that he'd asked for permission rather than told her what to do.

"An open symposium," he explained. "Held at a place where the public can gather, so that everyone can hear from the Platinum Collective. It won't be an attack on the Sterling Society, but rather offer proof that your group is far more relevant. It's a stronger position to play and turns the focus on the good the Platinum Collective can do, rather than appearing defensive."

She turned the notion over in her mind, carefully weighing the prospect. "A way to show that the Platinum Collective was created by the people, and is *for* the people."

"And everyone will see you in action. Your determination, your intelligence, your dedication to something so vitally important."

"The Sterling Society never opened its meetings to anyone," she noted, stunned by the notion.

"Which is why the Platinum Collective is a massive step forward," he explained. "A symposium could show London that your group is different. A necessary change."

"I think it's a good plan." She dared not believe, and yet what he suggested could truly be the answer. It could secure the Platinum Collective's position in society, despite Sir William's efforts to undermine them. "If the group agrees to it, I'll place an announcement in the *Hawk's Eye*." She pulled in a rough breath. "Thank you for the suggestion."

They stared at each other, and it felt as though the distance between them stretched vast, deep, and dangerous as an ocean full of monsters and whirlpools.

Even so, she was grateful, incredibly grateful that Finn had possessed the courage to come to her with the idea.

"When I said those terrible things to you . . ." He swallowed thickly, and his eyes were damp. "I couldn't have been more stupid."

"You *aren't* stupid," she said fiercely. "You're astoundingly intelligent—and you also did something that hurt me."

"There isn't going to be a moment in my lifetime that I won't regret that," he answered, voice vibrating with self-recrimination, "that I failed to see *you* in that moment."

The pain in his eyes, in his words, made her throat burn. She pressed a hand to it as if she could somehow staunch the misery that engulfed them both.

"Understand this," he went on, voice cracking, "I

did something terrible. I cannot apologize enough. And I don't expect or demand your absolution."

"I was at fault, too," she said thickly. "I spoke cruelly, and I'm so very sorry for it."

He nodded, and yet they each remained where they were, too wounded to meet in the middle. A long, agonizing silence followed.

She was trapped in the amber of her fear, as frozen in time as an ancient butterfly caught in the moments before flight. He had apologized, as had she, yet the pain remained. Now they each seemed to know the damage they could do to the other, and trembled in its wake.

They could not go back, but going forward seemed impossible.

"I came here to offer my help," he went on, his words rough, "and now I've given it. I won't trouble you anymore tonight. Good night, Tabitha. I'll see you at the symposium—and then you needn't fear ever encountering me again."

He wrested open the door and disappeared into the thick, heavy fog.

For a moment, she gazed at the space where he'd been. It almost glowed with the afterimage of his presence and she reached out to touch the place he had occupied. But her fingers encountered only nothingness.

Pure instinct made her move. She went after him, though she had no idea what she would say or do if she caught him. It couldn't end this way . . . could it?

By the time she reached the middle of the block, he had vanished into the murky mist. She stopped, and stared into the gray night for a long time. Yet Finn never came back.

Chapter 27

❧ ✳ ❧

Nervously, Tabitha scanned the Imperial Theatre as more and more people filled the pit and seats. Everyone appeared animated and eager to see what was about to transpire, no doubt intrigued by the public nature of the feud between the Sterling Society and the Platinum Collective.

"A stroke of brilliance, to this notion for a public symposium," Diana murmured, standing beside Tabitha in the wings. Clearly, she and Tabitha were of the same thinking.

"That was entirely Finn's doing," Tabitha answered as she peered out from behind the curtain. She gave him all the credit for this—though the sheer number of people filing into the Imperial made her stomach leap. Never had she suspected that so many citizens of London would be so keen to take part in a symposium with an intellectual society, but then, surprises both terrible and wonderful unfolded every day.

She prayed that today would be a wonderful surprise.

"Is Mr. Ransome here yet?" Chima asked, joining their group.

"Not that I've seen," Tabitha replied.

She craned her neck, hoping for a glimpse of his tall, dark figure. Only two days had passed since he'd appeared at her door, suggesting this symposium, and in that time, she'd rehearsed and discarded countless speeches. Yet she'd never had the courage to go to him and tell him exactly what she wanted from their future together. Much as she wanted to give them another chance, fear that they might hurt each other again kept her at home and silent.

Even so, she needed to see him today and hold firm to the courage he gave her. He'd wanted this symposium to not only show the world what the Platinum Collective could do, but that she had been working to make this dream happen. Whatever happened, she would find the strength to keep moving forward.

As the theater continued to fill, she glanced toward the stage itself. Two rows of chairs were arranged on the boards, half of them on risers so they could be seen by the audience, and a desk stood to one side for the moderator. The collective had met twice before today, discussing how the symposium would unfold. A moderator would introduce the Platinum Collective, outline its intentions and plans, and field questions from the audience.

They had also voted as to who would play the important role of moderator: Tabitha. She'd demurred, believing that she oughtn't be the one to speak for them, but the group insisted that at the least, as one of the founding members, she could open the discussion to ensure everyone was able to have their voices heard.

Now the eighteen current members of the Platinum Collective gathered in the wings. Faces of every hue eagerly looked at her.

"Is everyone here? Everyone ready?" she asked.

There were nods and murmurs of agreement, though she noted that some looked as nervous as she felt.

"Thank you for being a part of this," she said, humbled to her core that these incredible people believed in the Platinum Collective as much as she did. "Let's take our places and we'll begin."

There were nods of assent from the group. In a single file, they exited the wing and walked onto the stage itself. A bit of scattered applause rang through the crowd, but mostly, there were whispers of curiosity.

Tabitha felt both fully present and also oddly removed from herself as she crossed to the waiting desk. But before she could sit, the noises from the crowd grew louder, more excited. People began pointing to the boxes filling with men.

She gulped when she saw that they were members of the Sterling Society. An ironic smile curled her lips as she noted that they had specifically chosen the boxes where Society's elite sat to watch theatrical performances. The Sterling Society had spoken quite clearly: they were above the people in the seats and filling the pit.

Even across the distance of the theater, she could make out Sir William as he took a seat at the railing of one box. He threw her a disdainful look, as one might throw the contents of a chamber pot onto the pavement below.

Very well, if Sir William wanted to try to take down the Platinum Collective, he'd have a fight on his hands. She'd already pummeled him in her imagination, thanks to her trip to Finn's pugilism academy.

She tipped her chin up in response, and the baronet

scowled, clearly hoping that she would be cowed by his presence alone.

But she wouldn't be afraid. This meant too much, and in backing her and the Platinum Collective, Finn had shown Tabitha that she was never a force to be underestimated.

"Tabitha," Diana hissed from her seat. "Look."

Her friend nodded toward the back of the theater, and Tabitha's pulse fluttered when she spotted Finn making his way down the center aisle. He was taller than most of the people in the audience, so she easily followed his progress as he moved toward the very front of the pit. Amidst the multitudes, she saw him and only him, and the pure admiration in his eyes as he gazed back at her.

He smiled at her, a small, encouraging smile, and it resonated all the way to her toes.

Then one of the members of the Sterling Society yelped, "Good Gad—the Duke of Northfield. And the duchess."

More excited sounds rose up from the audience as a black-haired man with a piratical air moved down the aisle. A woman with Mediterranean features walked proudly on his arm, though she smiled cordially at many of the people they passed on their way. The duke and duchess reached Finn's side, greeting him warmly.

When she caught Finn's eye, she motioned to the duke, silently asking him, *Did* you *invite him*?

Finn gave a tiny, almost shy nod.

Tabitha's heartbeat knocked in a frenzy. God above, Finn *had asked a duke* to their symposium. Both the Duke and Duchess of Northfield were known for their progressive stance politically, the duke a known advocate for tolerant immigration policies, while the duchess ran several schools for girls across the city.

He'd never said anything about bringing a duke to the symposium. Tabitha never expected to have such powerful people in attendance today.

And then, to her astonishment, *another* duke appeared.

The imposing Duke of Greyland walked with purposeful strides, his elegant blonde duchess beside him. They stood next to the Duke and Duchess of Northfield, with all of the men shaking hands and the two ladies waving to each other.

The crowd was in a veritable frenzy. Not only had two dukes joined the symposium, but they were in the pit, rather than sitting up in the rarified air of the private boxes.

Tabitha could scarce believe her eyes. She gazed at Finn with astonishment and gratitude, and he gave her a tiny, pleased look. She mouthed, *Thank you*, but he held up a finger, as if to say that she should bide a moment longer.

She gasped when the Duke and Duchess of Rotherby came forward. Followed by the Duke of Tarrington, the Earl and Countess of Ashford, the Earl and Countess of Blakemere, and Viscount and Viscountess Marwood. The viscountess looked rather pleased to be in the Imperial but as a visitor, not in her usual capacity as playwright.

The last time Tabitha had seen so many powerful aristocrats had been at a ball, *not* standing at the front of the pit in a theater so they could participate in a public symposium. Yet they were here. Because Finn had gone to all of them and asked them to come.

Her head spun. She looked to Finn, who, smiling

enigmatically, tipped his head toward the boxes where the now extremely unsettled and irate Sterling Society sat. Sir William looked particularly unhappy at the sheer number of influential aristocrats that had appeared to take part in today's discussion.

Lady Ashford pulled out a notepad, and was busily scribbling in it. Come to think of it, there were several people in the crowd doing the same—they had to be members of the press. And they were all here, covering the Platinum Collective.

Tabitha snapped to attention. She couldn't keep the audience waiting any longer.

She stood, her legs only *slightly* shaking beneath her, and walked to the footlights downstage.

Raising her hands, the throng quieted. She gulped at having so much attention paid to her—there had to be over a hundred people in the audience—and when she spoke, her voice came out slightly thin.

"Thank you all for—" Inwardly, she winced at the reediness of her voice. She glanced at Finn, who sent her an encouraging smile.

Britain's Cleverest Woman, he mouthed.

A smile sprang to her lips as her fear calmed.

"Thank you all," she began again, her voice much stronger, "for joining us today. As you read in the *Hawk's Eye*, we are the members of the Platinum Collective, an association of individuals who, we hope, represent the breadth and scope of the people of England."

There was some applause, with the bass notes of muttering from the Sterling Society.

"It is our intention to never close ourselves off from your voice and your needs," she went on, "and, with that in mind, we have opened our doors so that everyone can speak and be heard."

Another round of clapping rose up, more forcefully.

"I'm Mrs. Tabitha Ransome," she said with pride once the applause quieted, "and I shall moderate today's discussion. With that in mind, we'll begin at once."

She walked to the desk, her legs now much steadier beneath her, and when she took her seat, she waited for questions from the audience.

Silence.

She waited. And waited.

Someone coughed. A few chairs creaked. But no one broke the quiet.

Nervously, she looked toward Iris, Diana, Arjun, and Chima. Perhaps this whole experiment was doomed, and she and the rest of the Platinum Collective faced humiliation.

That possibility was driven home when Sir William laughed derisively. The sound echoed in the theater, landing like a burning coal in Tabitha's stomach.

How could she salvage this awful situation? Perhaps she ought to talk more of the Platinum Collective's aim, and that could spark a discussion. Anything had to be better than this terrible silence.

"I've a question," a man's deep voice asked. The Duke of Rotherby.

"Yes, Your Grace," she said. Hopefully, her voice didn't betray her relief at having *someone* talk, even if it was that extremely intimidating duke.

"An education bill is coming up," the duke said, his words ringing with authority. "I've a particular direction I intend to vote, but I want to hear what the Platinum Collective believes are the long-term ramifications of this policy, should it be enacted."

Tabitha straightened in her seat. Her own words

steady and clear, she said, "Educating more individuals, rather than a select few, benefits everyone and ensures that fewer and fewer fall into the trap of poverty—which can perpetuate itself.

"However," she went on, over the crowd's interested buzzing, "there are many other members of the Platinum Collective with far more expertise than I on the topic. Miss Goldstein, would you be so kind as to answer His Grace's question in more detail?"

Diana nodded at Tabitha, then said in a steady voice, "To begin with, Your Grace, if boys *and* girls are given equal education, the standard of living for *everyone* increases."

As Diana spoke, and other members of the Platinum Collective added their own thoughts on the subject, the audience grew quieter and quieter, including the aristocrats. The entire theater was caught up in the direct and purposeful arguments presented.

Everyone, except the Sterling Society.

"This is balderdash," Sir William bellowed, interrupting Diana, who was citing statistics about the rate of population growth amongst the literate. "Decisions of this scope cannot be left to people who don't even possess a university education. It's—"

"Not you *again*," someone in the crowd shouted, annoyed.

"You already said your piece," another audience member snapped when Sir William attempted to interject once more. "And it was more than anyone wanted to hear."

Sir William turned red. "But, you can't—"

"Quiet!" a woman retorted. "We didn't come to hear *you*. Or *any* of you," she added, waving dismissively at the agitated members of the Sterling Society.

"A little more silence would suit you better, Sir William," the Duke of Rotherby said coldly. "My eyes are being opened today, more so with this group of individuals than any *other* intellectual society has done. It's time for the people to speak."

Tabitha held her breath as she watched this exchange. She wasn't above feeling a surge of triumph when the very men who had ridiculed and dismissed her lumbered to their feet and stormed out of the boxes, their angry mutterings trailing after them like a rotten smell.

She barely managed not to gleefully clap her hands together. Looking to Finn, she saw his own eyes glint with triumph. When she silently said her thanks, he shook his head and pointed at her, as if to say, *This is all* your *doing.*

"Go on, madam," the duke encouraged Diana.

"Yes, go on, Miss Goldstein," Tabitha added, smiling at her friend.

Diana resumed talking, with Mr. Rowe and others adding their expert opinions, and by the time they reached their conclusions, there was a moment's silence. Followed by booming applause. Even the audience members who were in the seats got to their feet to add to the ovation as all the members of the press wrote furiously in their notepads.

Joy burst in Tabitha, as bright and life-giving as sunlight. No matter what happened after this, she, Finn, and the rest of the Platinum Collective had done their very best. Judging by the appreciative clapping and whistles from the crowd, their very best had been more than enough. They'd done it.

The discussion continued for a full hour. At the conclusion of it, the audience's ovation was thunderous, and every member of the Collective bowed.

Eager to share this victory with the person who'd helped make it happen, she looked to Finn.

Her heart sank as she saw him making his way toward the exit, as if he believed that his presence was no longer required.

Tabitha immediately walked to the center of the stage and raised her hands, asking for silence. The audience quieted, and in that stillness, she spoke clearly and directly.

"You've met most of the members of the Platinum Collective," she said, her voice ringing all the way to the back of the theater. "But there's one individual whose contribution has been invaluable."

Finn froze and slowly turned to face the stage. He was too far away for her to make out his expression, but his posture was alert, as if he held himself in waiting.

"Not only did this person help with the genesis of the Platinum Collective," she continued, and while she wanted everyone to hear her, *his* attention was what she needed the most, "as well as organize all the complex matters surrounding the creation of a group such as ours, he recommended today's symposium. All of his contributions have been invaluable, and he's an extraordinary addition to our collective.

"Friends," she said resonantly, "I would like to introduce you to one of England's finest minds, Mr. Finn Ransome."

Chapter 28

❧ ❋ ❧

Standing at the back of the theater, Finn jolted. The moment had been bittersweet, because Tabitha had achieved everything she wanted—precisely his intention—and yet that also meant that he'd had no reason to linger, or watch the exultant joy on her face, or continue to hear the applause she and the Platinum Collective so rightly deserved.

And yet here she was, telling the hundreds of people in attendance how important *he* was. How intelligent. How valuable.

His heart lodged firmly in his throat as the crowd turned to look at him. But it was *Tabitha* that he saw, her and her alone, smiling at him with happiness and gratitude and adoration.

"Will you join us on stage, Mr. Ransome?" she asked.

He moved without thought, cleaving through the parting audience, going to her because there was no earthly way of keeping him from her side. The applause barely registered—all that mattered was her.

He dimly felt the pats of hundreds of hands on his back as he strode forward. Someone guided him to the stairs beside the stage, and in moments, he stood next to Tabitha, who seemed to glow with joy as she took his hand. The press of her skin to his shot through him like pure molten gold.

Tabitha named each of the members of the Platinum Collective, who all took bows, until she got to Finn. "And, of course, Mr. Finn Ransome," she added.

The ovation continued as, in a dreamlike trance, Finn bowed.

"Mrs. Tabitha Ransome," he added, gesturing to her.

Her eyes shone like gems as she curtseyed to the crowd. Then, before the clapping could die down, the Platinum Collective left the stage, including Finn and Tabitha.

Continuing to hold his hand, she led him to a quiet corner of the wings, away from the other members, who were eagerly chattering about the day's success.

Finn and Tabitha looked at each other for many moments, the din around them fading away. He drank her in as though he'd never had a drop of water. She looked both weary and energized, the way a gambler might appear after a long but successful night at the tables. But there was uncertainty in her gray eyes, too.

His stomach pitched. Perhaps her gesture of bringing him onstage had been a final one, signaling the end of their relationship. Living without her would be hell, yet if that's what she wanted, he'd abide by her desire.

Before Tabitha could speak, he said, "It wasn't necessary to have me come to the stage, but I thank you all the same."

"Of course it was necessary," she insisted. "None of this would have been possible without you."

He inclined his head, appreciative. He'd take her gratitude with him to keep him warm on the cold days and nights ahead.

"And," she continued, "I couldn't let you go without saying something. Something I've been wanting to say to you for a very long time."

He braced himself. Surely now, she would tell him that they'd each achieved their goals, and now she no longer had need of him.

She drew in a breath. Then said, her voice vibrating with emotion, "I love you."

He gaped like a cursed man who'd been dealt an ace and a ten. "I know I'm rather dense, but I can't have heard you correctly."

"I'll tell you this again. Finn Ransome," she said vehemently, "you are *not* stupid. You're wise and intelligent and so bloody perceptive you outshine the stars. I will tell you that with my last breath. But not before I tell you once again that I love you."

He stilled. Barely able to believe it, he rasped, "Truly?"

"I do, Finn." She closed the distance between them and cupped his face with her hand. He leaned into her, absorbing the wonderous feel of her against him.

"I love you so much," she continued, her words strengthening, "I haven't words to fully capture the depths of the love I feel for you. And," she added, her eyes gleaming, "you know how adept I am with words. Yet none of them can measure the utter adoration I feel for you."

"Tabitha . . ." He leaned forward, resting his forehead against hers. His heart pounded so hard it was a miracle the whole building didn't crumble around them from its force.

"And it's not predicated on what you can *do* for me," she went on. "It's *who you are* and who you allow me to be. It's all of those things, and more. So much more. I love you, Finn, and I couldn't wait another moment to tell you, but I had to stop you before you fled. I was afraid that you didn't want to see me."

"Oh, love," he answered hoarsely, "I *always* want to see you. I live to behold your eyes, or even a glimpse of the hem of your dress. I could look at the space where you *had* been and be happy, because I knew you'd stood there." He blinked back the moisture gathering in his eyes. "I was leaving because I'd done what I had come to do. The rest belonged to you alone."

"It's *ours*, Finn," she insisted. "Everything is *ours*."

"I love you, Tabitha." His voice vibrated but he didn't care if he showed her how exposed he was. There was no shame in that vulnerability—she'd shown him that. "It's part of me, what I feel for you. There is no me without that love, and it will live on long after I've departed this world. And I'm so sorry for dismissing you."

"I will always regret how I spoke to you," she said solemnly. "But what happened showed me something."

"What's that?"

"That this is a *true* marriage," she explained. "We may have entered into it because it was advantageous to our separate goals, but it's grown and changed. People in true marriages make mistakes, and those mistakes hurt because they care about each other.

Because they love each other. Then they move forward, stronger. Together."

Curving his hands around the back of her head, his lips found hers, and she kissed him back fiercely, and *God*, how he cherished her and her passion. She was the beginning and end of him. That he might have the gift of her for the rest of his life was almost too much—but he was greedy enough to take whatever he was granted.

"I want you to come home," she said when they finally surfaced. "I want you back where you belong—with me. That is," she added, almost bashful, "if that's what you want."

"It's *you*, sweet," he answered hotly. "What I want is *you*."

Epilogue

❧ ❋ ❧

One month later

Evergreen garlands adorned with red velvet bows
scented the air in the Duke of Northfield's ballroom
with crisp pine. Servants circulated through the
guests with platters of honey-dipped fried dough,
called struffoli, in honor of the duchess's Neapoli-
tan heritage. The duke and duchess themselves
were mingling with their guests in the vast, sparkling chamber, offering their holiday greetings and
thanking everyone for attending their Christmas
ball. It was a measure of the Northfields' devotion
to each other that they were never far from their
spouse's side, and they often held hands in view of
everyone.

Smiling at the sight, Tabitha understood what it
was to adore one's mate. She glanced down at her
own hand, her fingers intertwined with Finn's, and
warmth spread from the contact, up her arm, and
through her body.

Full. Her heart felt full, almost to bursting. But somehow, there was always room for more.

She glanced at her deliciously handsome husband as he chatted with his brother. Finn was resplendent in his midnight-black coat, snowy waistcoat, and snug white breeches, and it was all she could do not to lift up on her toes and kiss him here, in front of the duke and duchess's guests. There were many conveniently placed alcoves around the Northfields' massive home. Surely Tabitha could steal her husband away for a moment and show him exactly how she intended them to celebrate the rest of Christmas Eve.

"The way your wife is looking at you," Kieran drawled to Finn, "I don't think our conversation is going to last much longer."

"I've been prattling with you for twenty-eight years. Surely we've said everything of significance to each other already." Finn turned a wolfish smile to Tabitha, making her belly leap in anticipation. "Shall we find somewhere to unwrap our presents?"

"I'd hate to ruin your festivities," she said, even though she burned to do exactly that. "And you and Kieran seemed to have so much left to talk about."

Finn made a dismissive gesture. "He's not interested in hearing about the financial intricacies of running an intellectual society."

"And he doesn't care about the steps I've been taking to start my own publishing enterprise," Kieran added.

"How tedious we are," Finn said with a roll of his eyes. "Two respectable gentlemen making their respectable ways in the world."

"As if the two of you don't have a bet going right

now to see which of the guests is going to be the first to kiss another guest beneath the mistletoe," Tabitha chided with a laugh.

"My blunt's on the Duke of Rotherby and his wife," Kieran confided.

"I wouldn't take that bet, my love," Tabitha said to Finn. "Since I have every intention of dragging *you* under the mistletoe so I've a convenient excuse to kiss you."

"As if you need an excuse," he said, gaze growing hot as he raked it over her.

She reveled in his unabashed desire. It was almost frightening, how truly wonderful life with Finn was. They were both incredibly busy with their work. The Platinum Collective had in fact been so inundated with requests for meeting with Parliamentarians and other influential men, they'd recently hired Chima's fiancée to manage and coordinate their calendar. Since Ifunaya already had considerable experience managing the appointments for her family's construction firm, she was a dab hand at keeping everything organized for the society.

The day following the symposium had been a grand one for the Platinum Collective, but a dire one for the Sterling Society. Newspaper headlines read, *Sterling Society Tarnished as Platinum Collective Shines. Platinum Collective Ascendant, Sterling Society Loses Its Luster.*

They had done it. She and Finn and the others of the Platinum Collective. They were making their voices heard.

Ever since the disbanding of the Sterling Society, they had been in more demand than ever. Meanwhile,

Finn managed the operational concerns. She and Finn were so engrossed in their labors, they often didn't see each other for hours.

But their reunions at the end of each day were worth it. He was worth everything.

She reached for her husband, but stopped when Celeste appeared, looking agitated.

"What is it, darling?" Kieran asked his wife. "Has Dom showed up and challenged everyone to a bare-knuckle battle royal?"

It was a distinct possibility. Over the past month, Dom had retreated further and further into grim silence, and often sported bruises and cuts from the brawls he seemed to seek out in London's seedier corners. He no longer came to social events, yet one never knew where his bad-tempered humors might take him.

"He *will* likely detonate when he hears what I've just seen," Celeste said. "Or rather *who* I've just seen." She looked at each of them in turn. "Willa is back."

"My God," Tabitha breathed. Turning to Finn, she asked, "Did you know your sister was returning from the Continent?"

Finn and Kieran looked both downcast and uneasy. "No one spoke a word to us," Finn said heavily. "And she hasn't responded to any of my letters."

Tabitha's chest knotted. Her husband had spoken at length about the remorse he carried for creating such chaos and unhappiness in his sister's life, but so long as Willa remained abroad and didn't reply to his correspondence, he'd no way of expressing this, or finding a way to atone for the wrong he and Kieran had done her.

"What *will* Dom do when he learns that she's returned?" Tabitha asked anxiously.

"Heavenly angels are already girding themselves for war," Finn said, his expression tight. "Either he'll level the city, or he'll disappear into the deepest, darkest cave, and never be seen again."

"I don't care for either possibility," Celeste muttered.

"There she is," Kieran said tautly, nodding toward an elfin-looking woman with black hair and thick, straight brows.

Willa hovered at the edge of the ballroom while glancing around the chamber, as though in search of someone.

If she saw her brothers, she didn't seem to show it. Instead, with a frosty, hard expression, she vanished into the crowd.

A tense silence fell between the Ransome brothers, until Finn shook his head and his expression cleared.

"We'll call on her tomorrow," he said decisively, "but tonight is too fine to spend mulling over future battles. There is something I haven't done with my wife that must be remedied immediately."

"Sophisticated as the guests here might be," Kieran said wryly, "I don't think they'd appreciate the sight of you and Tabitha—"

"We're *dancing*, you ass," Finn snapped. Then, with a warm smile on his face, he turned to her. "Shall we, love?"

Her heart leapt into her throat. Even as excitement pulsed through her, a hint of nervousness prickled across her arms. Uncertain, she confessed, "I haven't danced at a ball in . . . well . . . ever."

Understanding and affection shone in his eyes. "That all changes tonight."

Her anxiety eased, loosening her limbs. In his arms, she knew exquisite shelter, magnificent happiness. She was, and always would be, safe with him.

In response, she took his arm. He smiled down at her as he smoothly led her onto the dance floor, his reverent smile never wavering as they took their position for the waltz. The music began, and they started to move.

"Of course," she said with a laugh. "Of course you're a splendid dancer."

"Only with you, love," he answered tenderly.

As they glided across the floor, Finn looked at her with so much love she could fly with its strength.

"What makes you smile, sweet?" he asked, turning her in his arms.

"Once, I was a wallflower," she answered as she beheld him. "And in my fashion, I'm still a wallflower. A wallflower who permitted myself only thought, no emotion. Now I can be everything. Heart *and* mind, because of you."

"You never needed me to be the marvelous creature you are now," he insisted. "That was you all along. Yet *you* helped me realize that I was not so worthless as I'd believed." He held her tighter, his strength all around her, shared love encircling them both.

"We're worthwhile apart," she said, soaking in all that he was, and all that they were, "and we're wondrous together. It was a gamble, this marriage."

"It was." Finn spun her, the room whirling around them, his gaze upon her as though she was the star at the center of the universe. "And we *both* won."

Our final scoundrel has one last chance to make things right . . .

❧ ✳ ❦

A ROGUE'S RULES FOR SEDUCTION

Dom's story coming Spring 2023!

The Argeneau Novels from
#1 *NEW YORK TIMES*
BESTSELLING AUTHOR

HUNTING FOR A HIGHLANDER

978-0-06-285537-5

IMMORTAL ANGEL

978-0-06-295630-9

MEANT TO BE IMMORTAL

978-0-06-295639-2

MILE HIGH WITH A VAMPIRE

978-0-06-295640-8

IMMORTAL RISING

978-0-06-311154-7

LYS11 0622